BETWEEN TWO FIRES

BETWEEN TWO FIRES

Mark Noce

Thomas Dunne Books
St. Martin's Press *New York*

This is a work of fiction. All of the characters, organizations, and events portrayed in this novel are either products of the author's imagination or are used fictitiously.

THOMAS DUNNE BOOKS.
An imprint of St. Martin's Press.

BETWEEN TWO FIRES. Copyright © 2016 by Mark Noce. All rights reserved. Printed in the United States of America. For information, address St. Martin's Press, 175 Fifth Avenue, New York, N.Y. 10010.

www.thomasdunnebooks.com
www.stmartins.com

The Library of Congress Cataloging-in-Publication Data:

Names: Noce, Mark, author.
Title: Between two fires / Mark Noce.
Description: First edition. | New York : Thomas Dunne Books/St. Martin's Press, 2016.
Identifiers: LCCN 2016002481| ISBN 9781250072627 (hardback) |
    ISBN 9781466884434 (e-book)
Subjects: LCSH: Nobility—Wales—History—To 1063—Fiction. | Great Britain—
    History—Anglo-Saxon period, 449-1066—Fiction. | Wales—History—To
    1063—Fiction. | BISAC: FICTION / Historical. | GSAFD: Historical fiction.
Classification: LCC PS3614.O33 B48 2016 | DDC 813/.6—dc23
LC record available at http://lccn.loc.gov/2016002481

Our books may be purchased in bulk for promotional, educational, or business use. Please contact your local bookseller or the Macmillan Corporate and Premium Sales Department at 1-800-221-7945, extension 5442, or by e-mail at MacmillanSpecialMarkets@macmillan.com.

First Edition: August 2016

10 9 8 7 6 5 4 3 2 1

For Laurel

To endure a dilemma is to
stand between two fires.
—CELTIC PROVERB

PART ONE
A.D. 597

I

Today I will marry a man I have never met. My stepmother orders the servants to brush the dust off my white gown. Father, our King, is already well into his cups as he and his warriors sing bawdy songs from the mead hall. Beneath my chamber window, the sea crashes into the hill fort walls. My head aches as the rolling surf bangs against the slick rocks far below, wearing away the fortress crags with the endless patience of the tide. I've half a mind to throw myself over the ledge.

But I don't. I am Branwen, daughter of King Vortigen, ruler of the Kingdom of Dyfed. I have a duty to the honor of my ancestors, and I will not be the first of my line to blemish it. Nonetheless, at times like these, surrounded by my stepmother's dawdling servant girls and their barking lapdogs, I wish I wasn't an only child. That's not entirely true. Father has countless bastards, many of whom are no doubt carousing with him down in the dining hall this very instant. But I have no siblings born on the right side of the blanket, no one to confide in. No one to take my place in this betrothal to a distant king.

The floorboards of my solar shudder beneath my feet. My stepmother grimaces, annoyed by the boisterous celebration of Father and his warriors drinking, brawling, and merrymaking with the peasants and scullery maids in the adjacent hall. I can hardly blame them. The people of our tiny seaside kingdom are euphoric. Not because they long to see me wed, but because my marriage means a lasting peace and an end to the war. My soon-to-be husband has an army of six thousand men outside our gates who have laid siege to our kingdom for the past two moons.

All I know of him are the six thousand spears that dot the green hills from the landward side of my window. That and the stories about him. I know less than a common dairymaid thanks to my stepmother, the Queen. She forbids any of the servants from telling me much of the outside world. But I have overheard a few rumors, from women in the kitchens and the horsemen who run Father's stables. They call him the Hammer King. He wears an iron mask into battle and wields a war-hammer said to have slain a hundred foes. My nightmares of late consist of a shadowy, faceless blacksmith. Each evening he swings a massive hammer down upon the anvil of my heart. I often awake in sweats that soak my bedcovers.

I tap my foot, glaring at my stepmother.

"Please, leave me be. I need to make water."

The Queen frowns.

"Do not muss your dress. A lady doesn't raise her voice or stomp her foot."

I roll my eyes. She ushers her bondswomen and their small dogs out of my bedchamber. Sometimes I envy those little hounds. At least my stepmother pets them and says nice things to them. She continually mistakes me not for her stepdaughter, but for some porcelain doll she can dress up and paint as she pleases. After the door closes, I wait until the last of her footfalls diminishes down the stairwell.

I collapse on a footstool and put my head on my knees. I can't weep. My stepmother will see the tearstains and Father will backhand me for having bloodshot eyes on the day of my wedlock. It seems just yesterday I played along the windswept beachheads, making tracks in the damp sand. The heft of my crepe wedding gown weighs me down as I look out my bedroom window for the last time. I'll be wed to the Hammer King by sundown.

Composing myself, I descend to the main dining hall. I hide my palms within the folds of my gown so that no one will see my hands shake. Father and his warriors cheer when they see me, banging their mead cups against the tabletops. Liquor sloshes from the brims of their drinks. They're too drunk to notice how I look. My stepmother's servant girls snicker behind their hands. Crow Face. Raven Head. Blackbird. The same old names. My stepmother makes no move to stop them. In our kingdom, even the slaves mock me.

My pale cheeks burn. My stepmother's golden hair shines by torchlight, just like a noble lady's ought. Even the bondservants have tawny or brassy locks. My midnight tresses and forest-green eyes reflect in the polished shields hanging on the wall. Black hair. Peasant hair. Amongst our kingdom, only the commoners and barbarians have jet-black sheaves like mine. It doesn't help that I'm thin as a stick and the bumps on my chest are small as flat cakes. No wonder my stepmother and Father are so delighted. The miracle of all miracles has happened. The day they marry off their ugly daughter.

And to a mighty king no less. I labor under no illusions. I am part of a bargain, a peace settlement that will bring stability to the warring kingdoms. The man who plans to marry me tonight has never seen me before, nor did he ask to. I only hope the war doesn't start anew when he sees what an ebony-haired scarecrow he has for a bride. I've reached my sixteenth summer and already my life seems to be over.

Father motions for me to take a seat on a mead bench across from him, a checkered board laid out on the table between us. His thanes give us a wide berth. Father clearly wants a moment alone with me. He may look all mirth and smiles, but he flashes a wolfish smirk from behind his frothing drink.

He makes the first move with an onyx pawn, his strategy always aggressive when we play chess. Celtic Chess, known as *fidchell* in Ireland and *gwyddbwyll* in parts of Wales; playing the game connects us to our roots, an ancient stratagem originating with the Old Tribes whose blood runs in us still. It's the only pastime Father and I ever shared together, the only moments when I saw something other than a stern monarch always frowning at me. Sometimes before the chessboard, he even let down his guard and talked of Mother. Not today though.

I defend with my druids, pieces called "bishops" by the clerics who play the game today. I prefer to remember things as the Old Tribes called them, as my mother would have known them. The King grimaces as he strikes one of my pearl pieces down with his horseman.

"You always hold back. Don't just defend, learn to strike."

"Maybe I'm laying a trap." I smirk.

"Not likely."

He glances from side to side, doubtlessly ensuring no one lingers within earshot as he leans across the board and lowers his voice so that only I can hear.

"I don't need to tell you how much hinges on this alliance with the Hammer King. I've no son born on the right side of the blanket, and my wife's womb lies empty. You're all I have left, so we must make do."

There it is. A not-so-subtle dig that had I been born a boy, things might have been much better for everyone. But now, he must make do with a raven-haired urchin like me. I swallow, trying to focus on the board while I listen.

"You've no wiles to put on him, no way to seduce the Hammer King, even if he was that sort of man," Father explains. "But you will be privy to private councils and words that pass in the halls of his castle. Things that may never reach my ears. It will be up to you to look out for Dyfed's interests."

"You want me to spy on my new husband?"

"I want you to keep your eyes and ears open, and your mouth shut."

I sigh, taking a deep breath. This may be the last time I see Father for a long, long while. I might as well be honest.

"Is it all worth it, Father? Wedding me to this stranger to save our people?"

Father grimaces at me like I'm some idiot child.

"Better to be at the right hand of the devil than in his way."

Within a dozen moves, he eliminates half my pieces on the game board despite losing his horsemen and his queen. Father was always good at sacrificing a queen when it spoke to his advantage. His sea-gray eyes gaze into mine, the look of a man more king than father. He takes my king piece to win the game, his voice flat and even.

"One game ends, another begins."

A knot tightens in my stomach, knowing that he refers to more than just the chessboard.

War trumpets blare outside. My heart stops up my throat. The clanking din of iron greaves and heavy chain mail echo from the hall entranceway. The Hammer King has arrived.

Father's men push back their mead benches, grabbing their spears and shields. Even though peace has been declared, they plan to look their fiercest before the Hammer King's men. Several guardsmen surround my stepmother and her ladies, but only one soldier thinks to stand by my side.

Ahern shoulders his spear and shield beside me. His stout frame and ochre beard bear a strong resemblance to my father. Even though he is one of Father's many bastards, he almost seems a full brother to me at this moment. I would reach out and take his hand, but right now I can hardly keep my knees from wobbling.

The Hammer King's thanes fan out into the torch-lit mead hall, the ever-present roar of the nearby surf thundering through the bones of the castle. Despite the crashing waves, my heart drums louder within my ears. The Hammer King's men wear iron helms and vests of mail, their thick teardrop-shaped shields bigger than our people's light calfskin bucklers. Although I know it would be treason to say it, the Hammer King's warriors look big enough to swallow ten of Father's men for supper. So I say nothing. My stepmother often reminds me that a lady keeps silent poise. Father always chides me that no one wants to hear what a little girl would say, especially when kings and lords are present. A herald blows on a curved horn once more, before raising his voice for all to hear.

"All hail, King Morgan, Lord of South Wales, Master of castles Caerleon and Caerwent!"

I murmur the name of my future husband. Morgan. I half-forgot the Hammer King had a real name, just like any other Christian soul. He is just a man, after all. My heart lightens until a lone figure appears in the hall entranceway. He wears a crown made of forked stag antlers, beneath it a metal helmet with a steel mask. Despite the tiny mouthpiece and eyeholes, the mask resembles the grim visage of an iron goblin. I cannot move, frozen by the hollow stare of the Hammer King as he stands on our darkened doorstep. Even Father's mouth hangs open, speechless. Only the sound of the sea and guttering torches fill the vast stone hall.

Morgan's footsteps clack heavy as horseshoes across the cobblestone floors. He carries a huge iron war-hammer, slung behind his back. I doubt any men in the room would have the strength to lift it. He pauses first before Father and my stepmother before turning toward me. The Hammer King removes his riding gloves as he looks me over. Even through the eye slits of his mask, I feel his gaze appraising me as a knight might observe a horse. My cheeks burn hot as I dig my fingernails into the flesh of my palms. What did I expect after all? He is a warlord called the Hammer King, not some charming troubadour with a harp. He has not come to woo me, but to bed me. The King removes his helmet-mask and smiles.

I swallow. He wears his brown beard short and well trimmed, his gray eyes sparkling with a hint of starlight. Morgan flashes another friendly grin. He even has all of his teeth! Other than an old scar along his left eye, he has an unblemished face. My stepmother's ladies-in-waiting would surely blush if he ever glanced their way.

Bowing slowly, I regain my composure. He is a king, after all, and is only being courteous. It must make him retch, to have an ugly youngling like me for a bride. Morgan has at least ten years on me, maybe more. He could have any queen he might desire, but he has chosen a crow-faced girl barely halfway through her teens. I can guess his thoughts. Morgan sees my father's lands when he looks at me. He sees all the green pastures, windswept rocks, and stout spearmen of Dyfed in my eyes. I represent an extension of his ever-growing kingdom, nothing more.

Father clears his throat. Were the situation not so tense, I might stifle a giggle at seeing my father so lost for words. He and the Hammer King bow to one another, their warriors leering at each other across the room. Father never takes his eyes off King Morgan.

"I present my daughter, Lady Branwen of Dyfed. May she bear you many sons!"

I flush from ear to ear. The Hammer King frowns with approval and nods. He takes my hand, his fingers so much larger and rougher than mine. I feel small as a mouse in his grasp. Father raises his hands, signaling to the minstrels that they may resume playing their lutes and pipes. The din of clanking drinking horns and mirth making fills the hall. Serving wenches smile as they bring mead to soldiers from both armies. Father leans in close to Morgan's ear.

"Let us retire to my private chambers, Lord Morgan."

The Hammer King bristles at Father calling him "lord" instead of "king," but he nonetheless nods in reply. He seems a silent sort of man. What must my boisterous father make of his new son-in-law? The Hammer King releases my hand, but I remain beside him, uncertain what to do next. My stepmother intrudes with a curtsy, batting her eyelashes at King Morgan.

"My liege, I summoned a banquet from our larders for your wedding feast. Forgive our unprepared tables, but we had little warning of the newly announced betrothal."

"No need, Queen Gwendolyn. I march at dawn back to Caerwent. My bride and I will be wed there."

"Oh, I—I see," my stepmother stammers.

She curtsies again, her eyes glazing over with distracted thoughts. Morgan's words clearly disappoint her, but I can't help from flashing a dark smile. At least I won't have to deal with any more of my stepmother's pomp and fuss, struggling to make me a lady after years of neglect. At the same time, the finality of my wedlock weighs down my steps. Come tomorrow, I'll leave my childhood home beside the sea forever, belonging to a strange man in a strange castle far to the east.

Father detects none of his queen's disappointment, nor my own foreboding, as he ushers Morgan toward his chambers. I trail after them, still not knowing what to do with myself. Father gives me a sharp glance. He clearly doesn't want anyone disturbing his meeting with Morgan, but I loathe the thought of remaining behind with my stepmother and the other chattering serving girls in the main gallery. I've never been one for festivities. Reading one of Abbot Padraig's books beside the fire, alone in my solar, has always appealed to me more than the drinking songs of the mead hall. As I stand alone, save for my guardsman, Ahern, King Morgan turns back and takes me by the hand.

"I would have my Queen-to-be remain at my side. I brought an army all the way to Dyfed for her hand, and I don't intend to let her out of my sight."

He smiles again, and I find myself stupidly grinning back. Hopefully, he doesn't notice my crooked eyeteeth or the pockmark of acne on my left cheek. Did he really assemble an army just to make a woman out of a stick-thin girl like me? Father raises a stern eyebrow before he shrugs. He mumbles under his breath.

"Womenfolk are too dim to betray secrets they do not understand anyway."

The three of us snake up the spiral staircase to Father's solar overlooking the cliffs. Ahern remains at the foot of the stairwell, guarding the entrance. Father shuts and locks the door.

A chill runs down my spine as a fell wind blows in through the window. Icy stars glimmer over a rising blue moon. Father rarely allows anyone inside his private quarters. Although a Welshman to the bone, Father is proud of the blood of Romans and Irishmen in his veins, distant though those ancient links may be.

An imperial eagle standard from a long-lost legion of defeated Rome hangs in one corner. Celtic tapestries with knot-work deck the stone interiors. Father lights a candelabra beside his desk before unfolding several parchments and charts. He stoops down beside the chamber hearth, rekindling a fire in the glowing embers. Morgan pores over the largest map on the desktop, a drawing of Wales sketched out by long-dead monks with insect ink on calfskins. I've seen the Abbot's clerics do as much when they recopy the tomes of the ancients in their chapel by the sea. I retreat to the corner of the chamber, more comfortable in the shadows where I can see without being directly seen.

The fire in the grate blazes to life, lengthening the shadows that line Father's face. Without warning, he brings his fist down hard on the center of the map on the table. I jump back at his snarling face, but Morgan doesn't move, almost as though he expected this outburst. The two kings stare one another down as the blaze in the fireplace snaps and crackles across the peat logs. Father breaks the silence first.

"Do you think to steal my throne from under me? My lineage is twice as ancient as yours!"

"*Might* will unite Wales under a single king someday, not pedigrees,"

Morgan replies calmly. "And I've more than enough spears to drive your tiny kingdom into the sea, Lord Vortigen."

Father sneers at Morgan in turn calling him a mere lord in his own castle. Backing against the wall, I suddenly wish I hadn't poked my nose into Father's affairs. If only the Virgin would provide me a tactful way to flee the room. Foolishly, I placed myself in the corner opposite the door. With Father's blood up, I've no intention of crossing his path while he and Morgan stare one another down. Father bangs his fist against the tabletop again, raising his voice loud enough to shake the rafters.

"Aye, you might, *might* scale our walls, but we'd bleed your army dry if you tried it!"

"I've no intent of shedding blood before my wedding night. Nor do I wish to interfere with your castle and kingship. You knew what type of alliance I wanted. Your daughter's hand unites our houses."

"But I still rule as sovereign in my own lands!"

"Of course. Dyfed belongs to you and your sons ever afterward, but when I call on you, I expect Dyfed's spearmen to join my army. I am a patient man in many things, Vortigen, but in the days to come, you either stand with me against the Saxons or not. That promise I will keep in blood."

At mention of the Saxons, my heart sickens. Those cruel pagans have conquered more than half our lands and every year eat away at the borders of Wales. Their hordes of bloodthirsty warriors have filled every cemetery in the Welsh Lands with countless men, women, and children. I ball my fists at my sides and shut my eyes. Only once have I seen the Saxon brutes up close, long ago. The flames of the longhouses and the screams of womenfolk still ring in my ears from that night. Father's stern face sobers with sadness at the mention of the Saxons. He glances at me as I bite my lip in the shadowy corner.

"Ever will I stand against the Saxon invaders, Morgan. It was they that took my first wife and nearly made an orphan out of my daughter the night their longships arrived on our shores."

I look Father in the eye, my own green eyes burning hot as embers. Almost never do we speak of Mother, not after that night all those years ago. Suddenly, Father's mild contempt for me becomes so plain. He lost my mother, a beautiful wife of the Old Tribes with midnight locks and emerald eyes. In her place, all he has left is me. A daily reminder of a lesser, uglier version of the queen he lost. Who can fault Father for despising me? He only managed to save me that fateful night, not Mother. The Saxon swords did the rest. Morgan steps between us, for the first time really looking at me without the pretense of a half-forced smile.

"Not a family in Wales hasn't lost someone to the Saxons," Morgan begins. "Since my father was slain by their chiefs, I have ever waged war against them to keep my kingdom and all of Wales safe."

Morgan faces Father again.

"We are natural allies, Vortigen. Every year the Saxons push our borders back. Lands that the Welsh once peopled peacefully now lie burnt and broken under Saxon rule. We must unite all the Welsh Lands or it is only a matter of time before the Saxon war-chiefs push all our kingdoms into the sea."

"You'll never unite all the Welsh," Father says, hanging his head. "Not since the days of Arthur has it been done. Maybe these are the last days of the Free Welsh. Perhaps the Saxons come to bring about the end of the world as the priests have foretold."

Rarely have I seen the wind knocked out of Father so, and never have I seen him show his despair before a stranger. Despite still wearing my white wedding gown, I throw a horse blanket around my shivering shoulders. His words chill me to the marrow. All our once-great castles and sacred sites have fallen to the Saxon invaders in the last few generations. Londinium, Camelot, and Avalon are all mere memories in the folklore of our people now. Far to the west, on our rocky peninsula of Dyfed, it seems easier to sometimes forget the Saxon threat that daily besets the eastern borders of the Welsh Lands. But I sometimes wonder whether I'll ever live long enough to sprout gray hairs on my head, before the Saxons extinguish our race from the free kingdoms in the west. According to the priests, it has been nearly six hundred years since the coming of Christ and already it looks as though the End of Days is upon us.

Father collects himself and grimaces at the map. The mountainous, wooded terrain of Wales has helped defend us just as much as the sword and spear, but the many rivers and valleys also divide us into separate fiefdoms all calling their own lords king. From the northern realms of Gwynedd to the southernmost territories of Gwent, no Welshman acknowledges a single monarch as ruler over all Wales. Father shakes his head.

"Even with you and I united in the South, the rest of Wales will never bend the knee to you, Morgan. Belin the Old rules North Wales with an iron fist, and the Free Cantrefs in between are just as likely to raise the sword against us as they are the Saxons. Our Welsh love of independence and infighting may be what helps the Saxons to finish us off in the end."

"Leave Old Belin and the Free Cantrefs to me," Morgan assures him. "Climb one mountain at a time."

Father nods and grasps Morgan's hand in the Roman fashion, the two noblemen clutching one another's forearms firmly. Goose bumps cover my skin. Only yesterday, Morgan's armies were our enemies, and tonight they become our friends.

Morgan lost his own father to the Saxons and so we both know what it means to lose a parent. Perhaps that should comfort me, but instead a prickly feeling rises in my gut. Something about this unnaturally calm Hammer King unsettles me.

By wedding me, he has united Father's kingdom with his own, obtaining control over all South Wales without losing a single soldier. Whether Father knows it or not, he has for all intents and purposes bent his knee to Morgan. The spearmen of Dyfed will now fight beside the knights of Morgan's army. Like a spectator of a chess game, I've watched Morgan put my father into checkmate and Father doesn't even seem to know it. This husband of mine is no fool to be trifled with. Perhaps he will someday be king of all the Welsh. Perhaps.

Both men look at me as I clear my throat. It takes a moment to find my voice. What do the likes of kings care for the thoughts of a sixteen-year-old girl? But I've the blood of Celts and queens in me, and among our people, women still have the strength to speak up. Even a tiny mouse like me.

"There is one thing you wise men have forgotten."

Morgan and Father exchange looks.

"It will take more than swords to defeat the Saxons," I continue. "Their numbers are greater than ours."

"Speak when spoken to, child," Father fumes, before apologizing to Morgan. "She reads too much from the Abbot's books, and you can see how it addles a feminine mind."

"No," Morgan interrupts with a hand. "I would hear what my Queen has to say."

Father gives Morgan a sidelong glance, probably wondering why he indulges me so. The Hammer King looks me up and down, not as a horse this time, but sizing me up as though I were a man. Before either of them can change their mind, I press on with my point.

"Suppose you do the impossible, and unite Wales, and push back the Saxons. We will be too weakened and new infighting will begin. New invaders will come. Whether Saxons or Picts at our gates, an iron fist will not keep the free-spirited Welshmen loyal to any man's crown."

"Bah!" Father protests. "Let us worry about that day whence and if it ever comes."

"No, the lady is right," Morgan says, still looking at me. "What would you do, Lady Branwen?"

My gaze falls and I feel hot in the face for having brought the subject up. I see the problem too clearly, but a solution does not arise in my mind. My voice dies down to almost a whisper.

"I know not, my liege. I only know that bloodied spears and swords are not enough to bind the Welsh people together. You must do something else to unite them . . . something that speaks to their hearts, to earn the love and admiration of all Free Welsh folk."

I straighten my spine. Father blows air between his lips and turns to stoke the fire. Morgan says no more, observing me with his unfathomable gray eyes. Just like the people of Wales, I too would prefer Morgan win my heart before claiming my loyalty. I know not whether my words have touched him or if he thinks me more the fool. Probably just some little, insignificant girl, whose only purpose is to provide a bedmate and heirs for the royal line. Just what a proper lady ought to be, my stepmother would say. I grind my molars, half-mad at myself for speaking my mind and half-frustrated that my stepmother's view of a woman in this world might be right after all. But she doesn't have the blood of the Old Tribes running through her veins like me.

Without another word, the two kings descend the stairwell toward the din of boisterous revelers in the mead hall. Traversing the stairs, I feel Morgan close to me and smell his musk, a hint of pinesap and peat smoke on him. He must spend many a day in the field, under a tent, rather than at home in his castle. My palms sweat, feeling his breath so close to mine own. Will he wait until our wedding before putting me in his bed, or will he take me aside tonight? Wed by a priest or not, I'm to be his property soon enough.

Descending the turret steps, Father and Morgan outpace me as the two of them resume speaking in low tones. At the foot of the stairs, I head down an adjacent corridor, needing a moment to myself. A salty evening breeze cools my face as I stand beside an arrow slit overlooking the orange glow of the chapel windows down by the cliffs. Hymns from the monks' and nuns' evening vespers reverberate along the dark moors as the clerics pray to God.

A pair of footsteps shuffles beside me in the dim corridor.

"I hope I'm not too late to wish the bride-to-be congratulations and a long, happy life."

"Abbot Padraig," I reply, smiling at the balding holy man. "What brings you up from the abbey?"

"A little memento for my best pupil," he says with a grin.

He pulls a large tome out from beneath his brown robes, opening to the first page. I put a hand to my mouth at the sight of such a magnificent manuscript, fine yellow vellum replete with perfectly tilted script. An illuminated image of a dark-haired woman wearing a crown shows on the opening page, her gown painted with bright azure, beryl, golden, and ruby hues. The Abbot places the heavy book in my hands.

"It's written in my own hand, a record of the ancient days of the Old Tribes, and Queen Branwen the Brave."

"Branwen the Brave? My mother named me after her."

"Because Queen Branwen was the most beloved queen of all Wales," he says, beaming. "Wise, good-hearted, and courageous."

I raise a curious eyebrow.

"She also met an unfortunate end, if I recall."

"Sometimes sad stories teach us the most. But I pray that you will draw inspiration from this book when you live in your new castle, far from home."

I reach out and take the old man's hand. Books are rare as gold, and this is no small present even for the head of a monastery. No one has ever given me such a treasure before.

"Thank you, Padraig. I shall read it often, and when I do I will think of you, my friend."

He smiles and bows, still vaguely formal in his mannerisms, despite the two of us having been student and teacher for years. His vestments smell faintly of crushed herbs, doubtlessly having just come from the monastery apothecary. The patient monk spent many hours not only instructing me in scholarship, but also in the ways of the healing arts. I'm going to miss his steady voice and fatherly countenance.

The hymns from the abbey down by the sea gradually change their tune, the new melody perking my ears. An ancient lay in the Old Tongue. I swallow a lump in my throat, recognizing the familiar evensong. They only chant like that when a woman begins childbirth, using the song to draw the babe into the world. Local womenfolk heavy with child often go to the abbey to receive help and blessings as they bring their newborns into the world. Of course, not all mothers survive the ordeal.

Morgan will surely expect me to bear him sons before long. How many moons before I find myself on a birthing bed? Will the nuns sing of my deliverance or my funeral dirge? A knot forms in my throat.

Father and Morgan's suddenly harsh voices echo down the hall. I beg Padraig's forgiveness as I excuse myself and hurry back toward the foot of the turret stairs. The guardsman Ahern bows toward them, his face flushing with color.

"Forgive me, sires, but a rider has arrived bearing ill news. The East Marches are under attack! A Saxon army has crossed into the Welsh Lands."

I feel the color drain from my face. Several other guards exchange worried looks. The roar of wenches and soldiers in the nearby mead hall reverberates off the ceilings. Most of the revelers still do not know of the evil tidings. Tomorrow many of them may be widows or dead. Perhaps this alliance between Father and the Hammer King has come too late.

Morgan loosens his giant war-hammer from his back. He hangs his head and speaks under his breath, although whether praying to God or cursing the Saxons, I cannot tell. His war-hammer seems nearly as tall as I am. He turns to Father as he dons his helmet, the mask portion still drawn up so we can see his face. Whatever his feelings, he speaks with the stoicism of a veteran soldier.

"I leave posthaste, Vortigen. My army is needed elsewhere, but I will call upon the spearmen of Dyfed before long."

"God go with you." Father nods.

A hush falls over the entire castle and I no longer hear the minstrels playing. Word has clearly reached every corner of the keep. Morgan orders his warriors about. His men scurry out from alcoves to get their armor on whilst maidens pull on their disheveled shifts and wipe fresh kisses from their tender mouths. A few older soldiers guzzle down the last mead in their drinking horns.

As I step back quietly, others bustle about without seeming to notice my presence. It looks like I won't be going anywhere after all. Morgan is halfway out the hall entranceway, his thanes saddling their horses. A mixture of relief and regret bubbles up inside me. With a war on, the Hammer King hardly has time to make a wife of me just now and take me away from my childhood home. At the same time, it will be another monotonous month or more of listening to my stepmother's chatter and the snide remarks of her ladies-in-waiting.

I set down my new book from the Abbot on a nearby table, gazing at the image of the ancient Queen Branwen on the first page. What would she do in my stead? I'm no great matron of the Old Tribes as she was.

Morgan calls out above the chaos of mingled soldiers and serving wenches, drawing my attention with his commanding voice.

"Lady Branwen, we must make haste."

He speaks politely, but firmly, and at first I do not understand. Morgan beckons me forward while drawing his black mount nearly to the lintel of the hall entrance. My eyes widen before I cross the floor and take his hand.

He means to take me with him. Tonight. This very minute.

My pulse jumps in my throat. I move to speak, but nothing comes out. With one swift motion, King Morgan hoists me atop his dark stallion.

He mounts the monstrously large beast and wraps an arm around my middle. His massive war-hammer dangles from the other fist. A single kick of his heels jolts the horse forward as we gallop off into the night. Dim torchlights and the whoosh of the sea fade behind us.

I've not even had a moment to say farewell. To Father, Ahern, the Abbot, or even my stepmother. I've nothing but the wedding gown I'm wearing. And my new book still sits half-open on a mead table in the main hall! Curse my empty-headedness.

Morgan and his horsemen canter through the darkness, neither sparing a glance toward me nor each other as they follow the old coast road east. An argent moon emerges from the clouds, lighting our path ahead. Despite the cool night air, I sweat like a roast. My temples ache as I glance back at my new husband, holding me astride his horse like a stolen bride. Morgan grimaces as though already deep in thoughts of battle. He intends to take me with him against the Saxons, and into the heart of danger.

2

My wedding gown hangs in shreds. A night astride a warhorse has reduced my linen dress to frayed ends and torn, mud-flecked skirts. I wince as a red sun rises in the east, my bloodshot eyes and sore joints worn from a sleepless evening in the saddle. Rocky coves and gray-sand beaches stretch across the seafront, the naked borderlands between Dyfed and South Wales. Once I wed King Morgan, these will remain borderlands no longer, but will lie within the heart of the Hammer King's ever-growing dominions.

In a single night, I've ridden farther than I've ever been from home. Far from the goose-feather pillows and sealskin coverlets of my solar bedchamber. Instead, my new husband holds me by the waist as I loll in the saddle, the ever-present rumble of hooves thundering in my ears. Morgan brings our steed to a halt as one of his thanes raises his sword in salute. The King frowns.

"Why the slowing pace? We're halfway to Caerleon already."

"Apologies, sire," the soldier replies. "Your horsemen have outpaced the foot soldiers. Half the army is strung out several leagues behind us."

"Then we continue on with just the horsemen!" Morgan barks. "Every moment we delay, Saxons steal deeper into the East Marches."

"My lord, if I may," the soldier says with a bow. "Even the horses grow fatigued and need water. At this pace, we will reach the Saxons completely worn out and hardly able to lift our heads, let alone our swords and shields."

Morgan grimaces, looking away toward the distant sun in the east where he wishes he and his army already were. My head sags down onto my chest, heavy as a lodestone. I can hardly stomach another half hour atop this bucking stallion. Morgan tightens his fists on the reins, ready to ride on. He has the stamina of iron and the will to match it. My future husband seems content to ride his horse to death if it gets him to the East Marches faster.

Just before he digs his heels into the flanks of his steed, I reel back in the saddle. Moaning at the ache in my limbs, I can no longer hide my discomfort. I never rode farther than the length of the beach outside my bedroom window before today. Morgan reaches out for me, but everything in my vision turns into a groggy blur. He dismounts and lowers me down from the saddle, speaking tersely to his guard.

"We'll wait for the rest of the army to catch up. Everyone must gather their strength."

If I could move my hand, I would cross myself in thanks to God. Morgan must carry me, because I don't feel my feet on the ground. He lays me down beneath a small grove of trees. The dry scent of oak leaves and acorns pervades the soft grass around me. My eyelids sag heavy as church bells as I succumb to the happy oblivion of sleep.

Thoughts of Father cloud my murky dreams. I stand on a chessboard shrouded in mist, petrified as though I were a giant queen piece made of stone. Horsemen and druids line up around me, but I cannot move. A large king piece advances through the fog, its stony base grinding along the ground and hurtling toward me like a swift torrent. But I cannot budge, cannot even move as the king piece comes down on me like a sledgehammer in the mist.

I awake in a sweat, the blood pounding in my ears.

To my astonishment, I lie on a large cushion with quilts thrown over me. I pinch myself until I wince, but this is no dream. Still muddled with sleep, I palm the screens of the box-like contraption I now seem to inhabit. The floor sways like a cradle, the plush confines of my tiny, coffin-like box suddenly starting to make sense. I'm inside a litter.

Outside the mesh screen, rows of marching spearmen wear iron helms with horsehair plumes. Soldiers of South Wales, King Morgan's men-at-arms. A quartet of brawny servants carries my litter along the dusty coast road in the midst of the army. The King's men must have put me in a litter after I collapsed beneath the oak grove along the main roadway. Wherever did they find such a luxurious carrier out here in the wilderness? I gasp at the sinking sun outside. Have I slept an entire day? My arms and legs ache as I sit up, the servants bringing my jostling litter to a halt. Footsteps approach and stop beside the mesh screen. I swallow, sensing danger.

The hasp slides back and a bearded man sticks his head in, nearly nose to nose with mine. I flinch, yet his voice sounds familiar.

"My lady, are you all right in there?"

Ahern! My heart lightens at the sight of my kinsman.

"Ahern, what are you doing here? And where is here? What has happened?"

"Little much, my lady. We're still a half day's march from the Hammer King's strongholds at Caerleon and Caerwent, which I can only assume is where we're headed. Your father left orders for one of his Dyfed spearmen to ride ahead and accompany you. I volunteered. A queen should always have some kinsmen close by, no?"

He smiles before resuming his stoic stance. Despite being born to different mothers, he is now the closest thing to family I have left. I impulsively stretch out my arms and give him a peck on the cheek. He blushes while standing at attention, straightening his shield and spear. He may have only seen half a dozen more summers than me, but he is a seasoned warrior. Just having his watchful gaze over me lifts a weight from my chest.

Ahern passes a small wooden box through the opening in my litter.

"A token from your father," he explains. "To remember your home and your duty, he said."

Unfolding the box in my hands, several black and white chess pieces clank together along a checkered board. I flash a half-grin, knowing that this little keepsake is Father's not-so-subtle way of reminding me to keep my eyes and ears open. Nonetheless, this little game remains one of the few bonds he and I share. The windswept crags of Father's castle may not seem like much, but it's the only home I've ever known. And my father couldn't have sent a better guardsman than Ahern. I stick my head outside the litter in order to take in some fresh air.

"Where is my betrothed, Ahern? I'd step out and look for him myself, but I fear I look somewhat indecent in my bedraggled robes."

"I know not, my lady. King Morgan rode ahead of the main army with five hundred horses. We've no word of him since midmorning."

My face flushes hot as a blacksmith's forge. Here I am worrying about my tattered clothes while my future husband gallops headlong into the jaws of death. It seems he couldn't stand to remain idle after all. Heaven knows how many Saxons crossed into the East Marches. Without the bulk of his army, Morgan's tired horsemen might ride into an ambush. They might be captured or tortured. Or worse. My heart starts to pound as I shake my head. Best not to dwell on such things. As the Hammer King said to Father, *climb one mountain at a time.*

If only I had a book to pass the time. I could curse myself a hundred times over for leaving Abbot Padraig's wonderful book back at Dun Dyfed. Clerics can spend an entire lifetime copying out a handful of books, every drop of ink, every vellum page crafted painstakingly by hand. It may not be listed amongst the Ten Commandments, but to leave behind such a treasure is surely a sin.

In my mind's eye, I still see Padraig's cherished library inside the abbey walls. More than a score of full volumes of books, and the kind Abbot let me read each one. My stepmother had me learning books with the monks and nuns when she first married Father. Probably hoping to put me in a nunnery, not knowing her womb would prove barren. No young princesses or princelings came along to replace me. Nonetheless, I miss those dusty tomes inside the Abbot's stone chapel. Tales of biblical miracles, Greco-Roman poets, and legends of the fairy folk from the bards of Ireland and Wales. And of course, tales of romance. Guinevere and Lancelot, Deirdre and Naoise, Dido and Aeneas. Yet the thought of such normally enjoyable tales unsettles my stomach now.

I may be plain to look upon, but I am still a girl, soon to be a woman. My palms sweat as I contemplate my soon-to-come consummation night. Surely, Morgan will return safe and sound, but what happens after that? The monks' books left out the part about how a man and woman should love one another in the marriage bed. My stepmother merely dropped vague hints about submission and bearing a pleasing demeanor. My skin itches with doubts.

My litter jolts to an abrupt halt, jarring me against the bulkhead. *Och!* I stick my head outside to see the commotion, but Ahern begs me to stay put. The entire army has halted in its tracks. My heart hammers faster, my tongue suddenly parched. Ahern shoulders his weapons.

"I'll see what the delay is, my lady. I'll come back quick enough."

I don't want him to go, but he disappears into the throngs of men before I can raise my voice. Probably nothing to fret about, but a nagging fear prickles my spine nonetheless. Soldiers sit down in the roadway to rest, several thousand of them lining the highway in opposite directions. What could've made them all stop so suddenly? I thumb the ring on my finger, a small bluestone trinket from my mother. It has always brought me luck. My nerves gradually still as they oft do when I remember my mother, telling myself to think calmly and collectedly as she always did. All seems well and peaceful outside. Nothing to fret about.

A pair of arrows embeds themselves in my litter.

Each arrowhead stops barely a hair's breadth from my cheek. I cry out. The servants carrying me topple over, each riddled with arrows. My timber litter collapses to the ground, sending me tumbling out of the battered box. I wince as I prop myself up on one elbow, the bitter taste of blood on my tongue. Crawling through the dust, I pass several crimson-stained bodies that cover the path. Men who will never rise again.

A deathly roar of howling men emerges from the woods. The King's soldiers linger in scattered fragments along the winding roadway, forming thinned ranks against the unknown foes. I've only read about war, but even I recognize an ambush when I see one. The bellowing warriors from the woods close in on both sides. Grizzled, bearded wildlings, clad in animal skins and vests of armor. Some bear helms with eye slits and nose guards. My heart stops up inside my throat. Saxons!

Where did they all come from? We're still many leagues from the East Marches where King Morgan has gone to do battle. None of this makes any sense. A Saxon army should never have gotten this deep into the Welsh Lands without being noticed.

A javelin grazes my right temple, drawing blood as I stagger to my feet. Time enough to sort everything out later. If I live to see the next hour. Scores of charging barbarians rush toward me. My knees tremble yet I cannot budge my feet.

Ahern is nowhere in sight. The men-at-arms around me on the roadway collapse in heaps, deafening cries rending the air as they grapple with the swarming Saxon horde. Picking up a fallen spear, I try to remember how Father practiced arms in the courtyard at home. If only I had paid more attention to such things!

A barrel-chested behemoth of a warrior leers at me from across the throng of clashing shields and spears. The Saxon wields a notched ax in hand, rushing toward me with a confident sneer. I've no chance. He bats my purloined spear away easily, snapping it in twain like a matchstick. Collapsing backward, I trip over my rigid feet. I shield myself with my arms, not knowing whether this barbarian intends to slay or violate me. Maybe both.

He suddenly frowns, dropping his ax and cradling his chest. A childlike expression crosses his face, as though something strikes him as unfair. He collapses at my feet, his backside split wide open and bloody.

A swordsman finishes the Saxon off, his blade longer and darker than any steel I have ever seen. My breath stops as my rescuer leans closer. He wears only light leather armor and has several streaks of green war paint across his cheek. He is no soldier of my husband-to-be nor of Dyfed. The swordsman grins, his azure eyes mischievous and almost carefree despite the battle raging nearby. He extends a hand toward me.

"Well, well. What have we here?"

"Don't touch me!"

I swat his palm away, but he merely laughs. Despite looking unkempt as a barbarian, he speaks perfect Welsh. Dozens of men like him, clad in green, rush to battle the Saxons. I grab a broken spear to defend myself, warily eyeing the strange swordsman. He freely looks me up and down. Despite the nearby murder and mayhem, I blush when I realize how much skin shows through my tattered white gown.

A horn blares across the dell, and soon the remaining Saxons retreat to the woods. Small pockets of Welshmen chase them back to the tree line. The swordsman's rough companions gather near him as my husband's soldiers re-form their lines farther down the roadway. He raises his sword in salute before flashing a cocky grin.

"You sure you don't wish to come with us, fair lady? You'd be safer than with this lot."

My chest swells as I summon what courage I can, still unsure whether this Welsh woodsman means to make a war prize of me or not. Father always taught me that a noble must force confidence into their voice even if they don't feel it. Let's hope these ruffians don't realize my bark is worse than my bite.

"Mind your tongue!" I rebuke. "I am betrothed to King Morgan, and he will reward or punish you accordingly."

"The Hammer King's queen?"

He laughs toward his companions, many already returning to the cover of the woods. His face might almost be considered fair to look upon if not for his ungodly war paint and that blasted self-smug grin. I tighten the grip on my broken spear shaft. My husband's men-at-arms should come to my aid at any moment. The dark-haired swordsman smirks before turning his back on me.

"Tell your husband he owes me for saving his bride. Tell him Artagan of the Free Cantrefs always collects on his debts."

The swordsman disappears into the woods with the rest of his companions, whether to pursue the Saxons or distance themselves from my husband's soldiers, I know not. Perhaps both. I stand awhile with my broken shaft in hand even though all the remaining foes nearby lie dead or dying. Both the surviving Saxons and the stranger named Artagan have fled. I breathe easier and lower my broken weapon. Saying a silent prayer, I shut my eyes a moment and thank my Heavenly Father that I can still draw breath.

My head aches, trying to make sense of what just happened. How odd that Artagan's motley company fought against the Saxons, and yet they clearly bore no love for the Hammer King's men, either. Father always says the Welshmen of the Free Cantrefs are queer folk. Until today, I never saw one up close.

Ahern rushes to my side, a quartet of men-at-arms following behind him. The guardsman pants hard, his face marred with a few nicks, but he seems no worse for wear. His voice nearly cracks with relief.

"My lady, did the brutes harm you? When the ambush began, I feared the worst."

"The Saxons very nearly had me, but some Welshmen of the Free Cantrefs intervened."

"Jesus of Nazareth, I'll never forgive myself! Those ruffians are almost as bad as the Saxons."

Ahern looks at my broken spear, a mixture of admiration and self-reproach in his eyes. As my bodyguard, he will doubtlessly see this as a stain against his honor. Nonetheless, he seems genuinely pleased I at least made an effort to defend myself. I smile and place my hand on Ahern's shoulder. What did I ever do to deserve such a loyal guardsman?

Knots of soldiers slowly re-form their ranks. A party of horsemen gallops headlong toward us. Judging by their shields and armor, they must belong to my husband-to-be's retinue. Rearing up beside me, one doffs his helm. His trimmed brown beard and shapely jaw remind me of my betrothed, but he appears to be a few years younger than Morgan. He has a similar build, but his eyes blaze hazel instead of gray. The nobleman bows with a fist clenched to his chest.

"My lady, I am Prince Malcolm, the King's younger brother. Did the Saxons lay a hand on you?"

"Very nearly, my Prince, but all is well. Have you word of King Morgan?"

"Only his orders to take you directly to Caerleon myself, and to keep you safe until his return."

Malcolm impatiently snaps his fingers before several serfs bring forward a new litter. So that's where the first litter came from. Prince Malcolm must have remained behind to command the infantry while his elder brother rode ahead with all the horsemen. I start to politely protest, seeing all the trouble he goes to in bringing up another litter, but he shakes his head.

"Ladies are fragile things, my Queen. Let men decide what is best and care for you."

Taken aback, my voice deserts me. Does he mean to compliment me or put me in my place? Too tired to argue, I acquiesce to his request and step into the litter. Four fresh servants lift me up. Malcolm waves them along, exasperated with the poor serfs no matter how fast they move. Although similar in looks, he has a haughtier temperament than his elder brother. Malcolm stops to examine the dozens of slain Saxons and Welshmen lying along the highway, the dusty track stained vermillion with pools of blood. It takes an effort for me not to retch. The Prince orders Ahern and more guardsmen to surround my litter. Malcolm remarks to himself and his men, probably thinking I cannot hear.

"Look at the dead! The Saxons blocked up the road with fallen trees farther ahead, but the worst fighting was right here. This was no mere ambush. The Saxons were after something. They meant to take my brother's Queen."

My skin goes cold. The litter lurches forward as the foot soldiers resume their march. My lips tremble, my nerves frayed from my first brush with death. The Saxon savages had me in their power. But how did they know I would be here? Just yesterday, I myself couldn't have even imagined that I would be traveling the old coast road with the Hammer King's army.

If not for that swordsman Artagan, and his strange Welsh woodsmen, I might be a captive in some Saxon's camp by now. Or worse. As I succumb to a fitful slumber, my litter bobs through the crowd of soldiers toward the castle strongholds of my husband's kingdom. There I should be safe, at least for the time being.

I awake to the scent of soapy water and hot steam. My torn clothes have vanished and I lie naked on a pillowed cot. Warm vapors cloud the large, stone-walled room. I try to hide my nakedness with my bare hands. This seems like some strange dream. So much has happened in the last few days, nothing seems impossible now. Rising from my cot, I find a short hallway that ends at a window, offering me little in the way of escape. My pulse quickens as a soft breeze wafts through the archway. Green fields and a shimmering river loom several stories below. May the Virgin save me, I'm higher than a hawk! My palms sweat as I back away from the windowsill, still trying desperately to hide my private areas with two pillows from the adjacent bed.

"I hope you don't intend to take cushions into the bath with you, m'lady."

Startled, I turn around to find a young serving girl with her hands on her hips. Although she looks to be about my age, she stands a full head shorter than me. She points toward a large vat. The steaming waters fog my face as she gently strips me of my pillows and ushers me into the tub.

"No need to hide God's creations, m'lady. Just me here, and I gots them too. Call me Rowena."

At first I resist her hands, but the first shock of the heated water runs like wildfire through my flesh. I let out a heavy sigh as I sink up to my shoulders in the warm bathwater. All the weariness in my bones dissolves in the lavender-scented tub. Rowena suds a brush with an ivory bar and soaps up my back. Whatever has befallen me, I have surely landed in paradise. Breathing in the warm steam, I stop Rowena's brush with my hand.

"Where am I? Is this a bathhouse?"

Rowena cackles, resuming her scrubbing.

"This is the castle of Caerleon. Prince Malcolm's seat, m'lady."

"This isn't my husband's castle?"

"Well, I suppose they all are, dearie, but the Prince garrisons this one and less than a day's ride to the east lies the King's castle at Caerwent. Have you ne'er been in the kingdom of South Wales before, Your Grace?"

I give Rowena a sidelong glance. Our ways may seem odd to the Saxons and Romans, but we Welsh consider it a matter of pride that everyone from servants to kings may speak their minds freely. I'm sure our enemies would scoff and remark that our people's free, independent-minded ways will doom us in the end. But take away that freedom and you take away what makes us Welsh.

Rowena busies about the bath towels while I continue soaking up the hot waters of my tub. So this is the Kingdom of Gwent. I may never have journeyed more than a day's ride from Dyfed before, but I've seen enough of maps to know that the twin castles of Caerleon and Caerwent lie at the heart of the Hammer King's realm. Each stronghold stands about a day's gallop apart within the southeast corner of Wales. With the advent of our marriage, Morgan's fortresses of Caerleon and Caerwent will continue to shield South Wales as well as Dyfed from the Saxon invaders to the east.

Rowena hums to herself after washing me down and toweling me off. Despite being about my age, her hands are rough as an old woman's from working with lye soap. Her honey-brown locks lie piled atop her head in a fascinating chignon, which must be the current fashion for damsels in this part of Wales. The influence and styles of the ancient Romans run strongest in the castle towns of the South, or so my stepmother always says.

After putting me in a soft, green gown with a fur collar, Rowena shows me a mirror. The ivy cloth brings out the green in my eyes and the slim fabric makes even my sixteen-year-old body seem queenly. The royal wardrobes of South Wales put my old linens from Dyfed to shame. As Rowena belts a gold-threaded sash around my waist and pins two silver earrings on me, I begin to feel like a true queen for the first time. She combs my hair, rubbing a hint of jasmine into my dark locks.

"You look like a right proper princess now," Rowena says, smiling back at me in the mirror. "Won't be long before you've got little princesses and princelings of your own."

My stomach tightens at her mention of children. She surely means it as a compliment, but I cannot help recalling the many birthings of lambs and foals I've assisted Abbot Padraig with in Father's stables back in Dyfed. Nonetheless, I've never had a hand in the delivery of a woman heavy with child. All I know are the cries of anguish echoing from the nunnery once they begin their songs to draw the newborn into the world. Such was the way my mother brought me into the world and every mother of the Old Tribes before her. Only many such mothers didn't survive the ordeal. I swallow the lump in my throat, trying to push such thoughts from my mind.

I constantly keep thanking Rowena for tending to me, unaccustomed to having my own handmaid. Back in Dyfed, Father always considered it a frivolous luxury, even though he allowed my stepmother to indulge in several ladies-in-waiting. Even now, I feel a touch guilty. Betrothed to a king or not, I'm still perfectly capable of dressing myself. Nonetheless, Rowena seems to have an eye for fashion, which I unfortunately lack, so I happily smile at my reflection in the mirror as she works wonders with my green garment.

Outside the tower window, the red-tile-roofed houses of Caerleon surround the castle and crowd the banks of the nearby river. Never have I seen so many people all living together before. Girls herd chickens and sheep through the narrow sandy streets while young boys help their fathers shod horses in the smoking blacksmiths' shops. Mothers with babes in hand gather produce from the boatmen unloading their wares along the waterfront. A bustling settlement, Caerleon makes Dyfed look like a backwater by comparison. Rowena gives me a quick tour as she points out sights from our windowsill.

"King Morgan's castle at Caerwent be just as big as Caerleon if not grander," she says. "The twin citadels lie near each other, with the King's Wood betwixt them. To the east, the old Roman road traverses the forest."

Folding my arms, I survey the pleasant scene of well-tended gardens and fields. Beyond lie the tall oak groves of the King's Wood and the brown Roman road cutting through it. Somewhere down that path lies my lord's castle and my new home.

A herald's horn blows from the battlements. Small dust clouds rise farther down the roadway. A long column of cavalry canters down the winding path, bearing the red dragon banners of South Wales atop their lances. Morgan! It must be. The cavalcade of riders comes on slowly, their mounts clearly tired. I cannot make out more than specks of horsemen in the distance as I squint over the windowsill. Peasants all along the citadel gather to see the approaching riders. Doubtless, many of them have husbands, brothers, and sons amongst the Hammer King's troops.

An arm bangs on the door of our castle apartment. The thud of a metal fist on the solid oaken door makes me jump. Rowena cranes her face next to the keyhole.

"Who begs entrance to her ladyship's chambers?"

"I am Lady Branwen's guardsman! Who the devil has barred this door?"

I recognize Ahern's voice and nod to Rowena to loosen the hasp. My brother bangs on the door again. She reluctantly lets Ahern in, prodding him in the chest with a thick finger.

"Her Grace was taking a bath, and I'll lock whatever doors I bloody well please! For her privacy."

Ahern grumbles under his breath, but says no more beneath Rowena's challenging stare. The cuts on his face have small bandages, but look to have begun healing well. He turns to me and stands at attention, honorable and formal to the last even though we've known one another since childhood.

"My lady, the King's horsemen have been sighted near the castle walls."

"We know that, you oaf!" Rowena butts in. "We've a better view than you."

Despite my efforts to hide it, I smile at the two of them sparring. Rowena already clucks like a mother hen around me. I stifle my giggles at seeing Ahern's feathers so ruffled.

Rowena glances back out the window, her cheeks suddenly turning pale. A leaden weight sinks in my stomach as all the color drains from her face. She points at the approaching horsemen and their dragon banners, much like the old Pendragon flags King Arthur once flew over his armies. Something about the way the dragon banners flap in the wind, their staffs tilted forward at an awkward angle, only deepens my foreboding. My hands turn cold as I begin to understand. The serving girl raises a hand to her mouth, barely speaking above a whisper.

"They've dipped their banners, m'lady. Someone has died."

3

Shuffling feet echo under the castle gateway. The soldiers bring Morgan in on a pallet, his face pale as a ghost. Prince Malcolm rushes toward his injured brother as the procession of downcast warriors passes under the main gate. My gut clenches tight when they halt in the entranceway. Morgan's eyelids flutter, a few faint breaths escaping his lips. Even wounded, he clutches his great war-hammer as though its weight can keep his soul weighed down to earth. Although the King still lives, his men dip their banners anyway. Not even they expect him to last the night.

Malcolm demands to know what happened, but I only catch pieces of mingled replies from the guards. One soldier's voice manages to rise over the others as he reports to the Prince.

"We hit them hard, my liege. The Saxons didn't expect us so soon, but our numbers were near equal. The King crossed arms with their captain, the Chieftain Beowulf."

Malcolm suddenly turns as pale as his wounded brother. I grab the Prince's sleeve, still not understanding.

"Who is this Beowulf? Was he the one who did this to my betrothed?"

The host of armed men exchange silent glances. Malcolm growls at his men.

"Everyone out! Except for the healers."

The troopers' heads sink, their shoulders sagging as they leave amidst the shuffle of chain mail. I do not move. My husband-to-be is badly hurt, and I refuse to leave his side. His mangled body reminds me of a broken bird unable to fly. Whether he was a king or peasant, I could not find it in my heart to abandon such a man at death's door. Abbot Padraig taught me to be a Good Samaritan as well as a healer, and I'll not neglect such lessons now.

Decked in white cleric robes, several healers lift the King's makeshift mattress of straw and sticks before heading toward a tower stairwell. Morgan groans with every tilt of his pallet. When I move to follow the healers upstairs, Malcolm restrains me by the wrist. His grip tightens hard enough to make me wince, but he looks past me almost as though he forgets I am there. The two of us stand alone in the deserted alcove.

"This is the Fox and the Wolf's doing," he says with a growl.

"My Prince?" I ask, confused.

"Brothers. Saxon chieftains, both of them. Cedric the Fox is crafty as the devil himself and his brother Beowulf is so strong that the soothsayers think him a wolf born into man's flesh."

"And so Beowulf did this to the King?"

"Aye. And I believe his brother Cedric must have led the raid that was meant to capture you, my lady."

I swallow hard. For the life of me, I cannot understand why these two chieftains I have never met should bear such ill will against me. But then I realize that I can no longer think of myself as insignificant Branwen of Dyfed. I am soon to be a queen of South Wales. A valuable chess piece for a conniving Saxon foe, especially if I were taken hostage by our enemies. I succeed in gently removing Malcolm's hand from my sleeve.

"Then two traps were set today, one for my soon-to-be husband and the other for me?"

"Leave these matters to men, my lady. Your prayers are all that can help my brother now."

He turns away, ignoring me with a raised palm as he saunters out of the room. Twice now, he has shoved me away like a petulant child. I ball my fists even as my stepmother's voice inside my head checks my tongue. No lady would speak ill to her lord's kinsman, no matter how discourteous he may be. The shock of seeing his brother so bloodied seems to have temporarily addled Malcolm's thoughts. Alone in the alcove, I summon what poise I can as I draw in a deep breath. I'll show the Prince that this lady can do more than a knight at times like these.

Scaling the turret stairs, I find my husband-to-be in the uppermost solar. A quartet of clerics huddle around him, all of them men with balding tonsure haircuts atop their pallid heads. One monk sharpens a blade whilst another settles a bowl under the unconscious king. The clergymen exchange looks as I enter the room, the eldest of them scratching his white beard.

"My lady, what are you doing here?"

"What do you intend to do to him?" I ask, pointing at the King.

"Why, bleed him, Your Grace. We must purge the ill humors from his blood."

I raise an eyebrow. Surely, this old holy man jests. Haven't the Saxons' swords drawn enough of Morgan's blood already? Unfortunately, the monks' grave faces seem quite serious. Clearing my throat, I try to sound as commanding as Father does when he is cross with his servants.

"Put away your tools! Bring me freshwater, needles, and thread. Now!"

"Your ladyship—"

"I've tended wounded men and beasts alike before. I am also a king's daughter and soon to be a king's wife. Now do as I say and fetch my serving girl as well. Or do you wish to explain to the Prince why his brother died whilst you were busy bantering words with his brother's widow?"

The monks quickly get to their feet and scuttle down the turret steps. Alone for a moment with Morgan, I peel back his bloodied clothing to examine the wounds. I've seen livestock mauled by wolves before, but the sight of the King's open gashes makes the room start to spin. A pair of open slashes runs the length of his torso, like claw marks from a bear. I steady myself with a hand on the bedstead.

Thankfully Morgan sleeps deeply, else he would be roaring with pain right now. This Chief Beowulf must have wielded a large ax. Something like the weapon of the Saxon who tried to capture me. A shudder runs through me, thinking that I too might have ended up cut to pieces like this. I put a palm to Morgan's forehead, his scalp hot and bathed in sweat.

Rowena creeps up the stairs, carrying all the items for which I asked. She gasps upon seeing the King's injuries. The serving girl curtsies before jabbing a thumb over her shoulder.

"Some grumpy clerics told me to find you. Do you truly know how to heal such wounds, m'lady?"

"In my father's kingdom, I used to mend the cattle and horses when our livestock were attacked by wild beasts."

She gives me a blank, unreadable look and for a moment I wonder if the clerics were in the right after all. Perhaps I should relinquish my future husband's care to them. Then the thought of Malcolm's dismissal of me boils my blood. No, I must try to save the King's life if I can.

Rowena says nothing, but we both know the odds are slim for my betrothed tonight. It may not matter after all who tries to save him. Whether under the care of the monks or myself, King Morgan's fate lies in God's hands.

We set to work, cleaning and sewing up the King's bleeding wounds. The candle burns low in the bedchamber while the sky outside turns from red to purple to black as night falls. Even as I work bent over the wounded King, I take a bit of Prince Malcolm's advice, and say a silent prayer over Morgan for both his body and his soul.

For two weeks, I hardly sleep. Rowena and I take turns at the King's bedside while the castle kitchens brew soup and herbals at my instruction. When not cleaning bandages or taking a catnap in an armchair, I write letters to the abbey in Dyfed asking for Brother Padraig. I trust his skills in medicine far more than these South Welsh clerics, who daily insist on new remedies that make my skin crawl. Bloodletting, leeches, and salting wounds with the sign of the cross. I'd trust an old hag in the woods before I'd let these misguided "healers" anywhere near the King. Prince Malcolm has only borne with my insistence because my efforts have somehow kept his brother from slipping beyond our reach. Yet Morgan still remains very weak and does not yet have the strength to rise from bed.

I awake with a groggy yawn, unsure what day it is or the hour. Horseshoes clack along the cobblestones of the castle's front walk outside.

Rowena and the King both lie asleep on their pallets. Bending over the tiny upstairs window, I squint under the blinding midday sun at a lone rider cantering atop a donkey. His voice carries on the wind, strong as a sermon in a cathedral.

"God bless all under this roof, Your Grace! I hear you have need of me?"

"Abbot Padraig!"

Rubbing my eyes, the sight of my former mentor brings my weary limbs back to life. The guards let him upstairs and soon Padraig stands beside me, leaning over the King's bedstead. Balding as ever, his old skin wrinkled as crumpled parchment, Padraig thumbs through the books in his satchel. He nods and hums to himself, as though deep in conversation with someone I can neither see nor hear. Padraig clicks his tongue in disapproval.

"The steel that did this to him had something on it, a rust or mold or poison. You have cleaned his wounds and kept him fed marvelously, Lady Branwen, but it is a malady within his flesh that the Hammer King now battles."

"Will he live?"

"It depends. If the festering comes from rust or mold, he will recover. If poison, it remains but a matter of time before his lifeblood fails."

"When will we know for certain?"

"You've tended him these past few weeks. Either his humors have been healing inside him or they have been wilting. We should know which whenever he next comes to."

My heavy eyelids sag, the Abbot's words making my heart sink all the more. Morgan sleeps, his pink eyelids flickering, yet I'm certain he knows I am here. His hand grasps mine firmly as I put my palm in his. In his weakness, I have come to know my betrothed in a way that only a nurse or a mother might. The King lost his parents years ago to the Saxons, and now, in a way, he has no one to watch over him but myself. Without Rowena and me, those castle clerics would have probably killed him by now with their misguided doctoring.

Padraig elbows me with a large book.

"You seem to have misplaced this."

My eyes alight on the Abbot's wedding gift to me, the tome I foolishly left on the mead bench back in my father's castle. I press my lips to the monk's bald head, making the old man blush.

"You brought it all the way from Dyfed? Thank you, Abbot! I promise never to let it out of my sight again."

He smiles before retiring across the room.

"I wish I could be of more use, my dear. But it seems I've come a long way for nothing. All we can do now for King Morgan is wait."

"At least we now know the cause of his malady, thanks to you. Just having you here raises my spirits."

Rowena awakens and I soon introduce my new friend to my old teacher. The two talk in low tones for a while, making polite conversation whilst I watch over Morgan. With little more to do than wait, I open my book and caress the first page as I read the opening lines written in Padraig's steady hand.

> In the Year of Our Lord Five Hundred and Ninety Seven are written these ancient tales of Branwen the Brave, Queen of the Old Tribes in the centuries before the coming of the Romans and Christ. Praise be his name.

As the hours pass, I read by a sliver of waning sunlight cutting through an arrow slit. It has been some time since I first read such stories as a child. Of how Branwen was born by the sea, in the days when women ruled the Old Tribes as equals to men. Mothers became druidesses and daughters ruled as high chieftains beside men who were warriors, smiths, and bards. It was an era of magic and wisdom long since obscured by the mists of time.

Despite my fascination with the narrative, my eyelids start to sag just as I reach the pages that describe how and where Branwen met the man with whom she would fall in love. I yawn, my head growing heavy. Before I know it, the Abbot puts his hand on my shoulder. The light in the arrow slit grows dim.

"Get some rest, Branwen," he whispers. "The book and the King will still be here on the morrow."

Too tired to protest, I stagger to my own cot against the far wall. I nod off the moment my head hits the goose-feather pillow. My mind passes out of time and thought.

When I finally rise, a snuffed-out candle smolders beside me. A cold wind whistles through the castle, the first breath of winter heavy on the autumn wind. The purple haze of dawn glimmers through the arrow slit overhead. I sit bolt upright in bed, realizing I've overslept.

Voices murmur in low tones across the chamber. Throwing a blanket across my shoulders, I suddenly realize that the room is full of silent strangers.

Malcolm, the clerics, Brother Padraig, and several servants all gather around the King's bed, obscuring my view. My throat tightens. It looks like a cloistering for a funeral. Padraig must guess my mind, but oddly enough he smiles and guides me to the bed as he clears a way through the crowd. I blink, finding a small pile of mutton legs at the foot of the bed-stead. King Morgan grins at me as he sits upright in the sheets, gnawing on a bone.

"Forgive me, my Queen, but I did not wish to awaken you. I arose with such a hunger and the kitchen women have been kind enough to provide me with enough lamb shank to make me belch."

I laugh, relieved to see him alive and well. He eats as a man might after a long fast. The clerics all offer humble "amens" and make the sign of the cross in the air. Morgan takes me by the hand.

"I know it was you who stood by me and nursed me back to health, my lady. Although I could not stir to speak, I remember you hovering over me like a guardian angel."

" 'Twas not just I, my King. My serving girl, Rowena, and Abbot Padraig watched over you as well."

"And they shall be rewarded, as shall you. Our betrothal has lasted long enough. You and I will wed tonight!"

He squeezes my hand fondly. I find myself warm in the chest, both alarmed and excited at the suddenness of his declaration. The other South Welsh clerics protest all at once, their mingled voices decrying the King's still feeble strength. Just to prove them wrong, the Hammer King puts both feet on the ground and drags his war-hammer toward him. Everyone takes a step back from his bed, the King grinning with a challenging look as he lifts his massive weapon. It clearly pleases him to see the others cower back from his sickbed. Even on his deathbed, a king must seem strong and invincible to his thanes. He turns to Padraig, pointing with his hammer.

"Make the preparations, Abbot. What day is this?"

"The day before Hallowmas, my liege. Well into autumn, and if memory serves, also the anniversary of Lady Branwen's birth."

All eyes turn to me, making me squirm. What with all our labors and sleepless nights watching over the King, the number of days has slipped my mind. Today marks my seventeenth name day, and now it seems, the day in which I shall wed a king. Perhaps Morgan's recent brush with death has made him impatient to hold me in holy wedlock. And so the first night of my marriage bed shall be in his brother's castle at Caerleon.

Ushering me from the room, Rowena plucks and prods me as she chitters away happily as a spring bluebird. Her expression oscillates between broad smiles and thoughtful frowns. Much work remains for us to do before the ceremony.

Herded into one room after another, I acquiesce to her demands. Heated water for a fresh bath, crushed red ochre for my nails, beet juice to rouge my cheeks, and a buttermilk plaster for my already fair skin. Afterward, she slips me into a crepe and topaz gown, draping gold rings, silver bracelets, and a pearl necklace over me. I catch glimpses of myself in a bronze mirror as she stuffs wheat stalks and berries into my headdress. I can't tell if I look like a beautiful bride or some kind of harvest goddess. Rowena gaily smoothes out the wrinkles in my gown as she makes last-minute alterations. Despite my approaching wedlock, I can't help but dwell on thoughts of my birthday as well.

On that fateful Hallowmas Eve night seventeen autumns ago, Father doubtlessly paced back and forth outside my mother's solar, waiting to hear the first cries of his much-awaited son. Instead, he got me. Only once did he ever tell me of that night, and in an offhand way, while in one of his drunken reveries. He recalled the broad smile on my mother's face the evening afterward, she belonging to the Old Tribes who prized daughters more over sons. A primitive custom, Father called it.

The sun sets outside the castle. Rowena and the other women close up every shutter, bolt every external door, and turn every mirror to face the wall. All Hallows also marks the time when the spirit world crosses over into our own. A time when apparitions appear in the mists, and grave-yards murmur with the revelries of those beyond the grave. Tonight, Rowena makes sure to turn in three circles and spit each time she crosses a threshold. Christian or no, some beliefs from the Old Tribes never die.

In a way, I actually prefer to have my marriage on this night. Perhaps my mother herself will watch over me as her only daughter weds the greatest king of South Wales. Assuming the spiritual realm cares for the pains and joys of mortals anymore.

When I reach the chapel in my new dress, my footsteps jingle with silver bracelets that bedeck my damask gown. I hide my trembling palms under my bouquet. Everything has happened so fast. Morgan seems a good man, but in so many ways the Hammer King remains a stranger to me.

Morgan awaits me at the stone altar. He steadies himself on his up-ended war-hammer, using it like a makeshift cane. A broad smile creases his face, a bronze crown and several golden chains belying his otherwise plain linen tunic. Padraig stands beside him with a Bible in hand, the chapel crucifix peering down at all of us. A dozen witnesses join the quiet ceremony, Ahern and the clerics filtering into the pews. Rowena looms close by my side while Prince Malcolm stands at a respectful distance from his brother.

As I approach the sacristy, I admit that this is not at all the way I en-visioned royal marriages. No laborious ceremony, flower petals, or throngs of cheering onlookers throwing grains and chaff. The simplicity of the ceremony makes me breathe easier, as though an iron weight has lifted from my shoulders. Boisterous crowds have never much appealed to me. Tonight the chapel sounds quiet as a monastic library. Just my groom and me, a few witnesses, and God.

Morgan smiles as he takes my hand. Padraig turns to the altar and invokes the Almighty in Latin, the language of long-ago Rome. I know the tongue from all my reading lessons in the Abbot's care. Brother Padraig turns to Morgan and asks for the rings. Only when Morgan hesitates do I realize the King doesn't speak Latin. I gently whisper to him in Welsh.

"If you have a token, my King, you may present it now."

He pats my hand, seemingly pleased at both my translation and my discretion, even in front of so small an audience. Morgan pulls out a pair of golden rings and slips one onto his finger and the other on mine. Its golden heft weighs heavy upon my hand. Padraig makes the final incantation in the air, spreading sweet-smelling incense. Before I know it, Morgan has his lips on mine, his brown beard tickling my cheeks. With a single kiss, I am now made a queen.

Our guests smile as they offer congratulations. Morgan and I soon find ourselves alone in his brother's private chambers, set aside just for us tonight. I keep my gaze to the floor, feigning interest at cracks in the limestone tiles. I've only vague notions of what to do next. I fold my palms, wiping the perspiration from my fingers.

Morgan kisses me on the neck, his hands gentle as they unlace my gown. I gasp at the cold touch of his skin against mine, unused to pressing myself so closely to another. His heavy thighs soon find mine on the bed, our kisses and tongues mingling until I can't tell him from me. A fiery pain pierces me to the core and I cry out against my will. Morgan stops.

"Are you all right?"

I rightly don't know how to answer him. Despite the mingled pleasure and pain, I nod and we continue.

Before I know it, the consummation ends and Morgan snores in the darkness beside me. He proves himself to be a gentle lover, if somewhat hasty in the bedchamber. I toss and turn beside him, feeling the bedsheet wet beneath me. So the deed is done. For some reason I blink back water in my eyes. I am a woman now, a wife, and a queen.

We ride into Caerwent the next day at the head of a procession of mounted knights and an endless train of foot soldiers. Morgan did not wish to waste any time getting to his capital, and after the rumors of his purported death, he needs his subjects to see their leader alive and well. Thousands of inhabitants line the roadway to greet us, cheering and waving while Morgan and I ride side by side atop a pair of tall mounts. I wince in the saddle, my thighs still sore from last night, but I wave and smile at the cheering crowds, pretty as a painting. My featherheaded stepmother would be proud.

The local maidens wear long skirts and bonnets, whereas the men have hose breeches and woolen shirts. A far cry from the tartans my kins-folk prefer in Dyfed or the skins and furs of the Free Cantref Welsh. Morgan has his full armor on, shining like a polished silver coin. I canter beside him in a pure white garb like the virgin I no longer am.

Caerwent's tall towers loom before us. Red-tile-roofed homes crowd the streets, and stone chapels surround the old Roman amphitheater. The fortress walls themselves stand much taller and broader than those at Caer-leon. Their stone bastions bear pockmarks from fire and battering rams. Caerwent is a base of war first and a settlement second. No doubt, the fortress has seen many sieges in its time.

As we enter through the western gates, red banners hang above every tower, window ledge, and archway. The crimson dragon standard of the Hammer King's realm flies everywhere. Only when the iron grating of the gates closes with a thud behind us do I realize I have arrived at my new home. A prickly sensation rises along my scalp. These lofty towers and gray stone keeps will never let me out.

Shaking such childish thoughts from my head, I dismount in the main courtyard between the outer defenses and the interior halls. High above, pikemen patrol the upper embrasures, keeping watch over the East Marches. Rowena accompanies me as Morgan and Malcolm lead us to our new accommodations. My serving maid beams with rosy cheeks, sporting a new dun-colored dress. She is now my permanent lady-in-waiting, a wed-ding gift from my new brother-in-law, Prince Malcolm.

Wide stone arches reinforced with wood support the interior halls. The sheer volume of these cathedral-like interiors takes my breath away. I recall reading in ancient monastic annals that the bulk of all South Welsh castle walls were laid down by the Romans centuries ago. Unfortunately, our people no longer know how to erect such monstrous stone battle-ments anymore. One of many arts lost to our wise men since the coming of the barbaric Saxons. Even though Father calls our hill fort in Dyfed

a castle, it seems like little more than some rocky walls and wooden palisades compared to the majesty of Caerwent. I run my hand along the cool
interior bulwarks, touching worn inscriptions carved by heroes and knights
long dead. Only fragments of chiseled words within the stone remain.
SPQR. AP ARTHUR. CYMRY.

With arms spread, Morgan presents his pride and joy within the castle.
His throne room, or atrium as he calls it in the old Roman fashion. A
large, circular chamber several stories above the heart of the complex, it
has tall open archways that overlook the greens and rivers beyond the city
walls. Our footsteps echo off the whitewashed pillars and polished marble floors. Miniature statues of Arthurian knights carved into the stone
columns look down at us like silent sentinels. Only the twittering birds
reach us this high above the city floor. At the center of the room stands a
pair of thrones, one large chair of black schist and another, smaller seat
made of cream limestone. Morgan pats the smaller stone chair.

"I had it installed before I set out for your hand in Dyfed. Give it a try,
my Queen."

I flash Rowena a wry, sidelong glance before reaching out for the
limestone chair. Cold to the touch, I recline in it as I would a pool of water.
Once in the seat, the entire atrium seems dwarfed beneath me, save for
the King's seat to my right. I tap my slippers against the base of my perch,
betraying a giddy smile. My very own throne.

A child comes running into the throne room, a young boy with dirty-
blond locks. No more than ten years old. At first I think the youth one of
the serving staff until I notice his silken collar and well-tailored tunic.
The child leaps up into Morgan's arms.

"Father!"

The room suddenly contracts as though I stare down a long narrow
tunnel. Nothing but Morgan and this little boy stand at the end of it. The
child glances at me suspiciously. How could I have been so naïve? Morgan has ten years on me. I should have expected he would know women
and have sired heirs of his own. Did Father know of Morgan's young son
when he betrothed me to the Hammer King? Of all the possible outcomes that could befall me, I never envisioned myself as someone's stepmother. And at seventeen years of age no less. Instead of being the put-upon

child, *I* am the strange new woman in the household. My palms begin to sweat.

Morgan ushers the child forward, the boy sliding reluctantly toward me. He has the King's straight nose and regal jaw, but the yellowish hair must come from the mother, whomever she was. Morgan ruffles the boy's hair.

"Allow me to present my son, Arthwys. My only son and heir to the throne of South Wales."

Arthwys, a Welsh variant of Arthur. By the time this boy grows up, his father may very well have made him the next King Arthur of a united people. Still seated, I bow from my throne toward the boy. He forces a crooked smile, glancing up at his father as he hides behind the King's frock. My own smile must look equally forced.

Across the atrium, Prince Malcolm folds his arms as he smirks at me and the boy in our first encounter. My brother-in-law is actually enjoying my discomfort for some reason. Why, I cannot imagine, but he only flashes his eerie grin when his elder brother's back is turned. His brief sneer quickly evaporates into his usual smile, and I wonder for a moment whether I simply imagined it.

King Morgan soon excuses the boy. Arthwys bounds away into the arms of a serving woman, eyeing me warily as the lady ushers him out of the throne room. Morgan folds his hands behind his back, frowning thoughtfully.

"Let's show you to our solar."

Morgan and Malcolm walk ahead to a set of turret stairs. They climb the steps before I've even risen from my limestone seat. Rowena hangs back with me, keeping her voice low.

"His previous queen perished in childbirth last winter. They've only the one boy. I thought you knew, m'lady."

"Evidently, there is much my father did not tell me."

"Look at the silver lining, m'lady. With a male heir, the King's less likely to set you aside should you not produce a son soon enough."

Her words cut me as deeply as they comfort. True, Morgan has a son, and feels secure in his heir. But he will doubtlessly expect more children before long.

My skin turns uncomfortably hot. Some lords set their wives aside if no heir comes forth during their marriage. Such sonless marriages of noblemen the Church annuls, leaving the king free to seek a new wife. There are no ex-queens. Either childbirth kills them or a nunnery accepts them, and never do they venture out into the world again. The very walls of the castle suddenly seem to close in on me as we ascend the staircase. I've not been wed yet a day and already all eyes watch my womb for any sign of quickening.

Lush burgundy pillows cover an expansive curtained mattress inside the bedchamber. A warm fire in the hearth illuminates a tabletop full of pewter plates, silver carafes, and fresh bread. Rowena and I sit at the benches, filling our bellies after our long ride. With fresh wine in my goblet and warm bread in my stomach, I can finally stretch my limbs after having spent hours in the saddle. Morgan and Malcolm seem to have forgotten us entirely, the two brothers giving one another stern looks as they converse across the room. Morgan leans in close to his brother, nearly beard to beard.

"Impossible! How could the Saxons have known where my bride would be on the road?"

"Isn't it obvious, King Brother? We have a spy in our midst."

"No Welshman would spy for the Saxons."

"But not all Welshmen wish us well, and might let the Saxons do their dirty work for them."

Morgan shoots me a glance across the room. Pretend as we might, Rowena and I keep our eyes to our food even though we now hang on every word between the two men. Morgan lets out a heavy sigh.

"Then we've only one choice," he begins. "To call a gathering of rulers here at court."

"You mean to invite the North Welsh and those of the Free Cantref folk inside our walls?"

"Better to have our rivals close where we can keep an eye on them. We'll propose a united alliance against the Saxons, all Welsh kingdoms acting as one."

"Psh!" Malcolm scoffs. "They'll never agree to such a thing!"

"Of course not, but by their words and looks, we might discern which of them betrayed us."

Both men look one another over, their gazes meeting in agreement. These princes have clearly dealt with deceptive foes before, both on the battlefield and in the shadows of courtly intrigue. Mesmerized by Morgan's cool, calculating logic, I wish I had such insight into the hearts of others. With the two lords of South Wales more at ease, I venture to add my own thoughts.

"Perhaps the Welsh *are* ready to unite with us. After all, it was a band of warriors from the Free Cantrefs who saved me the day the Saxons attacked my litter on the King's Road."

The two men exchange looks, but I carry on nonetheless.

"Their leader called himself Artagan. He seemed a self-assured sort of man, and he had a message for you."

"Artagan Blacksword?" Morgan replies, raising a dark eyebrow.

"Artagan. Yes, that was it. He told me you now owe him for having saved your bride."

Morgan brings his fist down onto the tabletop so hard it cracks one of the wooden planks. Rowena and I jump back in our seats, spilling wine and bread crumbs across the floor. He leans in close to me, the Hammer King's voice graver than I have ever heard it before.

"I put a price on that blackguard's head not two summers ago for stealing my cattle and women's virtue! You're telling me that I owe this *outlaw* anything?"

It takes me a moment to shake my head. Whatever my husband's history with this man, I have a prickly intuition that he does not tell me all. Nonetheless, his stern face has taught me an abrupt lesson. No matter the circumstance, never mention the name Artagan Blacksword in the King's presence ever again. A thief and a violator of women? So much for the warrior who saved me from the Saxon savages. Prince Malcolm smirks in the corner, though whether at me or his brother, I cannot tell.

"Looks like we know the man who betrayed us?" Malcolm remarks.

"Call the gathering anyway," Morgan replies. "We'll learn more secrets if we get all of these snakes into one room together."

Both the King and Prince leave the chamber. Rowena and I pick up the pieces of splintered wood and chipped crockery. Wise as Morgan and

Malcom may be, they have failed to ask one very important question. If this brigand Artagan Blacksword really meant me harm, why did he spare me? Why save me from the Saxons? It nettles my thoughts like a splinter in my mind. Why, indeed.

4

His hand lies across my naked skin. Morgan rolls over in his sleep as the first sliver of sunlight cuts across our bedsheets. Over the past few weeks, the King has come to my bed with the predictability of a water clock. Around sundown each evening, his caresses and lips rise pleasingly over my body before he loosens his belt and takes me to the bed. His ardor matches his efficiency and within a few dozen lightning strokes he dispatches with his kingly duty for the night. Sleep comes upon him quite suddenly afterward, but I find myself lying awake and staring up at the scarlet canopy of our bedstead. My courses have come upon me this morning and I have hidden the towels in my chamber pot. Once the servants clean out my toiletries, the news will doubtlessly disseminate throughout the castle. Another moon passes and the Queen has not yet conceived.

As I roll out of bed, I frown at my scarecrow frame in the brassy mirror. Lords like their ladies thick and plump, but my ribs still show through the skin in places and my bust lags several years behind the other young womenfolk at court. Small wonder why the King goes about our lovemaking with such a businesslike demeanor. The same cool logic that convinced him to take my hand and bind together the southern kingdoms also compels him to get another heir upon me. Not so much for passion's sake, but for the good of the realm. I sigh as I watch a pair of starlings nesting alongside my bedchamber window. Birds may mate for love, but kings and queens have their duty to attend. Far be it from me to dishonor the tradition.

The blare of silver trumpets reverberates along the castle walls. Morgan rises beside me, both of us looking out over the windowsill. Beyond the gates of Caerwent, two separate processions approach the citadel, one from the north road and another to the west. The leaders called to the gathering have come. Both companies bear dragon banners, one contingent with green dragons and the other black. Guardsmen from the citadel greet them beneath the red dragon standard of the Hammer King. All the kingdoms of Wales bear dragon flags like King Arthur once did, only differing in the colors they choose to follow. Red, green, and black. Every warlord wishes to be the head dragon of the land without bowing down to the others. I shake my head at the iron-headed pride of the Welsh. A blind man could see why the Saxons continually prevail against such a brave, but divided people.

Morgan pulls on his clothes, fastening on his best gold brooch and crimson cape. His crown hangs on the bedstead beside his large warhammer. He grabs them both before descending the stairwell to the throne room. The King calls back to me, his voice echoing along the turret steps.

"Put something impressive on, my lady. Kings judge each other by the manner of their queens!"

My heart convulses as I turn toward the mirror. Disheveled raven hair and a threadbare nightgown make me look more like a peasant's daughter than a monarch's wife. Rowena arrives with a basket full of linens and shawls, rubbing her sleepy eyes as the bugles outside sound again. The entire citadel must know by now of the approaching envoys and their armed escorts.

After cycling through several gowns that could hardly pass for horse blankets, Rowena threads my arms through a beige woolen with azure fringe. I bite my lip as Rowena runs a brush through the tangled knots of my midnight locks, every stroke burning like fire at the roots of my hair. Morgan calls for me from the atrium. I shuffle into a pair of fur-lined shoes, our guests' horses whinnying inside the castle courtyard far below. Our visitors dismount and approach the throne room. Morgan's voice booms across the hall again, reverberating up toward my tower solar.

"Branwen!"

I scurry down the tower steps, Rowena holding up the train of my garments. We both nearly trip half a dozen times, descending the stairwell two steps at a time. As I settle into my seat beside the King, my face flushes enough without any artificial rouge. Rowena curtsies to leave, stopping to pluck a few stray threads from the hem of my gown. Morgan looks me over quickly, his face betraying none of his thoughts. I cannot tell whether he approves or disdains my choice of attire. No time for alterations now. The footsteps of our guests clack along the tile floors of the entranceway. Rowena finishes pruning my skirts and exits the atrium just as the first heralds announce their lordships.

"Belin the Great, King of North Wales! And his sons, Princes Rhun and Iago!"

A man with a sable cloak and a snowy-white beard approaches King Morgan's throne. "Belin the Old," as Father and most others outside the North call this king. Although not to his face. Two young men flank either side, both with dark hair and beards, their plate-mail shirts jangling with every step. Rhun and Iago, I presume. Judging by the sackcloth tunics beneath their armor, these horsemen must have ridden under the black banners. I inwardly chide myself, knowing I ought to spend more time studying the bloodlines of the royal houses to determine who is related to whom. These first guests follow the Black Dragon sigil of the North. Best not to forget such things.

Belin and his sons nod toward Morgan, showing respect, but not quite stooping to bow either. After all, in the northlands of Gwynedd, they rule supreme and bend their knees to no one. Morgan returns the gesture with a cordial nod.

From a side entranceway, the tardy Prince Malcolm shuffles into the throne room while tying up his belt. The Hammer King throws him a sharp look before Malcolm reclines in the shadows. Thank the Virgin I did not show up late to the atrium. Morgan will doubtlessly have a long talk with his younger brother later. The herald announces the next batch of envoys.

"King Cadwallon of the Free Cantrefs! And Lady Olwen, daughter of King Urien in the northern Powys Free Cantrefs!"

A large, round man with thinning red hair and a beard to match saunters into the atrium with a woman holding his hand. King Cadwallon looks large enough to swallow a wild boar for breakfast. His green doublet, bristling with buttons, leaves little doubt as to which company rode under the green banners. He turns to the lady holding his arm.

"King Urien is ill, and although I do not rule his lands, I offered to escort his daughter, the Lady Olwen, to these proceedings that she might stand in his place."

Morgan edges forward in his seat while the onlookers of the court murmur amongst themselves. Goose bumps rise along my forearms. A woman to stand in a council of men? These Free Cantref folk follow the ways of the Old Tribes even more than I first thought.

Lady Olwen wears a white linen gown and has dark locks like me, only hers hang straight whereas mine wave slightly. Our similarities end there. She has a full-bodied figure of a grown woman, and God as my witness, her irises twinkle with a hint of violet. Every man in court stares at her, and who wouldn't? She is a Welsh Venus.

Cadwallon clears his throat, his face turning the same shade as his auburn beard. I cannot help but stare. These Free Cantref folk are simultaneously a fascinating and yet strange lot, harkening from the wilds of the mountains and forests. Cadwallon looks angry, but keeps his voice marginally calm as he eyes King Morgan.

"Amongst the Free Cantrefs, our womenfolk may speak amongst men in council. I would expect to find that same right honored anywhere in the Welsh Lands."

Morgan leans back in his seat, staring at Cadwallon until every other onlooker in the room begins to shift uncomfortably. Tapping the arm of my chair, I can hardly remain still. My husband flashes a curt smile.

"For such a gracious noblewoman, we would be honored to have Lady Olwen listen in her father's stead."

"Thank you, King Morgan." Olwen nods. "You do my father great honor."

Her voice runs deep for a woman, and rich like one gifted with song. Morgan's polite smile turns into a genuine grin, and I find my own neck flushing hot. Lady Olwen has charm enough to mold even the likes of the

Hammer King to her whims. My fists tighten, contemplating how many men only value a woman for her allure and beauty. Though it be unchristian, a seed of malicious envy takes root inside me. A crow-face like me doesn't even have half the good looks Lady Olwen possesses. I bite my tongue until it smarts.

Morgan's guardsmen line the walls, each man-at-arms bedecked in chain mail vests and crimson capes. They clutch their spears and shields tightly, as though preparing to use them. All three parties eye each other warily, their red, black, and green dragon pennants nearly touching the domed ceiling of the spacious atrium.

The herald clears his throat to announce a final guest.

"Also, hailing from the Free Cantrefs, Sir Artagan Blacksword!"

My heart freezes up as the dark-haired swordsman strides into the throne room. Morgan rises from his seat and Malcolm quickly rushes to his side. The King grips his war-hammer and the Prince reaches for his large mace as they leer at the Blacksword. Artagan takes his place beside the other Free Cantref members, King Cadwallon and Lady Olwen. His longsword hangs in a cinch diagonally down his back. He smirks at the Hammer King's and Prince Malcolm's livid faces before turning his striking sapphire eyes on me. I blush scarlet as the black-haired swordsman stares unabashedly at me, his gaze running from my eyes to neckline.

"Lady Branwen, or Queen, I should say. It has been too long since our last meeting."

He bows toward me, ignoring Morgan and Malcolm. I slink lower in my chair, wishing for the world he hadn't brought me into the center of this. Why does he have to speak to *me*? I suddenly wish I could simply disappear. The Hammer King aims his weapon at Artagan, clenching his teeth.

"I've a price on this brigand's head! Guards, seize the devil where he stands!"

A ring of crimson-cloaked guardsmen level their spearheads at Artagan. The swordsman merely grins, not even drawing his blade. Instead, King Cadwallon steps between the knight and a dozen men-at-arms, the girth of his belly urging the soldiers to stand back. Cadwallon's roar seems to shake the rafters.

"This is a knight of the Free Cantrefs and he comes to this gathering under my protection! Any hand laid against him is a hand laid against me, and will answer to my archers for it!"

Several bowmen clad in green tunics and brown leathers draw back their creaking bowstrings. In response, a dozen more red-caped guards tromp into the room, the din of their chain mail murmuring off the ceiling. Belin's lot from the North do not draw their swords, but instead stand apart, flexing their fingers along their black ash lances. Clutching the sides of my throne, I wonder whether this limestone seat will shield me from spears and arrows if a brawl takes place. Morgan stands at the center of the throne room, his gray-eyed stare never flinching from Artagan.

"This so-called knight," Morgan begins coolly, "stands accused of crimes against my people."

Cadwallon steps between Artagan and Morgan, his stomach nearly touching the Hammer King.

"And half the men in this room stand accused of crimes against the Free Cantrefs! Did you call this gathering to talk peaceably or to cross swords?"

Morgan seethes through his teeth before calming his breath. My husband's hot rage subsides. He stands a full head taller than Cadwallon as he stares him down, raising his voice for all to hear.

"While at this gathering here in Caerwent, I grant temporary amnesty to all present!" Morgan declares. "All grudges must be set aside until after all parties have safely returned to their respective provinces. But once this conference has concluded, each lord may seek justice as he sees fit."

A silence pervades the room. Cadwallon and Belin exchange looks before they both nod in agreement. Artagan makes no move, his mischievous azure eyes glancing from the Hammer King to me.

Morgan bangs the handle of his hammer against the tile floors, echoing throughout the hall. At this signal, bondservants enter the chambers carrying carafes of wine and pewter goblets. The various parties retire to their new quarters in order to refresh themselves after their long journey to Caerwent.

King Morgan and Prince Malcolm quickly exit the atrium. I soon find them speaking in confidence at the foot of the turret stairs, their voices low and tense.

"I cannot believe the gall of that Blacksword!" Morgan fumes. "Provoking strife in my own court!"

"We should strip our visitors of their arms before the conference this afternoon," Malcolm replies.

"Try to take away their weapons and violence will ensue. No, little brother, you would only be playing into the Blacksword's hand."

Neither man seems to notice me as I stand in the alcove with them. Perhaps I seem too harmless a personage to eavesdrop on their secrets. I put a hand on Morgan's shoulder, rubbing his knotted shoulders and speaking soothingly in his ear.

"Why does King Cadwallon protect this outlaw, my King?"

"Because Artagan is rumored to be Cadwallon's bastard, and clearly his favorite knight."

Morgan turns back to his brother, his voice running cold once more.

"And where were you, Prince Brother?"

"Forgive my tardiness." Malcolm sheepishly shrugs. "I was delayed."

"You dabble under milkmaids' skirts too often, boy. Do *not* be late again."

The recollection of Malcolm tightening his belt as he entered the atrium earlier suddenly resurfaces in my mind. Lords have always had a taste for pretty women regardless of rank. The Prince has not yet taken a wife, but I had not imagined him the sort to dally with serving wenches to excess.

I clench my jaw, suddenly imaging Malcolm cornering some poor serving girl who is too afraid to defy the nobleman who haunts her steps with a lustful eye. And my husband allows such injustices under his roof? I take a deep breath. Perhaps I am being too hasty, imagining crimes I have not even witnessed. Still, I cannot help but eye my new brother-in-law a touch more warily than before.

Outside, armed companies of newcomers stable their mounts in the castle yards, covering the cobblestones with small beds of hay. Northern cavalrymen with tall, black lances sit astride armored chargers, coolly eyeing the green-clad bowmen of the Free Cantrefs who sheath their longbows beneath mantles of animal skins. All the while, King Morgan's red-caped foot soldiers keep close watch over their new guests, their short-swords concealed behind broad shields. The tension in the armed camp is palpable even from the safety of my window.

My palms sweat. It would take little indeed to set these horsemen, archers, and men-at-arms at each other's throats. With all these lords and ladies gathered together under one roof, more than a few secrets will doubtlessly pass from ear to ear over the next few days.

Morgan and Malcolm continue to whisper about the gathering of leaders scheduled for later this afternoon. Would that I were a fly on the wall in that council, to sit in a circle with lords and kings deciding the fate of our people. If only I had been born a man. But what am I thinking? Moments ago, I flushed scarlet when the Blacksword came into the atrium, drawing attention upon me as he purposefully ignored my husband. What would the ancient Queen Branwen have done in my stead? I doubt she or any other woman of the Old Tribes would have stood idly by and blushed. Clearing my throat, I summon what courage I can as I interrupt the two royal brothers.

"My King, I notice one important group absent from this gathering. None from Dyfed have come."

Both brothers exchange looks.

"Dyfed is part of my realm now," Morgan replies coolly, clearly perturbed by my interrupting his conversation with Malcolm.

"Your guests already show much distrust," I press on. "Better to show proof of Dyfed's allegiance to you."

"Speak plainly, my Queen. What proof can I offer, other than my word?"

"I will join you at the council this afternoon and represent Dyfed. Showing solidarity with your kingdom. That is why you wed me, is it not?"

Morgan's eyes widen, doubtlessly surprised by my insistence. My father told me to look out for Dyfed's interests, and I cannot do that if I'm shut out of the gathering of Welsh lords. While Morgan contemplates my proposal, Prince Malcolm scoffs beside him.

"You cannot seriously consider this, Morgan? A girl in the council!"

"Lady Olwen represents *her* father!" I retort. "And I shall stand in place of mine. My presence shows that Dyfed supports my husband, reminding the others that King Morgan now has the largest combined kingdom in all Wales. No small feat."

Morgan looks me over as though trying to pierce me to my soul. He folds his arms and slowly nods. His voice brooks no argument.

"Vortigen breeds sharp-witted queens. You will listen in council, and not speak. Understood?"

I nod, not sure whether I have gained a victory or simply entered a lion's den. Malcolm sulks, leaving without another word. Morgan ignores him and places a hand on my shoulder, his voice almost fatherly, yet stern.

"Remember, Branwen, we call this council to discuss a united front against the Saxons, but we also must keep our wits sharp toward a more immediate threat."

"The spy now in our midst?"

"Precisely. One of those sitting in this council tried to have me killed and you kidnapped. Although the Saxons were the instruments of this plan, they must have had Welsh help. I'm sure of it."

My throat runs dry. Memories of the Saxons and their bloody steel on the King's Road make my skin turn cold. To think that I will sit at table with someone who wished me such harm gives me an inward shudder. But I am a daughter of kings and a wife of one too now. I cannot play the part of a child forever. My husband doubtlessly suspects Sir Artagan, yet I am not so sure. The Blacksword saved me on the King's Road, and that doesn't sound like the act of someone plotting my demise. Of course, since when is anything in this world as simple as it first appears? Unlike the chess matches I once played with Father, this game of kings and queens is real, and the losers may forfeit their very lives. I swallow hard, watching the sundial by the window, counting the hours until the council begins.

A cleric chimes the evening vespers with the chapel bells, announcing the commencement of the council. Ahern escorts me through the atrium to the side room containing Morgan's round counselor's table. The large alcove overlooks the verdant pastures and blue rivers of the East Marches, the circular room itself replete with marble archways and stone columns that recall the architectural majesty of Rome and the Holy Church. At the entranceway, a pair of stone sentinels leer at all trespassers with gargoyle eyes, as though the dead kings of old sit in council with the living still. I squeeze Ahern's hand before leaving him at the door and entering the council chamber alone.

Most of the others have already gathered around the large oaken table, the members of North Wales and the Free Cantrefs among them. Morgan and Malcolm arrive last. I make sure to sit just to the left of my husband. On my other side, Belin's sons, Rhun and Iago, nod cordially to me, both men silent as their white-haired father. Directly across the tabletop, Lady Olwen and Artagan whisper in one another's ears, every so often glancing my way. I fight the urge to squirm in my seat. To the others, I probably seem as out of place at this gathering as a sheep amongst wolves. Nonetheless, I hold myself erect in my seat. For once, my stepmother's lessons in propriety have some use as I channel my nervous twitches into sitting with perfect ladylike posture. My hairline begins to bead with sweat, but I dare not move to wipe it away lest one of the others notice.

Morgan calls the council to order as he raises his voice.

"I've asked you all here so that we might gather all the Welsh might together and unite our forces against further Saxon invasions."

Before my husband can finish, Cadwallon bangs the table with the flat of his meaty hand. Morgan pauses to glare at the fat monarch.

"Something troubling you, Lord Cadwallon?"

"And I suppose you think *you* should lead this grand alliance against our foes?"

"My kingdom and my armies are now the largest in all Wales."

Morgan glances my way, silently reminding them that Dyfed's spearmen now number among his troops. All eyes rest on me, but every face might as well belong to a mask. All nine members of the council remain silent. Belin the Old raises his gravelly voice.

"Our enemies are likewise divided, splintered by their own success, rivaling each other."

"Aye!" Cadwallon seconds. "West Saxon tribes and the Anglo-Saxon kingdom of Mercia, under King Penda, sometimes fight one another."

"And sometimes they join hands as allies," Morgan retorts. "If the West Saxons and Penda combine forces, they will easily outnumber us. All of us."

Cadwallon stands, pushing back his chair with his wide thighs.

"I can fight Saxons without your help and I'll be damned before I bend a knee to any man here!"

The entire table erupts into overlapping arguments. Cadwallon shakes his fist at Morgan. Malcolm and Artagan exchange curses from their ends of the table. Olwen speaks cordially with Rhun and Iago, all of them nonetheless frowning at one another. Only King Belin and I remain silent. The old king looks at me with his pale-blue eyes before raising his hands. Gradually, the other members at the table cease talking so that the old man may speak.

"Queen Branwen of Dyfed has not yet voiced her thoughts. I would hear what she has to say."

"My lord?" I reply, eyeing King Belin with a raised eyebrow.

Morgan's eyes bore into me like hot coals. His order to listen and not speak in the council still rings in my ears. I've a sinking feeling Old Belin may have guessed as much and perhaps hopes to throw my husband or me off balance with his supposedly innocent question. I have to say *something* to make this meeting more peaceable, yet at the same time not offend my husband, nor reveal our intention of weeding out the traitor in our midst. I blurt out the first words that come to mind.

"I think the best way to kill a frog is to cook it slowly."

The other noblemen exchange looks, their blank expressions slowly giving way to grins and guffaws. Cadwallon bangs his fist on the table in mirth and even Old Belin flashes a smile. Everyone's shoulders relax as they recline in their chairs. Lady Olwen leans across the table, her violet-blue irises fixed on me.

"Is that some witch's spell, your ladyship?"

"It's something my mother used to say. One of the few things I remember about her."

My throat stops up a moment, and I push back the water behind my eyes. I can't recall the last time I mentioned Mother to anyone, let alone strangers. I cannot let them see this part of me, so I lower my voice in order to make it steady.

"Many a countrywoman may cook a frog caught from the bogs," I begin. "If she throws it in a boiling pot, the creature hops out, knowing it's in peril. But if she places the frog in lukewarm water, and gradually heats the cauldron with a growing fire, the creature will be cooked to death."

"How informative," Prince Malcolm mumbles dismissively.

"It is meant to be," I retort, my gaze boring into him. "We are all frogs, gentlemen and ladies. If the Saxons invade with a large army, we might unite against them, but instead they peck away at our separate kingdoms year by year, whittling us away one realm at a time. All Wales is a frog being slowly cooked to death, only we refuse to see it."

Silence pervades the room. Morgan puts his hand under the table and softly squeezes my palm with a smile. He approves of my words. I nearly smile back until Sir Artagan leans across the table toward me, an earnest expression on his usually roguish face.

"So what would you have us do, Queen Branwen?"

"Heed my husband and exploit the great weakness of the Saxons. They fear our unity, for it spells their doom."

Artagan and Morgan lock stares, neither one revealing anything with their expressions. I wonder whether my words have made an impression or if these two antagonists merely play chess with one another in their minds. Cadwallon takes up the conversation again, both he and Prince Malcolm debating the finer points of a possible alliance, mostly in disagreement, but neither with heated overtones as before. Morgan and Artagan remain silent, both watching one another while their kinsmen continue the debate. The brothers Rhun and Iago occasionally speak up, insisting on their own interests just like the other barons. Their father, Old Belin, coolly watches me. I pretend not to see the white-haired king as he evaluates me with a sharp eye.

When the bell tower tolls at the approach of the next hour, King Morgan adjourns the gathering in order to resume on the morrow. No one has agreed to anything in particular, but at least no blades have been drawn. Everyone here knows that we share a common enemy in the Saxon hordes, yet so much remains unsaid amongst these calculating men. I doubt these lords say or do anything without ulterior purposes.

As we exit the chamber, Lady Olwen accompanies me out the doorway, not saying a word. She merely looks me over before making a slight bow. I nod back and watch her go, her dark skirts trailing after her down the long stone archways. As the only other woman from the meeting, I wish I might follow her and share her thoughts. Perhaps over a cup of warm mint tea by the fireside. Then I remind myself that she comes from the Free Cantrefs, and probably opposes the alliance my husband is trying to form. Graceful or not, she may even be the one who plotted my capture by Saxon raiders. Anyone in the council chamber might have. My shoulders sag when I realize I'm no closer to discerning the truth than before.

When I return to my solar, neither Morgan nor Malcolm is there. The two probably sequestered themselves somewhere so that others might not hear their plots, not even me. Rowena pours me a decanter of mulled wine, clearing her throat as she motions toward the far end of the bedchamber.

I give a start, seeing a child standing beside my bed. Arthwys.

A little elfin boy, he seems entranced by the rouge coverlets where my husband and I sleep. I smile at Arthwys, but he does not look back. He speaks without moving his gaze from the bedsheets.

"Mother and Father used to share this bed."

I cough up the wine in my throat, wiping the spittle on my sleeve. Darkness begins to creep in through the tower window beside me, and the evening breeze raises the fine hairs along my arms. Without moving a muscle, Arthwys shifts his gaze upon me.

"You are *not* Mother," he says in a stern, eerily calm voice. "This is not your bed."

"Child." I try to smile back. "Your father and I have married. You and I are now . . . family."

"This is not where you sleep! This was *her* bed! It's not yours!"

His calm, changeling face runs with tears. My heart contracts like a fist while my eyes glaze over. His voice sounds so much like my own might have when my stepmother first wed Father. Only now I stand in my stepmother's place. It's as though I've stepped through the looking glass, my life turned inside out. Arthwys moans into his hands as he scampers out of the room, his muffled cries fading down the turret steps. I reach after the boy, trying to think up some words of comfort, but he has already gone. Poor child. What can I say? Life does not always turn out as we think it ought.

The clang of crockery from the kitchens downstairs announces the approach of supper. Every visiting lord and knight will attend the feast, and doubtlessly Morgan will expect his queen to attend and play hostess. I draw in a deep breath, the final gasp before the plunge.

It still feels as though I am merely pretending to be a queen, that some other woman will appear from the shadows and tell me to return to my father's castle. Rounding the turret steps, I wring my palms absentmindedly, dreading having to play lady-of-the-castle. I know about as much about being a host as my old stepmother knows of books. Which is to say, nothing at all.

I bump into a man on the dim stairs, apologizing for my clumsiness. My eyes suddenly widen. Artagan stands before me, his hair dripping wet and his chest bare.

He wears nothing but a damp towel wrapped around his middle. Almost against my will, my gaze darts to his muscular chest, his skin pink from the baths. I look away, trying to sidle around him on the narrow stairwell. The rogue grins at my discomfort.

"Queen Branwen, you have me at a disadvantage. I'm not quite dressed for the banquet yet."

"You must be lost," I reply, averting my gaze. "This turret leads to my private chambers."

He shrugs sheepishly.

"Easy to get lost in such a large palace. But your Roman bathhouse is well worth the journey. Baths are the one good thing the Romans brought to Wales."

His ever-cocky grin starts to wear on my nerves.

"Hmm, I didn't realize folk in the Free Cantrefs bathe at all," I lie. "You could have fooled me."

I frown at the half-naked hedge knight, still trying to get around him without tripping down a flight of narrow stairs. Will this shameless vagabond ever let me pass? What is his game, showing up on my tower steps nearly undressed? Morgan would have this brigand's head if he could see us now. Despite my attempts at indignant propriety, Artagan refuses to turn wroth with me, merely smiling as he lets me pass.

"Pardon me for keeping you, my lady. I've never a dull moment in your company."

I roll my eyes as I brush past him, my thoughts still muddled by glimpses of his brawny forearms and bare, slightly freckled shoulders. I quickly shake such images from my head. A married Christian woman should only see her husband so underdressed. Leave it to a Free Cantref ruffian like Artagan to wander the halls like that, wet and naked as a savage. Was he indeed lost? Or perhaps eavesdropping about the castle?

Thankfully, I find my lady-in-waiting down the next passageway. Rowena accompanies me into the main hall, most of the guests already well into their cups and gnawing on legs of mutton served up for the occasion. Morgan remains absent, but his brother sits beside the King's empty chair. Malcolm talks to Belin's sons over a joint of lamb, eyeing the serving girls between bites. His wandering eye makes me cringe. Time someone got that Prince a wife. He'll leave a dozen bastards behind in Caerwent if Morgan doesn't find a match for his younger brother soon.

I sit on the opposite end of the hall with Rowena as we partake of the feast. Barely a few minutes later, Artagan joins the other members of the Free Cantref delegation across the hall, his long dark hair still wet from the baths. Even under his loose tunic I can still picture his unclad, supple body. My cheeks suddenly flush hot. A few moons after my husband's initiation of me into the bedchamber and already my mind wanders too freely upon such avenues.

Artagan Blacksword's strikingly blue gaze follows my every move, but fortunately his party sits far across the room. Whatever his plot may be, I wish he would leave me out of it. Cadwallon bellows gaily beside him, his pile of bones and empty wine goblets higher than anyone else's. Lady Olwen converses with the many knights who pay her attentions throughout the night, but she never strays far from Artagan's table.

They must be lovers. The realization washes over me like a wave of saltwater. I cannot help but notice how she shares Artagan's drinking cup, always putting her lips to the rim where his lips have been. Olwen keeps a hand on his forearm, coolly eyeing the serving wenches who bring him drinks. She laughs coquettishly at his jokes.

My chest tightens, knowing I've never looked at Morgan with longing like that. Lady Olwen has something more precious than gold in her hands. My face flushes with heat at my own thoughts and I drown my mind in a chalice full of spiced wine. Artagan's rough-cut looks may appeal to Lady Olwen and the serving girls, but he still wears furs like a barbarian and has a nest of wild black hair to match.

I turn away and listen to Rowena's gossip about the kitchen maids and their midnight trysts with guardsmen in the haystacks out behind the King's stables. Her stories provide a welcome distraction.

Abbot Padraig sits on the other side of me, his conversation with another cleric seeping into my ears. Even as Rowena rambles on about scullery maids taking tumbles with knights in haylofts, I cannot resist the urge to eavesdrop on the Abbot. He speaks with the bald-headed Bishop Gregory, the King's head clergyman. The Bishop cannot mask the rising heat in his tone.

"Nevertheless, *Abbot,* you should have waited to perform the ceremony here, in Caerwent!"

"The King would not wait, *Bishop,* and so I obliged and wed them in the eyes of God."

"I crowned King Morgan in the Caerwent cathedral and I ought to have wed him and his bride here too! You overstep your place, little monk. Whence do you return to your monastery of rocks?"

"I serve Queen Branwen and God, Bishop Gregory. If you have a problem with that, I suggest you call an audience before your liege, the King. I doubt that news of your strangely afflicted altar boys has yet reached his ears."

The Bishop nearly gags on his wine. Padraig continues supping his bread and broth as though nothing happened. I bite my lip to keep from giggling. No one backs Brother Padraig into a corner. Not kings nor bishops, not even the Pope himself. I wish I had half the Abbot's poise.

Rowena suddenly cries out beside me, her hand on my sleeve.

The crash of crockery mingles with raised voices across the hall.

I jump up from my seat while Rowena ducks behind me. Chalices and clay bowls across the feast hall clatter to the tile floors. A crowd of men tumble over upended tabletops while guardsmen try to pull the bloodied brawlers apart.

A fight.

At the heart of the fray, two men grapple over a fallen serving girl. Both young men swing fists at one another with the experience of veterans. I step closer to the combatants, both curious and dismayed all at once. Prince Malcolm and Artagan Blacksword have their hands at one another's throats. So much for our hopes of peace.

5

Morgan enters the hall with his war-hammer in hand. He thrusts himself between the two unarmed combatants. Artagan nurses a split lip
while Malcolm holds a palm up to his black eye.

Lords and knights shout at each other, some holding their comrades
back from the fight. Every guardsman in the castle tries to keep the bickering antagonists apart, but I doubt even they can prevent all these trained
warriors from getting at each other's throats. Morgan keeps a hand pressed
against his brother's chest, all the while prodding Artagan back with the
head of his war-hammer.

A lone servant girl lies on the floor between the two brawlers, clutching
a bruise on her left wrist, the skin turned purple. Her disheveled sandy
hair hides her face. The poor girl seems like no more than a bone disputed
between two snapping dogs. Something inside me starts to boil over at
the sight of this poor defenseless girl in a room full of drunken louts.

My stepmother would doubtlessly remind me that no proper lady in
her right mind would intrude into such a fray, especially with more than
a few hidden daggers bulging beneath every man's tunic. But the sight of
that lone bondservant huddled on the floor shames me. Am I the lady of
this castle or not? Its citizens are my responsibility. If I don't speak up,
who will?

I stride into the circle of menfolk and raise the young woman to her feet, her eyes going wide when she recognizes the thin diadem crown on my head. She curtsies, wincing as she clutches the welts on her arm. Rowena comes to my side, shooing away warriors as she might a barnyard full of roosters. The knights and lords halt their quarrel upon seeing me and the wounded girl in their midst.

"What is your name, fair maiden?" I ask her.

"Una, Your Grace."

"And who did this to you, Una?" I say, pointing at her arm.

Every man in the hall turns silent. The fight that had been all about Artagan and Malcolm's spat suddenly turns into a solemn trial over a wronged serving girl. Una gives the onlookers a sidelong glance, like a mouse surrounded by a herd of hungry cats. How foolish of me to ask such an open question. A servant girl dares not point a finger at men who carry blades and call themselves knights. Una lowers her eyes.

"I tripped, my Queen. Must have banged into one of the fallen table-tops."

The men immediately recommence hostilities, throwing insults and a few wild fists at one another. Rowena and I draw Una aside before more guardsmen gradually pry the two sides of bickering knights apart. Artagan and Malcolm glare back at one another. If not for King Morgan and his fifty men-at-arms crowding the hall, we would have bloodshed aplenty in the very heart of Caerwent tonight.

Rowena and I bring Una up to my solar chamber, away from the roaring din of the mead hall. Whatever the cause of the brawl between Artagan and Malcolm, Una must be at the crux of it. She remains silent while Rowena tends to her bruises with a damp washcloth. The girl has been through enough tonight already and needs no interrogation from me, but I cannot escape the nagging feeling that she knows something more. Something important enough to cause the Prince and the Blacksword to come to blows. Una bows her weary head.

"Pardon, Your Grace, but I should get back to the kitchens now."

"No, you shan't." I smile. "I've need of a second lady-in-waiting to serve me. If you'll agree, of course."

Una and Rowena exchange equally surprised glances. My needs are few, but hopefully I haven't offended Rowena by bringing a second servant into our midst. Rowena can certainly handle all the chores about me, but something in my heart demands that I shield this girl Una. How many women just like her have been manhandled all across Wales, by barbarians and locals alike? Besides, I'm not a terribly demanding queen and whatever tasks I set Una to doing, it ought to be easier than slaving away in the castle kitchens. At least with me she should be safe from further reprisals, whatever the cause of her misfortune in the mead hall tonight. Una eyes me hesitantly before nodding and agreeing to my request.

As the night wears on, Morgan does not come to my bedchamber. Perhaps he stays up late, trying to heal the rift between the bickering lords down in the banquet hall. Cold blasts of wind hit the castle, whistling through chinks in the walls and gaps in the shutters. Both Rowena and Una share the large bed with me in order to conserve heat, each of us lying head to toe.

At daybreak, the whicker of horses from the courtyard outside awakens me. Nestled between my snoring servant girls, I roll out of bed. I clutch a shawl around my throat as I peer through the window shutters.

Two columns of troops snake down the roads leading away from Caerwent, the black banners of North Wales going one way and the green dragon flags of the Free Cantrefs marching the other. A few watchmen in red tunics look on from the bastion towers, but no bugle calls or friendly goodbyes ring from the battlements. It looks as though the great gathering has ended already.

Heading toward the stairs, I open my bedchamber door to find a guardsman posted on the top step. I gasp, nearly running into the spearman before recognizing Ahern. I smile at my half brother, but he merely frowns back at me through his beard.

"Sorry, my Queen, but all royals are to remain in their quarters this morn. King's orders."

"Ahern, what do you mean? Am I prisoner in my own bedchamber? What's going on?"

Ahern leans closer, pleading with me.

"Stay up here in your solar, safe and sound. Please, Lady Branwen."

My voice fails me upon seeing such worry in his normally placid eyes.

A draft from the tower window chills my skin. The only royals in this household are myself, Arthwys, Malcolm, and the King. What madness is this? I doubt Morgan has confined himself to any particular room. Whatever vexes my husband this morning, I do not see why it applies to me. I've done nothing worthy of punishment, nor do I intend to be kenneled like a dog in my own home. I lean in close to Ahern, nearly nose to nose.

"Brother, you are a warrior of Dyfed, guardsman to the Queen, and part of *my* household, not my husband's. Either you will stand aside, or you will be my guardsman no more."

The spearman blinks, taking a half step back. He narrows his gaze and for a moment I fear he has seen through my bluff. Instead, he stands aside with his spear and shield at attention.

"As you wish, my Queen. I will die before I betray a noblewoman of Dyfed and my own blood."

I put a gentle hand on his forearm.

"Thank you, Ahern. You are a good man, and an honorable one."

Although he tries to hide it, Ahern's chest puffs out a little broader at the mention of honor. He may not hold a knighthood, but Ahern's sense of duty gives him more chivalry than any knight in Wales. He keeps his lonely vigil, guarding the door to my solar as I descend the stairs.

Now to find out what mischief is afoot in the castle this morn. My husband has tried to cage me like a rat, and I must find out why.

Avoiding the archways leading to the atrium, I steal down to the kitchens. Morgan will not think to look for me amongst the servants' quarters, hiding amidst the foggy steam of boiling cauldrons. Whatever has happened, the Hammer King is still accustomed to having his orders obeyed. I wonder with a sinking feeling what will happen if Morgan finds me creeping about the castle against his command.

The long tunnels beneath the main floor of the castle allow servants to navigate Caerwent easily and out of sight, running their daily errands without clogging the narrow hallways used by knights and lords. But today, the corridors appear almost empty. I peer around each corner, never spying more than an occasional scullery maid passing by, going about her chores. Since the Welshmen of the North and Free Cantrefs left, the fortress seems eerily silent. Perhaps I'm behaving foolishly, tiptoeing around my own castle like a thief.

I reach the south end of the castle where several apartments of the King's knights and household keep their beds. Ducking into one room, I find the walls covered in tapestries of boyhood squires and pages in battle. Wood and clay toys cover the floor, a set of dull-pointed sparring spears leaned in the corner. A young noble boy's room. Above the doorway hangs the red dragon crest of the Hammer King. This must be Arthwys's bedchamber.

I peer about his bedroom, but find no one within. Where are the guards that should be posted outside the doorway? Ahern said that the King ordered all royals confined to their rooms, and my brother has no reason to lie to me.

I scoff at myself for acting like such a child. I should march right into the throne room, just as I ought to have done in the first place, and confront Morgan face-to-face. Turning to leave Arthwys's room, I gasp as a hooded figure looms in the doorway before me.

"Who are you, sir?"

The cloaked man stalks closer, silent as a wraith. I back up against the cold stone wall, cornered beside a tapestry of young Arthur pulling the sword from the stone. I'd give half my dowry to have Excalibur in my hand right now, or any blade for that matter. I put on my haughtiest face, failing to keep the tremors out of my voice.

"Ex-explain yourself, st-stranger, or I'll call my guards outside!" I lie. "Guards!"

Under his hood, a crooked grin spreads across the stranger's thin cheeks. He removes a long, shiny dagger from the folds of his cloak and rushes toward me. I cry out, dodging the steel blade aimed at my throat.

I reach for the nearest object with which to defend myself. Tearing at the fabrics on the wall behind me, the large tapestry tumbles down on both of us. The man curses, his dagger ripping through woolen seams.

The world turns dark and heavy beneath the drapes of woven thread.

I scream, hoping someone will hear me. The assailant's blade slashes at my legs and sides, each thrust getting closer to my vitals. I kick and grunt and head butt the foe tangled in the draperies with me, but he only tightens his grip through the thick woolens. He draws me closer despite my flailing arms and legs, our limbs tangled in a heap of shredded tapestries on the floor. In a matter of moments, he'll have coiled around me like a snake, ready to strike. Then I'll be dead.

A din like thunder rumbles through the castle. My attacker suddenly stops, pushing the last shreds of covering off us both. He pins me to the floor with one hand and wraps his fingers around my neck, drawing back his dagger high above his hood. I shut my eyes, still pushing hopelessly against his chest. Blood pounds in my ears. I don't want to die.

Opening my eyes, my palms still press against the stranger's chest. A spearhead opens up inside him, its razor-sharp edge coming up through the breastbone. His blood runs down my fingers. The cloaked man wets himself, dropping his blade as it clatters harmlessly to the ground. His lifeless body slumps over me as Ahern draws the spear out of the man's corpse.

"Branwen! Speak to me!"

Ahern helps me to my feet. Blood runs down my torn shawl and nightgown, but aside from a few flesh wounds, none of it is mine. My brother keeps asking me whether I am all right, but I cannot even nod in reply, still transfixed by the bleeding corpse lying across the floor. A dozen more men-at-arms flood the room, their chain mail jangling loud as a storm.

"I followed you when you left the tower," Ahern says between breaths. "Nearly lost you in the servants' quarters though. Then I heard the noise in here."

Morgan pushes his way into the chamber, his hammer in hand and his vest of mail on as though he expects to go into battle. He puts a hand on my shoulder and shakes me, but I do not hear him, my tongue still tied. The King looks to Ahern.

"The Queen's had quite a fright, sire," Ahern reports. "But she seems well enough."

Morgan reluctantly releases me, bending over the bloodied body in the corner. The Hammer King folds back the dead man's hood. A bluish snake tattoo runs along the cadaver's eyebrow.

"An assassin!" Morgan says with a hiss. "Pictish by the look of him. The would-be killer waited in my son's room, and then fell upon my unsuspecting bride."

He picks up the crimson-stained ribbons of Arthwys's boyhood wall hangings, the image of a young King Arthur dismembered in scraps of bloodied cloth. The thought of Arthwys jars my mind to life. A little boy against the likes of this assassin wouldn't stand a chance. I grab Morgan by the sleeve.

"Arthwys, the young prince, where is he?"

"Safe with his uncle in Prince Malcolm's care."

"But then . . . you knew some danger was afoot?"

"I suspected. You should have stayed in your bedchamber as I ordered."

The King flashes Ahern a stern glance and leaves. I trail after Morgan, Ahern's footsteps following close behind. My torn and bloodied rags earn me more than a few curious stares from soldiers and servants throughout the halls, doubtlessly drawn out of hiding by my earlier screams. No one dares to meet the Hammer King's eye as he marches through the fortress, his metal greaves clacking loud as horse hooves along the stone floors. We wind our way up to my solar chamber where Malcolm and Arthwys await us. Like his brother, Prince Malcolm wears full armor and clutches his battle mace. The young boy rubs his red eyes. He has been crying. Ahern shuts the door behind me and stands watch outside. Where Una and Rowena have gotten to, I have no idea.

I splash cold water on my face from the washbasin before hiding behind my changing screen. The two men and young boy drink at the table while I strip out of my bloodied gown and put on a clean robe. Malcolm glances my way a moment before eyeing his elder brother.

"Well?"

"Dead," Morgan replies. "Before I could question him."

"Damn! I would have tortured him for days, whether he talked or not."

"He would have talked," Morgan replies grimly. "I'd have made him talk."

Stepping out from behind my screen, I tighten my robes and approach my husband.

"You confined me to quarters with no explanation. Why not tell me of the assassin?"

"I do not always have time to explain my decrees, but I expect them to be followed."

Morgan gives me a stern sidelong glance and I say no more. Husband or no, he rules as king in South Wales and his word is law for all subjects, including me. The Hammer King brings his fist down hard against the table and for a moment I fear he will strike one of us. Malcolm, Arthwys, and myself stand silent as statues. Morgan slumps down into his seat, his eyes glazed over in thought.

"At this moment, I trust no one outside this room," he begins. "Someone has betrayed us."

"Give us time and we'll weed out the traitor," Malcolm replies. "We should raise an army."

"And do what? Attack who? Winter approaches and my men have returned to their farms."

Stepping between the brothers, I pour them each a new drink, trying to soothe their tempers. I pet Arthwys on the head, but the boy pushes away from me and sulks in the corner. Sighing, I let the child go. Will I ever be more than a stranger to him? My hands still tremble a touch, my nerves worn from my encounter with the assassin. If Ahern had not followed me, I would be cold as a corpse now. I pour myself a drink, quickly finishing the cup.

"The assassin had a Pictish tattoo," I begin. "Who would hire a Pict?"

"Old Belin wed a Pict queen once," Morgan recalls. "He has certain ties to those barbarians."

"The old king's not fool enough to use a Pict!" Malcolm scoffs. "It's too suspicious."

Morgan remains silent.

"You think someone used a Pict assassin to make it look like Belin was behind the attack?" I ask.

"The Blacksword is behind this," Malcolm says with a growl. "I'd stake my life on it!"

"It could be the Saxons too," I reply.

"Use your head, foolish girl!" my brother-in-law retorts. "There's no Saxons here. Someone from the gathering left an assassin behind after the council broke up. Artagan's had it out for us since we put a price on his head."

"Is that why you fought with him last eve in the mead hall?"

Malcolm clenches his jaw, the skin around his left eye still swollen purple. I've only asked a simple question, yet my brother-in-law looks like he would like to take a crop to me. The King and the Prince exchange looks before Morgan intervenes.

"Last night doesn't concern you," my husband says to me in a flat voice. His rebuke stings and I speak out without thinking.

"If it's the reason why an assassin almost killed me today, then I believe it does concern me!"

"Mind your tongue, wife."

"I can't help it. I'm just a *foolish girl* after all."

Throwing Malcolm's words back at them both, I glare at each man until the meat behind my eyes hurts. I stomp out of the room, heading past Ahern and down the stairwell. Neither King nor Prince makes a move to stop me, continuing their privy council behind closed doors. With both of them using my chamber, I've no place to go for privacy, no room to shut out the prying eyes of servants and soldiers that fill the halls. Against my will, tears run down my cheeks, blurring my vision. I sit down in a deserted stairwell and dry my cheeks.

The horror of the assassin's knife renews itself again in my mind. All seventeen years of my life nearly came to an abrupt and bloody end, and with so much left undone. No children or family or whatever else I am supposed to want. I'd be replaced tomorrow by a new queen, and all the while the wise lords of Caerwent call me a foolish girl!

Gentle hands caress my shoulders. Rowena and Una sit on either side of me, wrapping a blanket around me as the three of us crouch in the stairwell. My sniffles gradually subside. Rowena offers me a hot mug of mint tea, neither woman asking me any questions. Whether a commoner or a queen, it goes without saying that a woman has little weight in a world of kings and knights. We are all chess pieces in the hands of men. Una smiles, trying to brighten my spirits.

"At least you're not lying on the floor while two big oafs brawl over you, m'lady."

I fake a half-smile, recalling Una huddled on the ground between Malcolm and Artagan. I venture to see if Una will tell me the truth about last evening. No lords or knights can overhear us now.

"My husband would not tell me what the fight between his brother and Artagan was about."

"Small wonder, it was over me."

"I don't understand."

"Prince Malcolm has a wandering eye. I did not reciprocate his . . . *advances* last evening."

"I feared as much," I reply, cradling her bruised forearm. "And he actually did this to you?"

"Sir Artagan saw and told the Prince to leave me be. The rest of the fight you saw yourself."

My head begins to hurt. Malcolm certainly has a taste for servant girls; Morgan chides him about it often enough. Nonetheless, I had hoped I was somehow wrong about my brother-in-law's transgressions. Yet Una's purple welts are damning proof that Malcolm is indeed the kind of man to force himself upon a maiden. Why would Artagan Blacksword, of all people, defend Una? That doesn't sound like the act of a cattle thief and a purported violator of women, as my husband accuses him of being.

Rowena adds her own bit of common sense as she leans closer to Una.

"Them two probably just wanted an excuse to get at each other. You was just the spark that set them off."

"It was enough to dissolve the council from convening again," I add. "That spark dashes any hopes of an alliance against the Saxons, and brings us no closer to discovering who tried to have me kidnapped or assassinated."

Assassinated. The word rings in my ears. It's as though I'm talking about someone else, somebody far away. But this is my life we're talking about and there's no guarantee it will have a happy ending. I almost lost my life today and nothing under heaven could have brought me back. I reach out and clasp Rowena tightly by the hand, my fist trembling in hers. The words spill out of me before I can stop them.

"I'm so scared, Rowena," I confess, biting my lip. "God help me, I'm scared."

She pats my hand, sidling closer beside me. Una hangs her head in sympathy with us. Perhaps I burden these two serving girls with my tales of woe, but they're the only women in the entire kingdom I can talk to. I've known Rowena only a few moons, and Una is practically a stranger, yet I trust them as much as Padraig or Ahern. Odd and inexplicable as that may seem, my heartstrings will burst asunder if I don't confess my fears to someone. Rowena pats my hand.

"There, there, m'lady." Rowena smiles. "You're not alone. You got loyal folk like Una and myself, and powerful men like your father and husband to protect you."

"But it is because of my relationships to men such as Father and my husband that my life is in peril," I reply. "Both of them scheming and plotting, not caring who gets hurt."

Rowena shrugs.

"Me Pa oft took a stick to me whether I 'twas good or bad. Especially after me Mum died of the plague one winter. But I lived through it and through all the fellows trying to put their paws on me when I worked at the castle back in Caerleon."

Una looks up, her voice faint and unsteady at first.

"Leastways you two had parents," Una begins. "Saxons took both of mine, and did worse to me before I got away. Being a scullery maid doesn't erase the nightmares of what they did to my village."

Both women exchange looks, taking the other's hand.

"You see, your ladyship," Rowena says to me with a sniffle. "We be plenty scared too. We just push on best we can. Haven't much choice really."

I straighten my spine as I draw in a deep breath, the tears from earlier already dry on my skin. What a self-centered fool I've been, brooding over my own misfortunes when these two women have endured just as much as I or worse in their young lives. Beaten, manhandled, and God knows what else, yet they persevere despite their hardships. I squeeze Rowena's fingers with one hand and Una's in the other.

"The Abbot once told me that no one can be brave if they aren't first scared. So at least the three of us can all be brave together."

Both girls beam back at me.

"Well, fret no more, m'lady," Rowena replies in a jovial voice. "We'll share your bed from now on so as you're ne'er alone, and I'll sleep with a poker in one hand and a kitchen knife under the mattress."

"I feel safer already." I grin.

All three of us laugh, but in truth Rowena's words comfort me better than any tonic. Until I married, I never feared assassins, mainly because no one paid much heed to an ugly daughter living along the crags of Dyfed. Only now do I see that no matter what I do, I must live my life under perpetual threats both from within and without. Such is the burden of a queen.

Her black doll's eyes gaze back at me. Perched atop my gloved arm, the spotted brown plumage of the falcon stands out against the gray sky. Padraig tells me that female falcons are the most prized. Stronger and faster than the males, she-falcons also hunt better and produce healthy broods. The Abbot calls this particular variety of falcon a Merlin. Standing atop the uppermost tower bastion of Caerwent, I survey the ivy fields, quicksilver rivers, and dark woods beyond. With a flick of my wrist, I release the Merlin, her cry piercing the heavens as she dives to earth far below.

"Good!" Padraig says beside me. "She has taken to you, Your Grace."

"Only because you've taught me how to handle her so well," I reply. "I think I'll call her Vivian."

"Vivian, my Queen?"

"After my mother."

The falcon descends through the air, gliding over the meadows in search of prey. Her tapered wings spread wide as she circles the fields below. I sigh. What a joy to soar like that, to be so light and free.

Someone clears his throat behind us atop the tower bastion. King Morgan lingers in the shadowy archway. Padraig politely excuses himself.

I wish the Abbot would stay. Morgan has visited my bed infrequently these last few weeks, and never to stay the night. I shiver in my cloak as the autumn winds run their fingers through my dark hair.

"I've a request, my Queen."

"Not an order?" I snap, still peeved by our last conversation after the assassin attack.

"My easternmost vassal, Lord Griffith, requests additional troops to watch the borders."

"So send him some."

"I've none to send. Most men in my army serve in summer, returning home for winter."

"So what do you need from me, my liege?"

"I want you to go to Lord Griffith's fort in my stead."

My green eyes narrow on my husband's brown-bearded face. He seems serious. From the corner of my eye, I see that Vivian still circles the meads below. I pace around my husband, keeping my gaze to my feet.

"Why not go yourself? You're his king."

"Peasants in one of my other cantrefs refuse to send their yearly tithes of bread and grain, so I must take what few men I have and go there to set things aright."

"And you would send me on this important errand to Lord Griffith instead of Malcolm?"

"Malcolm sails for Cornwall. I've an offer for him to wed a Cornish lord's daughter."

He points at a ship heading downriver toward the estuary and the sea beyond. A small sail disappears on the horizon and Prince Malcolm with it. So, Morgan has decided his wild-oats brother needs to settle down after all. An alliance with Cornwall would behoove Morgan's growing kingdom as well. My husband always thinks of everything from multiple angles.

But none of this explains what I ought to do if I go to see Lord Griffith. I've heard the man guards a small fort along the Forest of Dean beside the Sabrina River, the extreme eastern edge of the South Welsh kingdom. Saxons lurk on the opposite shore there. I shake my head, knowing that my presence alone will not satisfy a war-captain who has asked his king for reinforcements.

"If your vassal asks for troops, he won't be happy with just me. What do I tell him?"

"Your royal presence will calm him and assure him I have his interests at heart. Besides, he doesn't need any new troops now. It's halfway through autumn and the fighting season is over. Living on the border with the Saxons makes Lord Griffith jumpy. He sees Saxons in his soup."

"Why me, Morgan?"

"You've a calm head and I believe you will do well. Besides, it's a chance to get out of the castle walls for a change."

"No, I mean, why do you offer me this?"

"To mend the rift between us. To show you I value your diplomacy as much as a man's."

We stand only a few paces apart, our breath fogging the space between us. Although he has not said it, I know he offers this as a way of apologizing for the words between us, when he and his brother thought me a "foolish girl." Perhaps this is the closest a monarch comes to saying he is sorry. Morgan takes my hand, his cold fingers rubbing warmth into mine.

In the days of yore, the Old Tribes often sent women as envoys, but since the coming of the Romans and Saxons, such traditions have faded in the Welsh Lands. Morgan of all people would be the last kind of man I would suspect of honoring such an age-old tradition. Perhaps making amends with me supersedes any concerns he may have about contemporary propriety.

The day the assassin struck, and Morgan sequestered his brother, son, and me together, he said he only trusted the three of us and no one else. Now I see in the intensity of his stare that he meant it. He entrusts me to settle issues along his eastern frontier, the gateway to his kingdom. I don't know whether to feel honored or put upon. It is a chance to prove myself, yet also a nearly impossible task.

Nonetheless, I firmly clasp Morgan's hands and look up into his gray eyes with gratitude. I never wanted to be just a bed warmer to a king, and it lightens my heart to see that Morgan understands.

"When do I leave?" I ask.

"Today." He smiles, kissing my palm.

Morgan leaves me to prepare. Rushing down to the stables to saddle a mount, I find Brother Padraig squatting in the hay amongst the stalls. I cock my head to the side, wondering what on earth the monk is doing down in the sty of a horse bed. Without looking up, the cleric waves me over.

"Lend me a hand, my lady. This mare's time is near."

"Abbot, I leave within the hour on an errand for the king. You should be with me."

"Plenty of time for that. I've trained you as a healer of both man and beast. Or are you too good to get down in the muck now that you're a queen?"

He says this last part with a wink, but I put on a feigned smirk of indignation anyway. I bend down beside him as a mare lying in the hay begins her labors. The Abbott loves all of God's creations, whether man or animal, and I've helped him when whelping everything from pups to lambs before. We let the mare do most of the work, shifting her legs and flapping her lips as she pushes her foal into the world. With a gulp, I wonder if I might not groan or worse if I found myself in childbed.

With a splash, the foal's hooves spill out onto the earth, followed by the body and head. The Abbot and I cut the cord and push the afterbirth aside before the mother can eat it. Padraig insists that horse placentas have healing properties necessary for certain potions. I hope I never have to drink one though.

Despite the muck and gore, I cannot help but smile as the youngling struggles onto its wobbly feet. Within a matter of minutes, the foal can move about and suckle from its mother. The Abbot elbows me with a grin as we share a washbowl for our hands.

"God made mankind stewards of the earth. If more kings and knights realized the effort it takes to bring a life into the world, they might not be so swift to snuff it out with steel and iron."

I beam with pride at the balding holy man. Few men, clergy or otherwise, glow with grace as often as my Padraig does. I'm not worthy to unlace his sandals.

Yet despite all the wondrous things Padraig has taught me over the years, there is one lesson he left out. Taking advantage of the good mood, I try to broach the topic.

"When are you going to let me help you deliver a human child?" I ask with a smile.

"When you're ready," he replies noncommittally.

"And when will that be?"

"You'll know."

I frown, trying to hide my disappointment. Despite all the healing arts and calvings in which I've assisted him, he has left this last mystery to me without explanation. Perhaps it's no easy thing for a monk sworn to God to discuss the medical facets of handling a woman's parts when in labor. Nonetheless, I cannot help a nagging fear that he perhaps doesn't believe I'm ready to help with something as important as bringing human life into the world.

Without a word, the monk cleans his hands as he exits the stables. Some mysteries must simply wait for another day, I suppose.

Before the next chapel bell from the cathedral tolls, I saddle my mount beside the castle gates. Morgan comes alone to see me off, apologizing that he cannot spare a large escort for me, but assures me that the journey will be short and the roads clear of foes this time of year. The cold weather keeps the enemy at bay better than a thousand spears. I lean down from my horse and give Morgan a kiss. He pats my mare on the rump and waves as my small party rides east.

Only four companions join me, my personal household all on horseback. Ahern, Padraig, Rowena, and Una canter behind me as my falcon, Vivian, descends to my gloved hand. My heart beats with the rhythm of horseshoes padding along the muddy highway. Not since I left Father's court at Dyfed have I been at liberty to travel. I feel free as a hawk.

Just as Morgan promised, the day passes quickly and without trouble.

We arrive in Lord Griffith's territory just before sunset. I smile at the broad curves of the great sapphire Sabrina River and the emerald Forest of Dean beyond. Perhaps this errand will not be so trying after all.

Lord Griffith's fort consists of a wooden palisade with timber watchtowers set beside the river. Both the Welsh and Saxons mostly build their castles out of wood like this one. Stone fortresses like Caerleon and Caerwent are the exception, their quarried foundations first laid down by Roman engineers. Since those ancient days, the building of stonework has been lost to us. Such have I gleaned from Padraig's books of history and legend that he carries in his satchel. I wonder what other great things we have lost since the coming of the Saxons. Only the Almighty knows for certain.

Ahern hails the gatekeepers of the fort, announcing my title and that we come in the King's name. The guardsmen open the large, spiked doors. We trot inside the wooden keep, and dismount in the muddy courtyard.

A man helps me off my horse, careful to keep my skirts out of the mud. I turn to thank him when my voice fails me. Sensing my alarm, Vivian starts squawking on my arm. The man before me is Artagan Blacksword.

He unsheathes his longsword, its ringing steel flickering silvery one moment then onyx the next. A half dozen of his companions surround us with drawn spears and bows. Ahern raises his own spear and shield, but too late. Artagan checks him with the flat of his long blade. My brother halts, seething red at having walked into an ambush. The Blacksword laughs and aims his sword at me.

This fort belongs to my husband and should be garrisoned by his troops, but I only see Free Cantref warriors in greens and furs. My heartbeat drums in my ears, my palms moist with sweat as I stare down the length of Artagan's blade. The hedge knight smiles at me. God help us. We've been captured by an outlaw.

6

⬦─◦≻◦◦≺◦─⬦

Torches cast pools of light in the otherwise darkened timber keep, the tap of dripping water echoing through the cavernous hall. We stagger inside at spear-point. Half a dozen rugged archers and spearmen encircle us, decked in drab furs and green tunics. They smell of mud and the piney woods. A rawboned woman warrior amongst them watches me with disdain in her eyes.

Artagan eyes my falcon warily. With a piercing caw, Vivian ascends to the rafters. I glare at Artagan, unable to restrain my anger any longer.

"Unhand us! We come on the King's errand to his vassal, Lord Griffith. What right have you to bear arms inside an outpost of King Morgan's domain?"

"Because I asked him to," a deep voice answers from the darkness.

Several watchmen kindle additional torches along the interior walls, casting light upon an oaken throne. A lone man with a dark beard streaked in gray reclines in the half shadows atop his seat. Despite his stern appearance, he grins warmly at me.

"Be not alarmed, Queen Branwen. I am Lord Griffith of the Dean Fort and am honored to have you here. Sir Artagan is also our guest. He and his warriors generously offered to help garrison our walls."

"My husband would not be pleased to find you sheltering someone he deems an outlaw," I reply, pointing at Artagan.

Lord Griffith rises from his chair.

"Tread easy, young Queen. I serve King Morgan loyally as I did his father before him. I have scarce fifty men to defend this fort, and most of them farmers. I see no harm in allowing six Free Cantref warriors to lend us a hand."

"Then these are all the men Sir Artagan has?"

"More than you brought, my lady. As I recall, I urged King Morgan for reinforcements."

My cheeks sting at his remark. With only Ahern, a monk, and two serving girls, I hardly have much help to offer Lord Griffith. Perhaps Morgan should never have sent me. Somehow, I must appease a loyal vassal who needs troops that his king cannot provide. I must find a way to make bricks without straw.

Artagan stands uncomfortably close to me, flashing another cocky smile as though I am the butt of some joke. His unabashed stare makes me cringe. I approach Lord Griffith, doing my best to ignore Artagan.

"Then we are not prisoners here, my lord?"

"Far from it." Griffith smiles. "You must forgive Sir Artagan. He is not skilled in courtesies."

"Never claimed to be," Artagan gibes, getting a laugh from his men.

Lord Griffith claps his hands, calling for his servants to stoke the baking kilns. Artagan's warriors back away from me and my small retinue, Ahern still giving them the evil eye as they linger nearby. Griffith descends his throne and bows before kissing my hand.

"What meager fare we have we shall share with you tonight, Queen Branwen. Guests to the Dean Fort are never turned away, whether they be a simple hedge knight or the Queen of the realm herself."

Despite his mottled salt-and-pepper beard, and careworn face, I cannot help but smile back at Lord Griffith. His countenance reminds me much of Father, only less into his drink and far kinder in his speech.

He gives me a tour of the grounds while his people prepare the evening feast. The dusky skyline turns purple along the forest riverfront. The sweet scent of pinesap permeates the evergreens and small crofter fields. Such a tranquil place. I might mistake it for Eden if I didn't know it was a border settlement. If only the Saxons would let us alone, communities like the Dean Fort might flourish without the ever-present shadow of war.

Although he does not directly mention it again, I can see plainly why Lord Griffith needs more support from my husband. Dozens of women and children from every farmstead huddle inside the stockade as night falls. Hardly a man between fifteen and fifty mans the walls. The summer fighting has taken its toll on the settlement. I shiver as I tug my shawl tight about my shoulders. Thank God for the cold weather, the only thing keeping the Saxons at bay.

By the time we return to the main keep, the hall has transformed from a dank abode to a place of light and warmth. Women string meat and apples over the blazing hearths while minstrels pipe away at their flutes. A small circle of boys and girls begins to dance, some with legs of mutton still in hand.

I clap in time with the music while Lord Griffith offers me a seat of honor next to him at table. He cuts the choicest venison for me. Griffith politely excuses himself a moment, swapping drink and stories with his guardsmen across the room. His people seem quick to celebrate, probably accustomed to finding prosperity one day and death the next. Such is life along the Saxon border. And why not make the best of every moment? Especially when one does not know which moment may be their last.

Dancing revelers grab both Una and Rowena by the arms. My handmaids surrender to such persistence and join in. I nearly drop the goblet from my mouth, giggling at such a mirthful sight.

Rowena's jovial smile and ample curves earn her several dance partners, including a few Free Cantref revelers. Una grimaces, far more timid as she tries to keep time with the beat of calfskin drums. I cackle gleefully, both girls smiling at me by turns as they spin through the circle. For a moment, I forget I am anything but a girl at a country dance. I've no more worries than a dairymaid.

"Do you dance, my lady?"

Artagan sits beside me. I shift my seat, not wishing to be alone with the Blacksword. I keep my gaze to my food.

"Why are you here?" I demand.

"My followers and I travel the borderlands to guard against the Saxons, keeping the river villages safe whether they belong to the Free Cantrefs or not."

"No, I mean why are you *here*, sitting next to me?"

"Isn't it obvious, Your Highness? You're the only woman in the hall not yet dancing."

I pick at my meal, still not deigning to look at him. What must I do to make him leave me alone? Something Morgan once told me arises in my mind.

"My husband says that you steal cattle and ravish peasant girls. Is that true, Sir Artagan?"

He suddenly grows very still.

Perhaps if I get Artagan to show his true aggressive nature, Lord Griffith will see why Morgan wanted to lock up the Blacksword in the first place. Instead, Artagan pulls a thread of twine from around his neck, clenching it in his fist.

"I only took cows from rich barons, and gave them to poor villagers who didn't have enough meat to last the winter."

"And what of defenseless womenfolk?"

"The only girl I ever knew who was ravished was my sister, and that was the Saxons' work before they killed her."

Artagan presses the token into my hand. A small, soapstone figurine of a young girl. The tiny idol suddenly feels heavy as a boulder in my palm. I shut my eyes. The screams from the night the Saxons took my mother reverberate in my ears.

Artagan rises to leave before I put out a hand to stop him.

"That was unkind to say to a man who once saved me from Saxons. Forgive my hasty words."

"Your husband and I do not see eye to eye, but I thought you might be different."

"Because I come from Dyfed?"

"Because your mother was of the Old Tribes, like my own."

He departs without another word, leaving me speechless in my seat. I rarely hear mention of my mother by anyone, let alone from a stranger.

How could this hedge knight, of all people, know of my mother? Artagan has dark hair like myself and hails from the Free Cantrefs. I ought to have guessed that the blood of the Old Tribes runs strong in him.

My temples throb. I still hold the tiny figurine in hand when Griffith saunters back to my table, well into his cups. He downs another mouthful from his drinking horn before spying the soapstone figure in my palm. His gaze darts to Artagan across the hall.

"Don't judge Artagan too harshly, my Queen. He may run afoul of the laws of kings, but here in the borderlands he has saved many a villager from Saxon raiders."

"Are you not afraid I'll tell my husband that you harbor the Blacksword here?"

"Morgan knows my loyalty is ironclad. If he sends me the reinforcements I ask for, I won't need the help of outlaws like Sir Artagan, now will I?"

He gives me a fatherly smile. Griffith has a point, but Morgan has no troops to send. Not now, anyway. Perhaps I can convince Lord Griffith that my husband will send him more men once summer comes around again. It stands to reason Morgan will have more soldiers by then, especially between planting and harvest time when the farmers can leave their lands for a few months. But I must be careful not to make promises my husband may not be able to keep.

I rest my hand against my chin. Morgan should have sent someone else on this mission. Queen or no, I know about as much of diplomacy as a shepherd girl. No move I can make seems to be the right one.

Rising from the bench, I skirt the circle of dancing revelers. Both Rowena and Una twirl among them. Artagan has his back to me, sipping from a mead horn beside one of the crackling hearths.

Perhaps my husband and brother-in-law have heard false rumors about this hedge knight. The Blacksword admitted to stealing cattle, whether for good reasons or no. But how could a man who wears a remembrance of his fallen sister be a villain?

I sigh, unsure what to do. My stepmother always says a queen should seek to weave peace amongst rival knights and kings. If I can be nothing else, at least I can be a peace-weaver.

"I believe this is yours."

I hand the trinket of the soapstone girl back to Artagan. He turns, half-startled as the firelight reflects in his warm blue eyes. I offer him my other palm and motion toward the dancers.

Artagan blinks, looking me up and down with surprise. He nods with a cautious smile. The handsome hedge knight takes my hand, my fingertips abuzz under his touch. My heart pumps faster. The revelers make room for us in the circle, everyone clapping hands in time with the music of pipes and drums.

Rowena and Una exchange looks, doubtlessly amazed that I've linked hands with Artagan Blacksword, of all people. He proves himself light on his feet, staying right beside me as the circle moves faster and faster. Amidst the clapping and swirling tune, we gently collide more than once, our hips and hands touching at any given point. Artagan grins at me and I cannot help but smile back as the room spins around us.

Our steps quicken to the rhythm of stomping feet, each of us more than once hooking arms with different dancers before returning to our original partner. Thankfully, I manage not to trip over my own feet too much as Artagan leads me through the revolutions. He lifts me by the hips at one point, as though I were light as a feather pincushion. My feet don't touch the ground.

The set finally ends with a boisterous crescendo. I fall into Artagan's grasp, my heart drumming against his ribs. We unwind our arms from around one another, his muscles flexing beneath his threadbare shirt.

The two of us take a break beside a nearby table. I gulp down a chalice of mead as I catch my breath.

"I can't remember the last time I danced like this, not since I lived at Dyfed."

"You move swift as a pixie, Branwen."

"That's *Queen* Branwen to you, sir," I reply in a jovial tone.

He purses his lips in a half-smile as I turn away to pin back the loose ends of my hair. Rowena and Una give me sly, sidelong looks. Heaven help my brashness! Half the chamber must have watched us, and me barely wed a few months to my husband back in Caerwent. Every servant girl's tongue within a hundred leagues will wag over this.

So much for my cordial attempt to make peace. My husband will just as likely go to war knowing Artagan Blacksword held me in his arms, even if only for a moment. It was just a dance.

A bugle call interrupts the merrymakers as a herald races into the hall. Lord Griffith pushes his way through the crowd, demanding to know the meaning of the interruption. The guard's skin turns white as milk, his lips all atremble.

"My lord, we sighted torches outside the gates! The Saxons! They've come!"

A hundred balls of flame encircle the palisade, coiled around the fort like a fiery dragon. The Saxons surround us on every side. Lord Griffith, Artagan, and I observe the iron-helmed barbarians from between notches in the upper bastion walls. My stomach turns over at the scent of pitch and pine tar from the Saxons' smoldering torches. Griffith pounds his fist against a wooden embrasure.

"I warned the King of this! Little wonder no one believed me, I hardly believe it myself."

"I thought Saxons don't go to war this late in the season," I reply.

"They don't. Not in my memory, but that was before the Fox and the Wolf."

My skin turns cold at mention of the Fox and the Wolf. Along the dark riverfront, just before the tree line, two broad-shouldered warriors cluster beneath dripping firebrands. One sports red whiskers beneath his helmet; the other is immensely tall with a long bronze beard. The chieftain brothers, Cedric and Beowulf.

I stare at the two Saxon brothers across the glade, frozen like a hare before the hunter. Artagan pulls me down behind the stockade bulwarks.

"Keep down!" he whispers. "If the Saxons realize you're here, they won't lift the siege until they've taken you captive."

"Artagan's right, my Queen," Griffith adds. "I've hardly a skeleton force to withstand a siege anyway."

"It's almost as though they knew I would be here," I murmur to myself.

"But that's impossible," Artagan replies. "We didn't even know you were coming until you arrived this evening."

The spy. I thought I left such intrigues behind when I departed Caerwent, but evidently whoever continues to secretly plot my downfall has tracked me to the Dean Fort. I dare not voice my fears aloud, no longer certain whom I can trust.

Lord Griffith places a palm on my shoulder.

"We need to get you to safety," he says.

"I'm not going anywhere," I reply, trying to sound brave. "Besides, they have us surrounded."

"There is a way," Griffith says.

He leads us into a corner of the main hall. Servants dowse hearth fires while others rush by with spears in hand. I cross myself, knowing none of us may survive the night. It already seems like centuries since warmth and mirth filled these darkened corridors where we feasted and danced only minutes ago.

We crouch behind several casks that smell of dry grain. Lord Griffith pushes an empty barrel aside, pulling up a trapdoor beneath the dirt floor. He illuminates the hole with a torch.

"This passage leads out past the walls and into the woods. With any luck, you may escape."

"Me? What about you and your people?"

"My Queen, there's no time. Only I know of this passage and only a few can use it before the Saxons discover some have escaped. My men and I will distract them, defending this fort as long as we can. Sir Artagan will go with you."

Artagan and I exchange equally wide-eyed looks. Artagan aims a finger at Lord Griffith.

"I like you, Griffith, but I'm from the Free Cantrefs and I don't take orders from you."

"If the Saxons discover the Queen has escaped, she'll need someone to protect her. I can't spare any men as it is. No arguments! You two must leave now."

Artagan hangs his head. He seems to want to stay and fight. Maybe he just doesn't want to escort me through night woods overrun with Saxons.

Lord Griffith and I stare one another down. Does he honestly expect me to desert at the first sign of danger? Is that what a matriarch of the Old Tribes would have done? Part of me would surely like to make a run for it, the part of me that just wants to live and breathe another day. But Griffith and his people are my subjects now, and as such they are my responsibility. I cannot just leave them here to die.

A heavy clanking of metal on wood thunders from outside the fort walls.

Clack, clack, clack.

Dust falls from the roof beams. Peeking through a chink in the timber bulkheads, I glimpse the horde of Saxons outside banging their weapons against their round shields. My heart races as the deafening sound abrades my eardrums. The savages' torches loom closer.

Artagan whistles loudly between two fingers. His small band of green-clad warriors joins us in our dark corner of the main hall. They nod grimly as he explains the situation to them, their eyes falling on me.

My palms begin to sweat. Artagan draws his sword and grabs my wrist, motioning for me to follow him into the tunnel. I pull against him as I shake my head.

"I'm not going. I cannot leave my household thanes!"

"We haven't time for servant girls and a priest!"

"They're like family to me."

The Blacksword grimaces, but loosens my wrist. To my surprise, he goes into the yard and calls out to my companions. Ahern, Padraig, Rowena, and Una soon cluster beside us. I meant what I said about them being family to me. Lord Griffith puts a palm on my shoulder, his insistence starting to wear down my resolve.

"Please go, my Queen. Someone must get word to the King about what's happening here."

With a heavy sigh, I admit that Lord Griffith has a point. I gaze up at my falcon in the rafters. Although I am loath to part with my bird, Griffith needs her more than I do.

"Send my falcon to Caerwent with a note as well," I reply. "She might get through to my husband if we do not."

Of course a Saxon archer may well shoot her down, and I may perish in the woods first.

"Go, Branwen," Griffith says calmly. "We still stand a better chance of alerting your husband if we loose the bird *and* send you through the forest. I'll not have my king's new bride captured on my watch."

Realizing that time is wasting and neither Griffith nor Artagan plan to budge, I reluctantly nod in agreement. Griffith wraps his arms around a large barrel.

"I'll seal the entrance once you enter the tunnel. After that you're on your own. Godspeed."

Artagan ushers me into the tunnel while I call back toward Lord Griffith.

"I'll get word to the King," I promise. "He'll send help to save your fort."

He smiles at me like a man who knows he is doomed, but will soon see heaven.

"Farewell, my Queen."

One by one, we each pile into the dark hole. Lord Griffith places the first barrels over the tunnel entranceway behind us. The last thing I see is the older man's face, the eyes of a man who will meet his maker tonight.

My vision slowly adjusts to the dark tunnel, devoid of light save for a sliver of twilight glowing at the far end of the passageway. Groping our way through the subterranean corridor, my hands brush wet earth and gnarled roots. The heavy thud of countless footsteps rumbles overhead as the Saxons besiege the fort. Our small company snakes single file toward the dim light.

Gasping for air, I pray I won't perish inside this narrow tomb. No one should ever see the inside of their own grave.

My palm brushes something slick, a worm or grub. The clamor of battle rages through the ground overhead as the Saxons storm the palisade with a roar. Artagan stops when we reach the end of the passage.

"Wait here."

He disappears, crawling up out of the hole. I start to follow, but a deluge of pebbles and dirt collapses in his wake. The earth stinks like a pigsty. I cover my nose, my eyes tearing up at the stench. Where on earth does this tunnel let out? After what seems like an eternity, Artagan returns and sticks his hand down toward me.

"Quickly! The Saxons linger close by."

Rising up out of the pit, I claw to the surface while Artagan lifts me up by the arms. Coughing as I crawl into the moonlight, I look up to find myself surrounded by woods and several gray mounds. The buzz of flies leaves little doubt as to our location. We've come up in the middle of a dung heap. Despite the fetid smell, I must give Lord Griffith credit. Who would ever search a dunghill for a secret entranceway?

As I roll over in the grass, gasping for fresh air, Artagan clutches me close to the ground with a palm over my mouth. I struggle under his grasp, trying to breathe. He shushes me and points toward the torches of the fort, only a few hundred paces away. All the air seems to rush out of me.

Less than a stone's throw from us, a gang of Saxon warriors observes the fort while a hundred of their kinsmen scale the battered walls. Two war-captains converse in their barbaric tongue, shouting commands to their underlings who loosen torches of fire toward the timber palisade.

It's the Fox and the Wolf.

Artagan gradually removes his palm from my mouth. Cedric the Fox and Beowulf the Wolf stand close enough for me to count every link of their chain mail. All they have to do is turn around and they will see us.

The rest of our party ascends from the tunnel, quietly fanning out into the trees with Artagan and me. A few of the Free Cantref warriors eye the backs of the two Saxon war-chiefs, brandishing their spears under the moonlight. Artagan shakes his head and motions for them to get back. His men reluctantly retreat deeper into the woods. Fine as it would be to strike down these two Saxon war-chiefs, if we did so, hundreds of their howling warriors would be upon us in an instant.

Creeping slowly back into the trees, I cannot take my eyes off the burning fires kindled along the fort walls. Scores of good Welsh men and women will die tonight, all the while trying to protect me. I should be there, standing beside Griffith and his thanes.

Instead, I stop in my tracks as a large twig snaps underfoot. My blood seems to freeze in my veins.

Cedric and Beowulf turn around. Their eyes widen, possibly guessing who I am by my dark locks and green eyes. Artagan grabs me by the hand as we both bolt into the depths of the forest.

The Saxons raise a cry behind us. Arrows whistle after us in the dark, embedding themselves in trees mere paces from our heads.

Artagan shouts commands to his men, pairs of us splitting up into separate groups as we descend into the timberlands. The better to confuse our pursuers and hopefully divide their numbers in order to even the odds a bit. I catch glimpses of Rowena and Una, both paired off with other men as they go different directions into the nocturnal groves. Artagan and I separate from the others as we run through dark thickets and briar patches. Thorns snag my hair and claw at my cheeks, but I do not stop. The torches of the Saxons glow behind us.

Months of sitting on pincushions and sleeping in feather beds have not prepared me for a midnight run through the wilderness. Despite my heaving breath, I push on until my lungs burn. I used to run all day as a child along the strands of Dyfed's shores, and I'll not lose a footrace now that my life depends upon it. I pause only to tear the hem of my gown beneath the knees, lengthening my stride as I take to my heels once again and follow Artagan through the labyrinth of trees. The clash of swords and spears echoes through the woodlots behind us. I do not stop to look back.

We finally stop at a stream trickling through a quiet dell. I sink to my knees, bent over the brook as I cup mouthfuls of water in my palms. The frigid water stings my throat, but I cannot swallow enough of it. Artagan searches the woods with his eyes, the distant murmur of battle fading. He grabs me by the arm and pulls us into the creek, cold water splashing about our ankles.

"What are you doing?" I demand. "We have to find the others."

"We'll cross paths with them later. First, we have to move upstream to cover our tracks. I need you to trust me."

Staggering to my feet, I follow him through the shallows. I've little choice but to trust him anyway. Without a guide, I might wander these woods in circles. I stumble blindly over river stones while the stars glow fiercely overhead.

Numb from the shins down, I nearly twist my ankles in half a dozen places before we halt to rest. Fell winds cut through my tattered clothes, freezing me to the marrow. No fire tonight. We cannot risk it with the Saxon patrols wandering the woods. Artagan loosens his fur mantle and curls up beneath a stand of thick sedge. He motions for me to lie down under his furs. Worn as I am, I shake my head.

"I appreciate the gesture, but a married, Christian woman can only share her bed with her husband."

"Don't flatter yourself," he replies, trying to sound more jovial than either of us feel. "If we don't huddle for warmth, we may both freeze tonight."

I throw him a sidelong glance, but for once he doesn't flash one of his characteristic cocky grins. Instead, he rolls over in the dust, tugging his furry cloak over his shoulders. After a few minutes of shivering in the autumn winds, I kneel down beside the windbreak of thick hedges and crawl under the bearskin mantle with him.

Artagan stirs slightly, already half-asleep. His chest rises and falls in his slumber, comfortable as though in his own bed at home. I wince as I pluck several jagged stones from beneath me. This hedge knight must spend more nights sleeping out of doors than under a roof.

Despite my weary limbs, I toss and turn before making a small rut in the earth where I can curl up beneath our shared blanket. The cold eventually overcomes my sense of propriety as I spoon closer to Artagan. Even through the blankets, his skin runs hot. My shivering limbs seem to thaw somewhat beside him. The pleasant balsam scent of the woods permeates his hair and clothes.

My heavy eyelids begin to sink just as a lone wolf call murmurs in the distance. A shiver runs down my spine. It's going to be a very long night.

Daylight seeps through the treetops when morning arrives. The dawn air stings my cheeks as I curl up beneath the warm animal skin. I roll over to find the fur lies flat beside me, the earth beneath it long gone cold. I abruptly sit up.

Heaven help me. I'm alone in the middle of the wilderness.

Flecks of frost cover the fingers of the trees, the woods quiet except for the whistling breeze. The wooded highlands overlook a large snaking, sapphire river half a league distant. Tiny smoke trails rise along the greens. Far down by the waterfront, dozens of thatched roundhouses cluster beside the marshy banks. A village.

My heart beats more easily just knowing some human souls live nearby, whoever they are. We followed the North Star when we fled last evening so I can only guess that I have traveled deep within the domain of the Free Cantrefs. No old Roman road nor any signs of wheel ruts mar the landscape. The untouched forests and mountains look as rugged as the day God made them.

Fallen leaves crumple behind me.

I spin around, grabbing a rock to defend myself. Artagan laughs, crossing his bare muscular arms. I breathe a touch easier. So he didn't desert me after all. I still have half a mind to lob a stone right at him for startling me, but I'm just so glad right now not to be alone.

Without a word, he wends his way down the slope toward the distant village.

"Where are we going?"

He points mutely toward the small settlement of huts. A dark thought suddenly strikes me. The river below marks the borderlands between the Welsh and Saxons.

"What if it's a Saxon village?"

"Better than staying out here to freeze or starve to death."

He shrugs before descending into the woods. I drop my rock as I roll my eyes. What encouraging words. Do all hedge knights risk their lives so or is Artagan unique in not caring a fig for his?

An overcast sky blots out the sun, but I fear we continue to head northward, away from South Wales and home. Every step takes me farther from Caerwent and any chance I have of alerting Morgan of what has befallen Griffith and the Dean Fort.

I trail Artagan toward the village, observing him closely. He has not taken me to King Morgan's realm as he should have. But whatever Artagan's intents might be, I cannot yet guess. Holding Morgan's queen captive would certainly give the Free Cantrefs a large bargaining chip when next parleying with my husband. But would the man who saved me from Saxons twice now use me as a pawn again the Hammer King? A pang of guilt lances my chest for even suspecting him, yet at the same time I cannot deny the cold logic of such a plot. Saxon evils pervade the land enough without the Welsh constantly betraying one another.

By midday, we leave the foothills and reach the meadows alongside the riverfront. Artagan motions for me to crouch low as we stalk through the canebrakes toward the village. We squat in the mud, peering at the wattle-and-daub huts between gaps in the tall grass. When I try to speak, Artagan shushes me. His gaze never leaves the cluster of huts.

I sit and watch the settlement with him, wondering how we can tell whether they are Saxons or Welsh. I doubt we can linger here forever without being discovered.

A few people move amongst the hovels, their faces indistinguishable from a distance. Nothing more than a wicker fence surrounds the village proper. Meager defenses against marauders and thieves.

Artagan cups a palm around his mouth and hoots like an owl. What the devil? After several moments of silence a birdcall answers. Artagan rises from the bulrushes, a broad smile on his face. Two men emerge from the village, one with an ax over his shoulder and the other with a staff.

"Blacksword, is that you?" the axman shouts.

"Well met!" Artagan replies. "Keenan, how did you reach here before me?"

"It's my home village, isn't it?"

Artagan embraces the stout woodsman with the ax. A second man in a gray beard comes after him, leaning on a quarterstaff. I recognize the two men as some of Artagan's warriors from back at the Dean Fort. My heart nearly leaps in my throat, wondering what has happened to Rowena, Una, and the others. Artagan claps his two companions on the shoulders.

"Allow me to introduce my merry men, Keenan the Saxon Slayer and Emryus the Bard."

Keenan winks at Artagan before looking me over.

"I escorted a priest through the woods while you spent the night with a tart? Hardly seems fair."

"Show some respect," Emryus chides, bowing to me. "She is still a Welsh queen."

I rush forward at the mention of a priest. He must mean Abbot Padraig. I grab Keenan by his fur collar, drawing his youthful brown beard close.

"My people! Are they here with you? In the village?"

"Easy, woman!" Keenan replies. "We got the old cleric, though his slow feet nearly got us killed."

"And the others?"

"Others?" he says, glancing at Artagan, then me. "No others have yet returned."

I sink to my knees. Rowena, Una, and Ahern have scattered to the winds. Alone in the wilds or slain by Saxons or God knows what. Close as family, and now the three of them have vanished. Artagan rests a comforting palm on my shoulder, but I brush it away. I put my hands to my face, too distraught to weep.

7

The villagers whisper around me, never having seen a queen before. Darkness sets in amongst the dozen wattle-and-daub roundhouses, their smoking hearths filling the air with scents of venison and hickory. Artagan and his men stand watch at the edge of the flickering firelight. Padraig sits silent at my side. I hug my knees close to my chest, watching the flames dance along the hearth logs. We've still no sign of Rowena, Una, or Ahern.

Two village women offer me bowls of bone marrow broth. I nod and fake a smile, but only take a few polite sips. Despite the last two days of arduous travel, I am not hungry. The older of the two ladies calls herself Gwen, something of a village mother who already hovers over me as though I were one of her own. Her gray locks hang like ropes past faded blue tattoos that run down her cheek and neck. I stare, fascinated to see anyone alive today who still bears such marks of the Old Tribes. I thought such things only existed in storybooks. Padraig suspiciously eyes the pagan symbols along her skin, but says nothing.

The second woman, Gwen's daughter, introduces herself as Ria. Her long blond locks reach down to the small of her back. A young boy hides behind her skirts while she brings me a fresh jug of river water to drink. She has remarkable beauty, golden hair and hourglass curves. I almost say as much to her, but stop short as she stares longingly after Artagan.

Goose bumps rise along my forearms. Her child has dark hair and striking blue eyes. I look away as though accidentally stumbling onto someone
else's secret. Ria catches my glance.

"Something the matter, your ladyship?"

"I'm afraid I'm not much good company right now. My friends have
gone missing in a wilderness full of Saxons. Frankly, everything's the
matter."

"You still have your skin. In the borderlands, we prefer to dwell on
what blessings we have left."

"Like a beautiful son. What's his name?"

Ria puts a protective hand over the child's head.

"Art."

"Art? Named after an uncle or his father perhaps?"

Ria flashes a mask-like smile at my probing question.

"We follow the ways of the Old Tribes in the Free Cantrefs. A
mother's blood is all that matters."

She clenches her teeth as she smiles back at me. I've touched a sore spot
with her. Ria glances toward Artagan and the others on watch, the menfolk oblivious to the unspoken words between us women. Blind to the obvious, just like menfolk everywhere.

Ria's fair hair suddenly seems no longer pretty to me. More like the
color of dead grass. Nonetheless, her words about the Old Tribes give
me pause. Perhaps my mother's kinfolk once lived like the people of the
Free Cantrefs, free-spirited and independent if somewhat rough around
the edges.

Ria strides over toward Artagan at the verge of the settlement. She
watches me from the corner of her eye. As though I care. Only their silhouettes stand out against the twilight, their outlines close enough to
touch. Their muffled voices murmur amidst the chirping crickets. Ria
giggles at something Artagan says. The flirt. I know I'm being unfair in
my judgment of her, but something about this pretty village girl prickles
my skin.

Padraig shuffles closer to me, downing a bowlful of soup. Gwen bows
and gives him another before returning to her cauldron. The Abbot prods
me with a steaming cup of broth.

"You must eat, Branwen. Your hunger will not help our lost companions fare any better."

I put a hand on his arm.

"I'm glad you're here, my old friend. I don't think I could handle losing you."

"Hush, my child. Drink."

I gulp down a mouthful of piping hot soup. My belly rumbles as though suddenly remembering what it desires. Downing all the broth, I accept a second bowlful from Padraig before I finally pause for breath.

Emryus and Keenan join us by the fireside. Despite missing companions of their own, they jostle and joke with one another over their meal as though all is well. I want to rage at them for such callousness, gibing and supping by a warm hearth while their friends suffer the elements or the Saxons. But after a moment, I think better of it. Everyone copes in their own way. I prefer not to eat, but the gray bard and the jovial woodsman simply pretend that no peril exists at all. As though their friends had merely gone on an evening hunt and nothing more. Perhaps their way of dealing with grief is better, but I cannot force myself to laugh at their bawdy jokes tonight.

Excusing myself, I turn in for the night. My bones feel heavy as lead as I lie down inside one of the village huts. Turning on my side, I find just enough room on the floor between a village woman and a young boy. Everyone shares the same space in these communal dwellings, without so much as a curtain between them. I shut my eyes, pretending I recline upon my feather bed back in Caerwent. Despite my weary joints, sleep comes slowly to me in the crowded, smoky den. The last thing I hear before succumbing to slumber is Ria's girlish giggle outside.

At dawn, Padraig wakens me with a hand on my shoulder. Horses whicker from the village lawns. Shaggy mountain ponies paw at the earth, looking little taller than myself at the shoulder. I turn toward Padraig.

"We plan on going somewhere?"

The monk shrugs. Not one of these ponies has a bridle or saddle blanket, their long manes speckled with mud and catkins. Still, their muscles bulge strong and thick for such short beasts. I've ridden horses aplenty on the shores of Dyfed, but never have I seen steeds as wild-looking as these.

It makes me smile. In the Free Cantrefs, even the ponies call no one master.

Artagan ducks out of the adjacent hovel with Ria lingering behind him, her shift loose over a bare shoulder. I turn away, but not before Ria catches my stare. She grins as she ties up her wheat-colored locks, her womanly figure so much fuller than mine. My cheeks burn hot.

A good-looking hedge knight like the Blacksword must have a girl like her in every village. How freely these country girls give themselves up for a pair of bold eyes and a fair face. And what must Lady Olwen think? At the feast at Caerwent, she looked at him the way only a lover does. She must have known Artagan long enough to discover his dalliances with peasant girls. The scene suddenly reminds me of Prince Malcolm chasing serving girls like Una. What am I to make of a man who fights Saxons by day and philanders with farmers' daughters by night?

I should have been back in Caerwent by now, warning my husband of the Saxons besieging the Dean Fort. Instead, I'm stuck in some backwater encampment while Lord Griffith battles for his life. And to top it off, I'll probably never see Ahern, Una, or Rowena again. I hang my head. Some queen I've turned out to be. I can't even protect those closest to me, let alone my subjects or the realm. I can't even look after myself, it seems.

Artagan, Emryus, and Keenan mount three of the ponies corralled on the greens. Astride their bareback mounts, their legs nearly reach to the ground. The knights of South Wales would laugh at such shaggy ponies, no bigger than a small cow, but I find myself longing to reach out and pet one of their furry snouts. One nuzzles close to my outstretched hand, eyeing me curiously.

Not until the three riders begin to trot away do I realize they intend to leave without us. I dash in front of Artagan's mount, waving my arms. His steed whinnies as the beast halts and boxes the air with its hooves. He does not attempt to hide the fury in his voice.

"What in hell's name are you doing?"

"I should ask you the same question. You cannot leave Padraig and me behind. The Abbot and I will never find our way back home through this wilderness by ourselves. Besides, we have to warn the King of what befell the Dean Fort."

"We're going to find our missing companions first, and rescue them if need be."

"Then I'm going with you. Half of them are my people too. I'm responsible for them."

"We ride into the wilds, probably to cross swords with Saxons! This is no task for a pampered princess."

"I can ride a horse as well as any man. I'm Queen of South Wales, and a daughter of Dyfed. The only way you're leaving is either with me or over my trampled body!"

I fix my hands on my hips, nearly nose to nose with his snorting mount. Artagan's heels inch closer to the sides of his pony, and for a moment I fear he really intends to run me down. Every eye in the village watches us, probably wondering if all queens are as mad as I am. Artagan leans back in the saddle and laughs.

"The blood of the Old Tribeswomen runs strong in you! Ride with us then at your own peril, but you must do as I say when things get rough. No more behaving like Branwen the Stubborn."

"I am not stubborn."

Artagan makes a noncommittal grunt.

He whistles for two more ponies that canter up to Padraig and me. The Abbot gets one leg over his steed before the beast bucks him off into the mud. The villagers laugh while Ria's voice rises above the din.

"Outlanders can't handle our wild ponies. They haven't got the right touch."

Several more villagers guffaw. Helping Padraig to his feet, I wipe the mud off his cheek before assailing my own mount. None of Artagan's men make a move to help me. Biting my lip, I vault atop the pony, its spine arching as I wrap my legs around it. The little mare has more muscle than I thought, writhing angrily beneath me. I clamp my legs around her until my face turns purple. Finally, the she-pony neighs and relaxes. I pat her fondly along the neck, glancing back at Ria as she folds her arms and frowns. Artagan slaps his thigh.

"Just as I always suspected, so queens do have vigorous legs!"

Emryus and Keenan cackle behind him. The villagers seem less impressed. I lend a hand to Padraig, who respectfully declines before successfully mounting his pony on the second try. As our small retinue gallops into the woods, I suddenly question the wisdom of leaving this peaceful village behind. Suppose we do find our friends and suppose the Saxons have already found them first. What then? Artagan and his men seem like hardy warriors, but what of Padraig and me? We don't even have so much as a kitchen knife to defend us. The Abbot trained for a life of books and I for a king's bed. What in Christendom are we supposed to do in battle? My few glimpses of Saxons up close leave me little doubt as to who would prevail in a contest of brute strength. As though guessing my trepidations, Artagan lobs a longbow at my chest.

"Here," he adds with a quill of arrows. "Make sure to stick the Saxons with the pointy end."

He cackles and tosses a spear to Padraig. The bald clergyman catches it, but nearly tumbles off his mount, holding the upended spearhead backward. Riding amidst the tangled woods, I keep my head low beneath the gnarled tree limbs. Despite the thunder of hooves and the sweat rolling down my back, a pleasurable buzz rises through my spine. If we find our lost companions and must battle the Saxons, at least they will see a queen with a bow, unafraid to ride a wild pony with the best of them.

After days of trekking through misty woods, I awake in Artagan's arms. His lips hover over mine, his breath stirring my lashes. I gasp, trying to pull back, but even in his slumber Artagan has strong arms. Beneath our shared blankets I can do little but lay my head against his chest, listening to his heartbeat. He breathes heavily, relinquishing his grip before rolling over.

Emryus and Keenan sleep beside him with Padraig on my other side, all five of us accustomed to huddling for warmth by now. What a sight we must make. A queen, a knight, and a monk all cuddled together in the brush like a bunch of woodland beggars. The dawn light cuts through the recent rain clouds that have stormed for the past few days, turning the forest paths into bogs of mud. We still do not light fires for fear of the Saxons. While the others slumber, I sit up under the bearskin coverlet and watch the Blacksword sleep.

His placid face reminds me of a child's, so free of creases or cares. How often do Olwen or Ria look down upon his sleeping countenance? I've never seen Morgan's sleeping face, his features often hidden by the shadows of our shared solar chamber. How different Artagan's life seems compared to my own. He roams the wilds, sleeping amongst hedgerows and village huts, living under threat of Saxons and all with a price on his head, courtesy of my husband. Despite it all, he looks content in his simple, feral life. Never knowing what he will encounter from one day to the next, he lives a perpetual adventure. If I ever return to the comforts of Caerwent, I will certainly thank heaven for hot-water baths and good food, but I also know that each day will vary little from the next. I will play hostess, read books, and bear my husband sons. A cold numbness rises through my veins. I shake such useless daydreams from my sleepy mind. What woman in her right mind would choose the company of a rogue knight over the warm bed of a king?

The ponies whinny from their tethers beside an adjacent tree, awakening the men with the shuffle of hooves amongst the fallen leaves. After a quick breakfast of dried meats and waybread, we mount up and begin our winding trek through the woods. Dewdrops murmur through the damp dells as they drip from broad-leaves. My wet hair clings to my neck beneath my ruffled and muddied gowns. I've not had a fresh change of clothes since we left the Dean Fort, but none of my companions take any notice. Fashion does not seem to interest these Free Cantref men much.

Keenan halts ahead of our small company and dismounts. Artagan soon joins him on the ground while the rest of us keep watch over the surrounding woods. Keenan points to several worn indentations in the mud.

"Look at these tracks, Artagan. You see where they head."

"I'll be damned."

"You don't intend to follow them now, do you? It's too dangerous."

"Do we have a choice?"

My ears perk up at this first sign of hope and trouble. Maybe my brother and my serving girls still live. Artagan and Keenan both frown as they mount their ponies. I'm almost afraid to ask them why they look so glum, unsure I want to hear the answer. But I have to know.

"Do you think it's them?" I ask Artagan. "Have we found their trail?"

"If it is, then God help us," he replies. "They've gone to the last place on earth I'd wish to see."

The hairs rise along the nape of my neck. Before I can ask just where we are heading, Artagan digs his heels into the flanks of his mount and shouts into the beast's ear. Our small company gallops at a redoubled pace through the woodlands, following fresh tracks in the wet earth. Whatever dreadful den the Saxons have taken my people to I can only guess, but it cannot bode well for us if the thought of it makes Artagan blanch.

We ride the better part of the day until my thighs ache from clenching my mare. The canopy and overcast sky make it difficult for me to discern what direction we've taken. Whether we're on the Saxon or Welsh side of the border, I can only guess.

Under a brilliant flash of sunlight, we suddenly emerge into an open country of free rolling plains full of grass recently mowed by cattle. My eyes water under the sunshine and the unchecked wind. I blink in disbelief at a large gray silhouette in the distance, the tall outline of a castle looming across the river. I halt my horse beside Artagan, trying to find my voice.

"It's Caerwent! You've brought me home."

"That's where the tracks lead," he sighs. "And that's where I'm taking you."

"I best go myself. My husband has a price on your head, remember?"

"Whatever happened to your people, some of my men were with them. If they're alive and Morgan's got them, I intend to get my warriors back."

"Are you mad? The King's men will attack you on sight."

He ignores me as he urges his mount forward. His companions exchange worried looks, but they say nothing as we gallop toward the citadel gates. Padraig, God bless his wisdom, has the good sense to raise a pocket handkerchief over his head, flapping it about like a white flag. Filthy as we are from the woods, my husband's own guards might loose an arrow at me, thinking me just another dirty Celt from the Free Cantrefs. We halt beside the main gate, the crimson-garbed guards astonished at the appearance of the Blacksword on their very doorstep. Artagan's voice booms throughout the fortress.

"I've Queen Branwen of Dyfed with me! Tell King Morgan he owes me twice now for saving his bride."

Before I can blink, two dozen guardsmen swarm around our party, leveling their spears at Artagan and his men. Despite my rags, several soldiers recognize me and Padraig, ushering us away from the Free Cantref men. The guards pull Artagan and his men off their steeds, stripping them of their weapons as they call for shackles and chains. I dismount and rush toward the tumult, but several guards hold me back.

"No, wait! They come in peace! Sir Artagan has rescued me, he means no ill."

The clatter of armor and chain mail drowns out my words, the guards already clapping Artagan and his companions in irons. The soldiers rush Padraig and me away toward the atrium. Artagan looks my way, his bright-blue eyes dimming with sorrow as the men rob him of his famous longsword. Both Padraig and I keep shouting, demanding the guards listen to us, but not a soul heeds our words.

After the vivid greenery of the forests and wilds, the once-familiar stone hallways of Caerwent look whitewashed as tombstones.

Morgan and his brother stand in conference before the throne as his thanes bring me into the main chamber. The King blinks a moment before recognizing me.

"Branwen? Branwen!"

He opens his arms to embrace me, but I put a hand to his chest.

"My King, your guards have restrained Sir Artagan, who brought me here."

"When we heard he spirited you away from the Dean Fort, we feared the worst."

"He saved us! And how do you know of the Saxons attacking the Dean Fort? Have you word of my guardsman Ahern or my serving girls? Several Free Cantref men were with them."

"Calm yourself, my Queen." He smiles. "We have your people, all safe and sound. We rescued them on the King's Road from some Free Cantref warriors."

I shut my eyes and breathe with momentary relief. Ahern, Rowena, and Una all live. Over the King's shoulder, Prince Malcolm wrinkles his nose at the sight of my torn and muddied clothes. Before I can question either of them further, the King takes me by the shoulder.

"Are you all right, my Queen? Did the devils harm you in any way?"

"Artagan rescued me. That's what I'm trying to tell you! Where have you taken him?"

"To the dungeons, with the other renegades from his band. You sure he did nothing to you?"

"You're not listening!"

My thunderous voice silences everyone in the court. All eyes turn on me and I feel my neck flush, never having raised my voice so loud before the King. Morgan's smile fades, his words firm and deliberate.

"We received your bird from the Dean Fort. I led a sortie myself and relieved the settlement, chasing the Saxons out. Lord Griffith was down to his last man, but he and his household still live."

"God be praised, Lord Griffith will tell you the same as I. Sir Artagan led me to safety."

"The Blacksword has a price on his head, and he will stand trial for his crimes."

"For stealing a few cows and having evil rumors spread about him? He has saved me twice!"

Morgan snaps his fingers as a dozen guardsmen surround me and Padraig at once. Prince Malcolm flashes a crooked smile as soldiers on either side pin back my arms. Morgan does not look at me as he addresses his court.

"My Queen is overwrought from her odyssey in the wilderness. Take her to her chambers so that she may recover and compose herself."

The guardsmen usher me toward the turret steps, their grips so firm that my feet barely touch the ground. Clenching my jaw, I nearly speak out again, but think better of it. Manhandled by tall guards, with my husband's back already turned to me, I know I have no chance of further-ing Artagan's cause or my own by making a spectacle of myself. Instead, I murmur toward Padraig, loud enough for my husband and brother-in-law to hear.

"My mind is not unhinged. I know what I say and I speak the truth."

Morgan stops in his tracks but does not turn around. His men carry me up to my solar. Prince Malcolm leers my way before I disappear into the stairwell. The guards bolt the chamber door behind me, their shuffling armor on the stoop attesting to at least a pair of them standing watch outside. I stamp my foot, dashing an empty tankard at the locked door. Caged like a rat!

Despite the comforts of silken bedspreads and lavish food laid out on the tabletop, I merely find myself once again under lock and key in my very own bedchamber. I bang against the door with my fists, but the guards on the other side make no move to answer me. I've no idea where they took Abbot Padraig or where my guardsman Ahern has gone. A meek voice calls to me from the shadows across the room.

"Your Grace, is that you?"

"Rowena? Una?"

My serving maids emerge from the corner. They blanch at the sight of my ruined gown, rushing to the chest beside my bed in search of fresh linens. I tell them both to stop and sit down, pouring each of us a drink at the table.

"Thank God you're both unharmed," I say, sighing with relief. "How long have you two been in Caerwent?"

"For days, m'lady," Rowena replies. "We saw your arrival in the court-yard and heard the King's words."

"What happened to the Free Cantref men with you? And where's Ahern?"

"The guards put the Free Cantref warriors in the dungeon," Una answers. "Even the woman warrior among them."

"And the King won't let Ahern guard this room," Rowena adds. "Don't think he trusts him."

"So you're both prisoners here too."

"Nay, m'lady," Rowena says with a brave smile. "Not so long as we be with you."

Rowena's effort to raise my spirits brings a slight grin to my lips. God bless her. Blinking back the water behind my eyes, I find myself unable to say any more. Thank heaven both girls survived the forest and the Saxons. I feared that none of us would ever meet again this side of the grave.

Heavy rain begins to fall outside, thick droplets splattering along the stone windowsill. It takes Rowena and Una several tries to batten down the shutters against the howling winds. A shiver rises through me as I clutch a shawl tight about my throat. The first winter storms have come.

Daylight turns to darkness and still the guards do not permit any of us to leave my solar. They do relieve us of our chamber pots before bringing up fresh food and wine, even a vat of steaming water with which I can bathe. I know I ought to be grateful, but I stare coldly at the guards as they leave fresh woolens before bolting the door again. I doubt Sir Artagan and his men fare so well tonight down in the dungeons.

After ravenously eating my meal of cheese and mutton, I strip myself bare for my bath. Sliding into the wooden tub, I let out a heavy sigh. Inhaling the hot vapors, I descend up to my neck and shut my eyes a moment. The murky waters turn my skin pink with warmth. Rowena hovers over me with a bar of soap sudsed between her fingers. I wince at the heaviness in my chest.

"My bosom feels like two clenched fists."

"Thank the Virgin." Rowena laughs, touching my breast. "You've grown, m'lady."

"But I've had my courses this moon. I mean I can't have a . . . you know."

"Lass, you've just started flowering late 'tis all. You're already more a beauty than when you first came to live at Caerwent. Did your mother never say how old she was when she blossomed?"

I shake my head, sinking down deeper into the steaming waters. A little girl only knows so much of her mother. My memories of her consist of a few brilliant smiles and evening gowns, the feeling of a warm lap and a gentle lullaby. I wish I didn't remember her last day of life so vividly, the blood and the screams amongst the Saxon ships on our shores. Who knows how our lives might have intertwined had the barbarians never come. We might have fought, laughed, been close or distant, but a mother and daughter ought to at least get the chance to find out what they mean to one another.

Gazing down at the reflection of my wet locks and fair skin, I wonder if what Rowena says will come true. Could an ugly, crow-faced girl like me ever emerge from the cocoon of girlhood to look like the beauty my mother had been? But she had so much more, a wit and a voice that over-awed me even as a child. Father bellowed less in those days, either because Mother kept him in line or kept him happy in the bedchamber. Maybe both. From beyond the grave, Mother still gives me gifts, her green eyes and dark hair, and now even her figure. But how can I kindle the majesty of her mind and be a queen worthy of the Old Tribes? Somehow I must do her memory proud. But I find it difficult enough to rule as a queen when I don't even have someone here to show me how.

That night, Rowena, Una, and I share the large bedstead again, keeping warm while the winter wind beats against the castle walls. Morgan does not come to my bed that night or the next.

To pass the time each day, I teach the girls how to play Celtic chess on the game board Father gave me. I try to keep patient with them. After a lifetime of losing game after game to Father, it makes me feel like a mastermind to win match after match against these two novices. But they learn fast and soon we have some enjoyably challenging competitions.

Oft times, they try to distract me with gossip from the kitchen maids who bring us our daily allotment of soup. Apparently another serving girl is round with child. It doesn't take an Aristotle to guess that Prince Malcolm has not been obeying his brother's command to leave the local womenfolk alone.

Una shivers uncomfortably. Doubtlessly, memories of her encounter with Malcolm still linger in her mind. She abruptly changes the topic as Rowena and I take a turn at the chessboard.

"At least the Saxons have been driven back for the winter. Do you think they came solely for the purpose of capturing you again, my Queen?"

"How could they have plotted such a thing?" I shrug, moving my queen piece across the board. "I had only just arrived at the Dean Fort mere hours before the attack. . . ."

My voice trails off before I complete the thought. A coldness creeps into my limbs. How on earth could the Saxons have known I was there after only being in the Dean Fort a matter of hours? News by horseback doesn't travel that fast and it takes days to gather the number of warriors they brought to besiege us.

"It does seem an incredible coincidence," Rowena adds, trying to comfort me. "But they couldn't have known you were coming, could they?"

"Unless a spy from Caerwent told them beforehand," I reply solemnly.

There it is. The threat of a traitor in our midst, hanging over us like an invisible pall. The three of us sit around the chessboard in silence as we finish our game.

Perhaps the Saxons merely came to the Dean Fort that night to sack it for plunder or just for the joy of killing. But what are the odds they would attempt such an assault while I was there as well? It seems like far more than coincidence.

We keep the hearth roaring hot. Even though I sweat under the thick coverlets that night, I can't resist such a luxury. Not after all those nights exposed to the cold wilds with no more than Artagan's bearskin cape to keep me warm.

On the third morning of my captivity, I rise slowly, knowing I will spend another day wandering in circles inside the confines of my solar. Even a blind woman can see that Morgan has sought fit to punish me for my outburst in the hall the other day, isolating me with my ladies-in-waiting while Artagan and his warriors rot in the prison cellars. Opening the shutters a crack, I brace myself against the rain and the cold.

Padraig enters the chamber with a bow, a stack of books under one arm. The guards quickly shut the door behind him, locking the hasp. Brother Padraig wipes the morning dew from his balding brow as his peat-colored eyes glance my way.

"It's damp enough outside to drown a fish. I've slept on the chapel pews these past few nights, courtesy of your husband, who has denied me any other place in the castle."

"What?" I exclaim. "He can't do that! You're a man of the cloth. I can't believe Morgan could be so spiteful."

Padraig merely shrugs, resigned to the injustices of life. I grimace as I usher him toward the budding hearth in order to warm his hands. It's one thing for Morgan to punish me, but it's another disgrace entirely to keep a good soul like the Abbot living like a beggar. I rub my palms along the monk's worn digits, each of his fingers cold as ice.

"It does me good to see you." I smile. "I'm surprised the King let you visit me at all. He won't even let Ahern guard my door."

Padraig flashes an uncharacteristically wry grin.

"Like most kings, he thinks a simple cleric like me harmless. Shows what he knows."

He lets his stack of half a dozen books land on the tabletop with a thud, the sound waking both Una and Rowena in the nearby bed. The Abbot thumbs through the first folio, his normally placid features wrinkling under smiling eyes and a toothy grin. My brown-robed mentor is up to something.

"There," he says, placing a finger on an open page. "We've much to review today, so we'll begin here."

My eyebrows rise.

"You came up here to give me Latin lessons before breakfast?"

"We've an opportunity now. Imprisoned in style you may be, but we must learn to turn our disadvantages into advantages. Let us begin with the healing arts. I've copies of Hippocrates the Greek Physician, Saint Brigit the Irish Healer, and Taliesin the Welsh Shaman."

"Abbot, you taught me the basics of medicinals long ago. Why go into all this now?"

"You are a queen, and as such must know more than just the birthing of goats or the sewing of stiches. The health of the entire realm rests on your shoulders. The peasantry still believe that when a just lord rules, the people and the land flourish, but when a poor monarch rules, the people and the fertility of Wales suffers. The well-being of all your subjects is both your royal and ethical responsibility. Never forget that."

Padraig has a point. Regardless of what border some king draws on a map, we're all descended from the Old Tribes one way or another, all the same blood, the same Welsh nation. As a queen, I've a responsibility to protect them all, to care for them. Both my mother and the ancient Branwen the Brave would've certainly done the same.

As for the health of the nation, most commoners see the fortunes of the community as directly related to the kingship itself. Just rulers are favored by heaven and their people enjoy good health and good harvests. Bad rulers receive pestilence sent by God and his angels. A ruler who wishes to keep his or her throne more than a fortnight best look to the welfare of their subjects.

Thumbing through the books on the table, something in the flowery texts immediately catches my eye. Descriptions of women in childbirth, ancient druidic practices of purifying water, and diagrams of dissected body parts. These are not topics that a churchman like Brother Padraig should know about, especially women's organs and pagan charms. My round eyes glance up at the tonsured cleric.

"Abbot, where did you get these heretical books? The Bishop would make me say a hundred paternosters as penance just for reading such graphic descriptions."

The monk smiles.

"I was taught in the Irish school of monastic healing. The clerics there preserve some more . . . unorthodox methods of healing that were banned elsewhere in Christendom. It is these secrets that I intend to teach you."

By now, both Rowena and Una join us at the table. Neither one of them can read her own name, but the vivid illuminations on the pages leave little doubt as to the content of these forbidden medical tomes. Rowena puts a hand on each hip, eyeing Padraig with a smirk.

"And what, pray tell, does a monk know about what's beneath a lady's undergarments?"

Abbot Padraig blushes with a half-smile.

"I wasn't born a monk. I'm an Abbott, not a saint."

The girls exchange looks with stifled giggles. My jaw hangs open at this admission of guilt from my mentor. The man who first taught me about God seems to have a seedier past than he has let on. Before I can question him further, the jangle of chains from the main castle gates draws my attention to the window.

Down past the main gatehouse, a small band of soldiers marches out past the fortress walls. Several animals whinny in their midst. My eyes widen. Even from atop my tower solar, I would recognize those shaggy beasts anywhere. Mountain ponies.

Red-caped guardsmen back away from the mares, revealing a handful of men in furs and soiled green tunics. The prisoners! I lean halfway out the window, straining my eyes. Even from a distance, I can make out purple welts along their skin. The guards have not dealt easily with them. One by one, the men in green mount their ponies, but not one of them has the flowing dark hair or the longsword of Artagan.

The riders gallop toward the woods, leering back over their shoulders at the men-at-arms of Caerwent as they go. I wipe the drizzle from my brows, straining to see. Artagan is definitely not among them. But why would Morgan let his other companions go? Even Emryus, Keenan, and the she-warrior were released. My brows narrow as an iciness seizes my chest. My husband must have kept Artagan for some ulterior purpose.

Or else Artagan is already dead.

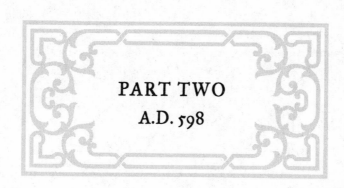

PART TWO
A.D. 598

8

By midwinter, I know I am with child. After weeks of confinement, Morgan allows me to join him for meals and walks about the grounds. He even visits my bed at night again. More frequently now especially since my bosom has filled out, heavy with milk for our coming son. My husband says he *knows* it will be a boy. I leave such divining to him. Only two moons have passed since I last had my courses, but every servant in the castle treats me like I am already nine months gone with child. Anticipation for another heir to the kingdom reverberates in every whispered conversation when I enter a room.

The toll of the bell tower calls me to supper. Una guides me down the winding stairwell by candlelight, my steps no longer guarded by anyone other than Ahern. He nods my way as he stands at attention, stoic as always when on duty. Crossing the castle toward the King's solar, I pass Rowena in the central portico. She stoops beside me, pretending to rearrange a bundle of folded linens. I lean down beside her, also pretending to help with the fallen sheets. We whisper without looking one another in the eye.

"What news?" I ask.

"He lives, m'lady."

"You certain?"

"Saw him me'self. He fares well enough, though the dungeons grow mighty frigid this time of year."

My skin runs cold, thinking of the deprivations he must suffer only a few rods beneath my feet. But at least Artagan lives. In reward for saving my life, he now rots in a prison cell, while I dine with his captors. I clench my jaw. Justice runs short within the walls of Caerwent these days.

Several of the Bishop's clerics pass, murmuring their evening vespers under their breath. Rowena and I pause, forcing ourselves to smile as she piles the spilled linens back into her basket, both of us pretending ours was but a chance meeting. Una clears her throat behind us.

Prince Malcolm watches us across the gallery. Rowena and Una leave me, trying to seem casual about it. We dare not risk saying any more while Malcolm lurks within earshot. Malcolm blocks my path to the King's solar. Morgan and Arthwys await us, sitting at table for a private dinner.

Malcolm ogles my serving girls as they depart. His eyes linger far too long on my low-cut gown, the cups of flesh once insignificant now proving increasingly difficult to hide. A prickly sensation rises along my spine as he leans down beside my ear.

"You look well, dear sister-in-law. How fare your servant girls of late?"

So the young rooster still watches the hens in my coop. I ball my fists beneath the folds of my azure gown, feeling undressed by his wandering eye. Summoning every ounce of poise I can, I smile cordially back at him.

"We all do well, my Prince. And what latest news have you from your betrothed in Cornwall?"

Malcolm's gaze darkens. I pretend not to notice his displeasure as we enter the small dining hall. Rumors of his betrothed heiress suggest she possesses as much girth as her landed inheritance. The heralds call her Lady Cordelia, but the peasant minstrels nickname her the Round Baroness. Her belt supposedly stretches long enough to saddle a horse. A great political match, engineered by Malcolm's elder brother, but surely a bitter draught to swallow for the self-proclaimed rake of Caerleon. The Prince says nothing, sitting at the far end of the table while King Morgan and Arthwys rise to greet me.

Servants fill our table with roast duck, beef stew, and enough warm bread to silence the growling in all our stomachs. Once the last serving woman retires, Morgan asks Arthwys to shut the door. The little boy does so before taking his place silently at his father's side. Morgan speaks without taking his attention from his food.

"Your appetite looks well, my Queen. Keep Arthwys's little brother well fed in the womb."

"I intend to, my King. Although I am not so very far along as of yet. I read to him, though."

"To the child inside you? I wonder what he hears."

"Abbot Padraig lends me books. Histories, poetry, and scripture. Tales of the Old Tribes."

Malcolm paws at his food across the table, looking past me toward his brother.

"No good comes from a woman filling her head with rubbish. The Old Tribes are dead."

"I've blood of the Old Tribes," I reply to Malcolm. "They live on in Dyfed and the Free Cantrefs. Even here."

"Well, we do our best to breed them out."

He and Morgan chuckle, little Arthwys following suit. I savage my bread with a table knife, ignoring all of them. Am I just a relic of barbarous heritage? Something to be diluted until less than a trace remains?

Let my husband and brother-in-law laugh. Padraig's books tell of a proud people, tribesmen and tribeswomen of the Celts who resisted the Romans. Despite the influx of Romans, Picts, and churchmen, the Welsh people themselves are still Celts to the core. The peasants in every realm have the dark locks and fair skin of the Old Tribes even if many of our nobility now have light-colored hair from centuries of invaders. Our Celtic ancestors possessed a rugged, independent spirit, a sense of honesty and honor that many subsequent conquerors of our island lacked. And the Old Tribes knew how to respect their women.

Laugh as they may, even Morgan and Malcolm's blood, peppered though it may be with Romans, still originates with the first tribes of Wales. They have forgotten who they are and where their people come from. But I do not.

Morgan and Malcolm relax. It always makes men in a good mood to put a woman down. I run a finger around the rim of my chalice as the brothers drink deeper into their cups.

They ruminate over their latest troubles, as only privileged nobles can. I half-listen, stabbing my food. Morgan put down a peasant revolt in the westernmost province of his kingdom, the serfs there beset by famine and disinclined to provide their yearly harvest tithes to the King. The Hammer King of course changed their minds, with a hundred mounted knights and an iron fist.

I sip from my goblet, trying to keep my food down. It turns my stomach to think that while I went on a peaceful mission to the Dean Fort, my husband was busy trampling villagers without a kernel of grain to their name. Is this the same man who came to fetch my hand from Dyfed less than a year ago? He certainly lives up to his namesake as the Hammer King. When Morgan mentions pulling his troops out of the Dean Fort, my mind returns to the conversation.

"I'm sorry, my King. Did you say you removed soldiers from the Dean Fort?"

"I only sent men there in the first place to rescue you, not to save a single outpost."

"But you sent me there as an envoy when Lord Griffith requested reinforcements."

Morgan levels me with his gaze. I swallow hard, suddenly understanding his meaning.

"You sent me there simply to buy time," I realize aloud. "You never intended to aid Griffith at all."

"If I send reinforcements every time he begs for help, the Saxons won't attack him. I want the Saxons to waste their manpower on a worthless holdfast like the Dean Fort. Lord Griffith fights best when cornered, and behind their walls his men kill three Saxons for every Welshman we lose. It's simple numbers. The Saxons have more and we won't beat them by playing nice."

It takes an effort to chew my bread as I try to hide my dismay.

"But you play with a man's life," I argue. "Griffith is loyal to you. You'd sacrifice him just to weaken your foes?"

"A king must make such decisions if he wishes to keep his throne."

Morgan downs another horn of wine, watching me closely. Even after a few bottles, he still has keener wits than anyone in the room. No wonder he is such a powerful warlord.

Heat rises in my chest as I clench my fists under the table where no one can see. My own husband used me as a pawn. I'm not sure what's worse, the fact that he lied to me or that he'd sacrifice Griffith. Or that he's locked Artagan in the dungeons. And I'm to have a child with this man? My gaze narrows on Morgan. He has yet to bring up that which continues to irk me most.

"Do you not find it odd, husband, that the Dean Fort was attacked mere hours after I arrived?"

"Not odd at all. The spy we've been trying to sniff out must have alerted the Saxons of your presence."

"But who?"

"Isn't it obvious? The Blacksword."

I do a double blink, barely keeping my rising voice in check.

"Preposterous! Sir Artagan kills Saxons, he doesn't sell them information."

Morgan eyes me like I'm a foolish dolt.

"I've had him locked up how long now? And not one single attempt has been made on your life in that time nor has anyone tried to kidnap you since. It's him, my Queen. Trust me."

I don't believe my ears. Artagan rescued me from the Saxons when he could have easily turned me over to them. For all his cunning, Morgan has let his personal hatred of the Blacksword cloud his judgment. The spy, the traitor in our midst, is still out there.

Before I can think of a reply, Malcolm interrupts by drubbing the tabletop with his fist. He aims a finger at his elder brother.

"We ought to hang the Blacksword and be done with it! Why do we wait, brother?"

Morgan sits stiffly in his chair. Neither brother has spoken of Artagan in my presence for many weeks. I down another mouthful of wine, trying to pretend I don't hang on every word. The last time I openly defended Sir Artagan, I got locked in a tower. I feign interest in my food as Morgan leans across the table toward his brother.

"You know why he lives. I set his men free to tell Cadwallon I hold his bastard son hostage."

"You mean to bind Cadwallon in an alliance, using his son as bait?"

"Very good, brother."

"But Cadwallon is prideful, he'll never bend the knee to us."

"He doesn't have to. So long as I hold the Blacksword prisoner I have leverage on Cadwallon."

Malcolm scoffs. Morgan stares him down with a frosty gaze.

"Artagan dies when *I* say, little brother, and not before. His time will come."

"So long as he never leaves the dungeons alive."

Malcolm belches and excuses himself from his seat. Morgan gives me a sidelong glance before dismissing all of us for the evening. We adjourn from our meal, each returning to our separate chambers.

My mind whirls as I stumble back toward my solar. The only thing keeping Artagan alive is his use as a chess piece against his powerful father, King Cadwallon. So long as Morgan holds Artagan in the dungeons, Cadwallon will not risk open war with South Wales. That would relieve Morgan's need for soldiers guarding the border with the Free Cantrefs. Men my husband could use against the Saxons. I don't know whether to congratulate the Hammer King for his statesmanship or slap him for his cunning. My husband truly is a ruthless chess player.

The bile turns bitter in the back of my throat, my skin suddenly hot. How have I become the slave-wife of such a man? A killer of defenseless villagers, a plotter of death, a man cold as iron. What kind of seed will such a man spawn inside me? My stomach churns as though a tiny dragon inhabits it.

I pause at the foot of the turret stairs, lost in thought. Most of the castle occupants have already gone to bed, leaving the hallways deserted. Only Ahern lingers nearby, still dutifully on watch outside my room. His gaze narrows.

"Are you ill, my Queen?"

"Ahern, do you ever feel like a pawn amidst a game of kings?"

"I'm not much of a chess player. But even a pawn can threaten a king, is that not so?"

"I no longer trust kings, not even my own husband. He seemed kind when we first met, but now the darkness in his heart becomes all too clear. He is the worst sort of villain, the kind that knows how to smile."

Ahern glances from side to side, making sure we stand alone in the deserted hallway.

"My lady, you are with child now, perhaps it has aggravated your fears."

I stomp my foot, my voice rising.

"My mind is sound, Ahern! I know what I'm saying. I should have listened to my heart long ago."

He bows, almost shrinking before me.

"I apologize, my lady. What does your heart tell you now?"

I shake my head. My heart asks the impossible, but how can I tell Ahern that? I hardly dare admit to myself what my own heart tells me anymore. How it wishes to flee this castle and the king who keeps me caged here. Such dreams are folly. I let out a heavy sigh.

"Morgan is only one problem. Three attempts have been made on my life. Two by Saxons and one by an assassin. Next time, I may not be so fortunate."

"Then you need a powerful man like King Morgan to protect you from such foes."

"And who will protect me from Morgan? God, if only I were a man, free to choose my own way!"

"If you were a man, Morgan would lock you in the dungeon instead of a plush tower."

I arch my eyebrows, my skin suddenly abuzz. The dungeons! Of course. I begin to pace, talking to myself.

"The enemy of my enemy is my friend."

"My Queen?"

"Something I read in one of Abbot Padraig's books once. 'Find an ally in the foe of your foes.'"

"But between Morgan and these assassins, you don't even know who all your enemies are."

"Then I suppose I need someone who's everyone's enemy."

He shrugs, rubbing his temples as though he has a headache. I snap my fingers, knowing for the first time in a long while exactly what I must do. I give Ahern a peck on the cheek.

"Brother, I need your help tonight."

He eyes me warily as I whisper in his ear. Even with half the castle asleep, we can waste no time. He looks crossly at me once I explain my intent. Ahern tries to talk me out of it, but to no avail. The guardsman bites his lip and shakes his head.

"We could both lose our heads for this."

"Please, brother."

He sighs before nodding reluctantly. I wait while he steals down to the lower levels of the castle. Minutes pass before I creep down the dark staircase after him. My soft slippers help muffle my footsteps, but I pause every so often to listen for sounds throughout the complex. Should anyone catch me, it may be to Ahern's doom and my own.

A hint of sulfur pervades the dungeons, the steady drip of water murmuring in the shadows. Ahern kindles a torch and ushers me to his side. He whispers as he takes a position by the doorway.

"I relieved the guard, but I will stand watch in case anyone comes. There's still time to reconsider, Branwen."

"Thank you, Ahern, but I've made up my mind."

Taking the torch, I proceed alone into the damp vaults. Empty cells line the walls. Rotten hay and gray puddles cover the stony floors, the occasional rat scampering across my path. Turning a corner in the labyrinth, I come face-to-face with a forgotten prisoner behind rusty bars.

A bleached skull and a mangled skeleton stare back at me from inside the cell. I jump back, barely stifling my cries. A voice murmurs in the darkness behind me.

"He's harmless, my lady. Old Bones, as I call him, has kept me company these past weeks."

"Artagan?"

He squints, raising a chained hand to shield his eyes as I bring my torch closer. His normally clean-shaven cheeks have sprouted a thin beard. Faded bruises mar his skin. It seems the guards who once roughed him up have now abandoned him to neglect. I sink to my knees before the bars, overcome by the sight of him chained like a hound. This hedge knight, who has saved me from more foes than my husband ever did, has more nobility in one little finger than all the kings of Wales. And he rots in a prison cell while Saxons roam the land and Welsh lords plot against one another. What kind of upside-down world do we live in? Seated on the floor, he looks up at me from behind the jail bars.

"Why have you come to visit me?"

"Because you are everyone's enemy." I smile warmly.

"Huh?"

"I'll explain later. Poor man. I must get better food sent to you, clean water, maybe even a shave."

He eyes me suspiciously before his features soften. His sad blue stare reminds me of the forlorn gaze of a baited bear that knows it will never escape its cage. He rises to his feet, the chains binding his wrists to the wall snagging taut as he approaches me.

"You grow more beautiful every time I see you, Branwen."

"Artagan, please."

"Can a dead man not speak the truth? Would that I had been born a king, or you a commoner."

I look away, not daring to lock eyes with him. Even in a dank dungeon, his azure eyes and chiseled face could make any country girl swoon. Why does he speak to me thus? Have I given him the wrong impression? I am still a married Christian woman, and to a vengeful king no less. It shames me to stand bedecked in silks and jewels while Artagan shivers half-naked in a cell.

When I finally meet his gaze, he makes a half-smile. Probably trying to put on a brave face for me even though he is the one in a cage. Beholding that soft grin and those honest eyes, I know I already trust him more than any man in Caerwent. I smile back, timidly, as though my soul were exposed before him. His grin quickly fades.

"Somebody's coming."

Footsteps clack down the corridor. I press my back against the cell bars. No way out and nowhere to hide. I raise the firebrand in my hand when the trespasser rounds the corner.

"My lady, come quick! The next guard will take his watch soon."

I heave a sigh of relief when I recognize Ahern. He takes my hand, but I do not budge, still transfixed by Artagan's gaze. Ahern tugs my arm.

"Come, my Queen. The dungeon fumes are not good for the child."

Artagan's cheeks stiffen, his gaze wandering down to my abdomen. My stomach balls into a tight knot. Although I have no right to, I frown at Ahern. Why did he have to mention my condition before Artagan? The Blacksword stares at me as my guardsman pulls me back down the hallway. Artagan's voice grows so faint I barely hear him.

"A baby?"

My mouth hangs open, but I've nothing to say. Artagan's gaze sinks to his feet. Before I can reply, Ahern has me moving up the stairs with him. He urges me to hurry, before the next guardsman takes his post.

Ahern sends me scampering off toward my tower. He remains behind so that the next guard will not grow suspicious. An unguarded dungeon would certainly raise eyebrows.

I wander through the empty halls, still lost in thought. Why did Ahern have to tell him? Now Artagan knows I carry another man's child inside me. I bang my fist into a cold stone column in the castle galleries, mad at myself for being mad at Ahern. What in perdition is wrong with me?

A married woman ought to bear children and feel pride in it. So why does an overwhelming bitterness rise in my throat?

I stumble up the stairs to my solar chamber, both Una and Rowena already abed. I fall into a dreamless stupor once my head hits the pillow. All of my thoughts turn to endless darkness.

The next morning, I lie half-awake in bed, not wanting to get up. I cling to a half memory in the fog between rest and wakefulness, remembering my mother. Barely a few years old, I sit on her lap as she combs my hair. Long raven-dark locks like hers. She talks to me, the warm timbre of her voice comforting as her soft touch. Her last words stick in my mind: *God is love and he lives in your heart. The cunning and powerful think the heart a weakness, but they are wrong, my child. Love is the greatest strength we have.*

My eyes open, the memory fading from my hazy thoughts. Love. Would that I knew where to find it, Mother. Men like my husband and brother-in-law seem to have forgotten God's greatest teaching.

With a sigh, I sit up in the blankets and greet the dawn.

I join Morgan and Malcolm for breakfast in the King's solar. They both ignore me, talking of the Prince's upcoming marriage to Lady Cordelia of Cornwall. Malcom bears no torch for the Round Baroness, but he eagerly rubs his palms together as the two brothers discuss the potential wealth to be made in trade and commerce with Cornish lands.

Despite lowering their voices, I overhear them discuss how advantageously Cordelia would be placed in line to the Cornish throne should the King of Cornwall's only son meet with a mishap. I nearly choke on a piece of blood pudding, but neither brother notices. To listen to these men plot against another man's child turns my stomach. I down a flagon of spiced wine, trying to clear my throat.

Since Malcolm's return from his visit to supposedly woo Lady Cordelia, rumors have circulated throughout the castle of how poorly Cornwall fares against the West Saxon tribes. We share a common Celtic heritage with the Cornish, but I fear they too shall soon succumb to the ever-present Saxon threat. All the world seems destined to fall into darkness. Even if Morgan and Malcolm held some sway in Cornwall, I doubt they would help the people there. Especially if the Hammer King won't protect his own border vassals at the Dean Fort. Just another chess piece in their game against the Saxons and each other. I excuse myself from the table, unable to breathe in this nest of vipers. I need some air.

Scaling the courtyard steps, I pace the bastion walls, alone save for the occasional guardsman on watch. Winter's cold breath feels like heaven against my flushed cheeks. Snowcapped peaks dot the mountains in the distance. Cradling my palms against my still-flat belly, I try to feel life stir within me. Instead, my stomach gurgles with this morning's breakfast. What kind of world will I bring this child into? A land where a child's father has other children murdered, and his own uncle chases scullery maids?

Something Ria once said gives me pause: *A mother's blood is all that matters.* Such is the way of the Free Cantrefs, and the Old Tribes before them. Perhaps my mother's wisdom speaks to me through the lips of that village girl. But the memory of Ria emerging from Artagan's hovel with her collar loose about the shoulder leaves a sour taste in my mouth.

Artagan is right. If only I had been born a commoner instead of a queen. At least then I might choose who I love.

Padraig calls out to me, his hands hidden in the folds of his brown robes. I stop to wait for him before the pair of us continue on a circuit along the castle walls. His bald brow creases with concentration, his gaze darting over his shoulder to ensure we walk alone.

"Something worries me. May I speak to you in confidence?"

"You know you can, Abbot."

"It regards the attempts on your life. They have happened with uncanny regularity."

"I know. That's why I fear a spy must still lurk in our midst, betraying our every move."

"Yes, but that's what troubles me, Branwen. I'm not convinced there is a spy, or ever was."

"I don't understand, Padraig."

"You were first attacked after your betrothal, on the road to Caerleon, but it was only the day after Morgan offered you his hand in marriage. What spy could have informed the Saxons of your whereabouts in just one day? It would take the Saxons several days at least just for their ships to land on the coast where they attacked you."

A leaden weight sinks in my gut. I never thought of the logistics involved in betraying such secrets before. I swallow hard as he continues.

"The second attack involved an assassin, but the assassin found you in your stepson's room, which you yourself had little intention of going to. If you never typically visit Arthwys's room, how could a spy inform an assassin that that's where you might be? Of all places, the killer should have gone to your solar, but he didn't."

Padraig speaks the truth. I never visited Arthwys's room before then, nor have I since. My running into the assassin there seemed like happenstance. I was so overwhelmed by the ordeal and so relieved simply to have survived that I never questioned why the killer would have waited for me in there of all places. I even thought at first that the assassin was there for the boy, not me. The Abbot further explains his reasoning.

"Thirdly, the Fox and the Wolf, the very same Saxons who sought to capture you on the King's Road, conveniently besiege the Dean Fort the very evening you arrive there. Yet, no one knew of your coming there. Even the King himself did not suggest the mission to you until the very hour in which you left. How could anyone have known such things, let alone some mysterious spy? How could a spy set so many plans into motion all at once?"

"But if a spy wasn't responsible for all these things, then how did they come to pass?"

Padraig sighs, his shoulders drooping.

"That is what I keep asking myself. My logic has only taken me so far. The incident with the assassin particularly befuddles me. The only person who knew of your whereabouts before the first and third attacks was King Morgan himself."

My blood runs cold as I halt in my tracks.

"Morgan has no scruples. Does my own husband want me dead?"

"I rule no one out, Branwen, but it makes no sense for the King to wish you ill. In fact, he has more reason than anyone to see you safe and well cared for. You give him a legitimate hold on the lands of Dyfed. For that reason alone, he cannot risk anything happening to you."

"He does covet Dyfed's lands and soldiers, and he only gets that through marriage to me."

"More than that, my dear. You carry his child, and will provide more heirs to his kingdom."

"So if not Morgan, who then? Who have I angered so? Who would hate me with such wrath?"

I wince at the idea of such unrestrained malice. Why must this happen to me? I hang my head. Padraig takes my hand.

"It is a cruel world in which we live, dear child. I doubt you've ever done anything wrong by anyone in your life, but your privilege and position as a queen make you a target for many."

"Even if I survive, how long before the Saxons come and cut all our throats?"

"Do not talk like that, Branwen! I did not tutor you in books and the Word of God just so you should lose faith when you need it most."

Even in his supposed anger, I sense him trying to lift my spirits more than chide me. He gently lifts my chin with his hand, the same way he oft did whenever I came to him with my troubles as a teary-eyed child. How I long for the quiet hours of books and the tranquility I had under the Abbot's tutelage back in my childhood days at Dyfed by the sea. I rest my hand on the monk's shoulder.

"I should've been a nun."

"No, my child." He smiles. "With your beauty, I don't think you should've stayed a nun for long."

We smile at one another, each trying to put on a brave face. A hot, sticky sensation suddenly wells up inside me. I take a step back on the parapet. Padraig's eyes narrow in concern, trying to steady me as I bend over at the waist. My vision starts to spin. I put a hand under my skirts and feel a wet heat between my legs. Pulling my fingers out from under my dress, I find my fingertips streaked with blood. The Abbot shouts to the guards for help as I reel in his arms. More blood runs down my legs before I collapse, the clamor of guardsmen and servants murmuring over me as the world turns dark.

Another moon passes before I can rise from bed without bleeding. The men in the castle keep away, fearing that they might somehow suffer ill effects from my womanly curse. Una keeps close watch over me, although I tell her I am fine, and would much prefer hawking with my falcon. The King once again forbids me to leave my tower. For my *health*, he says.

I pace the floorboards, my eyes tired from endless days of reading. Padraig left me some of my favorite classics to peruse, all of which lie open on the table. Dido and Aeneas, Deirdre and Naoise, Guinevere and Lancelot. But my most favorite, of course, is the one he gifted to me, the tales of Branwen of the Old Tribes. She too lost a child, and I find myself rereading those passages of her life, looking for some kind of solace.

Rowena brings me my evening meal of soup, which I sup while she returns to the door. The King questions her on the threshold, several of his men crowding the turret steps behind him.

"How long?" he demands.

"She's well now, Your Highness," Rowena replies with a curtsy. "But I suggest waiting another moon. Let her gather strength."

"In another moon, spring comes, and the war season with it. I'll not wait that long."

"Miscarriages are quite common, Your Grace. Give her time. You'll have another heir, surely."

"Do not lecture me, girl. She is *my* broodmare, and I'll ride her as often as I like."

A fire rises through my spine, my fingertips starting to shake. As often as *he* likes? Kings can never have enough sons, especially when pestilence or warfare constantly threatens the bloodline. But how many miscarriages has he suffered? I refuse to look at him.

Although Morgan continues to address Rowena, I can see he glares darkly at me from the corner of my eye.

"Bring her to my solar tomorrow night. No more delays. No more excuses."

Morgan descends the stairs with his men, the clatter of their chain mail fading down the tower steps. My jaw tightens. I stare at the shut door, my heart beating fast long after the King and his knights have left.

My God, the man actually intends to have his way with me whether I agree to it or not. Tomorrow, no less. He would actually violate his own wife on our marriage bed! My fists tighten at my sides, the bitter bile rising in the back of my throat. In the eyes of the Law and the Church, he owns me, like a piece of chattel that he may do with as he pleases. But I've seen Morgan's true face unmasked now, and no amount of pretty words or fine clothes can hide his inner darkness from me. He is no better than a Saxon brute when it comes to women.

I've lost the life of the child in my womb and nearly had my own life bled out in the process, and all he can think about is our next rut! I am no man's broodmare.

For more than a fortnight, I've wet my pillow with tears, some for my lost babe and some for myself. Better the child returned to God before it could come into the world. Is it wrong for a would-be mother to think such thoughts? God forgive me, but I'll not harbor another of Morgan's spawn inside me. Everything he touches turns to poison. Never again will I let him touch me. Never.

Finishing my bowl, I have the girls dress me before the open window.

The snowcaps on the mountains have shrunk and the frosted fields have turned to mud. The worst of winter has passed and soon the first buds of spring will appear. The cool air feels good on my hot cheeks.

"Braid my hair tonight."

"Braid it before bed, m'lady?" Rowena asks.

When I do not reply, both Una and Rowena exchange looks before acceding to my request. Together they section my dark locks into three parts, gradually folding it up into a single, long, thick braid running down my back. In the mirror, I eye my knee-high boots beneath the bed and my shawl draped over an armchair. I stay up reading until the girls dowse the hearth for bed. The three of us lie on the large single mattress, myself sleeping on the end tonight.

When the milky light of the full moon seeps through chinks in the window shutters, I rise from bed, careful not to disturb Una or Rowena in their slumber. I quietly grab my boots and shawl before descending the steps.

Ahern bumps into me at the foot of the stairs. He raises his eyebrows in surprise. I silence him with a finger to my lips before whispering in his ear.

"It's now or never."

He looks at me doubtfully, eyeing my boots. I put my hands on my hips and stare him down. He finally agrees and marches off to do as I bid. After he goes, I steal across the deserted hallways of the castle toward the King's bedchamber.

The door creaks as I push it open, yet I find no guard standing watch within. Small wonder, my husband is a formidable warrior and probably doesn't consider himself in need of a guard to watch over him while he sleeps. Morgan snores with his war-hammer leaned beside his bed. Even in his slumber he breathes like a lion. I squint through the darkness of the room, glimpsing his chest rise and fall beneath the covers.

Where is it? He must keep it here.

A glint of moonlight directs me to my prize, shining on the wall like a huge trophy. I gather it into my shawl and wrap it up tight. Morgan stirs as I stand over his bedstead. My heart stops until he begins to snore again. Even in his sleep he is a restless man. I tiptoe back toward the door, taking one last look at the man who calls himself my husband. After tonight there will be no going back.

By the time I reach the dungeons, Ahern has a torch ready for me.

"My lady, please reconsider."

I do not answer him.

Instead, I accept the firebrand from him and descend to the lower cells alone while Ahern keeps watch at the top of the stairs. The prize wrapped in my shawl weighs heavy under my arm. Threading a skeleton key into the rusty lock, the creaking hinges awaken Artagan as I open his cell. I tower over him with a dripping torch.

"Branwen? The guards told me about the child. I'm so very sorry."

I wince slightly. The sting of losing my pregnancy and yet the relief at not having to bear Morgan's child fill me with a mingled joy and guilt that I do not wish to speak about to anyone right now. But that is not what I've come to discuss with Artagan tonight. I thank him for his concern with a brief nod.

"Perhaps it happened as it was supposed to," I add.

He rises to his feet, his sapphire eyes looking me over.

"You look beautiful, Branwen."

Even in a prison cell, Artagan remains ever the charmer. I change the subject before his words make me blush.

"I see the guards let you bathe, and gave you better food. A shave too. Good, I bribed them to."

He steps closer, his muscles flexing beneath his rags. His gaze searches my face, his brows furrowing in confusion as I pull out another skeleton key and loosen his iron bonds. They clatter to the floor. Not too difficult to do really; the jailer leaves his keys by the dungeon entranceway. Artagan flexes his arms, rubbing his sore wrists. I resist the urge to reach out and touch him.

"Are you fit enough to ride?" I ask.

"Fit enough to fight my way past a hundred guardsmen."

"Good. You'll need this, then."

I unfold the shawl under my arm, revealing a long naked blade with darkened hues in its steel. Artagan's eyes alight on his longsword, before feeling its familiar heft in his hands once more. He starts to smile, before grimacing at me.

"Morgan and Malcolm will punish you for this, Branwen. I can't let that happen."

"They won't. I'm not just rescuing you, I'm rescuing myself. I'm coming with you."

My heart beats faster as I take Artagan's hand in mine. He leans forward, our lips only a breath apart. Ahern's voice echoes down the dungeon corridor. A shiver runs down my spine.

"My lady, you must hurry! The guards have been alerted! They're coming."

9

The peal of chapel bells rings in the belfry. I clasp a hand to my throat as the din of guardsmen's voices and jangling armor reverberates atop the dungeon stairwell. We've been betrayed.

Ahern grabs me by the shoulder.

"You know what to do, Branwen. Use the rear entranceway while I remain behind."

"No, it's too dangerous now. You'll have to come with us."

He shakes his head.

"Too late to change our minds now. If we stick to the plan, I'll be fine remaining behind. Besides, you need someone's ear inside this castle while you're away."

I put a hand on my brother's arm. He possesses a bravery worthy of the Old Tribes. I nod in agreement with his decision.

"Look after Padraig and my serving girls while I'm gone," I begin. "They may not understand. This is the only way I can keep them all safe."

"Please, Branwen. Go. There's little time."

The glow of torchlight looms brighter atop the stairs. Every moment we delay, the guards draw nearer. Artagan flexes his wrists, newly freed from their fetters. His gaze darts from Ahern's face to mine.

"Does someone want to tell me what in perdition is going on?"

"There's no time to explain," I reply. "I need you to knock Ahern out, quickly."

"Come again?"

"Hurry! It must look like he tried to prevent our escape. Now, Black-sword!"

Artagan and Ahern exchange looks before the Blacksword shrugs. He apologizes as he draws back his fist and slugs my brother across the jaw. Ahern slumps down onto the slick dungeon floors, his spear clattering behind him. Leaning down beside the welt on his face, I feel his pulse to make sure he still breathes. My poor, loyal kinsman. It seems a sin to leave my own half brother on the prison cell floor, but he agreed with me that it is the only way. The only way to save us all. I beckon Artagan to follow me.

"Quickly!"

"Where to now? We're trapped like rats down here."

He follows me to the opposite end of the cell block. Clearing a mound of damp hay away from a stone bulkhead, I find the warped iron lock of a small wooden door. Just where Ahern said it would be. The ancient handle comes away brittle in my hand. I scoff as I drop the useless metal shards to the floor.

"It's rusted shut!"

The guards' voices echo close behind us. They must have already dis-covered Ahern on the dungeon floors. Maybe this was a foolhardy plan after all. Once they round the corner, they will have us at their mercy. Artagan curses before kicking in the small door. Splinters fly every which way before the two of us duck through the low entranceway. We stagger into a dark room filled with damp straw. Artagan whispers in my ear.

"Where the blazes have you taken us?"

"To our salvation."

Feeling my way along a wooden stall, I reach out for a blanket on the wall. Shafts of moonlight penetrate chinks in the timber boards. A large beast paws at the earth, whickering as I shush the creature in a soothing tone. Artagan bumps into me in the shadows.

"The stables?"

"The King's stables to be exact. This is his horse, Merlin. Fastest steed in the kingdom."

"You mean you plan to just ride out the front gates?"

"My brains got us this far. I need your brawn to get us past the guards at the gate."

He helps saddle the horse before the pair of us mount up. Artagan grasps the stallion's reins in one hand, brandishing his longsword in the other. I clasp my arms tight around Artagan's middle as Merlin boxes open the stable doors and bolts into the castle courtyards.

In the darkness of the open yard, soldiers scurry about as they don their tunics and armor, some half-dressed whilst others fumble with scabbards and helmets. Several of them soon surround us in a circle of spears. Artagan roars in our mount's ear as he charges into the melee, hacking down guardsmen and lopping the heads off their spear-points. One man-at-arms grabs me about the leg, trying to pull me from the saddle. I cry out before shoving him full in the chest with my foot, sending him hurtling backward.

More soldiers spill out of the barracks, drawn by the commotion of clashing steel and Merlin's whinnying cries. I point Artagan toward the castle gates. Steel chains restrain the heavy grating that bars the main gateway.

"Aim for the hempen bonds below the chains! They connect to the gears in the gatehouse."

Artagan digs his heels into our steed's flanks, parting the crowd of soldiers at full gallop. With one slash of his blade, Artagan severs the hempen bonds attached to the iron links. The cogs within the gatehouse groan as pulleys snap and the chains begin to move.

The iron grating of the gate rises just enough for us to duck under its inverted steel spikes. Several spearheads hurtle past our heads, embedding themselves in the cobblestone walk. Merlin's muscles turn slick with sweat beneath the rising moon. Watchmen atop Caerwent's towers shout out to one another as we ride out of range.

Far behind us, moonlight bleaches the castle white, like a palace of crystal and ice. A lone figure looms atop the highest parapet, still as a stone gargoyle. His black silhouette stands out against the full moon, his dark crown and massive war-hammer unmistakable. Even from a distance, Morgan's silver eyes gaze right at me, like a pair of smoldering, burnt coals. A shiver runs down my back before I look away.

I'll not go back there ever again. Not inside those imprisoning walls. Never again in the Hammer King's bed.

Horse hooves thunder from the far-off citadel gates as dozens of horsemen pursue us down the old Roman road. Artagan guides Merlin off the beaten path and into the nearby woods, darting between trees as twigs and branches snap about our flanks. We gallop through a tunnel of dark oak groves, my hair whipping behind me in the wind. A familiar voice booms behind us.

"Blacksword! Blackswoooord! Run if you can! You are mine! Do you hear me, hedge knight?"

A chill overcomes me as I recognize Prince Malcolm's voice filling the shadows of the wood. He leads the King's horsemen and if he catches us first, I doubt either Artagan or myself will ever live to see the inside of Caerwent's dungeons alive. The Prince will gut us first.

Merlin trots to a halt in a moonlit glade, plumes of steam rising from his nostrils. I pat his slick sides, the valiant beast pushed beyond exhaustion. You gave it your best try, Merlin. We all gave it our best try. Artagan turns us around, lowering his blade.

"Ride on. I'll dismount and fight from here. They'll get no quarter from me. I've seen enough of dungeons to last me a lifetime."

"Merlin is spent and so are we. We'll meet our fate together."

Artagan's shoulders sink, too tired to argue. Malcom gallops into the wooded glen with at least a dozen riders behind him. So much for my well-laid plans. Artagan's sword got us past the fortress walls, but we cannot outrun the entire garrison even on the best of horses. If fault lies with any part of this escape, it lies with me.

Hurtling toward us, Malcolm swings his huge mace overhead as he growls through clenched teeth. Artagan raises his sword, bellowing back as he spurs Merlin to make one last charge. I clutch Artagan's chest tightly, wincing before the coming crush of bodies and horses.

Every steed in the cavalcade comes to an abrupt halt, shrieking with terror. Dozens of arrows hiss through the glade, downing riders and stallions alike on the forest path. Several figures emerge from the surrounding trees, loosing arrows and lobbing spears at the King's men. I blink in disbelief, my heart suddenly rising anew.

Archers of the Free Cantrefs! Green-clad woodsmen form a protective crescent around Artagan and me. I recognize Emryus and Keenan among those defending us under the moonlight.

The bowmen howl like savages as they surround Malcolm and his guards, the Prince's shield bristling with arrows. Malcolm's mount rears back, the Prince cursing all the while as he and his surviving riders retreat back toward the main road. Several red-clad men-at-arms lie lifeless on the trail, their riderless steeds dashing every which way into the woods. Artagan lowers his blade, looking with wide-eyed astonishment at our rescuers.

"Keenan? Emryus?"

"He sounds surprised to see us," Emryus remarks to Keenan.

"We kept watch long enough in these woods," Keenan replies. "I hoped to nab a king or prince, better to bargain for Artagan's release. Lo and behold, he spoils it by rescuing himself!"

"Actually, I'm the one who rescued him," I interject. "Freed him from his cell, at least."

His followers exchange looks, eyeing me like some quaint curiosity. Maybe they think me a liar. My husband underestimated me, so I see no reason why these wild-haired woodsmen should not. Artagan ignores me, embracing the gray bard and youthful axman like brothers. Only a handful of soldiers number amidst their motley company, and yet somehow they defeated a sizable force of Malcolm's men. These Free Cantref folk fight like banshees.

They corral several ponies from the woods and mount up beside us.

The rumble of hooves renews along the Roman road behind us. The citadel's cavalry will return soon and in greater numbers. My pulse quickens. Morgan and Malcolm will not give me up without a fight. Artagan calls out to his men as they part ways.

"Split up. Lead the buggers on a merry chase. We'll rendezvous at my father's keep. Godspeed!"

Darting into the next thicket, our horse picks up speed. Merlin may be tired from galloping at full tilt, but he can still trot at a decent pace. Artagan guides our stallion on a winding course through brambles and briar patches. We ascend into the wooded foothills before pausing along an outcrop overlooking the castle fields and woodlots far below. I shiver beneath the cold stars, listening to the distant whinny of horses. Scores of horsemen must be pursuing us into the forest, and by the sound of it, at least half of them now chase Artagan's companions in the opposite direction. Many still doubtlessly follow our own trail, Morgan and Malcolm perhaps among them. I tug my shawl tight around my throat, shutting my eyes against the night.

I've incurred the wrath of a powerful warlord. What price shall I now pay for it? Morgan may very well pursue me to the ends of the earth. He kept me well fed and cared for at Caerwent, but I was still a pet. A broodmare, he called me. I will never let him take me back to that gilded cage. Artagan may have been condemned to the dungeons, but every noble-woman in Christendom lives in a prison once she takes the vows of holy wedlock. I smack my fist into an open palm. I'll never be owned by an-other man again.

The Church may frown on divorce, but the Pope doesn't interfere in the shifting marriages of nobles so long as peaceful alliances are main-tained. The Old Tribes followed the Ancient Harmonies, cohabiting with whom they wished for as long or little as they wished. Is that not more sensible? Ever since the coming of the priests, queens have certainly wed new husbands once their old husband perished or if she was captured by another warlord.

My head starts to ache. No use mulling over this anymore tonight. I had to flee Morgan and his court before it suffocated me, before it killed me. Before whoever spied upon me made another attempt on my life. All the laws of man and God could not convince me otherwise.

I remove the gold wedding band from my finger. Probably worth a hefty sum. But I am not some nag to be bought and sold at market. I toss the golden ring aside into the muddy brush. May it never see the sun-shine again.

My hand rests on Artagan's arm, but a sticky sensation along my skin causes me to draw my palm away. My fingertips are red with blood.

"You're wounded."

"One of those spearmen got me when we tried to breach the gate," he admits with a shrug.

"Slow the horse."

I bend down in the saddle, eyeing a tall stand of overgrown weeds. Pulling a handful of green stalks, I select the softest ones under the moonlight. Poultice Plant, as Padraig oft calls it, using it when any of the lambs at the abbey is attacked by a lone wolf. A common enough weed, it grows year-round in most of Wales. I crumple a wad of green sprouts and chew them in my mouth. After a few moments, the bitter taste gives way to a slightly sweet flavor. Artagan winces slightly when I apply the green paste to his wounds, but he lets me go about my work without complaint.

"This will help mend your cuts and slow the bleeding," I explain.

He flashes a half-grin.

"You've some skill as a healer," he replies, impressed. "You're full of surprises tonight."

"I've only practiced this on lambs and cattle before," I answer, omitting that I once tended Morgan when he was badly wounded. Just one of many thoughts I would rather not dwell on now. Artagan flashes a wry smile as I staunch his cuts.

"Let's hope I live then."

How he can joke with such gashes in his arm I can only guess. I doubt I could sit astride a horse with such wounds. Nonetheless, I smile politely at his words, even though I don't feel much like laughing tonight. The seriousness of the decisions I've made this evening weigh me down. Too much has changed forever.

Merlin continues to keep a good pace, stout as any mountain pony despite his massive size. How odd it seems that the night I first met my husband we rode this very same mount out of Dyfed. Tonight, Merlin takes me deep into the mountains of the Free Cantrefs, to begin a new life, whatever that may be.

For one last time, I glimpse the tall towers of Caerwent on the plain far below. Rowena, Una, and Padraig must have heard about what has happened by now. I hope that Ahern can make them understand why I had to hatch my plot in secret, for all our sakes. Goodbye, my friends. I pray that we meet again in better times.

Artagan leads our steed deeper into the mountain passes. Even after the sounds of pursuing horses fade behind us, he still asks me no questions. He has the arms of a wrestler and the skill of a dancer with his long blade, but he seems given to unusually long silences as well. Does he think me a treacherous woman for leaving my husband? Or worse yet, a loose woman? The quiet drives me to speak up.

"I did not come to this decision lightly. I had to flee. Someone in Caerwent wants me dead."

"So how exactly does this concern me?"

"Don't you care?"

"Of course I care," he replies testily. "The Hammer King and I have been at odds for years, but this is pretty extreme even for the likes of me. I've never been involved in . . . wife stealing before."

My eyes widen. *Wife stealing?* Is that what he thinks this is? I'm not some sack of grain to be bandied about by whichever man happens to have me astride his horse. This conversation is going all wrong.

"Would you rather be back in the dungeons?" I say, a bit more grumpily than I intend. "You needed to get out of Caerwent just as badly as I did. I thought we were helping each other."

"We've saved each other's skins a couple of times now, for that I'm grateful. But you understand what this means for our peoples now that we've been seen riding off together? Morgan will summon his armies, and come springtime the South Welsh and the Free Cantrefs will be at war over this."

I swallow a lump in my throat, my brow breaking out in perspiration anew. I hadn't thought of that. If Morgan has a vendetta against me, he should only put a price on my head. Waging war against an entire kingdom simply because I no longer desired to live under his roof seems like the height of injustice. I reply in a small voice, looking down at my hands.

"I care for all the people of Wales, Artagan. We're all children of the Old Tribes. I never wanted to bring harm to anyone. Do you think me a fool for freeing you from the dungeons tonight and riding off into the wilds?"

He stops our horse, turning in the saddle to look me in the eye. My breath quickens under his direct gaze. Artagan flashes a half-grin, looking me up and down with his sapphire eyes.

"You've a fair face, a brave heart, and a beautiful mind, Lady Branwen. The Hammer King doesn't deserve you."

"That's not what I asked you."

He grins again.

"You did what you had to do."

He slaps the reins against Merlin's back as we canter farther into the night woods. The more leagues we put between us and Caerwent, the lighter my limbs feel, but a nagging fear remains in the back of my mind. If Artagan is right about open warfare between Gwent and the Free Cantrefs come spring, then such infighting amongst the Welsh Lands could easily spread. What will Father think once he learns of my running off? Some chess piece I turned out to be. His alliance with Morgan hinged on my betrothal.

As the night wears on, I lay my head against Artagan's back, my eyelids heavy as lead. His skin feels warm through his threadbare shirt despite the evening fog. Hopefully, the misty mountaintops will shroud us from the eyes of any pursuers. The steady clack of Merlin's hooves lulls me into a deep yawn. I sway in the saddle before succumbing to the numbness of a dreamless slumber.

When I awake, gray sunlight glows through the overcast clouds. I sit up with a start, no longer atop the horse, but buried in a bed of warm leaves and a fur coverlet. Artagan stands over me, eating an apple. He chews loudly as his lips smack together. The pitter-patter of raindrops taps the forest leaves.

"We should move on," he says. "I won't sleep well until I'm safe in my father's kingdom."

"Will we truly be safe at Cadwallon's court?"

"Safe as anywhere."

Rising to my knees, I try keeping my gaze to the grass. Artagan washes his arms and legs in a nearby stream, his skin flecked with goose bumps by the cool waters. Droplets run down his muscular arms and thighs, reminding me of a young Adonis. His eyes rise to meet mine before I look away.

He lays a breakfast of nuts and berries at my feet. Glancing at the deceptively gray sky, I wonder how long he has let me sleep. A twinge of guilt sticks in my throat. The first green buds of early spring dot the trees overhead. How different these wooded hillsides seem from the open fields of Caerwent. I speak without thinking, almost desperate to fill the silence between us as we finish our meal.

"After we fled the Dean Fort, you eventually returned me to Morgan. Why? Most men wouldn't have risked capture to bring me back to Caerwent in the first place."

"I'm not most men. Besides, he had some of my people held captive and I had to get them back. On top of that, I promised to bring you home, and so I did."

"And then you would have returned to Ria's village? Or Lady Olwen's court?"

Artagan stops midway through eating his apple, keenly observing me with his gaze. Men think their secrets are so safe, never guessing that anyone with half a mind can read their stories as easily as an open book. He clears his throat, looking away, almost as though embarrassed.

A crow caws from a nearby branch. Dark clouds of ravens and rooks circle high overhead, the cacophony of shrieking carrion birds deafening us both. Artagan grabs his sword.

"Something disturbs them. Something behind us in the forest. We must move on. Now."

Artagan whistles for Merlin. Whatever stalks the wolds behind us, whether the King's men or something worse, I pray it never finds us.

We ride on through rugged peaks and down switchbacks, away from the murder of crows swarming in the woodlands to the south. All the world seems turned to wilderness, as though Artagan and I are the only man and woman left. No longer certain of my bearings, I can only hope

Artagan knows where he takes us. Such thick oak and evergreen groves tangle our paths, ancient woodlots that I doubt have ever suffered from a woodsman's ax.

Finally descending from the wall of mountain ridges, we enter a series of river valleys equally awash in birch and hazel groves. Small wonder that neither the armies of South Wales nor the Saxons have ever conquered the people of the Free Cantrefs. With the ring of mountains that encircles their lands, scarcely a crow could invade without carrying its own rations.

As the day wears away, an evening mist descends from the mountaintops. Fog coats the valley floor as we skirt along the edge of a small river. A lone hill within the valley stands above the blanket of mists, its summit peppered with stone ruins. The skeleton of broken stonework shines like teeth beneath the rising moon. Reaching around Artagan's thighs, I grab the reins. We halt before the distant hillside.

"What is that place?"

"The ruins of Aranrhod. A stronghold of the ancients. That place is haunted."

"Haunted? You don't believe in ghosts, do you?"

"The magic of the Old Tribes built it. The Romans couldn't hold it, nor anyone after them. *Something* keeps people away. If not ghosts, what then?"

He spurs Merlin onward, not wishing to linger a moment longer beneath the shadow of Aranrhod. Although he clearly fears the place, Artagan shows wisdom in taking us this way. A native of the Free Cantrefs, even he hardly dares ride near the ruins. Certainly, no horsemen from Caerwent or the Saxon lands would come within a hundred leagues of this place. Nonetheless, as I gaze back over my shoulder at the moonlit walls, half-crumbling like a jagged crown, I cannot help but sense a presence watching over me. As though something with eyes looks out from those marred towers, something the Romans and Saxons could never understand. Something only a daughter of the Old Tribes might come to know.

We ride on far into the night, the constant pace of the horse rocking me to sleep like a cradle. Slumped against Artagan's back, I dream of the gray watchtowers of Aranrhod. A faint voice calls my name from deep within the ruins, a lilting feminine tone that lingers in the mists. *Branwen. Branwen.* It is the voice of my mother.

I awake with a start. Crickets chirp in the darkness. I must have nodded off in the saddle.

A hunting horn bellows through the night air. Figures with torches emerge from the woods, making Merlin rear up. My pulse jumps in my throat as the intruders surround us.

Artagan does not draw his sword, instead smirking over his shoulder at me. The people around us call out in shrill birdcalls and boisterous hoots. Beneath the flickering glow of orange firebrands, Emryus, Keenan, and the others greet us with hearty cheers. My eyes widen, adjusting to the dark before I see their green tunics and fur mantles by torchlight. Men and women, peasants and warriors all crowd around us, emerging from the woods like fairies in the night. I blink in disbelief. How could so many Free Cantref folk live in the thick of the forest?

Only when we turn a bend in the thickets does a narrow vale come into view. Sandwiched between tall woods and a snaking riverbank, a wooden fortress overlooks a small plain full of village huts and farmland. Artagan raises his hand in a sweeping gesture.

"Welcome to my father's domain. Cadwallon's Keep. Home of the defenders of the free folk."

Astride our tall mount, we part the throng of commoners crowding around the keep gates. Lookouts toot their hunting horns several more times. Villagers reach out to touch Artagan's bearskin cloak or grasp his hand. He leans over and smiles, calling many of them by name. These people are not merely thanes and serfs; they are his tribe, his family. Several bystanders hush and look at me between whispers. The Blacksword has brought home a queen of the Old Tribes, they seem to say.

Dismounting at the keep gates, the wooden castle reminds me much of the Dean Fort, only rougher in appearance. Blankets of moss and ivy grow upon the fortress walls as though the greenery of the forest seeks to turn the felled timbers back into living trees once more. Keenan and Emryus jostle merrily beside us as we pass through the palisade gates, gibing that they gave Morgan's Southrons a merry chase indeed.

The Hammer King's horsemen are probably wandering in circles in the mountains still. Keenan and Emryus's grins prove infectious. I cannot help but smile back at Artagan's warriors, each nearly as carefree and childlike as Artagan himself. A roaring voice hails us from the main hall.

"Merlin's Beard, my boy! It's not enough for you to break free from the dungeons, but you've got to steal away a king's bride to boot!"

"Sire, allow me to present the heroine who freed me from Caerwent, Queen Branwen of Dyfed."

Artagan bows to King Cadwallon and I in turn curtsy before the round monarch. With a mutton bone in one hand and a mead goblet in the other, Cadwallon steps forward to embrace me. The scent of liquor hangs heavy in his red beard, the girth of his belt nearly toppling me over. He winks at me as he speaks to his son.

"She's got a goddess's figure and the stamina of a filly, I bet. No wonder you let her rescue you!"

Artagan winces at the King's comment, while I color from ear to ear. Although I've not seen Cadwallon since the gathering at Caerwent last year, he seems somehow even wider and louder than before. The King claps Artagan on the back, his father laughing at something he seems to find particularly amusing. I smile back at the King, tickled to see the normally self-assured Blacksword so disarmed by his boisterous father. Already well into his cups, Cadwallon raises his drinking horn.

"A toast to Queen Branwen! For returning my son to me. Ever shall you be welcome under my roof, so long as it annoys the *mighty* Hammer King in Caerwent. I pray you may never leave us."

Artagan leads the other men and women in the hall as they all raise their cups, everyone replying with hearty "hear hears." He drinks from his chalice before handing it to me. Artagan watches me closely as I down his goblet of cider, tasting where his lips touched the rim. King Cadwallon has his minstrels start up a tune with pipes and drums, several men and women in green garb holding hands as they dance amidst the roasting hearths of venison and wild boar.

Artagan stands close enough for me to smell the fresh pine scent of the woods on his loose shirt. The cider must have gone to my head, but I cannot take my eyes off him. Firelight reflects off his high cheekbones and pearly grin. Drinking down the last of his cup, I hand Artagan his chalice back, our fingers briefly entwined. He leans down close to my ear.

"It seems only yesterday we danced together at the Dean Fort."

"I've danced with no other since then," I admit.

His eyes search mine before he glances at his feet, as though slightly nervous.

"I want to thank you, Branwen. For saving me."

"We did it together. We make a formidable pair, when we're not at each other's throats."

He laughs before his face suddenly grows serious.

"I've a confession to make. I lied to you."

I smile back, trying to laugh it off, but his comment stops my breath. This man and I have risked life and limb together against both the Saxons and Caerwent's legions. Even Ahern himself, suspicious of everyone, bade me to trust the roguish Blacksword. If Artagan has betrayed me, then whom can I truly trust? Artagan swallows a lump in his throat.

"I didn't just return to Caerwent to get my people back or because it was the right thing to do."

"No?"

"I couldn't bear the thought of returning you to the likes of the Hammer King. Whatever your fate, I didn't wish to be parted from you."

"Whatever for?" I joke. "Surely, the Blacksword doesn't lack for the company of women?"

"Women? Since I first saw you on the King's Road, I've known no other. Nor do I wish to."

As his words sink in, a sudden heat rises in my chest. His blue eyes seem to pierce my very soul, as though the two of us stand alone despite the crowded room. Why does he tell me this? I've seen the way Lady Olwen and Ria look at him. Commoner or noble, no woman in her right mind would do otherwise. He is strong, brave, and yes, even handsome. Mischievous and cocky to a fault at times, but honest as Abbot Padraig and loyal as Ahern to those he loves. I must have misunderstood him. No man in his right mind would want me now. I'm a runaway queen, probably disowned by both my former husband and father. I've no dowry, no fortune, no lands, not even my virginity to offer. I part my lips, but find my voice has abandoned me.

Artagan bows his head at my silence before excusing himself. He walks slowly from the hall, several of his half-drunken compatriots waving for him to come join them. The Blacksword shrugs them off with a friendly shake of his head. He gives me one last glance, lingering under the archway. I turn to go after him, stumbling over my numb feet as though rooted to the floor. A hand grasps me by the shoulder.

"Lady, I've been tasked with guarding you during your stay at Cadwallon's Keep. My name is Enid Spear-wife."

My mind is still awash with Artagan's last words as I try and focus on the woman standing beside me. She wears a bow strung across her green tunic and holds a large spear in one hand. A long brown braid runs down to the small of her back, her shoulders nearly as tall as a man. No wonder they call her "spear-wife." I recognize her as the warrior-woman amongst Artagan's war band of archers. These Free Cantref folk are the only people in Wales who still send their women to fight alongside their men as the Old Tribes once did.

Enid narrows her gaze. Even by the dim hearth light, I can tell she likes me little. I move to get around her, still looking for Artagan in the far archway, but he has turned away. Enid looks at him too, with loyalty and longing in her eyes. Another woman who would do anything for the Blacksword, if he only asked her.

I sigh with exasperation. Are there any she-devils in Wales who don't have eyes for Sir Artagan? By the time I push past her, Artagan has already gone.

"Come," Enid says briskly. "I'll show you your quarters."

Winding our way through the wooden complex, I peer down each narrow hallway, hoping to catch a glimpse of Artagan, but he has disappeared somewhere. With a frustrated frown, I force myself to keep up with Enid's long strides. What would I even say if I did find Artagan alone? My head starts to throb. Too much has befallen me in the last few days, too many brushes with death and enough conflicting emotions to befuddle the clearest mind. Why did he have to confess his feelings to me? I ought to be pondering the fate of my friends back in Caerwent. Nor have I deduced who the mysterious person is that continues to plot my downfall. Instead, I keep thinking of all the times Artagan saved my life in the last few moons, never once asking for anything in return. He has done so much for me and I've not even had the courtesy to thank him.

Enid halts outside an oaken door. Trying to bridge the gap between us, I smile cordially at her. I am a guest here, after all.

"Thank you for all you have done. Risking your life to aid Artagan and me. You are truly brave."

"Do not thank me. I have done a graver ill to my people than I ever imagined."

"An ill?"

"Are you deaf as well as dumb?"

Taken aback, I apologize if I have said anything to offend her, but she simply waves me away.

"You have endangered us all by coming here," she says with a scowl. "It will mean war with South Wales and many good free folk will die, all because of you. Whatever your reasons for taking refuge here, I hope they were worthwhile."

She leaves without another word, taking up her position as guardian down the hallway. I retreat inside my new quarters, shutting the door softly behind me. Water wells up behind my eyes as I think on my family back in Dyfed and my loyal household at Caerwent. I fled to prevent further harm, not to draw down destruction on those I love. *I'm* the one hunted by the Saxons, imprisoned like a broodmare by my husband, and stalked by an unknown foe who sends assassins to kill me in the night. I could not live another fortnight under Caerwent's walls, and yet I fear everyone I touch will only turn to ashes.

My small chamber is warm, complete with a soft bed and many furs. A tiny window overlooks the village longhouses surrounding the keep. Curling up into a ball, I sink into the downy skins of the bedspread. I can do no more tonight, my limbs and heart weary from two days of journeying on horseback.

Sleep eventually takes me, memories of Caerwent and even Dyfed growing hazy within my thoughts. I dream of the ruins of Aranrhod again, standing atop the rubble on the misty hilltop. My mother's voice has vanished, replaced instead by a lone figure in the fog. A mysterious man embraces me before placing his lips upon mine, his dark hair flapping in the wind. My heart rises within my breast as I kiss him within the mists of the old castle.

I awake with a start, finding myself alone in a dark room. Cadwallon's Keep stands silent, the revelers having long since fallen asleep. Reclining within the warm folds of blankets once more, I touch my lips, still warm with another's breath. It was a dream after all, wasn't it? I lie wide-eyed in the darkness, murmuring to myself. Just a dream. It was all just a dream.

10

A woman moans in the predawn darkness. I sit up in bed, taking a moment to remember where I am. The groaning grows louder, an all-too-familiar tone I recall from the women's quarters at Dyfed. Rolling out of bed, I wrap a loose shawl about my shoulders, tramping barefoot down the dark hallways of Cadwallon's Keep. My guardswoman, Enid, sits half-asleep outside my chamber, her spear leaned against a bulkhead. Startled, she rises to her feet.

"What are you doing?" she demands.

Ignoring her, I follow the sound of the wailing woman, her murmurs echoing like a ghost in the morning mist. Enid's footsteps trail after me as I exit the fort gates. The cold mud chills my bare feet. No time to turn back for slippers now. The wailing emanates from a nearby hovel, a faint smoke trail wafting from the apex of the thatched hut. Inside, an old woman and a little boy lean over a young woman on the floor, her belly round and swollen. I stop dead in my tracks, Enid bumping into me from behind. The woman on the floor clenches her teeth, breathing hard between moans as her blond locks spill across her face. Her eyes widen when she sees me.

"You!"

"Ria?"

My voice quivers, recognizing the old lady as Gwen and the young boy as Art, his azure eyes more like Artagan's than ever. Enid pushes herself between us.

"Why have you come?" she asks me. "Do you know this woman?"

"This woman is going to have a baby," I say to Enid before turning toward Ria. "But something's wrong. Why have you left your village?"

Gwen rises, half-shielding her daughter from me.

"We do not winter in the same place, better pastures here. But now the baby will not come."

"May I?" I ask.

Gwen and Ria exchange looks before the grandmother nods. I kneel down beside Ria, placing my palms on her hot stomach. The child convulses inside her, its limbs bumping against the skin. My palms begin to sweat, my pulse quickening in my throat. A real child, a baby who cannot come into this world without my help. Padraig always said I would know when I was ready to deliver a human child. My temples start to throb. I wish the Abbot were here now.

Ria looks at me with an almost animal fear in her eyes, half-eager for help and half-furious that I of all people have come to her in this most vulnerable of moments. I frown, turning to Enid.

"Fetch water, hot water. A needle and thread, and some fresh towels."

"Where'll I find all that? I'm a warrior, not a midwife!"

"You're a woman, aren't you? Sooner or later all women must do battle in childbirth."

Enid's face colors before she nods and rushes back to the keep. Whether my words shame her or fill her with a sense of purpose, I cannot tell. Queen or no, I still know how to deepen my voice and add the sound of authority to it. Gwen draws me aside a moment.

"Births were always a difficulty for me. Of all my children, only Ria ever lived. You've delivered newborns before?"

I swallow, lowering my voice.

"Many times . . . with lambs and horses."

Gwen's eyes widen. She glances back at her daughter with concern. Thankfully, Ria hasn't heard me as she groans again. My throat runs dry and I suddenly half-wish I hadn't stuck my nose inside this hut this morning. But what I feel now has become irrelevant. There is a human soul in need, stuck on the threshold of life itself. I draw Gwen's attention again with my steady gaze.

"I need your help, but we *can* do this. Together."

Gwen looks me over and for an instant I fear she will take a switch to me. Instead, she slowly nods her assent. The old woman gently ushers her grandson outside. The boy would probably only be in the way and whatever happens, it does him no good to see his mother in pain.

Alone with Ria a moment, I continue prodding her while she groans between breaths. Even sweating and red in the face, she still looks a beauty with her yellow locks and robin-egg eyes. She grasps me by the wrist.

"What's wrong?"

"The baby has not turned. Unless something is done, the child cannot be born."

"What will you do?"

"Just keep breathing."

I know I sound curt, but Enid and Gwen both soon return and we've much to do. More than half a year has passed since I last saw Ria, maybe longer. No one mentions who the father of the child might be.

Gwen holds her daughter, helping her breathe while Enid hands me the hot compresses I place upon Ria. Enid swallows, looking somewhat green, but she stays by my side. For someone who has gutted men, the sight and smell of blood now make her wince. I guess I'm not the only one who has never seen a woman in labor. Although I've never had to endure the trial myself, the monks and nuns at the Dyfed abbey still taught me some of the methods of helping women bring life into the world. Sweat runs down my temples as I try to recall the pieces of knowledge I've gleaned over the years. I begin to hum. Enid blinks.

"What are you doing?"

"It's a hymn. The nuns say it helps tell the angels to bring the baby forth."

Enid raises a skeptical eyebrow, but I continue chanting. Lowering my head close to Ria's legs, I hope that the child will turn toward the sound of the song. Come, little one, come this way to life and love. Whomever's child you are, please come safely into this world. Please.

Ria howls loud enough to shake dust off the thatched roof. She cannot help herself. The final push has begun. Was this what it was like for my mother? The pain and anguish, the fear and uncertainty? Gwen squeezes her daughter's hand, urging Ria to keep going. Ria clenches her teeth, her legs trembling. Gwen and Enid both glance at me, but say nothing. In a few moments, we'll find out whether the baby has turned or not. Ria and the child both hover along the precipice of life and death. We each take turns urging Ria on, first Gwen, then myself, and even Enid.

"Push, daughter!"

"Push, Ria!"

"Come on, push!"

My fingertips feel the tiny head crowning. In a few moments, the baby spills into my hands, its wailing cry piercing the cool morning air. Gwen leans down and cuts the cord with her teeth. I cradle the infant in my arms, cooing at the pink newborn. I place the babe in Ria's weary arms.

"Give thanks to the Virgin, Ria. It's a baby girl."

The child has fiercely blue eyes. Not pale blue like her mother's, but an almost silvery sapphire. Only one man in Christendom has irises like these. I turn, holding the sleeping babe in my arms as Artagan approaches down the narrow corridors within the castle keep. He stops and nods, not taking another step toward me.

"My lady."

"Ria is sleeping. She and her mother are outside."

"I came to see you. The village women say you saved the baby and her mother's life."

I frown, but Artagan does not seem to notice my clenched jaw. I turn away, unable to look into his azure eyes.

"I merely did what any good Christian would do," I reply. "Abbot Padraig taught me well."

"It's been a long time since a noblewoman here had such powers and knowledge."

"I'm no enchantress."

"To the people here you are. And to me."

I scoff, turning away. How can he talk to me like this? I'm holding his child by another woman! He had me half-believing him the other night, saying he thought of no other woman since he first met me. Although his boldness took me aback, I cannot remember my husband or any other man looking at me with such longing. Now I see, he's just like any other hedge knight. Brave, daring, handsome, oh yes, but more loyal to his hunting hounds than any woman born of Eve. I hand the slumbering child to him.

"This is yours, I believe."

"Ria said this?"

"I can see the truth plain enough with my own eyes."

He cradles the newborn girl in his broad arms, the child smaller than the length of his forearm. She even has his dark hair. God in heaven, he has two bastards here in his father's keep alone. How many more babies with startling blue eyes have been born across the Free Cantrefs thanks to the Blacksword? I bite my lip, wanting to hit him hard enough to make his cheeks sting, but I'll not lower myself to striking such a dog. It takes all my queenly bearing to keep my voice firm and cordial.

"You ought to stand with Ria before a priest. They've a name for children without fathers, and it's not a good one."

Before he can reply, I turn on my heel and walk back toward my chamber. Enid happens upon us, immediately trying to avoid me again when she sees Artagan following in my wake. He pauses and hands Enid the child before jogging after me. The Blacksword stops me just before the door to my room.

"I meant what I said before," he begins. "I've known no one but you since we met."

"If, *if*, that meant anything to me, I just delivered proof that you most certainly did."

"Count the moons back, Branwen. That's before I met you on the King's Road last summer."

Narrowing my eyes, I quickly tally the months in my head. Ria could've already been with child when I first saw her last year, perhaps not yet showing. Maybe. I shake my head.

"You'd make your own children live with the same shame as you? They'd be . . ."

"Say it: *bastards*. Before the Romans and the Saxons, we Welsh had no such name. A woman's child is hers, and that's all that mattered in the Old Tribes. You know that. In Dyfed and South Wales, they may have adopted Roman ways, but among the Free Cantrefs, a mother's blood is still all that counts."

Ria said as much to me once. I thought she was merely being evasive when I asked her who fathered her firstborn. Enid stands behind us, holding the child awkwardly in her arms. She looks like she'd rather be in the heat of battle than playing nursemaid while Artagan and I stare one another down. I ball my fists at my sides.

"You saved my life twice, and gave me shelter under your father's roof. For that, I'm grateful. But understand me, Artagan Blacksword, I gave up everything to escape my husband's realm and never again will I be subject to any *man*, in the marriage bed or otherwise. Even someone of the Old Tribes should understand that!"

I slam the door to my bedchamber before he can reply. Alone on my cot, I wait until Enid and Artagan's footsteps dissipate down the corridor. A wiser woman would flatter the son of the king who shelters me now, but I'll not heed even my own advice. A wise woman would also probably never run from her kingly husband either, even if he did intend to ride me like a broodmare until old age or a dozen birthings did me in. But how different might my fate be with a man like Artagan? Look at Olwen and Ria, even Enid. He has an admirer in every village and castle. What wife could live like that, sleeping with one eye open on the nights her husband is away? Not me.

Part of me wishes to bury my face in the covers and never come out again. But spring blossoms fill the air with their sweet fragrance and greenery covers the trees once more. It is not in me to cocoon myself indoors. Morgan shut me up in my tower for enough winter moons to last a lifetime. And even I am not dim enough to presume that King Cadwallon will give me my liberty here forever, just to spite his rival in South Wales. No, I must make myself useful somehow if I am ever to have a life of mine own.

For the next few weeks, I spend more time outside the keep walls than within them. Word soon spreads about Ria's recovery and her newborn.

Within the month, I deliver a dozen more babies. For some reason, Cadwallon has no lady of the castle, no living wife or noble daughter. Without asking, I begin to direct the servants and villagers alike, making them pull water from the fresh mountain streams upriver rather than farther down by the bogs where the people dump out their chamber pots. Whatever wisdom and learning I gleaned over the years under Abbot Padraig's tutelage seems like magic to these half-wild people.

Soon many ill elders recover their strength and every newborn lives past its first moon. I've done nothing but apply some basic knowledge to improve these people's lives, but already the villagers stoop and bow each time I pass. Under their breath, they call me "Mab Ceridwen." Something in the Old Tongue that I do not understand.

As I devour an apple for breakfast this morning, I exit the keep and nearly bump into Artagan. Unable to contain my curiosity any longer regarding the term *Mab Ceridwen*, I break my self-imposed silence toward him. I stop in order to ask him what the term means. He laughs.

"*Mab Ceridwen?* In the Old Tongue, it means 'Fairy Queen.'"

Coloring from ear to ear, I suddenly doubt his sincerity. Perhaps he jests. He watches me go, but I do not glance back. After all, what kind of Fairy Queen would I be if I let him see how easily his words get to me?

Enid follows a few paces behind me as she often does now. Cadwallon made it her charge to look after me, but thankfully she no longer gives me suspicious sidelong glances. She raises a skeptical eyebrow each time I insist on a new task, whether cleaning up the village latrines or making the cooks boil water before using it, but she makes a point of not openly questioning me. Enid sometimes prods the villagers back when they reach out to touch me, but I do not mind, often finding myself clasping an old woman's hand or a young boy's cheek as the locals thank me for helping some ailing family member. There is a heartwarming honesty to these Free Cantref folk that charms me to the core.

The villagers say I have the gift of healing hands. Maybe they are right. A golden warmth fills my fingertips each time I touch an ailing elder or seek to relieve a child in pain. Father always said my mother had a way with healing when she laid her hands on the ill and infirm. Perhaps I have inherited some of her gifts.

Enid's quiet loyalty reminds me much of Ahern, and if not for her presence, the loss of my half brother, the Abbot, and my serving girls would pain me beyond bearing. Oft times, I allow myself to think on them only a moment before burying myself in my work again. Some memories smart too much these days.

But I cannot afford the luxury of worry. Whomever haunted my steps at Caerwent, the traitor in our midst, might easily have done harm to one of my loved ones whilst trying to do harm to me. They are much safer without me around to endanger them. I still pray for them each night. What would Una and Rowena make of Enid and these rough Free Cantref women? The thought makes me smile.

After making my rounds this morning to the huts of several young mothers and their suckling babes, I take a stroll outside the village. Breathing in the fresh mountain air, I observe the crofters as they tend the green shoots of wheat and oats.

Just beyond the fields, a score of villagers treks eastward with their cattle and sheep in tow. Ria, Gwen, and her children number amongst them. I ask Enid to leave and return to the keep without me. I've something I need to do on my own.

Enid shrugs and heads back toward the keep. I walk down the road a ways and wait for Ria to pass. She sees me and stops, her growing babe suckling at the breast. Shading my eyes from the sun with my hand, I clear my throat.

"Returning to your village?"

"We've crops to plant, fields to tend, babes to raise. Sir Artagan gave me these."

She points back toward a small herd of cows, healthy beasts with udders full of milk. Artagan must have obtained the livestock from his father. Even for a hedge knight, these cows represent a fortune in wealth and a steady food supply. Before I can ask why, Ria answers my unasked question.

"He did not want me or my children to go without. He's not coming with us."

"Typical."

"Be not too hard on him, my Queen. He and I followed the Ancient

Harmonies in innocence before he grew apart from me. The better woman has his heart now. Be gentle with it, m'lady."

She pinches my shoulder before walking on, her touch both a caress and a subtle threat. Somehow I have difficulty believing the sincerity of her words. She doesn't think I'm the better woman and I certainly know I'm not. Ria will probably bide her time, waiting for Artagan's infatuation with me to run its course. To my surprise, Ria halts again and calls back to me over her shoulder.

"Thank you for coming into my hut that morning," she adds, raising her newborn in one hand. "My children and I will always be in your debt."

A dust cloud rises in their wake as Ria's kin trek back toward the East Marches. My heart rises in my throat, proud of the life I helped her bring into the world. And yet, a pang of jealousy lances my chest too. Ria has such a clear purpose and a family to keep her going. In many ways, her life is much richer than mine. She is a mother, a daughter, a farmer, and a lover. She is happy and fulfilled in who and what she is.

Enid jogs back from the keep, her shadow lengthening beside me. What brings her back so soon? My shoulders sag, as I'm still lost in thought about Ria and the bliss of knowing one's purpose in life. Enid pants, her chest heaving.

"The King summons you. A messenger has arrived."

My heart freezes up. Something is wrong.

Following Enid back toward the fort, I cannot help but wonder. Perhaps King Cadwallon no longer intends to shelter me under his roof. For the past moon, I've hidden at his keep deep within the Free Cantrefs, blissfully cut off from the tumult of the outside world. What a fool I've been to think that the mountains that ring these lands could keep my past from catching up with me.

Cadwallon waits in his near-empty hall, mud-splattered boots on the dais of his oaken throne. The large man breathes heavily, a massive two-handed ax lying across his thighs. Artagan stands behind him, wiping his longsword clean with a rag. The cloth is stained crimson. Enid bows and retreats to the doorway of the throne room. My voice echoes off the wide rafters.

"You summoned me, my King?"

"This morn, my men and I sparred with some South Welshmen trespassing in the mountain passes. We fended them off, but they doubtlessly came with a single purpose."

I swallow hard, exchanging looks with Artagan. A sortie of Morgan's horsemen on our borders can only mean one thing. My husband must have sent a task force of mounted warriors to steal me back. Evidently, the sweaty Cadwallon had more than one pony thrown from under him, judging from his breeches and ax marred by dirt and grime. Artagan sheathes his great sword behind his back.

"There's more. A herald arrived at midday. He waits outside. The man comes from Dyfed."

Mention of my homeland makes my heart leap and then go still all at once. The herald must have come from Father. I inwardly shudder, imagining his wrath with me. The peace between his kingdom and Morgan's hinges on my betrothal to unite their realms. Without me, their alliance remains tenuous at best.

Why did I have to be born the daughter of a king? Father will curse my name now that I have rejected the man he gave me to in holy wedlock. If only I could make Father understand. But the time for such understanding and compromise has passed.

Cadwallon gives permission for the herald to enter. A lanky warrior with thin brown wisps of hair falling along one side of his face, he bears a calfskin shield and long spear like most men of Dyfed. The color of his eyes and the set of his cheeks give me pause. Doubtlessly another one of Father's bastards. If only it were Ahern instead. The messenger doesn't even give me a glance as he addresses the King.

"I am Owen, herald of King Vortigen of Dyfed, ally of King Morgan in South Wales."

"Enough with the pleasantries, young pup," Cadwallon bellows. "What do you want?"

"My sire desires to negotiate for the return of his daughter, Queen Branwen."

"I'm right here," I interrupt. "If you want to negotiate, do so with me."

Owen keeps his gaze directly on the King.

"My liege gave instructions to treat with King Cadwallon and *only* King Cadwallon."

Pursing my lips, I've half a mind to wallop this little upstart right in the mouth. The smug foundling. I can't remember him from the countless illegitimate children Father peopled his castle with, but this newfound half brother of mine lacks any of the courtesy or loyalty of Ahern.

Owen smirks, giving me a sidelong glance. The young warrior actually seems to enjoy my discomfort.

Cadwallon leans his chin on his fist, closely eyeing the herald. A messenger arriving from Dyfed the same day that a sortie of Morgan's men assailed the mountain passes seems too coincidental for my taste. Father and my husband remain in league with one another for certain, hedging their best advantages. While Father negotiates peacefully for my recapture on the one hand, Morgan's men attempt to take me by force. One offers a peaceful solution and the other the sword, but their intent remains the same. They would have me back in Caerwent, a prisoner forever, a slave to bear Morgan more young brats in order to keep Father's lands tied to his. If it comes to that, I'll throw myself from a cliff first. I've come too far to be traded back to my father's people like some horse in the marketplace.

When King Cadwallon glances my way, I begin to sweat. I live under the protection of his household and his son. If he withdraws that shield, I'll be as defenseless as a beggar before the likes of Morgan and Father. Hunted into the bogs and wilds like a hare until they finally take me or I take my own life. My God, has it already come to that?

Artagan rests his hand on his sheathed sword. It suddenly occurs to me that whatever his father decides, Artagan has no intention of giving me up. Even if I never requite his affections, he'd rather defy his own kin than betray me. What have I done to deserve such a faithful knight? Ria was wrong. The better woman has not captured Artagan's heart. I've been as selfish and conniving as the men who seek to subdue me, and all the while the so-called renegade Blacksword has been the most honorable man of them all.

Owen steps forward, too close for comfort.

"What say you to my sire's offer, wise King?"

Cadwallon laughs in reply, his voice filling the empty hall. Owen begins to sweat, his shirt damp under the arms. The King pulls a hair from his head, splitting a single red lock on the razor-sharp edge of his ax.

"Among the Old Tribes, when the Romans sent a herald to parley, if that messenger proved himself to be a liar or dishonest in any way, they sent back his headless body on a horse in reply."

Beads of perspiration run down Owen's temples, his voice trembling.

"Great King, my liege wishes most honorably to compensate you for the return of his daughter."

"Codswallop! This very day a band of raiders attempted to cross my lands, doubtlessly intent on taking my guest here by force. Speak carefully, boy, your life depends on your next words. Are you saying that your noble lord had nothing to do with that?"

Owen takes a step back, bumping into Enid. Her spear urges him back toward the King. I cross my arms, repressing a grin as Father's herald squirms under their deadly gazes. No way out for the cocksure messenger boy now. He stutters before Cadwallon.

"But—but, Your Grace . . . those raiders bore the red banners of South Wales, not Dyfed."

"Did they? But how would you know that, herald? I never mentioned who the raiders were."

Owen gulps, knowing himself caught like a rat in a trap. He sinks to his knees while Cadwallon rises from his throne, his double-headed ax in hand. Artagan draws his own blade, surrounding the herald along with Enid and myself. Although I've no weapon, I step forward and grasp him by the collar.

"You have your answer, herald. Go back to your master and tell him that Branwen is no man's property anymore."

"You'd let him go?" Artagan asks in astonishment.

"With the King's permission," I reply, bowing toward Cadwallon. "Unless I'm mistaken, this Owen is another of my father's bastards. I may be many things, but I'm not a killer of my own kin, no matter how distant or dishonest they may be."

Cadwallon lowers his ax and nods.

"Because he is your kin and a king's son, however much a liar, we'll spare him. Make haste, boy! Before I change my mind."

Owen bows, nearly sweeping the floor with his nose. He throws me a dark look before hastening from the hall. Some gratitude.

Turning back to Cadwallon, I approach the throne and bow my head.

"Thank you for your continued protection and support, brave King. I'm sure it would alleviate many of your problems if you simply turned me over to my father or my former husband."

Cadwallon grins from ear to ear.

"And miss all the fun? No, I prefer to remain a thorn in the side of anyone who would do harm to a daughter of the Old Tribes, especially one as fair and gracious as you."

I color slightly, unused to such compliments. Cadwallon may like to eat and fight more than any king I've ever known, but he also has the most chivalrous heart of any ruler in Christendom. I'm fortunate indeed to have a friend like him.

Owen's horse whinnies outside, the sound of its hooves dissipating into the distance. Artagan and I step out onto the timber battlements, watching the dust trail from his galloping steed fade into the sunset. With the two of us alone beside the embrasures, I look up into Artagan's azure eyes as though seeing him for the first time. The wind whips through our hair.

"You had your sword drawn before your father even answered the herald. You wouldn't have let them take me even if your father hadn't opposed it, would you?"

"My allegiance, like my heart, can have only one mistress."

He takes my hand and kisses my palm. His lips feel soft as rose petals on my skin. As though abashed at his own forwardness, he excuses himself and descends the steps to the main hall once more. I've never seen the bold Blacksword suddenly so shy around anyone, let alone me. The brave fool. Today he tussled with warriors who sought to steal me away, and yet he seems more fearful of my reply to his advances. A smile steals across my lips.

The next morning, I arise early in my bedchamber. Fixing my hair in a bronze mirror, I ask Enid for a few odds and ends from the household servants. Dipping my hands in a bowl of rose water, I scrub my fingernails clean, polish my teeth, and wash the grime from my face. Enid returns with my requested items, giving me a sidelong glance in the mirror.

"I'm a warrior, not a lady-in-waiting. What do you need all these trinkets for anyway?"

"Just a little rouge for my cheeks and a touch of lavender for my hair."

"Aye, and a gown fit for a noblewoman. This used to belong to the lady of the castle."

"Who? Artagan's mother perhaps?"

"Nay, one of Cadwallon's other wives over the years. He's had many, some all at once."

She hands me the gown, green cloth with golden trim. A bit musty, but I clap it out before threading my arms through it. Fitting it over my slim frame, it clings tightly to my curves and runs low across my bust. Enid raises an eyebrow as I primp up my dark locks.

"You getting ready for a special occasion?"

"It's May Day, the start of summer. In Dyfed, the girls always dress their best on this holiday."

"Not dressing up for any man in particular, are you?"

She glares at me in the reflection. Despite bridging the gap between us over the past few weeks, it all evaporates in an instant. Boyish and plain as she may be, Enid's candle burns only for one man. Before I can reply, a horse whickers below the nearby windowsill.

Artagan looks up at my window from atop a chestnut steed. Merlin! The very same stallion that brought us safely through the wilderness. Artagan sits tall in the saddle, wearing a leather jerkin and a woolen tartan that rides up over his knees. His bare arms and thighs bulge with muscle as he steadies the powerful beast beneath him. His blue eyes sparkle like a pair of cobalt gems.

"My lady, the villagers are raising a maypole. They need a May Day queen for the festivities."

He extends his hand toward my window, his usual self-assured grin spreading across his clean-shaven cheeks. Enid frowns, but I cannot help from flashing a pearly grin down at Artagan. Lifting the hems of my skirts, I race down the steps and hallways, dodging serving girls before reaching the fort gates. I suddenly slow my pace.

Best not come running out of the keep like a hussy. Taking my time, I come up alongside Merlin and pat the horse's mane. Artagan looks me over, taking in my hourglass figure in my borrowed emerald gown. He stutters.

"Branwen, you look . . . you look so . . ."

"Are you going to offer me a ride or not?" I smile impishly.

He grins and lifts me into the saddle behind him. As Artagan kicks his heels into Merlin's flanks, we bolt from the keep walls and out into the open fields beside the woods. Villagers wave at us, wearing their brightest garments for the day. They pour milk and honey into the fields, celebrating the sunny start of summer. I cry out with glee as we skirt the river at full gallop, sprinting faster than the wind. My arms wrap tight around Artagan's taut abdomen as he slows to a canter beside the riverbank.

Artagan closes his eyes and draws in a deep breath, inhaling the balsam scent of the nearby woods. He recites something as though from a long-ago memory.

> *I've been many things:*
> *A sword to my foes,*
> *A shield to my people,*
> *A quivering string on a lover's harp.*

> *I've wept tears with the sky,*
> *I've been a flickering star at twilight,*
> *A rune carven on an ancient oak tree,*
> *A child born of the world's first kiss.*

His words set my skin abuzz, stirring something deep within me. I watch him a long while in silence, my arms still wrapped around his middle. It takes me a moment to find my voice.

"That's beautiful. I never took you for a poet."

"A warrior-poet," he corrects me with a half-grin. "Alas, I did not compose that one. It was sung by Taliesin the Great Bard, and is one of my favorites."

Just when I think I've figured out this hedge knight's quaint ways, he surprises me again by reciting poetry. I'm sure plenty of woodsmen know bawdy songs, but how many ruffians memorize poetry from Taliesin the

Bard? Taliesin won renown as the greatest poet and wise man of all Wales back in King Arthur's time. Today Artagan speaks with enough passion to do the old druid proud.

My heart beats fast against him as I lean close.

"I want to thank you, for bringing me to the Free Cantrefs, for saving my life."

"You rescued me, remember?"

I smile back at his playfulness.

"I still know so little about you."

"What do you want to know?"

"Where you were born, your family, your favorite songs, what you like to read. You do read?"

"Whoa, you can't just open up my life and start reading from the middle."

"You already know so much about me, my family and past. It's only fair."

We dismount and walk beside one another past the brooks that feed into the river, striding through the tall green grass. Merlin grazes in the bulrushes behind us, the two of us otherwise quite alone. The wooden keep looks like a miniature model of a castle beneath the woods and green peaks in the distance.

Artagan takes my hand. My fingertips warm under his touch, my skin rippled with goose bumps. He sighs.

"I grew up in a village not far from here. My mother raised my sister and me."

He only mentioned his sister once before, and she was taken by the Saxons like my mother. We've both lost so much to the barbarians, and I've no desire to dredge up our sad stories. I stroke his hand in mine.

"I've never heard you speak of your mother."

"She rarely leaves her home, something of a village chieftess. She still keeps strictly to the ways of the Old Tribes."

"Is she the one who gave you your good looks?"

"She certainly gave me my hardheadedness. And my sense of right and wrong."

I stop, turning away from him with our fingers still entwined. Right and wrong. With my life so upended in the last few months, the line between good and bad has blurred until I hardly know one from the other. I disobeyed my father and husband, breaking the bonds made by men who were supposed to be my betters. Instead, I stayed true to myself. Remaining a broodmare and pawn for Morgan and Father would've been a greater betrayal than I could ever stomach. But so many lives may suffer for my deeds. My eyes begin to water. Artagan touches my wet cheek.

"What's wrong?"

"Enid is right. I'll only bring destruction down on the people of the Free Cantrefs if I stay. Sooner or later the people here will suffer Morgan's wrath for having sheltered me. I must go."

"Go where? This is where you're safe. This is where you belong."

"I've come to care for the people here, but fleeing may be the only way to save them."

"The people here love you. Does that mean nothing to you?"

He leans over me, drawing me close. My hands rest on his chest, his heart drumming against mine. I part my lips to speak, but I've no words. No words at all. He wipes away my tears with his thumb, our eyes searching one another's. Our lips touch before I surrender in his arms.

II

"Riders at the gates!"

Enid bursts into my bedchamber, torchlight flickering in the nearby brazier. Artagan and I sit on my bedspread, several books open as we read by firelight. The warrior-woman narrows her gaze, probably wondering why she should find the two of us alone together and poring over dusty old tomes.

My pulse quickens at the sound of horses whinnying outside the keep walls. Artagan and I exchange looks as we dart to the windowsill. Outside the gate, several torches dot the otherwise pitch-black night. I place my hand on Artagan's.

"Raiders?"

"Too few of them, unless more wait in ambush."

"How did they get so close to the keep undetected?"

He frowns, undoubtedly wondering the same thing. Enid prods the open pages of yellowed parchment on the bed. Quickly gathering them together, I shut the book covers. Enid grabs one.

"What were you two doing?"

"Never mind," Artagan answers. "Wake my father and summon guards to man the walls."

Enid reluctantly obeys. Once she has gone, I hide the hardbacks under a blanket. Artagan unsheathes his blade, pausing in the doorway. He glances at the mound of hidden books.

"We'll continue this later?"

"I hope so," I reply, smiling.

He nods with a grin, darting down the dim corridors toward the main gate. I shake my head. He should not be so embarrassed. Even amongst noblemen, few warriors know how to properly read. It never occurred to me that Artagan might have learned all of Taliesin's poetry from listening to bards and minstrels instead of reading about it in books.

Nonetheless, Artagan learns quickly. A few more weeks of lessons and I'll have him reading as well as any monk. Tucking the last of the books away, I put on my shawl before heading outside.

I've no intention of hiding in my chamber while a potential enemy waits at the gates. Whatever fate has in store for me, I would rather meet it openly than cower behind closed doors. What gang of cutthroats has my former husband sent after me now? When I reach the lookout tower, Enid, Artagan, and several other guards man the battlements. The glow of torches emanates from a small company of horsemen clustered in the darkness. Artagan bellows down from the walls.

"Who goes?"

"Someone you once gave a cracked jaw."

My ears perk up. I know that voice. Leaning over the embrasures, I shout to the guards.

"Open the gates! It's my kinsman, Ahern."

Enid and a handful of Free Cantref men reluctantly unbar the large timber doors, letting the small cavalcade inside the muddy courtyard. King Cadwallon arrives as the riders dismount, their faces lit by torchlight. Rushing forward, I embrace Ahern and kiss his bruised cheek. He winces a moment, the old wound still not entirely healed. Nonetheless, he cannot help but smile at me.

"My lady, a queen ought not to be without her household, so I've brought them to you."

Three other riders dismount and step into the light: Padraig, Rowena, and Una. The balding cleric and my two serving girls smile broadly at me as I step forward to put my arms around them. Before I reach them, Cadwallon thrusts his meaty arm in my way. He shouts to his guards.

"Seize them! Guards, search them for weapons."

Enid and the other Free Cantref warriors surround the newcomers in a ring of spearheads. Ahern turns his own spear on them, bristling with anger. Of all the warriors in the yard, only Artagan does not draw his blade. I turn toward the King in disbelief.

"What's the meaning of this? These are my friends, my family, my sworn household!"

"Aye, and how conveniently they've been released from Caerwent just when all King Morgan's plots have failed. You really think they just blundered upon us in the dead of night by happenstance?"

Unarmed, Abbot Padraig approaches the ring of spears.

"We are no spies, Your Grace. Morgan does not even know our destination. We escaped three days ago."

"So you say, monk." Cadwallon frowns. "So you say."

"How did you find your way here?" Artagan asks, more curious than accusatory. "The mountains are treacherous."

"I can answer that," a voice calls out.

Keenan approaches from the shadows on horseback, Emryus following close behind as they enter via the main gate. The young axman dismounts and bows before Artagan and the King.

"Forgive me, my lords, but we discovered them while out on patrol and guided them hither."

"Why did you not lead them into the keep yourself?" Cadwallon demands.

Keenan clears his throat.

"Ah, I was . . . detained, sire."

Gray-bearded Emryus pushes Keenan aside.

"The young pup had a village girl to visit up the valley. I waited half the night for him to return."

"I figured it was no harm." Keenan shrugs. "These are friends of Lady Branwen."

Cadwallon and Artagan exchange looks, both hiding half-grins at the thought of Keenan detained by the likes of a willing peasant girl. Nonetheless, Cadwallon gives Keenan a stern glance before dismissing the youth.

"If you minded your duty half as well as you do a woman's skirts, you'd be a second Arthur by now."

Keenan sheepishly lowers his head before the King's rebuke. Artagan gives the youth a friendly whack upon the back of the head. Cadwallon turns to his guffawing men.

"Lower your weapons."

Enid withdraws her spear last, leering at Ahern. Moving between the guardsmen, I clasp Padraig's hands. He touches my cheek with such fatherly warmth that I have to fight back the water welling up behind my eyes. I feared I'd never see him again. Rowena and Una surround me, exchanging kisses on either cheek, each clucking like hens.

"We've brought some of your things, m'lady," Rowena begins.

"Gowns, slippers, cloaks, and such," Una adds.

Smiling until my cheeks seem fit to burst, I lead them all inside and offer them food and drink. We stay up half the night exchanging stories of what has happened to each of us since our separation. Much of it turns out to be fairly predictable. Morgan has restlessly roamed the halls of Caerwent, mad as a bull, and his brother, Prince Malcolm, has already put a hefty price in gold on Artagan's head.

Eventually, we find our way to my quarters, laying out bedrolls for the girls and the Abbot. Ahern insists on standing guard outside my room, even though Enid has not relinquished her post. I slip into bed, surrounded by my household like so many puppies in a litter. I begin to nod off to sleep, more content that I can remember feeling in a long time.

Unfortunately, Cadwallon has planted a seed of doubt in my mind. He has a point regarding the sudden arrival of my friends. Morgan surely would have pursued them when they escaped Caerwent to come and find me. Without a cunning woodsman like Artagan to guide them, how had they gotten so far? Morgan certainly could have detained them if he wanted to. Although I cannot unravel this riddle now, something tells me I have let in a Trojan horse.

Rowena draws a bath for me, the first real one I've had since coming to the Free Cantrefs. Even in the wilderness, she manages to keep me clean. She leaves me alone as I slip into the steaming vat, luxuriating in the warmth of my bedchamber. I shut my eyes and listen to the morning birds tweeting outside, the pitter-patter of rain on the roof only making me enjoy the comfort of my heated tub all the more. I recline in the waters, passing out of thought and out of time.

With my household around me once again, I feel truly at home for the first time in months. Only my falcon, Vivian, remains behind in Caerwent. If I could but somehow free that bird of prey from her captors, I might go hawking along the woods and meadows around Cadwallon's Keep. If only.

The door creaks open behind me. Startled, I rise and grab a towel. Artagan ducks his head inside, a mischievous grin spreading across his face when he sees me in the wooden tub. I aim a stern finger at him, trying to look cross even as I smile.

"Have you no shame, Sir Artagan? I thought Rowena locked that door."

"No lock could keep me from you, especially at a time like this."

"Turn around. You're worse than a young colt in season."

He enters and shuts the door, facing the wall. Stepping out of the vat, I wrap a towel around my middle, the cloth barely concealing me from bust to knees. My skin glows pink with the heat of the tub, my dark, wet locks dripping down my back. Artagan glances at me from the corner of his eye. I purse my lips.

"No peeking."

"Don't you trust me, Lady Branwen?"

He flashes a half-grin, slowly walking toward me. I wag my head playfully, pressing my hand to his chest. It's impossible not to smile back at Artagan when he grins like that. He really is just an overgrown boy. He puts his palms in mine, looking me up and down as I shiver under a draft. Artagan wraps his warm arms around me, pulling me close until our lips meet. He slowly devours me with his mouth, his muscles hard against my towel. I pull back, still a little unused to his free-spirited ways.

"Did you mean what you said yesterday? That I'd be safe here, that I could stay as long as I wish?"

"So long as I'm around." He winks. "You and I make a good team, remember?"

"When you follow my lead, that is."

"Of course, Your Highness."

He kisses me as we smirk at one another, his lips finding their way down my throat. The towel loosens around my waist. My eyes widen as his hands run down my bare skin. Artagan certainly likes to move fast.

I fondly slap his cheek and push myself away before adjusting my towel a bit more modestly. Artagan glances at me with a pained look, clearly not used to being denied when it comes to women. He may have the figure of a young Adonis, but this is one woman who will rule her own body. Only a few months out of the marriage bed, I've no intent of ending up right back in one so soon.

Artagan frowns and lowers his head. I'm not some filly in the field. I need time and I need to be sure. Why doesn't he simply understand that?

Reaching up, I put my palms on either side of his face, his eyes looking longingly into mine. We stare at one another a long while, no words, just two souls gazing deeply into one another. I run my fingers through his hair, calming him as I might a wild stallion.

"My heart is willing, but my love blossoms at its own pace. It's been trampled on so much before, it needs time and room to grow."

Artagan lowers his gaze and nods. He'd risk life and limb for me, but restraining his love is a bitter draught for him to swallow. He fakes a smile and kisses my forehead as he embraces me. I linger as long as I can inside his strong arms, listening to his beating heart. Caressing his brow, I tilt my face up toward him for another kiss, this one long and sweet. A knock comes from the door.

"Blacksword, are you in there?"

Enid pounds on the door. Artagan rolls his eyes and puts a finger to his lips. He murmurs in my ear.

"She's like an old mother hen. I best go out the back entrance."

He throws a leg over the windowsill. I stifle a laugh, still in my towel as I try to pull him back from the ledge. It's a long drop and he'll probably twist an ankle hopping out of my bedchamber window. Little does he guess, Enid doesn't concern herself so much with my own safety as she does with keeping Artagan and I pried apart. Halfway out the window, Artagan and I giggle as our arms entwine. Enid opens the door with Ahern right behind her. The warrior-woman freezes, her mouth ajar. Only Ahern manages to stutter a reply.

"We heard a struggle, my lady. Blacksword . . . what's the meaning of this?"

"At ease, kinsman," I reply. "I'll admit whom I wish to my chambers."

Enid frowns, glaring at Artagan.

"Evidently, you'll admit just about anyone."

Glaring back at her, I put both hands on my hips. How bitter she has become of late. Artagan laughs it all off, coming back into the room from the window ledge.

"They're just mad that I snuck by both of them. No secrets in this household."

Artagan gives me a peck on the cheek before excusing himself. He walks out the doorway, past Ahern and Enid unabashed. No secrets indeed. If the villagers of Cadwallon's Keep are anything like the servants of Caerwent, word will have reached every corner of the castle before noon. The runaway queen and the renegade knight, sneaking kisses behind closed doors. Just wait until rumor of this reaches Morgan in South Wales.

A shudder runs through me. The memory of his wrathful eyes watching me flee Caerwent all those nights ago flashes into my mind. The Hammer King is not the sort of man to rest until he gets even.

My cheeks sting as though I stand between two fires. Morgan's wrath burns on one side and Artagan's love on the other. Always, always I live in the space between two all-consuming flames. Saxons try to destroy my world from without, and traitors try to destroy it from within. And all the while I must decide whether I can save my people and yet still remain true to the desires of my own heart. Between two fires, indeed.

Ahern takes up his post outside my door, but Enid remains in the room. I can tell she wants to share a piece of her mind with me, and my experience thus far suggests that people of the Free Cantrefs seem even more inclined to share their minds than most. I turn my back to her, dressing behind a screen. Her voice is cold as ice.

"If your presence didn't bring war upon us before, courting Cadwallon's son certainly will."

"Conflict is inevitable. You don't know King Morgan or my father like I do. They'd have clashed with your people's kingdom sooner or later. I'm just the excuse."

Uttering these words, I realize the truth in them for the first time. Even if I played the mild lamb and remained in Caerwent, Cadwallon would never have bent his knee to the Hammer King. Morgan always planned to deal with the Blacksword's people sooner or later. But Enid's anger is more personal, and we both know it has nothing to do with wars or kings. She grimaces.

"Have your fun while you can. It matters not. Artagan is betrothed to Lady Olwen."

Half-clothed, I spin around on my heel and glare at her over the screen. Before I can call her a liar, her level gaze silences me. There is no falsehood in her. She turns and goes, leaving me alone with my churning stomach.

The rainfall outside my window subsides.

Lady Olwen? The Welsh Venus I met at the gathering back in Caerwent all those moons ago, a dark-haired beauty with violet eyes. I knew she looked upon Artagan with more than friendly knowing, but a betrothal? How could I have been so blind? Of course. Her father, King Urien, rules in the more northerly Free Cantrefs around Powys. An alliance between him and Cadwallon via their children would strengthen the Free Cantrefs against their enemies, both Saxon and Welsh. Balling my fists at my sides, I stomp through the halls of the keep, searching for the Blacksword.

In the fortress yard, a few dozen warriors dressed in green saddle their ponies. Keenan and Emryus number among them, stringing their longbows and stuffing their packs with provisions. Evidently some gathering of men is afoot. What else goes on these days that I don't know about? My garments are only half-fastened in place, my shoulder bare and my hair let down. More than a few warriors pause to look my way. Artagan laughs beside his mount, sharing a joke with his comrades as he preps Merlin. He smiles with surprise when I corner him.

"My lady?"

"Don't you 'my lady' me! Is it true? Your betrothal?"

The grin vanishes from his lips. His companions give him a wide berth. He glances over my shoulder at Enid, who stands beneath the eaves of the inner courtyard with her spear in hand. Artagan clenches his jaw, giving her a look that could curdle milk. I cannot help from seeing red. I need to hear it from his lips one way or the other. I want the truth.

"Answer me!"

"Branwen, you have my heart. The rest matters little now. I've no intention of going through with it."

"Does your father know that?"

"He will. No one can make me wed against my will."

"How easy it is then to be a man instead of a woman! What happens when your heart changes? Lady Olwen is a good match for you."

"Branwen, why do you talk like this? You know my heart."

"Yet you did not see fit to tell me about this small, little wife-to-be of yours? I've seen her beauty myself. The two of you should be quite happy together!"

Turning to go, tears well up behind my eyes. To think how close I came to letting my guard down with Artagan. His charm, his looks, all of it just a façade. Artagan growls at Enid, chasing after me as I return to my room. He grabs my wrist. The two of us struggle over the threshold before Ahern pushes himself between us.

"I believe the lady wishes to be left alone," my brother says in a stern voice.

Artagan shouts over Ahern's shoulder.

"Branwen, just listen! Please!"

I slam the door and press my back against it. Slumping down to the floor, I bury my face in my hands. Is there not one good nobleman left in all Wales? Father sold me like a heifer to Morgan who in turn planned to use me like a broodmare. Artagan alone seemed like a man with some sense of honor, and now I find him no better than the others. How long might he have led me on before he threw me over for his beautiful heiress waiting in the wings? Olwen! I never thought I could dislike a woman more than I did that village girl Ria, but the temptress of King Urien's court has outdone even her. Hugging my legs to my chest, I lie still a long while. I am done with being a plaything for men.

Someone knocks on my door. Rising to my feet, I smooth the folds out of my gown. Rowena's voice murmurs through the door frame.

"Your Grace, can I do anything for you this morn?"

"Assemble yourself and the others in the courtyard, Rowena. We're leaving."

"Leaving, m'lady?"

"You and Una must gather provisions. Have Ahern and Padraig saddle the horses."

Even with the door still shut between us, I sense the hesitation in her steps before she leaves. I rest my forehead against the wooden door. Half the world turns against me and the other half would sell me back to my husband to save their own skins. I clench my fist, banging it against the wood. I'll be damned if I spend another night under this roof! I never wish to hear mention of the name "Blacksword" ever again.

Outside, Ahern gathers the horses. Rowena and Una stand dutifully by their mares while Padraig frowns. The Abbot seems disturbed, but at least he has the good grace not to openly question me. Bystanders all along the inner keep silently watch us as my thanes mount up. Ahern leans down from the saddle.

"Take my horse, my Queen. We only brought four with us, and haven't a spare steed."

"Then take one of mine," a voice interrupts.

Cadwallon steps forward and hands me the reins of a mountain pony. He shrugs.

"She's small, but sturdy if you know how to handle her. The mare's name is Gwenhwyfar."

His sudden generosity stops up my throat, and my resolve to leave almost falters. Almost. Nonetheless, I repeat the name of the shaggy, cream-and-dapple mare under my breath. "Gwenhwyfar." A queenly Welsh mare indeed. I bow toward Cadwallon.

"Thank you, generous King. I've come to prefer mountain ponies."

"I would that you preferred mountain people a bit more. It saddens me to see you leave us."

He glances out the wide-open keep gates. Thirty-odd warriors decked in green depart through the open pastures. Artagan and his companions number among them. Their ponies whicker as gray storm clouds spread across the sky. The Blacksword gazes back at the keep before spurring his stallion forward. Enid brings up the rear of the company as they descend into the thickening mists. A tremor runs down my spine, as though I've just glimpsed Artagan and his warriors for the last time. Cadwallon helps me into the saddle.

"My troops must patrol the East Marches. The war season has begun, but the Saxons have been quiet. Nonetheless, I pray you take caution wherever you go, Lady Branwen. You are always welcome under my roof."

"Thank you for your shelter and hospitality, King Cadwallon. If only other men were as generous and honorable as you."

I lean down from my mare and give him a kiss on the cheek. The round monarch blushes until his cheeks match the color of his thinning red hair. He waves and watches us go.

Villagers line the greens to see us off, silently bowing or kneeling before me. Fighting the urge to reach out and touch them, my heart contracts as I recognize the familiar faces I've come to know over the past moons. Farmwives, milkmaids, and herdswomen cross themselves in reverence, some with newborns in their arms. What did I do to deserve the love of such honest, hardworking people? How odd I must seem atop my stout pony, a full head shorter than my follower's mounts. But the people of the Free Cantrefs respect their wild mountain ponies and only seem to look on me more as their true *Mab Ceridwen*. It almost makes me smile. Fairy Queen indeed.

Once out of earshot of the village and keep, Ahern rides beside me.

"Where do we make for, my Queen?"

"I'd hoped to go to the ruins of Aranrhod. I went there once . . . once before."

Nearly breaking my own rule about mentioning Artagan's name, I cannot lie to myself. We once went there together when we fled my husband's realm. Ahern and the others exchange pale looks at my mention of Aranrhod. Padraig sidles up beside me.

"That place is haunted, Your Grace. Surely, we can find refuge with the living instead."

"There is one other place, a fool's hope, but our last hope nonetheless. We could go to the Dean Fort."

The Abbot grimaces, but Ahern and my serving girls do not look quite as subdued or pale. I purposely mentioned Aranrhod first, knowing that if I suggested the Dean Fort outright, it would scare them just as much. Now with the choice being between ghosts and the living, the Dean Fort suddenly doesn't sound so bad. Nonetheless, in my heart the misty crags of Aranrhod still call to me with my mother's voice. Perhaps I might go there again someday. Perhaps, but not today. Padraig alone speaks up.

"Your Grace, the Dean Fort is not much better. Lord Griffith is still King Morgan's vassal."

"Griffith is a good man. He will shelter us."

"Only before returning you to your husband. Is that what you want, Branwen? He will have no other choice."

Turning to Padraig, I halt my mount.

"We have no other choice. This is the last alternative left open to us."

"We should've stayed at Cadwallon's Keep. I'm sure you have your reasons, my child, but your decisions of late seem rather hasty and ill-advised. It's not too late to turn back."

"Go your own way if you wish! I've made my choice. We make for the Dean Fort."

Padraig grimaces, stung by my words as he silently keeps pace. I dig my heels into the flanks of my mare as our tiny cavalcade bolts forward into the woods. Damn my quick tongue. I've crossed words with the only man who has ever been a real father to me. The wise cleric who gave me a love of books and taught me everything I know. Even he doubts me now. I turn to apologize for my harshness, but he has already let his steed drop several lengths behind in order to avoid talking to me. Dear God, what have I done? The path before me seems so twisted and dark.

The five of us ride on in silence throughout the rest of the day. Although we've no proper guide, I've ridden enough in the East Marches to know that once we come upon the River Sabrina, we need only follow it south until we reach the Dean Fort. Depending on where we find the river, we will undoubtedly come upon Ria's village halfway through our journey.

Will Ria smile smugly when she sees me riding alone with no Blacksword to accompany me? Perhaps I'm being unfair. Does she know of Artagan's betrothal? Would she even care if she did? She seems content to have Artagan's babies whether he ties the knot with her or not. Riding harder through the thick woods, I grit my teeth and resolve not to think on either of them.

At nightfall, we bivouac in a woodland glade. Rowena and Una try to keep my mind off my troubles, playfully disagreeing about the best way to cook rabbit stew in a cauldron in the middle of the woods. As they stir the pot for our evening supper, I stoke the flames with wood chips. Ahern stands watch by the tree line while Padraig immerses himself in his books, not once glancing up from the page. My courage fails me each time I try to work up the nerve to talk to him. Rarely have I seen the Abbot so cross. I've wounded him. Clergyman or no, he might curse me just as much as he'd accept my apology.

By the firelight, I look at my empty hands in my lap. Some queen. The last people loyal to me in all the world now camp with me beneath the open stars. Like vagabonds in the wilderness.

I close my eyes, using my folded cloak as a pillow. Memories of the hush of the unfathomably distant sea fill my ears. Once more, I can see the guttering candles inside the stony vaults of the monastery at Dun Dyfed. A younger version of myself sighs, reading illuminated manuscripts with Padraig looking over my shoulder. Despite the wintry draft outside, within the monastery, the tallow pages of each open tome glow with the colors of spring. Red ochre, hot saffron, and royal purple glisten from the inscriptions etched on warm-hued vellum. I still keep the book he gave me about Branwen the Brave tucked away in my satchel.

I awake with a start the next morning, finding myself back in the glade surrounded by my four companions. I pat my face and chest, no longer the young girl I once was by the shores of Dyfed. Now I'm just a lost queen in the wooded wilderness. Camp smoke rises from our smoldering fire pit.

We break camp at dawn, heading toward the rising sun. By midday, we reach a break in the forest. The teal curves of the great Sabrina River wind their way through the valley below. It almost makes me smile. Who needs a guide? Just follow the sun and the rivers. A couple years ago, I hardly knew much of the world beyond the rocky shores of Dyfed. Now I wend my way through the wilds like a seasoned scout. Smudged as I am with grime and dirt from spending a night on the forest floor, what would Morgan and his brother make of me now? Not quite such a helpless little woman anymore.

Ahern points eastward. Several columns of black smoke rise along the riverfront far below. A foul stench of burnt rubble and rotting flesh fills the air. A murder of crows circles high overhead. My heart rises in my throat.

I gallop headlong down the wooded slopes, heedless of Padraig and Ahern calling after me. My mare descends the foothills to the lowlands, fumes of dark smoke choking the woods. Coughing into my fist, I find myself alone in the black fog. When the trees part before me, I immediately recognize the place. Ria's village.

Heaps of ash and charred timbers remain where huts and longhouses once stood. Bloodied bodies litter the ground, peasants and animals slaughtered right outside their very homes. Crackling fires smolder so thickly they blot out the sun. The morning seems black as night.

I dismount and begin to search the bodies. Ahern and Padraig rein back their horses at the sight of such carnage, both Una and Rowena close behind them. Ahern looks furtively over his shoulder.

"My lady, we cannot linger here! It is not safe. Whomever did this cannot be far off."

"Have you any doubts who did this?" Padraig adds, pulling a broad spearhead out of a corpse. "This was done by Saxon steel."

Ignoring them both, I crouch over several mangled cadavers, some so disfigured that I cannot tell whether they belonged to men or women. The butchered livestock look like someone dropped them from an immense height. Wide, crimson stains cover the grass. Men could not have done such things. This looks more like the work of demons. Both Rowena and Una throw up behind their horses. I freeze, stopping over several bodies all laid out together. As I sink to my knees, my shoulders suddenly feel heavy as lead.

I touch Ria's white cheek, her flesh cold as ice. Recoiling as though death itself were somehow contagious, I clutch my palms to my mouth. Her clothes hang off her bloodied limbs in shreds. Beside her, the little boy Art lies next to his lifeless baby sister. The girl I first helped bring into the world.

My lips quiver with rage. They were only children! What kind of men could do such things?

Gwen's body lies a little farther off, a large reaping hook in her hand. She must have taken at least one Saxon brute down with her. These village women were made of sterner stock than I. Squeezing my eyes shut, I stop up my ears against the crackling of dying fires.

Ahern dismounts his steed and grabs me by the arm. Tugging me back to my mount, he suddenly stops as his eyes grow round with fear. A dull thunder of horse hooves murmurs through the smoky dells. Ahern barely speaks above a whisper.

"Someone is coming."

12

If only I had a knife. Or a spear or bow or anything other than just my two hands. On the run from Welsh warlords and Saxon raiders, I have little more protection than a common peasant. Standing my ground, I swallow hard as the rumble of nearing horses thunders through the smoke. Flames linger amidst the smoldering remains of the charred riverside village.

Ahern stands beside me, shouldering his shield and spear. A brave man, but only one warrior against God knows how many. If the Saxons take me alive it will be a fate worse than death. Many of the bloodied women's bodies at my feet testify to the savagery of these inhuman barbarians. I cross myself as the lead rider emerges from the smoke. A score of horsemen follow in his wake.

The motley cavalcade of rugged men comes to a halt, their garments bloodied and torn in places. Several horses limp, licking wounds on their sides. These men wear green.

Artagan dismounts, but doesn't seem to see me. My gut clenches tight. Not two days have passed and already our paths cross again. Despite my cool stare, he still doesn't look my way.

He staggers toward the bodies of Ria and her family. A fresh cut bleeds on his cheek, and a pair of new welts pockmarks his arms. He and his men must have crossed swords with the enemy. The Blacksword sinks to his knees beside Ria and her children. His children. Reaching out to touch them, he hesitates. His hands shake over their blank, lifeless stares. He balls his fists and looks up at me for the first time.

His piercing blue eyes seem to hold me against my will. How much more can the Saxons take from this man? First his sister, now his lover and their children. Whatever might have been, whatever wrongs he might have wanted to set aright, the chance for all of that has passed. Artagan hangs his head as I place a hand on his shoulder. Both his men and mine keep their distance.

"I'm so sorry, Artagan. My Abbot will give them a proper burial."

He shakes his head, pounding his fist into the ground. His knuckles bleed. He doesn't even seem to notice the blood on his throbbing hand.

"There's no time for burials. We move posthaste. You're coming with us."

"I was leaving the Free Cantrefs," I gently remind him. "I thought you didn't want me around anymore."

I suddenly feel foolish, our spat over his betrothal to Olwen seeming like such nonsense compared with the perils that face us now. But I sense that Artagan barely hears me, his eyes still glazed over from the destruction of Ria's village.

"You haven't heard then?" he begins. "Of course not. This isn't the only massacre this day. My father's keep has been attacked. The Saxons took him captive."

As I take a step back, my voice fails me. Cadwallon a prisoner? Heaven knows what the barbarians will do to him. And what of the people living near the keep, the place I called my home until only yesterday? Faces of every babe and elder I nursed back to health flash through my mind. The world has changed overnight. Artagan rises to his feet, his jaw clenched.

"Two Saxon armies crossed into the Free Cantrefs yesterday—one struck here and the other at my father's keep. We clashed with them twice, but my company is too small and the Saxons were too many."

"The Fox and the Wolf."

"Aye. Cedric and Beowulf each lead their own war bands. Rarely have the Saxons struck so deep into our territory before."

"Why now?"

"Isn't it obvious? They're looking for you."

My lower lip starts to tremble.

"But I only left Cadwallon's Keep yesterday, which means—"

"Which means the only way they could've known your whereabouts was if a spy was in our midst."

Artagan's words sink into me like daggers. This feels like Caerwent all over again, when assassins and intrigue surrounded me at every turn. Only this time, many innocent people have paid with their lives. All because of me. My heart suddenly weighs heavy as a brick. But I dwelt at Cadwallon's Keep for months without any danger, so why now does the enemy move against me? What has changed?

A coldness creeps into my bones as the four members of my household exchange looks from atop their mounts. Ahern, Padraig, Rowena, and Una arrived only a few days ago, and only since then has my life been in peril. It strains reason to assume such a thing could be mere coincidence. Had it not been for my hasty departure from Cadwallon's Keep yesterday, I would've still been there when the Saxons attacked.

My temples begin to throb. Oh, God, please let it not be true. Have one of my own betrayed me? It cannot be. It simply cannot. Artagan takes my hand.

"Mount up. The enemy is still close. Once the Fox and the Wolf combine their forces, they will be too many for us to resist them."

"But where will we flee to?"

"Flee? I intend to take the villains head-on, and crush one war party then the other before they unite. I will have their heads!"

My head aches fiercely now. The hot-blooded Blacksword, he only sees red. His men have exhausted themselves in two fights already. If he leads them into a headlong charge against the Saxons, they may take many down with them, but it will be the Fox and the Wolf who triumph. They will take Artagan's head, not the other way around. I prod my finger into his chest.

"Listen to yourself! You only want revenge, but your first responsibility must be to your people. By now entire villages of Free Cantref folk must be scattered across the mountains and valleys. They need a place to rally, a safe haven, a place to gather our strength."

"Where? Saxons are crawling all over my father's domain. There isn't a safe castle within a hundred leagues of us."

"There's one place we might go. A stronghold deep in the mountains. Somewhere the Saxons would be loath to follow us. We could go to Aranrhod."

Artagan blinks, looking at me as though snakes just sprouted from my head. The crackling fires dwindle around us. Once the smoke clears, the Saxons will surely come looking for us. We haven't much time.

"Aranrhod?" Artagan scoffs. "The place is haunted. It's nothing but a pile of ruins and rocks."

"It was once a refuge for the Old Tribes, and it can be once more. It was built by our ancestors. I will not fear something made by their hands."

"This is madness, Branwen!"

"It's this or we flee south to Caerwent and the Dean Fort. Would you prefer we throw ourselves at the mercy of my husband? I'm willing to swallow that bitter draught if it will help save the people of the Free Cantrefs, but that is our only alternative. It's that or Aranrhod. Make your choice."

Artagan makes a sour face at the mention of King Morgan. He takes a deep breath, peering at me as though trying to pierce my being to its core. I do not flinch. I meant every word I said. I care for all the Welsh, not just those in Dyfed, South Wales, or the Free Cantrefs. All of us are children of the Old Tribes one way or another, and despite our differences, we all share the same foe. Either we start looking after each other or Wales will perish under the Saxon hordes one kingdom at a time.

Every life we save is one more person who can help resist the ever-rising tide of Saxon barbarians in our lands. I am tired of running, from Morgan, from Saxons, and from the traitor in my midst. It's time we made a stand.

Artagan steps close to me until we are only a breadth apart.

"Whatever course we take, you would come with me?"

"It seems we're somewhat lost without each other."

He flashes a wisp of a smile before turning to his men.

"Send out riders and ravens to spread the word. We rally at Aranrhod. The Blacksword and the Fairy Queen will make their stand there, come what may."

Mounting my mountain pony, the same that Cadwallon gave me, I join Artagan's men as we gallop into the west. Emryus and Keenan nod toward me, both warriors sporting purple bruises. Enid does not glance my way once, although it gladdens me to see her alive.

My household trails close behind. Spies or no, I cannot bear to think ill of any of them. Someone has betrayed me, but I will not believe it one of them. I have larger tasks ahead of me now. We must reach Aranrhod and make peace with the ghosts there or risk becoming ghosts ourselves.

The crags of crumbling stone walls loom above the mists of Aranrhod. Our company has gained in numbers over the past few days as bowmen, stray villagers, and even a few spear-wives join our ranks. We've over a hundred followers, with more appearing every hour. If our riders and ravens successfully reach the other scattered settlements and homesteads of Cadwallon's domain, more refugees should come. Or so I keep telling myself.

Over the last two days, we saw signs of the Saxons' destruction that pockmark the countryside. Burnt-out huts, slaughtered livestock, and murdered peasants. Somehow we evaded the Fox and the Wolf, riding through the darkest thickets of the forest where even the bravest Welsh rarely go. The woods and mountains of the Free Cantrefs help defend us from the Saxons just as much as our spears and bows.

Thank the Virgin for guiding us here safely. The old fortress of Aranrhod sits on a lone hilltop in an otherwise misty plain, surrounded by a crescent of high ridges that wrap around the environs like a half shield. Artagan leans close as the two of us halt at the head of our company.

"The steep mountains will deter attack from most directions, but if the Saxons corner us here we will have nowhere to go. Aranrhod is as much a stronghold as it is a death trap. I hope you know what you're doing."

"The largest pass lies to the east. Set some keen lookouts there, ones that won't fall asleep."

"It's not just the Saxons that worry me."

He shivers, looking up at the green and rocky slopes. We ride toward the ruins together. The rest of our company holds back. Artagan and I trade looks. It seems this quest is up to us. If we don't emerge safe from the ruins, no one else will dare venture into them.

I draw a deep breath. It's now or never.

Artagan joins me as we gallop headlong into the mists. Whatever fate awaits me up in those ancient hallows, I will meet it head-on. As a free woman worthy of the Old Tribes.

Halfway up the slopes, we lose sight of all else but one another. Our steeds suddenly grind to a halt, boxing the air and whinnying fiercely. Bucking us off their backs, both Merlin and my mountain pony desert us in the fog. Artagan helps me to my feet as we dust ourselves off. Never have I seen Merlin or Gwenhwyfar so startled, the two horses retreating farther down the slopes. I wince as I rub my sore tailbone.

A deep roar from some unknown creature echoes off the heights. Loud as a lion, its unholy bellow sets my teeth on edge. Artagan draws his sword.

"You still convinced this place isn't haunted?" he murmurs.

We plunge ahead into the gray vapors that enshroud the hillside. Rocky walls emerge from the fog as we advance into the complex. Cracked battlements, overgrown archways, and several crumbling towers overshadow us like ancient stone sentinels. A cool breeze chills my skin. Every shadow and dark nook feels like it has a pair of watchful eyes. I never read about this ruin in any history book, but like much of our past, its memory has gone up in Saxon flames. Stalking silent as the grave, I whisper to Artagan, trying to ignore my wobbly knees.

"What happened here?"

"Amongst the Free Cantrefs, we've some scattered legends about this place, told around campfires on late nights, but nothing written down. Like I said before, it was the last stronghold of the Old Tribes. They resisted the Romans for years."

"But the Abbot's history books say the Roman legions conquered all Britain."

"Eventually, they captured the whole garrison, but the survivors used their magic to curse the grounds, and despite rebuilding the fortress, every Roman soldier here succumbed to a mysterious plague. Centuries later, monks came to build towers and make a monastery of Aranrhod, but the old magic held strong and soon they too abandoned the place to ruin."

"What kind of spell did the ancients cast here?"

"One that was not meant to be undone, but by one of their own. Alas, the secrets of the Old Ways are long since lost."

A baritone growl booms out from the mists.

Artagan and I freeze. We press our backs to one another. The deep howl reverberates off the stonework and seems to come from all sides before it fades. Maybe the others were right. Maybe we should never have come here. Whatever dwells inside these hollows, death itself seems to linger within them. Artagan descends into the fog.

"Wait here. Whatever hunts us, it is not human."

"Artagan, wait! Come back."

He disappears into the gauze of gray mist. The bravehearted hero. Unfortunately, I now stand alone in the middle of a haunted castle. Calling out as loudly as I dare, I hear no reply from Artagan.

A lilting voice rises on the wind. My skin turns cold, hearing the familiar song I've heard only once before. In my dreams. A woman's song rises in my ears. Turning around, a figure chants a melancholy melody from atop one of the broken towers. I gasp.

"Mother?"

The figure fades back into the mist, her voice fading with her. It cannot be. The Saxons took my mother years ago. Only a few years old at the time, I saw them strike her down. So much blood. No, it could not be her. Not here, not now.

A hand grabs me from behind. I jump as Artagan tries to shush me. I cannot keep still.

"Artagan, did you see her? Did you hear her song?"

"Huh? All I found were some animal droppings. Big too. Something lives up here."

"No, no. There was a woman. I think . . . I think she was my mother."

Artagan raises a skeptical eyebrow.

"I didn't hear anything."

Another forceful growl shakes the cobblestones. No need to ask, I know he heard that. Enough of this! I bend down and pull flint and tinder from my satchel. Artagan raises his arms.

"What are you doing?"

"Find some wood, dry wood. We must make the dark places light."

Within a few minutes, I have a fire going. Kindling a torch, I descend into the dark archways of the castle interiors. Artagan follows close behind, his longsword in hand. The flickering flames illuminate the strange mixed architecture of the ancient fortress. Rough-hewn stonework forged without mortar by the Old Tribes. Arches and aqueducts run through the veins of the complex, crafted by Roman engineers. Circular turrets and water cisterns constructed by the monks who failed to make the hilltop their permanent monastic home. Our footsteps echo far into the darkness. Such a vast place. It must have been quite a palace in the ancient days.

Turning a corner, I come nearly nose to nose with a pair of small, furry creatures. The tiny, four-legged cubs whimper and nuzzle us. I smile before Artagan abruptly pulls me back.

"It's no monster that lives here," he deduces. "It's become a cave for bears."

A deep growl emanates from behind us. We spin around on our heels, a huge she-bear snarling in our faces. Her claws cut deep gashes in the walls, her coal-black eyes reflecting the torchlight. Her fangs foam as she tries to get at her cubs, but within the confines of the narrow corridor, we cannot seem to get out of her way.

Artagan swings his sword, but the massive beast swats his blade away like a toothpick. I wave the flaming branch at the creature's snout, but to no avail. My heart hammers in my ears as the bristling predator charges us.

A woman appears behind the bear, raising her arms and voice. She coos at the two cubs, the baby bears scampering around us to lick her hands. Golden honey drips between the woman's fingertips. She chants toward the she-bear in some ancient tongue. Something like a spell.

My heart stops.

It is the woman from the mists. The mother bear turns to her, following her scampering cubs. Humming a soft lullaby, the woman leads the cubs and she-bear away.

Moments later she returns on her own. She has dark locks with faint streaks of silver. My voice shrinks down to a whisper.

"Mother?"

"No, child. Although, you have the look of the Old Tribes. No, I'm not your mother. I'm his."

Artagan frowns, lowering his blade.

"Annwyn? What are you doing here?"

"Is that any way to greet your own mother?"

"So you're the old ghost haunting the ruins of Aranrhod," he replies with a frown.

Doing a double-take, I grab Artagan by the shoulder.

"*She* is your mother?" I ask, still trying to convince myself that this lady named Annwyn is real.

"We haven't spoken in years," Artagan replies. "She isn't your typical mother. She follows the Old Ways."

"Old Ways?" I echo, remembering Artagan once mentioning such about his mysterious mother. I turn my gaze back toward Annwyn. "You're a pagan."

"I worship the old gods," she replies with a nod. "In truth, I worship nature. I'm a healer, much like your mother once was."

"*You* knew my mother?"

Now I know I'm dreaming. First this mysterious enchantress appears out of the mists and now she claims to have known Mother. Annwyn smiles as she patiently explains herself.

"Vivian was a chieftain's daughter from the Dyfed side of the mountains. Strong in the blood of the Old Tribes, although she followed the new religion."

"You're the one singing the song. I heard you, I saw you in the mists."

"I've many haunts, Aranrhod among them. I prefer the tranquility of quiet places, away from the prying eyes, torches, and pitchforks of Christians who are less understanding than yourselves."

Artagan steps between us.

"The reunion has been heartwarming, but we've a war on, *Mother*. Saxons may be coming this way and we've got to fortify this old derelict before they get here."

"Wars are the realm of men and folly, son. Have I taught you nothing? Only love can conquer hate."

Artagan winces as he turns to me.

"You see why we didn't get along? Saxons are pagans too, but no amount of love is going to halt their blades of steel."

"Some thanks I get," Annwyn retorts. "I just saved your lives, without the aid of any weapons but patience and love. I simply asked the bears to leave. Why not do the same with the Saxons?"

Artagan shakes his head, turning his back on his mother. I bow before Annwyn, trying to salvage the situation. This is not the time for some philosophical family dispute.

"Please, your ladyship. The people of the Free Cantrefs are depending on us. This place was a haven for their ancestors of old. We must make it a refuge once again."

Annwyn looks from her son to me, her dark hair and hazel eyes eerily reminiscent of my own mother. Despite having only just met her, I cannot help but feel my mother's hand guiding me to this wandering enchantress. Annwyn has a trustworthy face, but does that mean she will aid us in our hour of need? We certainly need all the assistance we can get right now.

She puts her hands on her hips, flashing a smile.

"How can I help?"

By dusk, a few hundred more villagers arrive in the valley. The westernmost survivors herd their animals through the mountain passes, their cattle, sheep, and hogs drinking at the small river that cuts through the valley floor. Fog still blankets the mountains, but clears enough along the plains for the people to find their way up the grassy path leading to the fortress gates. Or what used to be the fortress gates. Little more remains than crumbling archways of cracked stonework.

Artagan's woodsmen work by torchlight, digging in along the crumbling battlements. Every hour counts. A steady cacophony of clanking tools fills the night air. The Blacksword's bowmen shore up the defenses by piling up stones and timbers. Village women kindle bonfires for light whilst others gather water from the river. For the first time in centuries, the splash of freshwater fills the ancient cisterns. If the enemy does show up, we'll need every drop if we have to withstand a siege.

A constant stream of women and children trickles in throughout the evening, some bearing bindles whilst others have no more than the tunics on their backs. A few lucky peasants find family members or neighbors amongst the refugees, but far too many call out the names of missing loved ones in vain.

Directing the growing multitude from atop one of the bastion towers, I pore over a brittle, torn map with Annwyn. An old parchment, probably left over from the long-ago monks, it lays out a basic floor plan of the grounds. Rowena and Una sweep out the interiors of the old solar chamber behind me, cursing the animal droppings and cobwebs that fill the neglected chambers. I lean over the map as I address Lady Annwyn.

"We have to plug every gap in the defenses. We cannot risk any Saxons finding a way inside."

"I've visited this site for years and have still never fully explored the labyrinth of passageways beneath it," she replies. "This isn't one fortress but several, one built right atop the other. A Celtic hill fort beneath a Roman outpost, beneath a monastery of towers. Just be thankful there aren't more bears living inside . . . as far as I know."

Hanging my head, I scoff at the futility of it all. We've a matter of days, maybe only hours, to make habitable a castle that has fallen apart over the centuries. Regaining my composure, I point at the outline of the outer embrasures on the chart.

"What about the walls themselves? The gates are just gaping holes in the stonework now."

"Four walls and two gates that I know of," Annwyn begins, with a hand on her chin. "The west and south wall stand too high to assail, the best remnants of the Old Roman period. But the northern and eastern segments have crumbled so low in places that rabbits and badgers sometimes find their way inside. The ancient gates were made of wood, and of course burned down long ago, or so the legends say."

"Then that's where the Saxons will most likely attack us, the lowest walls and beside the missing gates. And they'll be a lot worse than a few rabbits and badgers."

"The Old Tribes rolled boulders down against the legions, routing the Romans many times."

"Did they run out of boulders eventually? Is that how they lost?"

"No, they were betrayed, by one of their own. The Romans captured everyone in a single night."

A knot tightens in my throat. How often have the Welsh been defeated by their own kind? Betrayed by spies from within. I shake my head, knowing that I must show some backbone. Nonetheless, I find myself watching Rowena and Una from the corner of my eye as they clean out our new quarters. Such young girls, they have followed me through thick and thin. I do them a disservice by doubting them in my heart.

A ram's horn blares from outside the walls. My pulse quickens. I race to the windowsill. Rowena, Una, and Annwyn all join me as we gaze eastward. A snaking column of torches makes its way down the valley toward the river fords.

No! If the Saxons have come already, we don't stand a chance. Our defenses look like rotten cheese in places, so many cracks and holes pockmark the masonry. Artagan's warriors drop their hammers and shovels, manning the broken ramparts with spears and longbows.

These new arrivals from the eastern passes crowd the fields outside our crumbling walls. Artagan calls out from the defenses, cupping his palms around his mouth.

"Stand down! Lower your weapons! They're Free Cantref folk!"

I sigh with relief. Thank heaven. Rowena and Una exchange smiles with me, each of us breathing a bit easier.

To my surprise, Annwyn hands me a quiver of arrows.

"Here, you'll need this. I've used it for game, but I confess I was never very good with it."

She offers me a bow of birch wood, its handle emblazoned with Celtic runes. Brimming with questions, I don't know where to start. No one has ever given me such a gift.

"Lady Annwyn, I cannot accept such an exquisite—"

She gently shushes me with a smile. "I think you shall have more need of it than I."

I bow, deeply humbled by such generosity. Despite her peaceful philosophy, Annwyn truly does adhere to the ways of the Old Tribes, who sent their womenfolk into battle beside their men. I pray I have the strength to draw the bowstring and do justice to this finely crafted piece of woodwork.

Gazing out over the windowsill, my eyes widen at the sight of such a large contingent of refugees. There must be a thousand of them! So many villagers and homesteaders. Entire stretches of the Free Cantrefs must be empty of people now.

A lone rider astride a white horse leads the swarm of survivors up the slope toward the missing gates. She must be some local noblewoman.

My gaze suddenly narrows on the unmistakable figure of a fair woman with long, straight, jet-black hair. Her violet gown glistens with fine silks and jewels. Only one woman in Christendom could match such beauty. Lady Olwen.

Artagan rushes forward to greet her. Straining my eyes, I can only see their distant figures meet amidst the crowd of refugees pouring into Aranrhod. The bottom drops out of my stomach. Both Una and Rowena glance my way with sympathy in their eyes. Why would Artagan want me now? Especially since I've rejected him and he has a perfectly gorgeous paramour that his father betrothed him to already. My ladies-in-waiting both abruptly resume their tasks, pretending not to have noticed the look of consternation on my face.

Throngs of more Free Cantref folk pass through the open gateways. We'll need all the room this old castle can afford us. Every nook and cranny within these walls will be filled by midnight. Descending the turret steps, I inspect the construction along the weaker segments of the walls. Artagan and Olwen are sure to be there. Natural leaders always throw themselves into the thick of things. I bring along my new quiver of arrows and my birch longbow.

Many of the new arrivals turn and wave to me, survivors from Cadwallon's Keep. Half the villagers from Cadwallon's settlement must have escaped to the woods in order to avoid the Saxons. I embrace several mothers and farmwives. It seems as though we haven't seen each other in years. Has it only been a matter of days since the Saxons turned the world upside down? My heart sinks when I realize how few of the elders have made it. The journey to Aranrhod must have been rough. Only the young survive.

Amidst the multitude, I hear Lady Olwen's voice before seeing her. Dismounted, she tugs her white mare behind her, her other hand upon Artagan's arm. Her deep, sensual voice could cast a spell on any man. She and Artagan suddenly halt before me, the rest of the crowd parting around us like a rock in a river. Olwen speaks to the Blacksword as though I'm not even here.

"Artagan, you didn't! Stealing another man's wife? That's bold, even for you."

The Blacksword shuffles uncomfortably. Lady Olwen keeps her hand on his arm. I stare down her haughty gaze.

"Actually, I rescued him," I reply matter-of-factly. "To what do we owe the pleasure, Lady Olwen?"

"I've come to rescue you, or at least your people. But they're not even that, are they? I suppose you're a queen of nothing now that you've thrown it all away."

My cheeks burn, but I've no reply. Despite her sharp words, she speaks the truth. I've no kingdom under my sway, no family nor husbandly ties to fall back upon. A queen without a country. Little better than a beggar-maid. Artagan removes Olwen's palm from his wrist, his gaze darkening.

"Branwen has done more for the people of the Free Cantrefs than anyone. She cares for every villager like a mother, and for no benefit but the goodness of her own heart. The people love her."

Olwen purses her lips. I glance at Artagan, unsure what to say. Such sternness has clearly taken Olwen aback as well. He nods toward both of us before excusing himself.

"Pardon me, Lady Olwen, but I've battlements to rebuild. Queen Branwen is in charge here. If you've come to lend a hand in our defense, I suggest you take it up with her."

He goes without another word, although he does glance back at my new bow with a curious expression. Olwen makes a sour face, her violet eyes lingering upon Artagan as he leaves. Puffing out her chest, she looks me up and down as she might appraise a horse.

"I brought as many survivors here as I could. The rest is up to you, Lady Branwen."

"You have my thanks," I reply cordially. "I'm sure we can find a useful task for you."

"I'll manage myself, thank you."

She motions to leave, but stops, as though remembering something she wishes to tell me.

"You've turned his head, Branwen. Nothing more. You think yourself the first? He'll come around, sooner or later. He always does. Always."

Olwen brushes past me, her shoulder glancing mine. My fingernails dig into my palms until they leave marks. I've a sudden, very unchristian urge to practice bow shots on her. But I've little enough arrows for our enemies as it is.

Striding back inside the fortress, I thumb the grip of my new longbow. Annwyn must be of a similar height as me, because when I pull back the bowstring, the nock comes right to my jaw. As though the bow was crafted for me. My skin buzzes with a thousand pinpricks, wondering what Mother would think if she could see me now. Me wielding a longbow in a strong-hold of the Old Tribes. I've no formal training in arms and none of the experience of a proper spear-wife, but I think I can at least manage to loose an arrow or two if need be. I suppose if the Saxons come, I'll find out.

Men and women nod to me as I walk the battlements. Artagan's war-riors erect a row of wooden pikes in the earth, angling them outward. With his naked blade, the Blacksword lops the heads off each log. Each wooden tip is razor-sharp. A row of sharpened timbers, these barriers will not stop the enemy, but may slow them down.

Amidst the burning bonfires and torches, everyone lends a hand. Keenan and Emryus cut wood, Rowena and Una dig entrenchments, while Ahern and Padraig pile rocks along the walls. Stooping beside them, I join the Abbot and my kinsman as they rebuild the walls one stone at a time. Padraig does not look up from his work.

"I thought ladies don't stoop to such menial labor," he says.

"Then I'm not a lady."

Hefting rocks beside him, we pile the stones higher at a low spot in the walls. The bald monk still looks cross with me, his brows tightly nettled. Who can blame him? I've played the part of a petulant brat the past few days, and yet Padraig and Ahern have stayed with me. Padraig stops his work, dusting off his hands. He looks me in the eye for the first time in days. Ahern and I pause in our work as the monk sighs.

"You've grown into a beautiful, intelligent woman, Branwen," Padraig begins. "You followed your heart when most of us would have balked and you've become a leader of our people, not just those of Dyfed or South Wales or the Free Cantrefs, but of all the Welsh. For these reasons and others, I'm proud to call you my pupil. You're the closest thing to a daughter an old man like me is ever likely to have. I may be a lot of things—cross, testy, and a sinner—but Branwen, my girl . . . I'm no spy."

I hang my head, his words bringing water to my eyes. I've been on the run for my very life for so long, my enemies have me seeing assassins and traitors everywhere I look. Even in the midst of my own household and kin. God forgive me, how I've let my fears blind me. I place an arm on Padraig's and Ahern's shoulders.

"It'll be a cold day in purgatory before I give up my trust and love in the two of you."

Padraig raises my chin with his fingertips, like he often did when I was a child. Ahern smiles at me, somewhat choked up himself. My guardsman's complexion suddenly turns pale, his eyes fixed on the dark horizon.

"My lady, look! The refugees . . . they've led them right to us."

Hundreds and hundreds of blazing torches fill the night woods surrounding the castle. The din of steel knives banging against timber shields murmurs through the darkness. Clasping my hands to my throat, all the air seems to go out of me. The Saxons have come.

13

Saxon war drums thunder in the night. Smoky pine tar from their torches fills the evening air. The ground shakes with the din of marching feet. Ahern and Padraig exchange looks, the firelight of a thousand Saxon torches reflecting in their eyes. They stare back at me like it's the end of the world. Perhaps it is.

"Get everyone else inside!" I shout, grabbing them by the shoulders. "Now!"

Nodding dumbly at first, Padraig and Ahern help stragglers in through the open gates. The Abbot and my guardsman seem to regain some composure after their initial shock, having something meaningful to do. My palms tremble along the wood grains of my bow. The black silhouettes of innumerable Saxon spearmen encircle the citadel, only a few hundred paces away.

Walking the battlements, it takes every fiber of will for me to tear my eyes away from the nearing danger. I remind myself that I must keep moving, I must stay focused. Pacing the walls, I keep my strides steady. I dare not stop. If I stop, I'll crumble just like these old walls.

The remaining refugees outside the walls usher their livestock in through the gates. Children cry out in their mothers' arms. Panic starts to fester on the faces of every Welshman and Welshwoman inside the citadel.

Artagan and his men form a defensive line along the eastern battlements, the jagged walls and timber palisades little better than waist high in places. I grab Artagan by the shoulder, his firm muscles steadying me. It takes a moment to swallow. My palate runs dry.

"Blacksword, how many Saxons are out there?"

"A thousand, maybe two. Maybe more, if both the Fox and the Wolf have come."

"We have just as many."

"Mostly women and children. I doubt we've more than three or four hundred who can fight."

"Plenty of women here can fight."

He nods, eyeing the longbow in my hands again. He must know it belongs to his mother, yet he still says nothing. Is there more to this bow than Annwyn first told me? Or perhaps Artagan is just getting used to seeing me with a weapon in hand.

Despite the impending arrival of our foes, he manages a cocky smile. His enthusiasm gives me courage. No wonder his men love him.

"Do we have anything resembling a plan, my lady?"

"Concentrate your warriors where the walls are weakest," I begin, remembering the map of the compound. "The east and north portions are particularly vulnerable."

"What about the south and west walls? They're high, but they still need defenders."

"We've villagers and stones aplenty. They'll hold those walls as well as a pack of she-bears. Let the Saxons come and see how well the mothers of the Free Cantrefs fight when their children are in peril."

Artagan raises an eyebrow, clearly impressed. Unfortunately, I already see a flaw in my battle plan. A pair of gaping holes remain in the east and north walls.

"We've still got another problem: the two broken gates. The Saxons will pour right through them."

"Let me handle that. Go rally your she-bears."

He grins, drawing his longsword. Carefree as a child, he looks as calm as he might at a country dance. Someday, he needs to tell me how he does that. If we last the night, first. Reaching out for him, I touch his arm one last time. So much I want to say, so much left unsaid. My voice falters.

"Blacksword . . . Artagan . . . look after yourself."

He winks in reply. I dart down toward the inner courtyard, scaling a shattered pillar in order to stand above the crowd. Glancing back, I catch my last glimpse of Artagan amidst the tumult. He urges his warriors into position, several dozen men upending a pair of oxcarts to block the open gateways. Good thinking, Blacksword. But how long will those rickety barricades hold? If our garrison is overrun tonight, no one will ever know what happened to us. The last stand of the Free Cantrefs.

When I raise my arms over my head, scores of villagers recognize me and pause. Mothers hush their young and the few elderly women scold young boys into silence. I clear my throat, fighting to keep my tone low, yet strong. If I sound afraid, if I squeak out a few hollow words, it will only spread despair. The people need to hear the voice of a queen.

"Free folk, hear me! The Saxons come to slay our children, to make corpses of our menfolk and slaves of our women. They are many, we are few. They have steel and we have stones, but we have something they do not. Our strength lies not in numbers, or arms, or the height of our walls. No."

I pause to gain my breath, and the entire castle falls silent. Men lining the walls and children poking their heads out of the dusty stables all have their eyes on me. Artagan's blue gaze finds me across the sea of people, his azure stare giving me strength. I renew my voice.

"We fight to defend those we love! As a cornered bear defends her young, so too shall we resist the Saxon hordes with every tooth and nail of our being. We are no barbarians. We do not fight for pay or loot or lands or captives or because some king orders us to. We fight for our children, for our mothers, for our friends, and for our lovers. We fight for *love,* and that makes us mighty!"

A great cheer rises from the crowd, rippling my skin in goose bumps. I'm out of breath, and my mind runs blank. I've nothing left to say, yet all eyes still focus on me. Artagan smiles, and for a moment it seems as though only he and I occupy the ruins together. Somehow, I find the words once more, my voice rising.

"Will you let the Saxons come and steal away your children?"

The crowd responds in unison. "No!"

"Will you let them ravish your women?"

"No!"

"Will you stand by while they kill your men?"

"No!"

"Then let them hear you, brothers and sisters! Let them hear the voices of a thousand Welsh inside the walls of Aranrhod who are still free!"

A deafening roar from the throng washes over the castle. Even the Saxons across the border must have heard that. Men beat their spear butts against the ground and women stamp their feet. The clatter rises as the people line the walls, taking hold of whatever weapons they can. Stones, pitchforks, spears, and bows line the defenses. Artagan nods at me with approval.

I lead scores of womenfolk up the open staircases along the highest walls. They tote rocks and small boulders between them, many stones simply scraps of the castle itself that have long since crumbled into heavy shards. Rowena and Una take up positions, and even Lady Olwen joins us along the bulwarks. Let's hope her spear is as sharp as her tongue. Only one figure remains among the children in the courtyard. Turning back, I find Lady Annwyn as placid as a sage in meditation. She raises a hand before I can question her.

"I do not believe in violence, young one," she says. "Peace remains my guiding star."

"But the Saxons—"

"I will prepare some medicines and bandages. I have a feeling we'll need both rather soon."

Nodding, I leave her to her ways. We will certainly require her healing skills before the night is through. Perhaps I should do the same, but with a bow in my hand and two thousand Saxons outside, I know that my place is on the wall. My loved ones man those walls, and I must join them.

Ahern and Padraig guard the north wall along with some of Artagan's warriors, and so I accompany them. This looks as good as any place to make a last stand. I draw back my bow, wishing not for the first time that I had more chance to practice. I must make each of my arrows count tonight.

My brother shoulders his shield and spear while Padraig makes a club out of an old walking stick. I almost grin at the sight of a monk playing the part of a warrior, but his grim tone soon drains all the mirth from my lips.

"Many monasteries have fallen to the Saxons over the years," Padraig recalls. "They do not favor long sieges. They will come at us with all their strength."

The Saxons drub their shields with knife handles and ax heads. The deafening clamor makes me wince. Their iron helms and long knives glimmer by torchlight, a pair of animal skin banners fluttering over their lines. A foxtail and a wolf skin. My hand trembles on the bowstring. The war-chiefs Cedric and Beowulf are out there somewhere. The very same who first tried to capture me once on the King's Road, and again at the Dean Fort. Tonight, they intend to make good their past failures.

As though in answer to the roaring Saxons outside our defenses, Artagan begins a chant of his own. His men take up the tune. The ancient verse pricks my ears, another line from Artagan's favorite poet, the old Arthurian bard Taliesin. My history of poetry may be a bit rusty, but if I recall correctly, it is an oft-forgotten line recording an ancient conflict known as the Battle of the Trees, when the people of the Old Tribes used both magic and swords to defeat their enemies. Goose bumps ripple my skin as Artagan's men repeat the mantra.

> *Call me sword, call me spear.*
> *Call me bow, call me fear.*
> *Call me harp, call me steel.*
> *Call me shield to all my people!*

The Saxons are quiet a moment and although they cannot understand Welsh, even they know a spell when they hear one. I smile at the Blacksword. Only he would think to use poetry as a weapon against our foes.

Our warriors' chants gradually fade as Artagan disappears from view, moving amongst the throngs of his men as he encourages them with his presence. His woodsmen continue to ready their positions, still piling a few last stones and buttressing the barriers with timbers. They pile dirt around the oxcarts that block the two open gates, makeshift barricades that will have to hold back our foes. They *must* hold.

The Saxons renew the clacking of their axes against their shields once more. The noise reaches a crescendo before suddenly dissipating. I don't know what it signifies, but I doubt it means anything good.

Two warriors stride out between the Saxons and our walls. Broad-shouldered and bearded, they wear long capes that snap behind them in the breeze. No one doubts who they are. The barbarians howl at the backs of their two war-captains. Together, the Fox and the Wolf raise a pike with something round atop its head. Squinting across the dark fields, I whisper to Padraig.

"What is that?"

"Not what, but who." Padraig frowns. "That is the head of King Cadwallon."

My breath withers inside me. Moonlight emerges from the clouds, illuminating the grizzled features of the former Free Cantref king. I look away, unable to shut out the image of his empty gaze and protruding tongue. The brigands could have traded a valuable man like Cadwallon back to us. They might have used him to barter concessions, maybe even offering to swap me for him. Lord knows, I might have done it to save the good king who once sheltered me. Cadwallon's head on a pike means only one thing. The Saxons intend to besiege us without further delay. There will be no quarter.

I can't see Artagan amidst the eastern embrasures, but I know he is there. Would he even want my hand on his shoulder now? If the Black-sword didn't see red before, he will certainly want to slake his blade in Saxon blood now. Ria, Gwen, their children, and now his father. Most of Artagan's family has fallen under the Saxon sword in the last few days. The Saxons haven't just come to raid and pillage, they've come to wipe us out.

A bloodcurdling battle cry pierces the air as the Saxon troops rush forward. Hundreds upon hundreds swarm toward Aranrhod from all sides, a ring of torches coiling about our walls like a fiery serpent. More than half of them concentrate toward the lowest defenses. Artagan's baritone voice booms out across the fortress, like the unseen voice of an archangel over the din.

"Archers! Make ready!"

A few hundred warriors in green drop their spears and axes, drawing back longbows at Artagan's command. Even some village huntresses and mothers have a spare arrow or two that they notch to their bows. I pull back my bowstring as far as it will go. The longbow, the famed weapon of the Free Cantrefs. Will it be enough against cold Saxon steel at night? May God guide our arrows.

The Saxon hordes draw closer. The clang of their armor and the musky odor of their unwashed bodies make me wrinkle my nose. What does Artagan wait for? The brigands will be upon us in moments! Artagan's voice roars above the crowd.

"Bowmen, loose!"

There is a hiss as hundreds of arrowheads soar into the darkness. Firing blind, I let my arrow go before quickly restringing another. By the time I notch my next feathery dart, the archers around me let loose at every Saxon they see. Some arrows thud harmlessly into timber shields or the soft grass. Others find their mark.

Howls and whimpers of pain surround me in the dim moonlight, like the lamentations of the damned. I never expect to hear such a sound this side of hell again. Bodies of Saxons collapse in heaps at the base of our bulwarks, some writhing with multiple arrows protruding from their chests and limbs. Others lie still in neat rows, piled like cordwood. I continue notching and loosing my arrows, pouring them into the crowd of foes below. As I draw the last arrow shaft from my quiver, my hand trembles so much that I cannot even string the dart.

The Saxons respond by lobbing their torches over our walls. Several fireballs crackle over my head, some landing in the yard behind me whilst others knock Welshmen down from the barricades. Women and children rush to dowse the fires with buckets, wineskins, and anything else that will hold water.

A series of large thuds slam against the stone ramparts. Long timber poles land along the wall beside me. My eyes widen. Ladders! Swallowing a knot in my throat, I stand back as I notch my last shot. My aim hasn't mattered much thus far, what with a multitude of enemies below. Why did I spend my arrows so freely? I'd give half a chest of silver for just a few more deadly quills. Blinking the sweat from my eyes, I raise my birch wood bow. I must not miss. I must *not* miss.

A grizzled Saxon emerges over the ramparts, his dirty-blond beard flecked with sweat and spit. With an ax in one hand and a round shield in the other, he leaps toward me. I loose my arrow toward his heart.

It thuds harmlessly into his wooden shield. I missed!

He swings his massive ax down toward me while I raise my empty longbow overhead. As though a thin birch bow could shield me from the weight of an ax head. I squeeze my eyes shut, wincing before the blow.

The Saxon pauses, his face contorting in pain. A spearhead rises up through his chest before disappearing in a fountain of blood. The barbarian keels over. Enid withdraws her spear from his huge corpse, wiping the grime from her cheek.

Bile rises in the back of my throat. The Saxon's blood pools around my feet. Bending over the back of the parapet, I spew what little food remains in my stomach. Enid pats my back as I wipe the spittle from my face. She knits her brow.

"Artagan sent me to look after you."

"What for?"

She shrugs.

"I didn't ask for the honor," she adds.

We've no time to argue. I stand shoulder to shoulder with her as more assailants scale the ladders below. I palm my chest and head, but find no wounds. I'm alive! Before I can blink, more Saxons swarm over the battlements. Enid tosses me the short-sword from her belt. She skewers invaders with her red spear tip while I fumble with the small sword. If only I had half her skill. All the book learning in the world does me little good now. My empty stomach churns over. The raw hate in the Saxons' wild eyes makes my skin crawl.

With my spent bow in one hand and a short blade in the other, I claw and hack at the bearded, oily-smelling Saxons struggling over the embrasures. Together, Padraig and I send one man tumbling backward over the defenses. Ahern and Enid grapple with warrior after warrior while Welshmen and Saxons fall all around us. Flagstones turn slick with blood.

Women and children pummel the assailants with rocks. Archers down enemies right in our midst. More than one spearhead or dart brushes my cheek, narrowly missing my face before lodging itself in a howling Saxon. An eerie bullhorn booms through the darkness, like a staccato Minotaur bellowing in the night. The wave of Saxon troops recedes from the walls, scores of warriors limping back to their own lines. Others drag wounded no longer able to walk. A cheer rises from our own lines. I raise my arms with the others, jeering at the retreating barbarians. Only Enid looks grim.

"They'll be back," she says with a grimace.

"You mean we haven't won?"

"Won? That was but their first assault. They'll come again."

My heart sinks, my limbs suddenly heavy as lead. Furry Saxon bodies litter the barricades, their animal skin mantles bloodied with arrows. A thin line of Welshmen in green remain standing along our own defenses, some with gaps of ten paces or more between them. The color drains from my cheeks. So few remain. Portions of the walls have so little defenders left that the Saxons could drive a herd of cows between our remaining spearmen.

Women carry the wounded down into the courtyard where Annwyn kneels over the maimed and dying, sewing up wounds with needle and thread. Padraig daubs Ahern's brow with a cloth, the guardsman's forehead bleeding from a wide gash. Ahern fakes a smile.

"It only looks bad, my Queen. I gave the Saxons worse."

He winces even as he speaks, stumbling before he sits down. With a dripping bowl, Padraig washes the blood from Ahern's hair. Enid stalks amongst the Saxon wounded, giving them a speedy end with her hunting knife. I shut my eyes. Some warrior I turned out to be. A frightened, childlike part of me would give anything to be elsewhere right now. But where is there left to go? We are the last bastion of Free Welsh in these mountains. The Saxons will simply wash over us like an unstoppable wave, until we are utterly defeated. Until we are no more.

Pacing the lines, I make my way down toward the east gate, searching every bloodied face for Artagan. He must live, he must. The overturned wagons meant to block the gateways look like no more than piles of drift-wood. The Saxons pummeled them to splinters trying to get inside. Life-less Welsh and Saxon foes lie in each other's arms as though embracing in death. Atop the crumbling walls, Keenan bends before Emryus as he puts the old bard's arm in a sling. My lower lip trembles as I approach.

"The Blacksword, where is he?"

Keenan hangs his head. My heart tightens like a clenched fist. Emryus's pained gaze leads me farther down the ramparts, where piles of corpses lie. Tiptoeing around the mangled limbs and skulls, I pause be-fore a lone figure at the apex of the slaughter. He kneels with his head in his hands, his bloody sword driven into the ground. Countless dead spiral outward from where he sits. Artagan looks up at me, his wet-marble eyes seemingly hard and soft by turns. Only Saxon bodies surround him. He must have slain more than a dozen barbarians all by himself.

"They killed him, Branwen. They took his head. They took my father's head."

Sinking down beside him, I wrap my arms around his bruised neck. He lays his brow on my shoulder, his breath warm against my skin. I shush him, patting his back. The brave warrior seems like a harmless boy in my arms, but moments ago he must have raged like an unchained beast. He silently weeps against my collarbone.

I run my hands through his damp hair, looking out over the carnage. A cold wind stirs the soiled green banners along the walls. Evening mists roll in. Less than half our warriors still stand. A shudder runs through me as I hold Artagan in the darkness. If the Saxons come again, we can-not stop them.

Dawn rises and still the Saxons do not come. Why do they wait? Perhaps they prefer to taunt us, lengthening our suffering as long as possible. Every man, woman, and child within the walls of Aranrhod now lives under the shadow of the Saxons. It is only a matter of time before they overcome our defenses and massacre us all.

Lady Olwen still lives. Somehow, she is the only soul inside the cita-del without a speck of dust or smudge of blood on her. She sits atop one of the old towers and scrawls endlessly on parchment, attaching notes to messenger birds. She has sent out ravens since midnight, in all directions, but none have returned. The Saxons probably downed a few and roast them over their morning campfires now. Their glowing hearths surround us in a ring, smoke rising over their besieging armies.

Who could possibly come to our aid? My husband? My father? Even if they had half a mind to, would that really be a better fate than falling to the Saxons? No matter. Morgan and Father will not risk their precious armies to save the renegade Blacksword and a faithless queen.

I sit up on the floor of my chamber, unwilling to move any farther. Outside the window, Olwen's scratching quill murmurs from the opposite tower. Does she really intend to spend her last hours penning correspondence that no one will ever read? The Saxons will wipe their arses with it after they've reduced this place to ashes.

Artagan slumbers beside me, the two of us having spent the night side by side. Just two weary souls, curling beside one another for warmth. A faint moon lingers in the brightening sky. To think, in only a few short moons I should turn another year older. I never thought I would perish before my eighteenth birthday.

I get up to make my morning water. Artagan snores on the floor behind me, his clothes still torn and bloodied from last evening's fight. Down the stairwell, the mingled voices of giggling women catch my ears. Narrowing my brows, I stalk down the steps. At the foot of the stairs, three figures lie beneath blankets covering a nest of straw. My footsteps give them pause.

Keenan sheepishly looks up from beneath the coverlet, Una and Rowena on either side. Coloring from ear to ear, I leave with a nod. Their giggles reverberate up the turret steps after me. I certainly can't begrudge them. Let them find what happiness they can in the hours that remain to us. Perhaps I'm a fool not to do the same.

When I return to my bare chamber, Lady Olwen awaits me. I glance back at the stairs. How could she have snuck by me? These old towers must have secret passageways within. Olwen flashes a wry smile at my discomfort. Artagan still lies sleeping on the floor between us, his chest rising and falling with the peacefulness of a child. I gaze past her as the sun rises in the window.

"Any news from your birds?" I ask.

"I've sent ravens in every direction. My father's motte in Powys lies closest to here."

"That's still days away. How many men could he possibly send to our aid?"

Olwen hangs her head.

"Not enough. Perhaps Dyfed or South Wales will save us."

I reply with a harsh laugh.

"Morgan is a calculating man. He will not risk his soldiers to save a rival kingdom."

"Perhaps Dyfed then."

"My father is like my husband. The bonds that once bound us have long since broken."

My gaze falls to the floor with hers as Artagan stirs between us. Olwen didn't come to my chamber merely to banter words with me. Perhaps she intends to have a last go with Artagan before the Saxons loose us from our mortal coils. She seems to sense my thoughts, watching me from the corner of her eye. I plant my feet firmly with no intention of going anywhere. Before I can reply, another ox horn sounds from outside the castle walls. Two riders gallop toward the eastern gate. Olwen sounds grim.

"The Fox and the Wolf. They've come to offer terms."

Artagan abruptly awakens and joins us at the windowsill, rubbing his sleepy eyes. He spits at the sight of the two Saxon war-chiefs before drawing his sword and descending the turret steps. His raw voice echoes up the stairwell behind him.

"Terms? They want terms? My blade will show them terms!"

Olwen and I dart after him, but he already has found his horse. He leads Merlin out the smoldering east gate, his greased dark hair streaming behind him. The hot-blooded Celt! He'll get himself killed, and the two Saxon chieftains will laugh over his grave. Leaping onto my mountain pony, I bolt after him. Olwen joins us on the greens outside the walls. Grabbing Artagan's stallion by the bridle, I bring his steed to a halt.

"Put that sword away before you make things worse than they already are!"

"Worse, Branwen? Worse! How could things possibly get any worse?"

Before I can reply, both Cedric and Beowulf halt their mounts before us. They bear a white banner overhead, signaling a truce for a parley. They still have axes and swords slung across their saddles beside many a bloody scalp. I clench my jaw. Maybe Artagan is right not to trust these barbarians, even under a flag of truce. These Saxons have no honor.

I swallow hard, never having been so close to the Fox and the Wolf before. They look even more fearsome than I imagined, their cheeks flecked with dueling scars and their arms thick as tree trunks. Cedric the Fox is the shorter of the two, with a reddish tint to his ruddy beard. Beowulf the Wolf sits tall as a mountain in the saddle, his sausage-like fingers pawing his yellow beard with one hand while gripping a massive battle-ax in the other. Their eyes focus squarely on me.

Each brother makes a grim smile. How long have these two brigands hunted me? And for what dark purpose, I can only guess. If not for Artagan and his drawn blade, I doubt either Saxon would restrain himself from laying hands on me this very instant, flag of truce or no. I sidle my pony closer to Artagan's horse, trying to look calm. It was a mistake for me to have come to this parley. Cedric breaks the silence.

"Beauteous Branwen and Lovely Olwen. Blacksword, you're a lucky ram between two ewes."

Artagan raises his blade, clenching his teeth.

"Speak your piece quick before I lop off both your heads!"

Cedric and his brother laugh.

"I've a thousand men ready to storm your walls. Is it just you, the women, and children left?"

"Come and see, Saxon dogs! We'll bleed two of yours for every one of ours."

"That still leaves me victorious by day's end. But I've a less bloody alternative to offer."

"Surrender the womenfolk as slaves and leave the men to rot? I think not."

"Nay, I ask only two things. Your people swear allegiance to us, and you become our permanent guest to ensure the peace."

"You mean captive! You'd just as soon lift my head from its shoulders. That's no offer at all!"

Artagan spits at his feet. The Saxon brothers exchange dark looks. Sweat beads along my forehead. We still have an opportunity here, an opportunity that is rapidly slipping away. Bitter a draught as it seems, the Saxons have offered us a way out of death. A peace that involves neither massacre nor slavery. Olwen seems to sense my thinking too, and leans forward in the saddle.

"What if one of *us* came with you willingly, instead of Sir Artagan?"

"Like Queen Branwen perhaps?" Cedric smiles.

The blood drains from my cheeks. He planned this. The Fox and the Wolf intend to get me one way or the other. Cedric only mentioned Artagan as a bargaining chip first because he knew we would never agree to it. But why have they striven so much to take me? Perhaps they plan to barter me back to Morgan in Caerwent or to use me in order to gain the submission of Dyfed. I'm still heir to one Welsh kingdom and wedded to the warlord of another. Maybe one of these Saxon war-chiefs plans to marry me himself. A sickening sensation rises in my throat.

Artagan flexes his fingertips along the pommel of his blade. This time he really intends to take one of the war-chief's heads. I raise a palm to stop him and Artagan stares at me with wide, unbelieving eyes. He really is just a boy. He does not understand. This is the only way. I try to steady my voice as a queen ought, looking Cedric the Fox directly in his yellow eyes.

"I must confer with my people first. We need time to discuss this amongst ourselves."

"I give you one hour. If I don't receive your answer by then, you shall certainly receive mine."

Cedric bows in the saddle toward Olwen and myself before departing. Beowulf sneers at Artagan, his bass laughter lingering behind him as he rides back toward the Saxon lines. Returning to the walls of Aranrhod, I feel Artagan's gaze boring into me. Once inside the castle fortifications, we dismount. Artagan grabs me by the shoulders.

"Branwen, you can't be seriously considering their offer?"

"Artagan, don't make this any harder than it already is."

"Listen to yourself! These men killed my father and your mother. You would put yourself in their power?"

"To save those I love, yes."

Looking up into his soft blue eyes, I've given up all pretenses. By now, all eyes from the battlements are on us, but I don't care. I've been fool enough not to admit my own feelings to myself. Now, at the end, I might as well be honest with those I love most. Artagan fights the water behind his eyes, drawing me into his arms. Despite his tight grip and bulging strength, he stammers like a helpless child.

"I . . . I won't let you go!"

"Yes, you will. Because I ask you to."

Cupping my palms around his jaw, I press my lips to his. Stubble flecks his cheeks and dirt mars my own, but his mouth tastes like paradise. The two of us linger in our shared embrace, awash in our mingled kiss and the small space between our beating hearts.

Untangling my hand from his, I remount my pony and make for the gate. By now, the castle inhabitants have guessed my purpose and begin calling out to me from the bastions. "M'lady, m'lady. Don't leave us. Come back. Stay." Brave, foolhardy friends, they would fight to the death rather than surrender one, lonesome woman to the clutches of the Saxons.

I cannot look back at Artagan. One glance would be enough to break my will. Goodbye, my love. Goodbye.

Rowena and Una weep from the walls while Padraig and Ahern stand silent. Olwen cannot bear to meet my eye. Farewell, friends and rivals. My life seems to have come full circle. Once given away by my father to make peace between warring kingdoms, now I am to be the peace-weaver once more.

I prod my mare down past the shadow of Aranrhod toward the spiked helms and tall spears of the Saxon lines. May the Virgin give me strength. I clench the reins with balled fists, willing myself forward with every step. Tears stream down my cheeks.

14

Cedric crosses his arms with a smug grin. Beowulf towers behind him, thumbing his razor-sharp battle-ax. Shifting uncomfortably in the saddle, I slow my pony to a trot. Best to get this over with. Barely a hundred paces from the Saxon lines, every breath seems like agony. My entire life stretches like an endless, deserted plain before me. I shall be a Saxon prisoner for the rest of my days, probably chained to some barbarian's bed. Wiping the tears from my eyes, I hold my head up high. The Fox and the Wolf may have me in their clutches, but I am still a Welsh queen at heart.

A high bugle call rings across the valley. Brining my mare to a halt, I stand alone in the center of the field between the Saxons and the walls of Aranrhod. My eyebrows knit together. That is no Saxon horn. More bugle calls reverberate from the woods and hills, the piercing blare of bronze trumpets shaking the trees. It sounds like the Second Coming.

Cedric and Beowulf exchange frowns, their men looking every which way. Figures crowd the heights of Aranrhod, equally furtive in their glances. Whoever keeps blowing those horns, they don't hail from the Free Cantrefs either. A deep thunder rolls across the foothills, beneath a mostly clear morning sky. Dust clouds rise above the ridges to the north.

Hundreds of horsemen emerge from the woods and gallop into the open fields between the Saxons and Aranrhod. Sunshine glints off their armor, the shuffle of chain mail reverberating throughout the glens. Every warrior bears a long pike as tall as the treetops. It looks like the wood itself is moving. Black banners snap atop their lances.

My breath stops up. Only one kingdom in all Wales flies black dragon banners. Belin the Old of North Wales! But have they come to treat with us or the Saxons? As the cavalcade comes to a halt, a pair of riders canters forward in heavy armor with black horse plumes running down their helms. Rhun and Iago, Belin's sons. It must be.

Their heralds lower their brassy trumpets. Lathered horses paw the earth, snorting and whinnying. They must have ridden hard to come this far south in so short a time. Both the Saxons and the people in Aranrhod take up arms, equally uncertain what these northern horsemen intend here. Rhun and Iago trot several lengths toward the besieged castle. They raise their spears in the air.

In unison, hundreds of riders dip their banners toward the fortress. The universal signal of respect and friendship. With a sigh, I begin to breathe again. The North Welsh of Gwynedd have come to lend a hand.

I'm still alone in the open field between three separate armies. The Fox and the Wolf glare at me across the open space.

I dig my heels into the flanks of my mare and bolt back toward the castle. A roar rises from the Saxon camp behind me. Several spearheads fly past my head. All bets are off now.

With another blare of trumpets, the northern men charge down the vale toward the Saxons. The rumble of their galloping stallions shakes the earth like an avalanche. The Saxons brace themselves, making a wall of spears as the wedge of horsemen near their lines.

Rhun and Iago charge forward in the lead, but I've little time to admire them. Javelins from Cedric and Beowulf's men rush by my ears. If they can't have me, they don't intend to let anyone else have me either. The walls of Aranrhod still stand a thousand paces away. In the blink of any eye, I will soon be at the center of a storm of clashing cavalry and spears. Ride, my stout mountain pony, ride!

The crush of spears, bone, metal, and flesh rends the air with a cacophony of cries and ringing steel. A wave of North Welsh riders cuts through the Saxon ranks, leaving a swath of trampled red bodies in their wake. Daring a glance over my shoulder, I glimpse a dozen Saxons running close behind me, Cedric and Beowulf amongst them. A Saxon spear embeds itself in my pony's hindquarters. She bucks me off with a shrill cry.

I hit the ground with a heavy thud, all the breath knocked out of me. My limbs sting from the impact. My mare, Gwenhwyfar, limps in circles, braying over her crippled leg. Cedric charges me with spear and sword in hand, Beowulf and his warriors following close behind. Trying to sit up, I feel my trembling arms and legs fail to rise, still stunned from the fall. I shut my eyes as Cedric towers over me, his yellow eyes burning bright as hot coals.

A roar of voices utters a strange battle cry over the din.

"Branwen, Mab Ceridwen!"

Opening my eyes, I see Cedric falter back before me. Artagan and the surviving warriors from Aranrhod have come out from behind their walls, charging headlong into the field on foot. The green-clad Free Cantref folk cry out as they loose stones and arrows at the Saxons. "Mab Ceridwen, Mab Ceridwen!" It takes a moment to realize they're chanting for me.

The Blacksword rushes over me, slashing at Cedric with his famous long blade. In an instant, Artagan runs his sword through the Saxon's chest before raising his weapon again. He severs Cedric's skull from his shoulders. The lopped-off head of ruddy-blond hair rolls over toward me on the ground.

Cedric's blank yellow stare looks up at me from the crook of my legs. His contorted face begins to swim in my vision. I stagger to my feet, Artagan steadying me with a hand on my elbow.

"Get behind me!" he shouts.

My head bobs, heavy as a lodestone, my palms still sluggish after my fall. A wounded color-bearer collapses beside me. An emerald dragon of the Free Cantrefs does not belong in the dirt. My blood starts to pump faster.

I lift the green banner up from the crimson-stained grass. Raising the ivy flag high, I hear the Welshmen cheer as I trail close behind Artagan. Even amidst the screams and clanging shields, their battle cry pierces the air. "Mab Ceridwen, Mab Ceridwen!" More and more fallen Saxon warriors cover the grass.

A Saxon ram's horn signals their retreat. Rhun and Iago's horsemen continue to pursue them into the woods, their cavalcade trampling wounded barbarians underfoot. While I wave my bloodied, green dragon banner overhead, the Blacksword continues lifting Saxon heads beside me.

Amidst the fray, Beowulf's towering figure glares back at me. I feel the searing heat of the Wolf's hatred on my cheeks. He disappears into the wood with the last of his fleeing countrymen.

Rhun gallops toward us, his armor dented and his lance splintered in twain. Iago nurses a cut along his thigh. Artagan raises his bloodied blade in salute. Beneath the mingled black and green banners, Welshmen from both the North and the Free Cantrefs cheer together over their fallen foes. Breathing hard, it takes some time before any of us have enough breath to speak. Dark-bearded Rhun halts his limping steed.

"We heard rumors of Saxon forces along our south borders when we received one of Lady Olwen's ravens. We feared we might arrive too late."

"You are most timely and brave," I say to both brothers. "Another few moments and I would have been in the clutches of the Fox and the Wolf."

Artagan raises Cedric's yellowed head.

"Here's one Fox that'll never haunt our henhouses again."

Iago frowns. "Aye, but I fear the Wolf has gotten away."

In the distance, a few dozen Welsh cavalrymen continue to pursue the Saxons into the forest. But both sides are already spent. Half the Saxons will probably make it back across the border. Beowulf included. The other half will never leave these fields where they fell. Wiping the blood and grime from my face, I steady myself against Artagan's shoulder. He leans his head against mine, whispering in my ear.

"I thought I'd lost you."

"You'll never lose me. Not now, nor ever."

He wraps an arm around me as Keenan and Emryus join us. The women and children of Aranrhod filter out the gates onto the field, nursing the wounded and embracing the victors. Young women kiss strangers while children pet the horses of the North Welshmen who rode to our aid. My skin buzzes from my toes to my fingertips. It feels so good to be alive! Wrapping my arms around Artagan's neck, I press my lips to his. Only when Rhun clears his throat do I remember we're not alone.

"It was bold of you to advance out of your walls, Sir Artagan."

"It was bold of you to come to our aid, Prince Rhun. We could not have won without you."

"My father would've come himself, but age prevents him. We may come from different kingdoms, but we're all Welsh and I'd rather see a Welshman rule the Free Cantrefs than a Saxon."

Artagan nods solemnly.

"Alas, the Saxons slew my father. We are without a king now."

Rhun and Iago exchange looks.

"Our condolences, Sir Artagan. Or *King* Artagan, I should say. You were Cadwallon's eldest."

Artagan blinks, glancing my way. Ever the merry-making hedge knight, I can see that the thought of kingship has never crossed his mind. Nor mine for that matter. My goodness, who would've ever imagined the Blacksword wearing a crown? Artagan shakes his head.

"My father never named an heir. He had many bastards besides me. We follow the Old Welsh Law here, where land is divided equally amongst all a man's sons, not just his eldest."

"That may be so," Rhun replies. "But it looks to me as though you've already won an inheritance here at Aranrhod. You have many loyal subjects."

"Queen Branwen led us to Aranrhod. If this victory belongs to anyone, it is her."

He squeezes my hand. Victory. The word has a strange taste on the lips. We saved our people and repulsed the Saxons, but I cannot resist my own selfish impulse. To stand here holding Artagan's hand, alive and well, means more to me than all the treasures under the earth. All the petty trivialities I fretted about before have fallen away from me. I nearly let the Saxons make me a slave for life. How quickly life can change in an instant.

Rowena and Una come down the slopes of Aranrhod. Rushing to greet them, their long faces stop me in my tracks. Something is wrong.

Behind them, Ahern marches down the grass with a limp corpse in his arms. My cheeks suddenly turn cold as death. My kinsman halts in front of me, his beard tinged with teardrops. In his strong arms, Padraig lies still and pale. A large scarlet wound runs down his side, bloodied by a Saxon spear. My lip trembles as I touch the Abbot's cold hand. I sink to my knees, unable to restrain my sobs. He sleeps with the angels now.

We bury Padraig in a mound beside King Cadwallon. Small piles of over-turned earth mark fresh graves along the western mountains where the people have collected our dead. The Saxon bodies we pile into a deep pit and set ablaze. Artagan holds me close as the smoke wafts over the barrows of his father and the Abbot. Padraig was like a father, at least in all the ways that matter. My own blood-sire wants me dead or living as a slave-wife to the Hammer King. Padraig gave me the gift of books and taught me that the loving voice in my heart was God. Hanging my head, I bury my sobs against Artagan's chest. My guide, my holy father, now Padraig is gone forever.

Nearby, Annwyn stares at Cadwallon's burial mound, her face a stony mask. Yet I sense an inner turmoil behind her wavering azure gaze. Long ago, Cadwallon was her lover, and although Artagan's parents never wed, surely some tender feelings still lingered between them. But now Cadwallon is dead, one of many souls now lost to us. I move to comfort Annwyn, but Artagan waves me off. Some folk deal with their grief bet-ter alone, and so we leave the old enchantress to her own thoughts as Artagan and I walk arm in arm toward the castle.

Planning the victory festivities has taken a toll on my hours of sleep. Rowena and Una scurry beside me, polishing stone floors and chipped tables that have gone to rot over the last hundred years. But God bless them. In a few days, we've resurrected this ancient ruin from the dead. Aranrhod seems like a castle fit for habitation once more.

I force a smile during the feast, still unable to fathom a world without Padraig. But I am not the only one to have lost someone dear to me. Artagan makes merry with his men, drinking from mead horns and jugs of fresh cider, even while his own father and loved ones now lie buried in the ground. Drowning himself in drink, Artagan mourns in his own way. I put on a cordial face for the sake of our people, who need mirth and merriment now more than ever. But my red eyes betray the tears shed over my prayers every night.

Scarce a soul inside Aranrhod hasn't lost someone dear to them. How selfish of me to wallow in my own misery when so many have had to bury kin, lovers, and friends. Preferring to bury myself in work, I bustle about the castle, attending to all the details of the feast. After centuries of silence, the main hall of Aranrhod echoes once more with laughter and turns bright under the warm glow of hearth fires.

In the main hall, I order the long tables to be arranged in a great circle. This way no lord or chieftain will feel slighted for having a place too near or too far from the head table. Much like Queen Guinevere's idea of a Round Table in Arthur's time. Although I draw inspiration from the past, I do not delude myself enough to believe that the glory days of our grandsires have returned. The Free Cantref folk and Northern Welsh are brave and true, but our disorganized rabble are a far cry from the Arthurian knights of legend. We do not even have a king to unite us.

Some of our most honored guests sit at my table, Princes Rhun and Iago, and of course Artagan. Lady Olwen joins us, smirking my way as Rhun offers her a seat between us. I smile cordially back at her. Her lavender gown shimmers by firelight. My own emerald mantle suits me well enough, one of the few pieces of clothes my serving girls smuggled out of Caerwent when they departed. Most members of the feast don skins and woolens. The Free Cantrefs may remain free, but they are still a poor people.

Emryus and Keenan stoke the hearth fires as the evening mists roll in outside. These hardened warriors grin like boys as they roast pigs over spits. With foodstuffs at a premium, nearly all the fare at our feast consists of wild game. Boar, stag, and geese sizzle over the crackling flames. I eat as best I can, but soon put down a half-gnawed bone. I'd give every silk in my clothes chest to have Abbot Padraig sharing tonight's meal with us.

Artagan rejoins us at our table, chewing on a haunch of stag meat. He banters with Rhun, Iago, and Olwen awhile. My mind wanders distractedly, thinking about Padraig. But something Rhun says perks my ears.

"With no king in this part of Wales now, my father Belin would willingly offer his protection to these people and its lands."

Olwen flashes her teeth in a not entirely friendly manner.

"And place half the Free Cantrefs under North Wales's rule? My father, King Urien, is the highest-ranking monarch in the Free Cantrefs now. Surely the people here would rather fall under his reign."

"If Urien lives out the year," Iago mumbles. "He's older than our own sire."

Olwen throws Iago a piercing stare, so unlike her usual demeanor. Artagan tries to smooth things over, drawing the subject onto more convivial things like the delicious venison on the table. If I could not eat much before, I now find my appetite gone entirely.

Suddenly, Rhun and Iago's rushing to our rescue becomes painfully clear. Not any simple do-gooders, they came at the behest of their father, intent on securing more lands for his northern kingdom. Belin the Old never does anything without expecting something in return. Meanwhile, Olwen hopes to secure these lands for her own kin, even though they never set foot here. Even in victory, our own fratricidal Welsh politics threaten to defeat us as much as Saxon blades. Without looking at anyone in particular, I raise my voice loud enough for all at the table to hear.

"These were Cadwallon's people and they are a free, independent lot. They will never follow someone who isn't one of their own. Not Saxon, nor even North or South Welsh."

All eyes turn on me, even some members of nearby tables putting down their table knives and plates to listen. Some of the Northern Welsh guests shift uncomfortably in their chairs. Rhun turns toward me, looking past Olwen.

"Who would you have rule here, Lady Branwen? Perhaps some of your Dyfed kin?"

"Nay. You said it yourself after the battle, Prince Rhun. Someone has already carved out a new kingdom here at Aranrhod. Someone who defended the people when no one else would, someone who has always fought for their welfare and enjoyed their loyalty and support. Someone of Cadwallon's line. Artagan Blacksword should be king."

This last pronouncement garners silence from the rest of the hall. Have I overstepped my bounds? My cheeks redden somewhat, but I stand and take Artagan's arm by the wrist, raising it up. In this mad world of wars and spies, I cannot feel shame for speaking the truth. Or common sense. Artagan is the best man to lead these people. The best man in many respects. He has more goodness and honor in him than any man I've ever met, so why can't I simply put that into words? When I say no more, Keenan steps forward to join me. He bends his knee before the Blacksword.

"By my life or death, I pledge my fealty to the man who led us at Aranrhod. Where you lead, I will follow."

Several men in green second Keenan's words with hearty "aye-ayes." Emryus takes a knee before Artagan, just like Keenan. Enid joins them. One by one, every Free Cantref man, woman, and child in the room takes a knee. Milkmaids I knew from Cadwallon's Keep, mothers who defended their children during the siege at Aranrhod, and spearmen who served in Artagan's company since before he was a knight. Even Ahern, Rowena, and Una bow before the Blacksword. I raise an eyebrow, but say nothing as I stifle a smile of surprise. When I move to bow myself, Artagan grasps me by the wrist in turn. He actually looks wide-eyed with apprehension.

"Not you too," he whispers. "You got me into this. You best stand with me now."

Lady Annwyn joins us and raises Artagan's other arm, her powerful voice carrying outside the hall to the throngs in the courtyard.

"All hail, King Artagan! Lord of Aranrhod, shield of his people!"

Cheers erupt from both within the chamber and without, the applause booming off the rafters. Some of the North Welshmen exchange looks, but clap politely with the rest. Lady Olwen plants a kiss on Artagan's cheek. Heat rises through my veins. She is still his betrothed. Have I just made her a queen as well? She certainly seems to think so. In my haste to support Artagan, it never occurred to me that I might be playing into her hand.

I sink back into the shadows as others rise to clap Artagan on the back and congratulate him. Lady Olwen hovers close by his side. I hang my head. Olwen and the Blacksword make a powerful match. Although I'd rather crawl over hot coals, I must admit it. Wedding Olwen would be the kingly thing to do. With her House allied to his, Artagan might someday unite all the Free Cantrefs under his sway, not just Aranrhod.

No nobleman in Christendom could resist bedding a woman both beautiful and well landed in fortune.

Artagan glances my way, searching for me in the crowd. I cannot face him. Swallowing the lump in my throat, I slip out of the main chamber and down a quiet corridor. I lay my forehead against the cool stone walls. Stupid girl! I've lost him forever. By my own hand I've put an end to my own happiness. Lingering in the hallway beside a guttering torch, I pound my fist into the stone bulwarks. Footsteps shuffle down the corridor.

"My lady, have I intruded upon you at an ill time?"

Rhun stands in the archway, his tall figure nearly touching the low ceiling. He politely takes my hand and kisses it. I fake a smile, something I seem to do more often these days.

"What can I do for you, brave Prince?"

"That was a bold thing you did back there. Not many women or men hold enough sway to make a king with a few simple words. Yet you seem troubled."

"These are trying times. A dear friend and companion of mine fell during the siege."

"You have my deepest sympathies, my lady."

He bows, placing a hand over his heart. His high cheekbones and trimmed beard cut a dashing figure. Not since we first met at Morgan's court has he ever spoken to me in private before. Why has he cornered me here in a lone corridor? He did not come just to banter about Artagan's impromptu coronation.

"You've something on your mind, Prince."

"You're as perceptive as you are beautiful, Lady Branwen. I confess, I did not ride to Aranrhod's rescue merely to fight Saxons. I came to ask for your hand in marriage."

I glance up at him with a start. Perhaps I heard wrong. His deep brown eyes search mine. Feigning something in my eye, I look away.

"My lord, I am flattered, but I need time . . . time to . . ."

He smiles, taking my hands in his.

"I know you have an eye for the Blacksword. What woman does not? But I am not a jealous man. As I understand it, he is already betrothed to Lady Olwen."

My cheeks burn hot, but I cannot look away with him standing so close. He cuts me to the quick with his words. With Olwen as Artagan's queen, there will certainly be no place for me here at Aranrhod. These people whom I have come to love and care for will be the ward of another queen, their beloved Blacksword the bedfellow of another woman. Rhun rubs my palm with his fingertips.

"Morgan treated you ill. You were right to run away from that life. But you've no nobleman to shelter you, no one strong enough to protect you from Morgan's wrath, and believe me, he will come for you again. You need someone to look after you, someone with as many strongholds and soldiers as your former husband."

"Why do you wish to wed me? I've nothing. I'm merely a runaway queen."

"You command the respect of the people, not only here, but across all Wales. Word of your good deeds has spread. The commoners love you. And you're still the only heir to the kingdom of Dyfed. Joining our two houses would bring peace between the northern and southern Welsh Lands, a peace that has not been seen since the days of Arthur."

So that's it. Belin the Old was wise to send his eldest son to come courting me. With one stroke, he would have the sympathy of the Free Cantrefs and the loyalty of Dyfed.

And my father's no fool either. Upon hearing word of my betrothal to Rhun, he would gladly switch sides in an alliance with King Belin. With their combined forces, they would equal Morgan's strength in the South. It would seem preposterous if it wasn't so true. Simply by putting a ring on my finger, Rhun would make his father effective ruler of half of Wales, with the other half likely to follow sooner or later. Morgan hasn't been the only one with designs on uniting all of Wales. Apparently, the wily Old King Belin has been plotting the same thing from his castles in the North.

Rhun combs back a stray lock of my hair with his hand, looking deeply into my eyes. I'd be a fool to refuse his offer. His father's armies and lands would keep me safe from Morgan. I'd certainly live in more luxury than I've had since fleeing to the Free Cantrefs. But am I simply trading one warlord husband for another? What do I know of Rhun?

Little more than I did of King Morgan when we first wed. I'll not be a broodmare again. Never. Rhun senses my indecision.

"I'm a patient man, Branwen. Think over my offer. I ride for home on the morrow. You can tell me your answer then."

He presses his lips to my knuckles once more, bowing before he leaves. Rowena finds me in the hallway while toting a fresh jug of cider close to her chest. I stare blankly past her, still absorbed by the full weight of the decision I must make.

"M'lady, are you well?"

"Prince Rhun has just asked me to be his wife."

Rowena raises both eyebrows, flashing a timid smile. She knows to whom my heart belongs, but she also knows the political realities of the age in which we live. She tries to make the best of it.

"Congratulations, m'lady. Do we leave for North Wales then?"

Still in a daze, I cannot find the words to answer her. Wandering the empty hallways, the boisterous revelry from the main hall reverberates throughout the bones of the castle. Retiring to my empty tower, I lean against the windowsill overlooking the valley. Bonfires dot the night, the survivors of the siege celebrating their newfound home and king. Many are undoubtedly happy just to be alive. With so much suffering, the people deserve a respite from all their grief.

Putting my chin in my hand, I breathe in the smoky peat fires and the wet fog coming down from the mountains. How straightforward the villagers' lives seem, despite all their hardships. Free to love whom they wish, to farm or hunt as their vocation demands, to keep their loved ones close to them all of their days. Queen or no, with Padraig gone, I am all but an orphan in this world. A world in which men only look at me based on what I'm worth, and how much land comes with my dowry. My eyelids begin to sag. Perhaps I've been unfair to think such thoughts. I'm tired and spent.

Footsteps murmur up the stairwell behind me. I know the sound of that brisk tread without even having to turn around. Artagan pauses in the chamber doorway. A cool evening breeze brushes my cheek as I keep my gaze to the window.

"How's your newfound queen, Lady Olwen? Neither she nor your people should be without their king on his coronation night."

"Branwen, why did you run off? One moment, you're declaring me the next King Arthur, and the next you've vanished."

Lowering my gaze, I still do not look at him.

"Prince Rhun proposed to me this evening."

"What?"

"He expects my answer in the morning. I suppose you'll wed Olwen soon enough yourself."

Artagan grabs me by the wrist, spinning me around to face him. Clenching my teeth, I push back against him. King or no, I'll not let some hedge knight manhandle me. I drub my fists against his chest, but he refuses to let me go. His knit brows and pursed lips nearly touch mine, his voice rough as gravel.

"My father arranged my betrothal to Olwen. But I'm king now and I'll do as I please!"

"No king can do as he pleases! You've a duty to your people now, to make the best match for their sake, not yours."

"Then I renounce my throne! You made me king. You want the crown so badly, you take it!"

"Don't be absurd!"

"I don't want to be king . . . I want you."

He releases my arms. His deep blue eyes search mine. Rubbing my wrists, I stand close enough to feel his breath on my lashes. Why does he ask the impossible of me? My heart and mind tell me two different things. Lowering my head, I swallow the knot in my throat.

"It's a good match, wedding Olwen. It will bring peace and stability to your kingdom, to all the Free Cantrefs. It's the right thing to do."

"And you wedding Rhun is supposed to solve everything? The people here need you."

"Whoever weds me will have a war on his hands! Morgan will never give me up!"

"I already have a war with the Saxons. I'm not afraid of the Hammer King."

"Then you are a fool."

"Do you care nothing for me?"

"Artagan . . ."

Biting my lip, I lose my voice when I look up into his flickering azure stare. I should lie. With all of my strength, I should tell him I care nothing for him, and send him out of my life forever. Instead, I let him kiss me. Surrendering to his touch, we hold one another beside the dark archway of the window. Artagan lowers himself down on one knee, taking my hands in his. His lip trembles before he steadies his voice.

"I love you, Branwen. I always have, and I always will. Be my bride. Be my Queen. Be my wife."

Pressing my lips tight together, I squeeze his hands in mine. Never have I wanted something more, to share my days with this carefree hedge knight. Together we've wandered the wilds, defied kings, and faced life and death side by side. If only the world of kings and Saxons would leave us alone. The two of us could be happy in a small cottage bower with no more than some thatch over our heads and warm woolens for a bed. I heave a heavy sigh as Artagan looks up at me with expectant, loving eyes. If only he understood. My heart rises in my throat because I know what my answer must be.

15

The North Welsh horsemen depart before dawn. Not a good sign. Word must have reached them during the night. Faint dust trails hang over the northern mountain passes as the rear guard of their cavalcade disappears in the distance.

Olwen's and Artagan's voices reverberate through the castle walls. Half the citadel must hear them. Crockery and pots clatter to the floor behind their closed door. The sun rises over my bedchamber in the opposite tower as I listen and wait. Olwen's tone raises the hairs along the nape of my neck.

"You bog-brained, black-hearted, no-good, lying dog! You made me a promise, Blacksword!"

"Our fathers made a promise, not me! Damn it, Olwen, don't act so surprised!"

With a grunt, Olwen hurls something metallic across the chamber. Artagan curses, no doubt ducking. Whatever kitchen implement she tosses his way clangs about the floor. Her raised voice scares a murder of crows from the tower rooftop.

"She's a trollop, Artagan! Her own father disowned her and her last husband will bleed half of Wales dry just to get her back! You'll be dead or a cuckold or *both* within a year, mark my words."

A door slams. Olwen emerges at the foot of the stairs, glaring up at my tower. Even from the shadows of my windowsill, her violet stare feels like frost in my veins. Her snowy-white mare whinnies before Olwen darts out the eastern gates at full gallop. Her figure diminishes in the distance. A weight lifts from my chest, but a shadow still gnaws at the back of my mind. What if her words come true? Have I signed Artagan's death warrant and mine own? I cross myself, praying to both the Virgin and Abbot Padraig up in heaven. Help me, please. Help us all.

Artagan saunters into my chamber, rubbing the back of his head.

"Well, that's over and done with."

"I fear we've made more enemies than friends."

"King Belin and Urien aren't our enemies. But they won't ride to our aid anytime soon."

He shrugs it off, wrapping his arms around me as though we hadn't a care in the world. Pressing my ear to his chest, his heartbeat stills my nerves. But a few lingering splinters stick in my mind. Belin's sons and Olwen will not forget the turn we gave them this day.

Outside, Keenan's and Emryus's voices boom off the archways.

"Hark, all welcome to attend the marriage of King Artagan and Queen Branwen, sovereigns of Aranrhod! Cider and mead for all!"

The two warriors slur their words, stumbling slightly and already well into their cups. I cannot help but smile as the two men raise their drinking horns up toward our tower window. Artagan rubs my chin with his thumb and kisses my brow. I sigh, letting all the tension out of my limbs. Lovebirds tweet from a nest in the tower eaves.

We gather for the ceremony in a small roofless chapel amidst the ruins of the eastern wall. Archways overgrown with ivy and honeysuckle blossom with wildflowers. A few puffy clouds dot an otherwise clear summer sky overhead. Although only a few dozen of us fit inside the shell of the old church, the murmur of crowds attests to the throngs outside. Gray-bearded Emryus strums a tune on his harp as I walk down the aisle in an emerald gown with lavender trim, the last of my old wardrobe from Caerwent. Artagan beams from the altar, his mother beside him with her arms upraised. An old priestess, inside an ancient chapel, wedding two Christian souls. I could laugh at the madness of it all, but it will do. All will be right in God's eyes, or so my heart says. Such is the voice Abbot Padraig always told me to follow.

Rowena and Una hold the train of my gown before retreating to the corner, exchanging sly glances with Keenan. I playfully roll my eyes. Many children will doubtlessly be sired in the revelries later tonight. Ahern and Enid cross spears with several warriors overhead. My half brother gives me a nod, ever the stoic soldier. Enid casts longing glances Artagan's way. As always, my beloved man is oblivious to the spear-wife's pining eyes. Poor thing. Perhaps God will grant her happiness someday with some other man. Perhaps.

Artagan takes my hand as we stand before the worn stone cross, overgrown with clover. Annwyn waves her arms over us, murmuring in the Old Tongue as she sprinkles us with water. If Padraig were here, he would have wed us himself, but the old priestess's ritual still seems oddly Christian. Blessed with holy water, we wrap a cloth around our wrists, bound and tied in a knot. Whatever Annwyn consecrates, in whatever tongue or religion, I know it carries the blessings of the divine. She finishes with a wand, making a sacred sign in the earth before smiling at us.

"You may now kiss one another."

Artagan cups my cheeks in his palms, his warm lips on mine. Smiling through our kisses, our audience hoots with approval. I thank God with a silent prayer. In the year of our Lord 598, I am finally married to the man who has truly earned and won my heart.

We march outside the chapel hand in hand and greet the people outside. Keenan bellows on a large ox horn, garnering cheers from the crowds as Artagan and I wave. A calfskin drum and minstrel pipes murmur through the vale, the villagers breaking into dance and drink. I smile so much my cheeks hurt.

Now this feels like a real victory feast. No more looking back at the sorrows of the past, but instead focusing on the bright future that lies ahead.

Artagan lifts me into his arms as we cross the threshold of our tower. He grins while I pepper his neck with kisses. Artagan scales the steps two at a time with me still in his arms, lifting me as though I weighed no more than a feather. He kicks open the door atop the stairwell. The scent of candles and incense permeates the chamber.

"What's this?" I ask as he puts me down.

"Our new home. Una and Rowena helped put it together."

A warm fire crackles in a brazier, casting a bronze glow across a makeshift bed of furs and woolens. My birch longbow hangs on one wall and a shelf with several books lines the other. Rushing toward the bookshelf, I thumb through the half dozen tomes. Classics, scripture, and legends all on vellum sheets bound by hardback. I recognize these stories. They're Brother Padraig's books from the abbey in Dyfed. He must have still had them on his person when we fled to Aranrhod. Each book took generations of clerics to ink, their heavy pages worth their weight in gold.

Even my book of the tales of Branwen the Brave is here. I fondly pet the spine of the book Padraig once gave to me. Another token from the man I loved as a father. For the first time since his passing, I can recall fond memories of my teacher without sorrow. His words and his legacy live on in these books and in me.

Artagan shuts the door behind us.

"I could think of no better place for the start of our castle library than by your bedside."

"It's wonderful—the books, the room, all of it."

"Maybe you could continue teaching me my letters."

"Is that how you wish to spend your wedding night, King?"

I flash a wry smile. Artagan loosens his tunic, dropping his mantle and shirt to the floor. In a few quick strides, he has me in his arms. The sap begins to rise behind his deep blue eyes. Pressing my mouth to his, I cannot get my own clothes off fast enough. We've put this off for far too long. How many evenings did we share a bed of wild rushes or a stone floor? Never doing more than cuddling for warmth. His lips travel down my blouse, nuzzling between my breasts. I pull him down onto our soft bedspread, running my palms along the hardened muscles of his back and thighs. Every stretch of skin toned and pulsating with life.

The rhythm of drums and pipes fills the dusk air outside, the music drifting up into our torch-lit lair. Artagan's manhood rises against the inside of my smooth legs, his fingertips in my hair and his kisses on my neck. I grasp his firm, clenched buttocks as he moves inside me, his hardened nipples brushing mine. Our mingled breath warms our cheeks as we move to the quick tempo of the drumbeat. Awash in the touch and taste of his flesh, I gasp.

"Artagan . . . *Artagan,* my love."

We move faster, my palms pressing against his hard abdomen. His hands cup my bosom. He arches atop me, his heat spilling inside me. I pant harder, clasping him tight as my core peaks under his feverish thrusts. Still short of breath, we gaze into one another's eyes, two pools of liquid love entranced with one another. I reach up and kiss him again and again, reveling in his love inside me. The first of many such times we shall enjoy one another tonight.

"No, no, more to the left."

I wave with half-feigned exasperation at the stonemasons. Workmen hoist large blocks of limestone from wooden rollers. The clank of hammers and chisels reverberates throughout the castle. Day by day, over the past few months, the towers and walls of Aranrhod have risen once again with the construction of stone buttresses and timber scaffolds. With a sketch in hand, I direct the laborers as they aright fallen columns and bulwarks neglected since the days of the Romans. Teams of lumbermen hack away at logs in the courtyard whilst carpenters plane wood for the new gates. Artagan folds his arms and shakes his head with astonishment.

"I've never seen such dedication in artisans before. The people must truly adore you."

"They labor for themselves as much as they do for us. This castle provides defense for them and their families in times of need. The granaries will safeguard their grain stores, and the smithies provide fresh forges for their tools."

"An allotment of land for each worker sweetens the pot too, no doubt."

"I don't expect them to work for nothing. No one has claimed the lands around Aranrhod for generations. Now we can settle crofters, herders, and huntsmen on parcels where good soil has rested untilled for years. Autumn should bring forth a good harvest."

"If we last that long. We had another skirmish in the south passes this morn."

Artagan's gaze darkens. My skin grows cold, as though a cloud had suddenly blotted out the sun. Steeling my nerves, I try to put on a brave face. It pinches my heart to see darkness in Artagan's normally sunny countenance. I speak low enough for only the two of us to hear.

"How many this time?"

"We lost two dozen men, but gave the bastards as good as we got. That's twice in the last fortnight. Morgan's raids grow more and more frequent."

"It's the summer season, the war season. Your merry men are no strangers to a tough fight."

"I've barely a hundred warriors left. The rest work on the castle or still recover from wounds after the Saxon siege. One day, Morgan will come over those mountain passes and I won't have enough men to stop him. It's only a matter of time, Branwen."

Sighing, I look back at the reconstruction of the fortress. Like so many ants, dozens of craftsmen move about the masonry and timberworks. If only we had more time or more men, or both. Ironically, the very Saxons who besieged us are probably all that keep Morgan's army from launching a full-scale invasion against us. Barbarians will harass Morgan's eastern borders this time of year, like so many gnats coming out in the summer heat. The Hammer King will have half his troops occupied defending his own settlements until the winter freeze, still many moons away.

Artagan's green-clad bowmen have bought us time by guarding the mountain passes, but even the best warriors cannot hold out forever against overwhelming odds. If Morgan's troops pierce the mountains and surround our fortress, we'll be done for. We cannot afford another siege so soon. The reinforced walls might protect us for a time, but our newly planted wheat and oats need time to ripen and flourish. A poor harvest will spell famine come wintertime.

A patchwork of green fields dots the open meadows amidst the woods that surround our emerald vale. I shut my eyes and say a quick prayer. God preserve us, God give us the time to grow strong once again.

Wrapping my arms around Artagan's neck, I lay my forehead against his. Fresh nicks mar his forearms, and he walks with a slight limp. How close did a Southron warrior come to wounding him today? Gaining a kingship has done nothing to curb his willful, hedge knight ways. He still leads every sortie against our foes, earning the love of his men, but making himself an easy target for our numerous foes. The thought of his steed returning empty haunts my steps every time he rides away. Courage makes Artagan an attractive lover, but it only adds lines to my face now. Why won't Morgan simply leave us alone? Artagan deserves to grow old with a loving wife, warm and safe in this happy valley tucked away in the highland fastness. I will remind him of all the goodness in the world to-night in our bedchamber. Flashing a half-grin, I take him by the hand as we retreat to our tower.

At the foot of the turret steps, a voice calls out to us. Enid storms the catwalk toward us, her spear stained crimson. I pause, my shoulders sink-ing. My foray into the bedchamber with my husband will have to wait, it seems. It's still daylight and the demands on a king and queen are many. Enid halts before Artagan, still muddy from the field.

"How many times must this happen before you'll heed my words? We need the beacons!"

"It hasn't been done in a hundred years," Artagan scoffs. "Who will man them? *You?*"

I raise an eyebrow. What on earth do they bicker about? Enid seems to find many a reason to argue with Artagan since he took my hand in marriage. She doesn't even look my way. Her tone toward her new king makes me bristle a touch, but then again Enid has fought by Artagan's side a long time and she is doubtlessly accustomed to snapping at him as she might an older brother. I step between the two of them, trying to shelter my exhausted husband.

"What are you two squabbling about? It's been a long day. Can't this wait until tomorrow?"

"It can always wait." Enid frowns, still glaring at Artagan. "We'll wait until it's too late."

Artagan sighs and looks my way, at least trying to answer my ques-tion.

"She wants to relight the beacons in the hills. In days of yore, the people set watchmen in the passes, each outpost with a large tinder pile ready to light at a moment's notice in times of danger."

"A chain of far-apart beacons can spread word of an enemy faster than horses," Enid interrupts. "If we set up new beacons in the hills, we would have better warning when foes come calling."

Artagan shakes his head.

"Unless there's a fog. Or no one left to man the beacons at all! I won't ask good men to sit and rot in the high mountain gaps just so I can sleep better at night in a snug, warm castle."

Enid stamps the butt of her spear hard against the floor.

"Then you're a fool, and no king at that! We've been lucky so far, but it's only a matter of time before Morgan's men slip past our nets and march on our gates. Beacons would give us early warning."

"I may be a fool, but I am King, huntress! And my word stands. The answer is *no*!"

Enid spins on her heel, stalking off in a huff. I rub Artagan's tense shoulders, his muscles tight as knotty roots under my fingertips. He sulks like an angry bear as we ascend to our solar. The Blacksword pours himself a tall goblet of wine and sinks down in a cushioned chair beside the flickering hearth. After he has endured a hard day's ride and a sharp fight with Morgan's men, I know better than to broach any serious topics with him.

Brave and truehearted, my Artagan can still easily forsake reason once he has exhausted his body. Loath though I am to admit it, Enid has a point. A wise ruler would take her advice to heart. Bonfire beacons may be just what our kingdom needs, but our new king does not want to hear it. He would not wish to guard a frozen outpost in the high summits and so he will not ask any of his warriors to. It makes him a worthy war-captain, but not a smart monarch. Sometimes a king must learn to send men to difficult fates for the greater good of his realm.

Trying to make small talk, I break bread at our table. Food always brings Artagan around sooner or later. He slices mouthfuls of cheese while I pour him some fresh wine.

"We're short of clerics here," I comment. "But several village women tell me they wish to become nuns."

"Probably promises they made to God if we ever survived the siege."

Artagan laughs between bites. I simply shrug. Some of these poor farm girls probably suffered much at the hands of the Saxons. Who could blame them for wishing to rid themselves of the world of men? I take a swig of wine myself.

"I put them to work, making copies of the few books we have."

"You're teaching them to read as well? Already a queen, do you plan to become an abbess too?" he gibes.

"I enjoy the fruits of this earth far too much to forsake them, dear husband."

Pinching his thigh with my hand, we exchange grins. Artagan has gotten much better at his letters, but he'll never make a scholar. He has a knack for remembering stories, reciting the words in each book more from memory rather than by deciphering the Latin script. What a bard he might have been, but he could never be a man of the cloth. Thank heaven.

I laugh to myself, trying to picture Artagan with a shaven head, repressing his manly urges behind a Bible. Ha! A monk's habit would fit him as well as ostrich feathers. Padraig would've rapped his knuckles with a stick if ever he had the Blacksword for a pupil. But that kind monk never struck me once. Always, his round face lit up when we read together at his abbey by the sea. Pressing my lips together, I look away as my eyes water. If ever we have enough tomes to fill a proper library at Aranrhod, I'll name it after St. Patrick. Abbot Padraig's patron saint. He would have liked that.

Downing a bowl of soup, I have to remind myself that life is for the living. Despite all those dear ones we've lost in days gone by, we do them no honor by brooding over the shades of the past. Carpe diem, as the Abbot's books would say.

At nightfall, I kick off my shoes and pull Artagan down to the bed. Our lips meet as I run my hands through his tousled hair, his fingers eagerly pulling the laces from my gown. I grin with feigned exasperation at the vigor with which my husband nearly rips our clothes to the floor. He has all the impatience of a stallion in season, his manhood already brimming wet. I put a soft palm to his chest and give him a lengthy kiss to ease his pace. He calms slightly, his heart still racing beneath his muscled chest. His strong arms lift my hips up onto his lap as we sit atop the bedsheets, our bare legs wrapped around one another. His lips travel down my bosom as I surrender to his rising heat.

Afterward, Artagan falls fast asleep, his chest rising and falling in his slumber beside me. Spooning beside him, I watch over him in the moonlight. Crickets chirp outside our window in the warm summer air. Exhausted, he looks peaceful as a cherub in his sleep. Caressing his brow, I plant a kiss on his cheek. How long can this bliss last? Finally having found the right husband, my former husband still hunts for me. In another two moons I'll be eighteen. God, that these evenings together might last forever. I almost don't want morning to come.

When I awake, the covers beside me feel cold. Sitting up, my heart begins to race. Artagan has gone. A rooster crows from the courtyard as the first rays of light pierce my tower window. Wrapping a shawl about my shoulders, I pad barefoot across the chamber. The cool morning air chills my skin. Rowena and Una enter my chamber, toting basketfuls of fresh bread. Splashing my face in the washbasin, I turn to Rowena for a towel.

"Where is my husband?"

"King Artagan's in the yard, m'lady. Inspecting his knights."

"Knights?"

"Yes, Your Grace. He gave his best warriors knighthoods today, Sir Emryus and Sir Keenan."

Rowena smiles. Her lover, Keenan, has risen in the world. A knighthood! I suppose as a king, Artagan has the right to grant titles of nobility as much as the next monarch. Una pours my bathwater in a large vat, steam clouding her face.

"And Sir Ahern," Una adds. "The King has made him seneschal of the castle."

"My brother, Ahern? Knight and seneschal of Aranrhod?"

Una nods. My dutiful half brother, although born on the wrong side of the blanket, has risen to the rank of a knight and seneschal of a castle. I smile to myself. He will make a superb castellan. It's quite an honor for Artagan to put my kinsman in charge of the castle guards and the bastion's defenses. Artagan did not even tell me. Perhaps he meant it as a surprise. I will do my best to feign happy shock when he breaks the news to me. It's not every day a woman's brother becomes both a knight and a majordomo. I furrow my brow, questioning my serving girls.

"Who will be my personal guard then I wonder?"

Both girls exchange looks before Rowena answers.

"Enid the Spear-wife, m'lady."

I grimace before they both look away. Perhaps it's time I learn to better wield my bow. Enid hasn't voluntarily guarded me since before I wed Artagan. I slip into the hot waters of my tub, barely noticing the heat seeping into my flesh. My mind churns. Time enough I learn to properly defend myself.

After my bath, I dress in a tight-fitting doeskin tunic and boots. Upon opening my chamber door, I find Enid already at her post. She has her back to me as she guards the turret stairs. Stringing my birch wood longbow, I nod politely toward her before marching down the stairwell. She trails after me without a word, both Rowena and Una accompanying us as we exit the castle gates.

Una and Rowena set up a target on the greens beneath the western wall. Setting my quiver down, I take my time notching my arrow to the bowstring. No need to rush. Wouldn't want to miss too terribly, what with the spear-wife herself watching. I suppose some pressure is good. I certainly didn't feel calm when the Saxons besieged our walls. My bow shot missed one barbarian, and if not for Enid, I probably would have had my head split in twain. Next time, I may not be so lucky.

My arrow lands on the edge of the leather target with a thud. Rowena and Una offer encouragement as I string another arrow. The steady thump of my feathery darts hits the calfskin. Enid keeps her gaze to the woods, saying nothing. My last bow shot veers astray, glancing off the stone ramparts.

Enid flashes a half-grin. I must seem quite the novice to a veteran like her. Retrieving my arrow shafts, I begin again. I inwardly vow to practice until my fingers blister. Let Enid see that I'm not just some pincushion queen. *Thump, thump, thump.* I loose my arrows faster, drawing the string back as far as I can. My shots dig deep into the calfskin target. Grunting with effort, I shoot arrows hard enough to pierce armor.

After working up a sweat all morning at my bow work, we return to my tower solar. Enid remains on watch outside the stairwell while my ladies-in-waiting busy about their chores in my bedchamber. I put down my longbow, my fingertips already sore and starting to callous over, yet the pain in my hand fills me with pride. Another few weeks and my hand should toughen enough so that I won't even feel the sting of the drawstring.

Rowena and Una look up from behind the table, sweeping the floors and cleaning crockery. They exchange grins. My temples throb. I hold a hand to my head before I snap at them.

"What could you two possibly find so amusing?"

"Can you not guess, m'lady?" Rowena replies.

"You're a touch moody of late, your ladyship," Una smiles. "Far more cross of late than usual."

"Am I?"

I did not realize I was more testy than usual. Is it so obvious that I want to impress Enid, yet am frustrated by her long silences? Una and Rowena snicker like village girls. Rowena in particular fights to control her bubbling giggles.

"When did you last have your courses, Your Grace?"

I blanch from head to foot, my eyes widening. Looking down, I flatten the wrinkles out of my tunic, resting my palms along my abdomen. Both girls stifle their chuckles. How many moons has it been? At least three. By the Virgin! I thought I was simply going to fat. Rowena and Una put their arms around me, congratulating me and patting my stomach. Me, a mother? Suddenly recalling my own mother, my eyes begin to water. Smiling through my tears, I touch each girl on the cheek.

"Tell no one, just yet. I want to break the news to Artagan myself."

Caressing my belly as though I might feel something, I chide myself for such impatience. Not even starting to show yet. Come little one, ripen and see the home that awaits you here.

A dark cloud looms in the back of my mind, thinking of my last pregnancy. With a different man in a different place. Perhaps this time, the result will be different too. Once Rowena and Una have left me alone in my room, I sink to my knees and pray.

Clasping my fingers together until they turn white, it takes me a moment to gather my thoughts. Counting the months back, I realize that I must have conceived on our wedding night. If all goes well, our child should come to us by late winter or early spring at the latest. *When* all goes well, *when*. Not *if*. Please, Heavenly Father, let the child be healthy and whole. So much death and destruction have beset us these past few seasons. Let the world fill with love and life once more.

Pacing my chamber, I cannot concentrate the rest of the day. Distracted by thoughts of motherhood, I leave my sewing half-finished beside the spinning wheel. On a settee by the window, I laugh to myself. Imagine Artagan as a father to my children! Gallivanting about with a boy or girl on his back. Despite having several years on me, he is still such a child himself. Our son or daughter will doubtlessly love him more, I contemplate with a playful smile. Just as everyone else does. But no matter. No one will ever love this babe as much as I. No one.

When a knock comes at the door, I frown, half-expecting Enid. Instead, Ahern enters. Resplendent in his new green tunic and golden brooch, he looks every bit the part of a castle seneschal. My old guardsman nods, not quite risking a smile as he clutches his spear and shield at attention. Ever the honorable soldier. I embrace him heartily, his eyebrows rising at such unusual closeness.

"I've something to tell you, kinsman. Something wonderful!"

"And I you, your ladyship. I've word of a merchant caravan on the west road."

"That's your news?"

"A rider told me they carry a strange bird for sale. A Merlin purchased from Caerwent."

"Caerwent? My falcon, Vivian! But how?"

"The Hammer King must have sold it, perhaps it reminded him too much of you. These merchants have it now. Free Cantref folk from the western coasts, I think."

After tossing on my boots and shawl, I make for the door.

"Have we any coin, Ahern? I must rescue her, if it's my old Vivian."

"I'll buy her for you myself, Your Grace. But you said you had something to tell me as well."

I pinch his bearded cheek, whispering low.

"I'm with child, brother. Two or three moons along already!"

Ahern turns pale. For a warrior recently knighted, Sir Ahern seems about as terrified of babes as ever I've seen a man. He struggles to congratulate me, his stutters low and incomprehensible. Protective as ever, he insists on escorting me to see the caravan. I happily consent. Enid trails us to the gates as Ahern and I gallop westward on horseback.

"No need for you to tag along," he shouts back at her. "I can manage the job just fine."

Enid folds her arms and halts, glaring at the new seneschal with a face fit to curdle milk. But he is officially in charge of the castle defenses now, so she does not contradict him.

Ignoring their tiny power struggle, I refuse to let anything dampen my mood today. Riding hard with the scent of wildflowers filling the meadows, we follow the western trail into the foothills. Aranrhod shrinks to the size of a miniature model in the vale below. I sigh with pleasure, my pony slick with sweat as we slow to a trot. Can this day be any better? A child quickens in my womb, sired by the man I love. And now, my long-lost falcon has returned. Once I get better with my bow, I shall teach our newborn to hunt and hawk like me. Well, once he or she reaches several years of age at least. Feeling my saddle, I realize that in my haste I left my bow behind in my room. No matter. I can always take up target practice again tomorrow.

The silhouette of a small caravan looms along a gap in the western mountains. Just a handful of wagons. Their mounts draw water from a mountainside spring. Ahern halts behind me as I dismount before the travelers' tents. None seem to be afoot just yet, perhaps napping after a long journey. Ahern motions toward the nearest canvas dwelling. I hope he brought enough silver. I'd trade my weight in bullion to get my falcon back. Brushing aside the tent flaps, I stalk inside.

The tent seems empty. An odor of fish and wet wood smoke makes me wrinkle my nose. Nothing but a few trinkets and horse blankets litter the grass inside. What manner of traveling merchants are these?

Hands reach out from the shadows, grabbing my wrists and covering my mouth. Struggling against hempen bonds, my muffled cries sound like no more than a whimpering mouse. A strong fist backhands me across the jaw. Staggering backward, I feel my hands knotted tight behind my back. A figure steps forward with a long spear in hand.

"Do you not recognize your own kin, Princess?"

Squinting at the swarthy youth, my eyes suddenly narrow.

"Owen?"

"*Sir* Owen now, herald and knight of King Vortigen of Dyfed. Father wants you home, Branwen."

He speaks with such malice. His wicked smile makes my flesh run cold. Bastard-born of my father, this Owen has no more brotherly feelings for me than he would a hound. King Cadwallon wanted to hack off this blackguard's head all those months ago, but I of all people spared him. I suddenly wish I had not been so generous.

A dozen Dyfed spearmen fasten my bonds tight, but forget to gag my mouth. I crush one warrior's foot with my heel, stumbling out the tent flaps and shouting at the top of my voice. My lips bleed.

"Ahern! Ahern, to arms! To arms!"

My guardsman stands aloof. He neither draws his weapon, nor shoulders his shield. He grimaces, his gray eyes welling with tears.

"I'm sorry, my lady. Dear Branwen, I'm so very sorry."

All breath seems to leave my lungs. Owen's heartless cackle rings in my ears before something heavy cracks against my skull. The world turns dark as I collapse at Ahern's feet. Why, brother? Why?

16

Horse hooves clack in the darkness. The floor of the wagon bed rolls like the deck of a ship. I lie prostrate in a nest of hay, my wrists chafing under the coarse ropes that bind my fists to my feet. Hog-tied like a piece of livestock. Lifting my pounding head from the straw, an all-encompassing blackness pervades the night. Crickets chirp while the cart bounces along the rough trail. We must be heading west toward Father's kingdom. The roads in Dyfed have never been good ones.

Worming my way out of the leather bag atop my head, I gasp for breath, careful not to draw the attention of my captors. At least a dozen riders trot alongside the wagon. Far too many for me to overcome or escape, even if my limbs were free and we didn't travel on a near-moonless night. Sir Owen's raspy voice murmurs through the dark as he gives orders to his confederates. My muscles cringe.

To think I spared this bastardly herald when King Cadwallon would have lopped off his head. I felt duty-bound to protect my blood kin, no matter how distant. A folly that a girl may indulge in, but not a queen. Now Owen has me in his clutches, taking me back to the father who first sold me in marriage to the Hammer King. But it's the memory of Ahern's contorted face that cuts me to the core. How could you, brother? What could have induced my loyal guardsman, of all people, to betray me into the hands of mine enemies? Has he been the spy, the traitor in my midst all this time? I sob without tears or sound, my limbs too spent and my eyes run dry.

None of the riders have Ahern's broad build. He does not number amongst my captors. Perhaps he simply took his thirty pieces of silver and went on his way. But Ahern never wanted for coin or honor or anything else whilst in my service. Time and again he spared me from Saxons, even helping me escape King Morgan's castle. He could have betrayed me then or any number of times thereafter. Why now? What has changed? My fists shake. Whatever the reason, the truth remains the same. My kinsman has sold me into slavery.

Artagan will not rest until he finds me. He and his men will cross hell and high water to get me back. My lips tremble. But how will my husband even know of my capture? He made Ahern seneschal of the castle. No one will even raise the alarm. No one saw the villains take me, and Ahern could invent any excuse regarding my whereabouts. Even now, my beloved Artagan may not know of my peril. Sitting with his socks by the fire, he may think me on some local errand to aid a woman in labor and no more. None will suspect me missing for hours, even days. Long after Father has me in a prison cell atop the crags of Dyfed.

The wagon suddenly rolls to a halt. My head glances off the timber frame and I let out a sharp whimper, savaging my lip. A spear butt jabs the small of my back. Owen towers over me.

"Awake, are we, Princess? Out of the cart!"

His men loosen my bonds just enough so I can shuffle over the lip of the wagon bed and onto the cold ground. Blood dampens my ankles where the ropes have scratched my skin. Limping toward a tree, I rest my back against the trunk. Owen's men give us a wide berth as he prods my skirt with his spear tip, lifting the hem of my gown.

"A fine jewel of virtue betwixt your legs. Don't think because we're kin that it would stop me from taking it from you, Princess. You're heir to the Kingdom of Dyfed. The man who mounts you mounts the throne."

My throat runs dry as he flashes another wicked grin. He can't be serious! Owen may be one of Father's bastards, but the same blood flows in my veins as his. I instinctively press my bare legs together but Owen parts them again with his spear butt. I fight to keep my voice calm. The firm, confident-sounding demeanor of a queen is the only weapon I have left.

"I'm with child. I carry King Vortigen's grandchild in my womb."

Owen sneers, giving me a suspicious glance.

"He has children aplenty, bastards and otherwise."

"But no grandson or granddaughter, born of his only legitimate heir. Whatever Father's feelings for me, he would want that grandchild safe and sound. The child I carry inside of me."

"You lie!"

"Ask Ahern, if you don't believe me."

"He's gone! He would not come with us."

Owen turns away in disgust, pacing back and forth in the dark. His men water their steeds by a trickling mountain stream while others repair a wobbly wheel beneath the wagon. We must have journeyed halfway through the mountains by now. Owen will not dally long in this glade. He'll whip his men with all possible speed toward Dyfed, knowing anyone else could steal me just as easily as he did himself only yesterday. My only hope of preserving my virtue is to convince Owen that the child in my womb is more valuable to King Vortigen than gold. It may be true or may not. Thankfully, Father is not here to say otherwise.

Sir Owen holds his spear over my belly, his brows knitted in thought. I repress a half-smile. Despite his ungodly urges, I've planted a seed of doubt in his thick skull. Owen raises his spear-point to my face.

"Back in the cart! We've a ways to go before we get you home, sister."

The wagon bounces forward as soon as I recline on the straw once more. Running my thumb along my abdomen, I cradle the unborn life inside me. I coo and shush the child, reassuring my babe as much as myself. The stars seem to swirl overhead. Whatever black fate awaits us in Father's realm, I will not let them harm my baby. If the mothers of the Free Cantrefs taught me anything during the siege of Aranrhod, it was that one mother defending her cubs was worth ten warriors fighting for plunder and booty. May the Virgin give me strength.

Half-asleep in the cart, my eyes stir as thunder murmurs through the foothills. Sitting up, I blink at the dim woods. The riders hear it too as they halt their mounts. Horses, more horses! Owen shouts to his men.

"Do not let them take her! If the battle goes ill, slit her throat first!"

Clasping one hand to my throat, my fingertips tremble as much for my own life as for the life inside of me. Does this bastard Owen have any semblance of a human heart? Before his spearmen can reply, a flurry of arrows whistles into the nocturnal glade.

Several arrowheads find their mark and topple spearmen from their horses. My heart quickens. Few archers in all of Wales could make shots like that in the dark. The bowmen from the Free Cantrefs have come.

Artagan roars loud enough to split the night in twain. Somehow, against all odds or reason, he is here! Enid's piercing war cry, along with Keenan's and Emryus's baritone shouts, mingle with the clash of steel. Silhouettes of dark figures wrestle on all sides of the wagon, the spearmen of Dyfed grappling with the archers of Aranrhod. Dim shadows fill the narrow wagon road.

Owen hurls his spear, its biting steel grazing my cheek. I gasp at the sting of metal on flesh, and my palm comes away red from my right cheekbone. I roll and stumble out of the wagon bed onto the ground, still bound and bleeding. Owen glares at me with wide, wildcat eyes under the pale sliver of a moon. He pulls a knife from his belt, racing toward me to finish the job.

I tug at my bonds until my wrists bleed. No, no, no! Even though I gnaw at the hempen bonds with my teeth, the ropes still won't relinquish their grip. Owen wraps one hand around my bloody cheek, his thumb pressing into the wound. I wince with pain. The knife flashes in his other fist.

Bound like a calf for the slaughter, a searing fire rises within me. Butting my head against his, I fight like a cornered animal. I bite Owen's flesh. His howl rises above the din of clashing warriors. The metallic taste of blood runs down my teeth. Owen stumbles backward, his knife clanging to the ground. Rolling onto my side, I grab the blade and begin sawing away at my ropes.

Owen stumbles around, his hand clasping his marred face. Blinded by pain, he circles me while I cut at my bonds. The frayed fibers loosen around my feet and hands. Breaking free, I rush him with the knife. Time the blackguard got a taste of his own steel.

I stab at his face, but Owen bats me across the jaw. I reel backward from the heavy blow. Beneath the starlight, he retreats to the woods. Staggering on my hands and knees, the pain makes me drop my knife. Unable to locate the dagger, I paw the earth in search of something with which to defend myself. A hand grasps me by the shoulder.

"Branwen! Are you all right?"

My pulse stops until I see Artagan's face. Wrapping my arms around his neck, I hold him close enough to feel his heart beating against my ribs. The fighting around us dies down. Only Free Cantref warriors surround us in the dark. Bathed in sweat, Artagan pants hard as he wipes the bloodstains from his longsword. I search his chest with my palms.

"I'm fine," he says, eyeing the bloody cut on my cheek. "My God, what did they do to you?"

"Nothing I didn't do right back to them. It was Owen of Dyfed, one of Father's bastards."

"I know. Ahern told me."

"Ahern? But you don't understand. It was Ahern who—"

"Who betrayed you. He told me himself. Confessed not long after he did it. If he hadn't told us, we might not have known of your capture until it was too late."

"Did he say why he betrayed me in the first place?"

"You'll have to ask him. I have him in the dungeons back at Aranrhod."

Artagan frowns, his hard-set jaw clenched tight. It probably took every fiber of his self-restraint not to gut Ahern when he learned the news of my capture. As I press my lips to his cheek, Artagan softens before lifting me onto his horse. He mounts Merlin behind me, grasping me tight about the middle. I seethe with frustration.

"Owen got away."

"With one less eyeball, I'll wager." Artagan smirks. "If you got him better than he got you."

"We're on the Dyfed side of the mountains. There may be more of them out there."

"Then we best make haste back to Aranrhod."

"Not too fast, my love. I wanted to tell you at a better time, but you must know. I'm with child."

Artagan's chest stiffens. The shadows hide his face as he sits like a statue in the saddle. I bite my lip, waiting for him to reply. Perhaps I should have waited until we returned to the castle. But I'll not risk this pregnancy to a bumpy road on horseback without speaking my mind. Maybe Artagan recalls his children with Ria, and the cruel fate they met at the hands of the Saxons. As a man, I only assumed he would welcome heirs with joy. But being bastard-born himself, childhood may not hold the fondest memories for him. I rush to touch his cheek.

"I'm sorry, my love. I should have waited to tell you until—"

He presses his lips to mine. His smile warms my mouth as his arms squeeze me tight. His eyes sparkle by twilight before he puts a hand on my stomach.

"You and I?" he asks.

"Yes, you and I, and a child."

Nuzzling noses, I let out a sigh of relief. Only moments ago I thought my babe would be born in captivity, under my father's thumb or worse. Now we shall live in freedom in our own castle, safe and sound. Artagan kisses me again. Enid scoffs beside us.

"Come on, you lovebirds, we've a long ride back to Aranrhod."

She digs her heels into her mare's flanks, leading the column of bowmen back down the trail into the mountains. Artagan grasps me gently, urging our steed forward at an even trot. Leaning my head back against his shoulder, I shut my eyes and breathe in the dry-grass summer air. Home, we're heading home to Aranrhod and our castle in the mountains.

I practice with my longbow in an abandoned corridor deep within the castle. Barrels line the walls, the servants utilizing this cool stony chamber as a wine cellar most likely. Alone by torchlight, I draw back my bow and loose another arrow toward a distant calfskin target at the far end of the dim passageway. My shot lands with a thud near the center of the bull's-eye. Months of practice have steadied my arm and my aim, but I do not smile.

Cool evening winds swirl leaves outside a chink in the masonry, allowing a hint of the fading light outside to seep into the otherwise dark abode. I instinctively pause to run a palm over my growing abdomen. A few months along, yet my pregnancy has not prevented me from improving my aim with a bow. But I know that I must be even better if I am to defend myself when it counts. If I am to protect my child whenever he or she comes into the world.

The sound of footsteps shuffles to a halt behind me.

"So this is where you steal away to," Annwyn says with a smile, a torch in hand. "At the rate you're improving, you'll be the best shot in the citadel in a few months' time."

"I'll be going into labor in a few months' time," I reply with a grin and a shrug. "The cold autumn storms outside would've ruined my outdoor practice schedule if not for this passageway I found. Come springtime I hope to be able to hit a target at twice the distance I can now."

Annwyn stands beside me with her dripping torch as I loose another shot at the rawhide target. The arrow lands a few finger-lengths to the left of where I wanted it, so I notch another feathery dart and try again. Annwyn watches me while I practice.

"How fares your brother?" she asks.

I pause between my shots before resuming again. Despite trying to pretend the conversation doesn't bother me, I find my aim going even wider of the mark. We do not mention Ahern by name any longer, almost as though he were dead.

"The prisoner, you mean?" I reply. "Still in the dungeons. He won't speak to me or anyone else. Artagan doesn't want me going down there anyway. Thinks the fumes are bad for the baby."

Annwyn nods solemnly.

"Were he not your blood, he probably would've been put to the rack by now. But I suppose languishing in a prison cell is torture enough."

"Artagan endured a stint in a dungeon himself once," I reply, recalling those dark days at Caerwent before I broke Artagan and myself free from Morgan's grip. "But I thought you didn't believe in violence."

She puts a steady hand on my bow, forcing me to stop my practice.

"Even I have my limits. My faith values all living things, yet I am still human. My own grandchild was threatened while still in the womb.

Even my vows of nonviolence would've been tested had we not gotten you back so soon."

I smirk at her in a jovial manner, giving her a sidelong look.

"What are you saying, Annwyn? That you would've come charging into Dyfed with a spear and bow to rescue me if your son hadn't already done it?"

Her lips smile, but her eyes do not.

"I thank the Goddess that I was not put to such a test."

This is a new side to Annwyn. Of course, I've only known her less than a year, and she has lived a long life. No telling what she might have been like in her younger days, before becoming a mystic and hermit. Back when she took up with men like Cadwallon and raised her son.

Annwyn makes a strange face, her lips caught between a smile and a grimace. Her eyes glaze over as though she looks at some distant scene that I cannot see.

"This bow was intended as a gift for my daughter," she begins. "Crafted by a skilled fletcher, who was my lover for a time. But my young Niniane was taken from me."

The longbow, its curves so familiar to me, now suddenly feels heavy as lead in my arms. No wonder Artagan said nothing when he first saw me use it during the siege. He must have recognized the longbow for what it was, for whom it was originally meant.

"Niniane, your daughter," I begin, making a guess. "Artagan's sister?"

"He does not speak her name, nor do I much, for that matter," Annwyn admits. "They were close, even though she was much younger and they had very different fathers. Her death nearly drove my son to madness for a time. The Saxons have lost a hundred men because they took that one girl from us. Painful as the memory is, it has made Artagan the warrior and leader he is today. And now the bow that seemingly had no purpose has found its way into the hands of someone worthy of it. A queen who rules in the manner of the Old Tribes."

I glance to my feet, unsure what to say. In the short time I've known her, Annwyn has given me so much. She gave me a bow intended for her daughter, she wed me to a son originally intended for another, and she even gave me a glimpse of a woman who may not have been that different from my own long-lost mother. Herself.

"Why do you tell me all this?" I ask. "These must be painful memories for you."

"They are. But even when things seem dark, there is a plan, a purpose to everything in our lives even though we may not be able to see it at the time. I think you are now in a place within your life where I too have once been. Beset by enemies from within and without, trying to bring a child into this cruel world, and all the while struggling to find the voice of God in all of it."

"God?" I reply. "I thought you worship the Goddess of the Old Tribes." She smiles knowingly.

"It is all one. That is something priests today will not admit. You know, when the first Christians came to these islands, they worshiped the Goddess side by side with their Christ God? They made our spirits into their saints, even applying the trinity of our goddess mysteries to their own religion. All true faiths in this world worship the same divine love."

It warms my heart to hear her say things aloud I've often felt all my life, but never had the words to express. She speaks true, for how many Welsh folk, particularly those of the Free Cantrefs, attend a Christian church yet still make offerings to spirits of their ancestors? Is not the Virgin the Mother of God just like the ancient Celtic Goddess who was mother to the spirits of the Old Tribes? I put a gentle hand on Annwyn's arm.

"You have a gift for expressing things in a beautiful way, Annwyn. Perhaps you could tell me more of such things sometime."

"I would like that," she replies, fondly squeezing my arm back.

She turns to go, leaving me to my archery. As I notch another arrow to the bowstring, she stops and calls back to me through the dark vaults under the castle.

"And Branwen. Your brother may have betrayed you, but take my advice. We only have so much time with those we love. Whatever he has done, he still meant something to you once. Do not let him pass out of this world without trying to make amends first."

Annwyn departs without another word. The tunnels beneath the castle suddenly turn cold under an icy draft. I twist my lips, trying to

conjure up an image of Ahern that does not remind me of the day he sold
me out to my enemies. I draw back my bow, launching an arrow at the
target so hard that it embeds itself up to the feathery end of its shaft. Whatever amends I have to make with him, they shall not happen today.

My belly has swollen to the size of a large melon. This afternoon I work
with needle and thread beside the fireplace in my solar. Rowena and Una
card wool in the corner as they chitchat. While I sew beside my tower window these many months, the fields outside have turned golden with autumn wheat, then frosty white under the first winter snowdrifts. I practice
archery by day and work at the loom by dusk. Despite my worst fears, I've
lived to see my eighteenth name day, and I'll soon be a mother at that.

My woven tapestry now spans half the room, running the length of the
wall on one side of the chamber. With Rowena and Una's help, we've
wrought the history of the rebirth of Aranrhod in spun wool and thread.
Three segments depict the Saxon siege, the arrival of the North Welsh
horsemen, and finally the crowning of myself and Artagan. Obtaining
proper colors has proved trying during this cold time of year, but trades with
passing merchants and monks have helped us manage. Every color was
painstakingly chosen. Fiery and golden silk threads for Artagan's crown.
Gossamer threads for the castle towers. Black sackcloth for my hair.

A knock comes at my bedchamber door. Una and Rowena look up
from their weaving as Artagan paces quietly into the room. He wears a
hard look and barely raises his gaze from the floor. Several days of stubble
often cover his cheeks nowadays, as though he is too weighed down with
other thoughts to remember to shave. My ladies-in-waiting instinctively
rise and curtsy before excusing themselves. The King waits until their
footfalls fade down the turret steps. I put down my needle and thread in
my lap as he paces the length of the room.

"What gives you that dark look, my love?"

"How fares the child?"

"We're both fine. We've a few weeks yet. But you didn't come here to
banter about birthing."

"He still will not speak. Your brother is a stubborn man."

"Half brother, yes. Stubborn, but strong as well."

It still cuts too deep to talk of him much. We skirt around his name as though he were a ghost. Languishing in chains for near on nine months seems as close to death as a man can come. Although many weeks have passed, Annwyn's advice comes back to my mind. I reach out and grab Artagan's hand.

"Let me try again."

"In your condition? I'll not let you down in the dungeons now."

"He's the only one who knows who's behind all the attempts on my life, when I lived at Caerwent and when the Saxons tried to capture me. I must know, Artagan. For my sake and our child's."

"He's kept silent all winter, what makes you think he'll talk now?"

"Let me try, Artagan. Please."

He squints into the frosty draft whistling in through the window. Without looking my way, he squeezes my palm before nodding. I put down my embroidery and give him a comforting peck on the cheek, then hasten down the steps before he changes his mind.

Enid accompanies me to the dungeons. Once the turnkey lets us in, the two of us stand alone with Ahern in his cell. Water drips in the darkness. Few shafts of light penetrate the depths of Aranrhod's ancient dungeons. Green sludge pockmarks the porous walls. A full beard and shaggy hair hide Ahern's face, his thick chains binding him close to the stone bulkhead. Enid glares at the prisoner.

"We should have put the screws to him."

"Chained in a dungeon is torture enough," I reply.

"Excuse me, Queen. I've a castle to keep watch over."

Enid hastens from the chamber. Since Ahern's disgrace, Artagan has appointed Enid as the new seneschal of the castle. Nonetheless, she has kept her duty of standing watch as my personal guard more often than not. Though I doubt so much for my safety as for the child in my womb. Enid's attitude toward me remains cool as ever, but I carry Artagan's heir and Enid often asks after my unborn babe as though it were her own. The spear-wife's loyalties flow in strange ways.

Alone with my half brother, a draft chills my skin. Tugging my shawl about my shoulders, I stand awhile in silence. Ahern makes no move to speak. He doesn't seem to breathe until his eyes finally blink. I heave a heavy sigh. My kinsman simply lets himself rot, silent as a crypt. Setting my torch in a brazier, it casts a bronze glow across the gloomy cell. Out of habit, I palm the sides of my rounded belly.

"The midwife says my time comes soon. All those birthings I assisted, yet I've never had a birth of mine own. I'm a little scared."

Ahern keeps his gaze to the floor, but I continue anyway.

"I'll ask the King to let you have a trim, and some fresh meat to keep up your strength."

"No."

Startled to hear his ragged voice, I crane my ear closer. His unused vocal cords make him sound hoarse as a frog. Leaning close to his face, I fight the urge to wrinkle my nose. His unwashed britches stink of refuse.

"What did you say?"

"No!"

He lunges forward in his restraints. Leaping back, I feel my heart race as his taut chains jangle along the wall. Unable to advance farther, he slinks back toward the floor. I wipe the sweat from my brow.

"Why won't you let me help you?"

"Because I deserve this! I betrayed you. Don't you hate me? Don't you feel anything at all?"

"You betray yourself, by keeping silent to protect whomever put you up to such folly in the first place."

He growls, facing the corner. His voice suddenly softens.

"Does the child fare well?"

"Stirs all the time." I smile. "As restless as its father."

"I wonder, will it be a boy or a girl?"

"We'll all find out soon enough."

Ahern hangs his head.

"I was supposed to go with them, Owen's men, and accompany you to Dyfed. But you told me only that morning you were with child, so I turned back to Aranrhod."

"To confess to Artagan in time to save my life. It seems there's some good in you still."

"There is no good left in me, Branwen. Leave me to rot."

I push the air out my nose. Pacing the floor, my heavy footsteps echo off the empty dungeon cavern. Around and around I go with Ahern, still getting nowhere. Is there no key that will unlock the secrets inside his heart? His mixed actions managed to endanger and save my unborn child all in one day. I'd like to kiss his furry beard and wring his neck all at once. Steadying my breath, I lower my voice.

"My child is in danger. Death stalks us already."

"Do you feel ill?"

"I've my health, but once my babe comes into this world, the same foes who sought to quell my freedom will seek to destroy this child. My girl or boy will be heir to the thrones of Dyfed and the Free Cantrefs. Every Welsh and Saxon warlord will strive to kill or capture such a child so long as men war over Wales. I doubt my babe will live to see its first year."

Venting my fears, I hardly know the thoughts in my mind until I speak them. Ahern stares up at me speechless, knowing that my words hide no deception. Still as a stone, I make no move to blink back the water welling up behind my eyes. Ahern moistens his lips, his neglected voice wavering and raw.

"I've been the Judas in your midst all along, although at first I did not know it."

"That makes no sense, brother."

"I've always been your loyal guardsman, but I remained loyal to Dyfed as well. When I first accompanied you when you wed King Morgan, I sent regular messages back to your father. I reported on your welfare and whereabouts as he asked me to. Only later did I learn that those messages had been intercepted."

"By whom?"

"At first I did not know. Believe me, Branwen. I had no idea."

"Ahern, you don't know how to read. Who wrote and deciphered these letters for you?"

"It wasn't the Abbot. I think Padraig suspected though. Bishop Gregory helped me."

"King Morgan's cleric?"

"Aye, he was the go-between, sending messages back and forth."

"So Bishop Gregory has been my enemy all this time?"

Ahern begins to chuckle, almost darkly.

"Nay, girl. Listen. The Bishop merely did the writing. Someone else was reading the letters. I thought the Saxon attacks mere coincidence, but after the assassin at Caerwent, I began to have suspicions. Your father had his own plots, but hurting you wasn't one of them. You were his prize, the bond that bound his kingdom to Morgan's. No, it wasn't King Vortigen who made you bait for Saxons and assassins."

"Then who? Ahern, tell me! If not for my sake, then for the sake of my unborn babe."

Ahern sighs.

"I don't rightly know. That's the rub. Word came from your father when Owen last visited Aranrhod. Owen told me himself. Your father realized someone had been reading his messages from the Bishop. The wax sealing had been tampered with."

As I pace the prison cell, the gears in my mind begin to spin. Each time Ahern reported my whereabouts to Father, whoever read those letters set the Saxons on me. First on the road to Caerwent for my marriage, then again when I rode to the Dean Fort. Every time something bad befell me, Ahern had always been with me or arrived only the day before. But something doesn't fit. My eyes suddenly harden, turning on Ahern.

"I understand your loyalty to both me and my father, and how that must have torn you in two. I understand that you were a pawn of wiser and cleverer men. What I don't understand is how you could betray me to Owen! By then you knew your spying had consequences. You knew what would happen!"

"Aye. Owen came to me in secret the night before, to set the trap for you. Saying your favorite falcon had resurfaced. Offered me land and a lord's title, but ultimately it was an order from my king. The last such one I ever intend to obey."

Ahern lowers his face into his hands, shivering as he fights the sobs. My temples throb. I don't know whether to pity or spurn the man. He saved my life more than once, and helped me free Artagan and myself from Caerwent's dungeons many moons ago. Divided by his loyalty to his king and myself, he was used by both. If only the mystery could have ended with his confession! Now I only have more questions. Who was reading his messages to Father? Who used Ahern's letters as intelligence regarding my whereabouts? Using each correspondence as a tool by which to lay the next trap.

The Bishop. No one, least of all myself, ever accredited Caerwent's high cleric with an overabundance of brains. Padraig often chided the man for paying more attention to his altar boys than to Holy Writ. But the Bishop must be the key. He read and wrote the letters, and he must have sent them. So who got to the Bishop first? A sickening, slithery chill uncoils in my stomach.

Gregory is Morgan's pet. He'd do anything his king asked of him. Morgan could easily have read every letter. So could his brother Malcolm, for that matter. But why? Morgan had every reason in the world to keep me alive as his bride and broodmare. Malcolm then? The Prince of Caerleon has a malicious streak for certain. But it still doesn't add up. I now know how I was betrayed, but I still don't know who was ultimately behind it all. The person who has been plotting my demise from the very start. Pursing my lips, I put a hand to my brow. My forehead feels hot and heavy as a blacksmith's anvil.

The room begins to swim in my vision. Ahern rises in his chains, trying to steady me. His voice trembles.

"Branwen, are you all right? Guards! Guards! The Queen is ill!"

Footfalls from the guards murmur down the stairwell. Ahern's eyes glaze over as he stares at me in wide-eyed fear. Foolish man. Does he not understand? Grasping my hands about my middle, the contractions surge up through my sinews and bones. The baby stirs inside me.

PART THREE
A.D. 599

17

The baby shifts from the left to the right breast. He nuzzles my bosom before suckling contentedly in my arms. Birds twitter outside the tower windowsill as I recline on a settee with my son, golden, warm sunlight pouring over his soft scalp. Tufts of auburn hair freckle his tiny head. Laughing to myself, I press my lips to his small brow. Little Gavin. Named after King Arthur's bravest Welsh knight, Sir Gawain. Artagan leans in the doorway, crossing his arms as he watches me feed our boy.

"Why do you laugh?" He smiles.

"How could two raven-haired folk such as us have a red-haired babe?"

"You've been saying that these past three moons. My father had auburn locks."

Gavin nurses contentedly in my arms, his eyes closing as though half-dreaming. Despite the sleepless nightly feedings, every morning I still marvel at the miracle that is my new son. He has my button nose and his father's sea-blue eyes. Gently stroking his soft cheek with my finger, I cannot help but breathe easier when my child is near. Artagan leans closer, eyeing his son.

"How fares Rowena?" he asks.

"She brought her newborn by yesterday. A little girl, named Mina."

"And Keenan's the father, eh?"

"I was told once that in the Free Cantrefs, a mother's blood is all that matters."

I smirk up at Artagan as he purses his lips, feigning indignation.

"I was merely curious. You ought to put Gavin to nurse with Rowena. I'm sure she's got enough milk for two."

"And not feed my own babe?"

Artagan's eyes flash down toward my bare chest. My bosom swells daily, heavy with milk. Artagan has barely been able to keep his hands off me, his azure gaze lingering long on my generous bust. Was it only a few years ago I was a flat-chested, crow-headed girl in Dyfed? I might laugh at Artagan's attentions, but his frisky palms rarely give me a moment's peace now that I have Gavin to suckle. From cradle to the grave, men really never change. They always want the tit, one way or the other.

With Gavin asleep on my lap, I fold up the lacing on my loose gown. Artagan looks away, seemingly disappointed as I tighten my bustle. Sitting in the warm sunlight, I bask in the verdant glow of spring. Green fields blossom around the castle grounds. Artagan stomps his foot in the corner, deep in thought. I put a calm hand against his chest.

"Something else is on your mind, love."

"A raven brings news from North Wales. Lady Olwen and Prince Rhun have wed."

I suddenly feel hollow to my bones. It's a powerful match. I never doubted a ravishing woman like Olwen wouldn't remain a spinster for long. Does my husband still think of her? Of course not, what a foolish notion.

Yet Artagan taps his fist along the lintel of the door, biting his lip. We've not seen Olwen or Rhun since the North Welsh came to our rescue during the siege of Aranrhod. More than a year ago now. It was tall, handsome Rhun who asked for my hand in marriage then. Lady Olwen assumed Artagan would make her the next Queen of Aranrhod. How strange that our fates should have reversed so. I keep my gaze to the floor.

"You wish that you had wed her instead?" I reply a touch impishly, indulging in my own insecurities perhaps more than I should.

"What?"

"It would've secured all the Free Cantref lands to you. Now Rhun will claim her father's territory as his own."

Artagan kneels down, taking my chin in his hand. His sapphire eyes search mine, one hand stroking my hair.

"I chose you then and I choose you now. My heart belongs to Branwen Mab Ceridwen, and no other."

I smile despite myself, hearing him refer to me as the Fairy Queen. Our local subjects still call me such. Although months have passed since the trial of childbirth, I clasp Artagan's hand now as tightly as I did then when our son first came into the world. Just the three of us in our solar chamber, with no need of anyone else in the whole wide world. I wonder. Had we been born commoners, with no more expectation than to farm and have children, would we have been any less happy? I kiss Artagan longingly, our mingled lips warmed by the streaming sunlight.

To think, we've a newborn son less than a year after our wedding day. The year 599 is already looking to be the best year of my life, thus far. I smile fondly at Gavin slumbering against my chest.

A bugle horn blares in the distance. Its piercing boom makes me shiver down to the spines of my feet. Gavin stirs in my arms. I rise in order to walk and shush him back to sleep. Artagan squints out the window, his hand on his sword. His voice sounds grim.

"The beacons are lit in the mountains. Danger approaches."

Three smoke trails rise over the foothills, the nearest bonfire flickering like a ruby set against the forest slopes. Thank heaven Enid made Artagan see reason and install outposts with beacon bonfires in the mountains. After my kidnapping, no one wants to risk falling unawares into an enemy's trap. Whatever peril approaches, at least it will come to us in full daylight and not steal upon us in the dark of night.

Artagan shouts down into the courtyard below. Dozens of green-clad bowmen scurry toward the battlements. Enid surveys the beacons atop the southern ramparts and waves Artagan over to join her. He turns to me and draws his sword.

"Stay here. Don't open the door for anyone."

Without another word, he disappears down the stairwell, and I bar the door behind him. Keenan and Emryus soon join him as he scales the wall where Enid and a score of other archers gather. Whatever the threat, it seems to originate from a southward direction.

A knock comes at my door.

Clutching Gavin close to me, I stand quiet as a mouse. A fist bangs against the door again. What has come over me? No queen in her own castle ought to fear to open her bedroom door. I'm being silly. Nonetheless, I put Gavin down in the cradle before stalking toward the door. I pull down my longbow from the wall before loosening the hasp on the lock.

"M'lady?"

I sigh, recognizing Rowena's voice. As I usher her inside, she holds her newborn close to her breast. Little Mina whimpers in her mother's arms. I shut the door behind her and bar it again.

"Rowena, what brings you here?"

"I'm still your lady-in-waiting, am I not, Your Grace? Babe or no, I had to look in on you."

"Where's Una?"

"I know not, m'lady."

"I'm beginning to worry. Una went on some errand to a neighboring village over a week ago and still no word."

"I wouldn't fret." Rowena shrugs. "I'm sure she'll be back soon."

Rowena looks away, hiding her face. She does not tell me everything behind Una's mysterious absence, yet I sense it is not over some life-or-death matter, so I let the subject pass. For the moment at least. Nonetheless, as little Mina stirs in her arms, a vague intuition forms in the back of my mind. Both Una and Rowena once shared Sir Keenan as a lover. Before he fathered Rowena's daughter. Perhaps the closeness between the two women is not what it once was.

Whatever the cause, it will unfortunately have to wait while we have mysterious strangers at our gates. Reassuring her, I sit my lady-in-waiting down on the bed.

"I'm fine, Rowena. But you should not be out of bed."

"Me own mum worked the fields the day after I was born. I've had rest aplenty, m'lady."

"Well, I'm sure there's nothing to be frightened of," I fib, trying to sound a bit more confident than I feel. "The castle's well protected."

"Do you not recognize that horn, my Queen? Only one lord in all Wales uses an ivory bugle."

My veins run cold. Turning toward the window, I steady my palm on the stonework. A large cavalcade breaks from the forest, cantering straight for the castle gates. I drop my bow to the floor, instinctively reaching back toward Gavin in his cradle. The crimson dragon banners of South Wales fly over the approaching horsemen.

"Rowena, has my old husband returned for vengeance?"

"I know not, m'lady. But that's not his horn, like I said. Only the Lord of Caerleon uses an ivory bugle call. That's Prince Malcolm, that is."

My hairline runs damp with sweat. Malcolm? Even worse.

The mere thought of that blackguard lurking outside the walls where my child sleeps makes me grind my teeth. Lifting my bow, I dart toward the door and sling a quill of arrows over my shoulder. Whatever black fate has come to our doorstep, I'll not hide in my chambers like a frightened sheep. Aiming a finger back at Rowena, my voice reverberates off the rafters.

"Look after my boy! Whatever happens, do not open this door."

Giving her the advice I hardly heeded myself, I close the door and descend the steps before Rowena can reply. I know my place now. On the battlements, defending my husband and my son. I'll put an arrowhead right into Prince Malcolm's heart if need be. Time those lordly knights of South Wales see how well a mother of the Free Cantrefs fights when cornered with her cubs. Artagan's eyes narrow as I scale the embrasures. He struggles to keep his voice low.

"The battle line is no place for a nursing mother!"

"I'll be the judge of what a mother can and cannot do. Why have we not loosened a volley of arrows yet?"

Still plum-faced, Artagan cannot find the words to rebuke me. Instead, Enid leans forward, her spear in one hand and a longbow in the other.

"They're flying a flag of truce. They wish to parley."

"I'll give those blackguards an answer," I retort, drawing back my bow.

"Hold!" Enid shouts. "Something doesn't make sense. They've brought maybe a hundred soldiers, not enough for a siege. If they meant us ill, they'd have brought more men."

"If they'd meant us well, they'd have left us alone."

Glancing at the woods, I wonder how many more troops Malcolm may have hidden behind those trees. It doesn't suit someone like

Malcolm to come under a white banner with his tail tucked between his knees. And why no Morgan? The Hammer King is up to something for sure.

Malcolm's riders fan out in a large crescent beneath our walls, their chain mail jangling in the early afternoon light. The South Welsh of Gwent have neither the fast steeds nor long lances like the horsemen of the North, but on foot, an armored Southron can often handle double his number in the melee. Let's hope our arrowheads can pierce Southern chain mail today if necessary.

Artagan descends the steps to the courtyard and mounts his warhorse, Merlin. The very same horse we once rode when we fled from Caerwent all those moons ago. The very same steed that once belonged to the Hammer King himself. Artagan orders the guards to open the gates.

"I'll go out to meet him. Alone."

"To be fodder?" I scoff. "Not likely. Whatever we face, we face it together."

Whistling for my mare, I mount Gwenhwyfar beside him. Enid, Emryus, and Keenan all saddle their own steeds and join us under the gateway. Artagan digs his heels into Merlin's flanks, trotting off in a huff. He mumbles under his breath.

"What good is it to be king when no one heeds your word?"

Keenan and I exchange grins. The young knight touts a green dragon banner over our small company. Galloping into the emerald pastures outside Aranrhod's walls, we halt before the cavalcade of Southern warriors and their bloodred banners. Local peasants look on from farmsteads and the castle walls, watching us behind closed doors and arrow slits.

Prince Malcolm looks the same as ever. A well-trimmed, chestnut-bearded version of his older brother. A scowl spreads across his lips when he sees me. His guardsmen stand around him at perfect attention, their dark eyes watching us through the eye slits in their helmets. Our ponies curl back their lips, flaring their teeth. Neither side speaks.

Malcolm's gaze runs the length of my silhouette. He still makes me feel naked before him. My neck flushes, but I clutch the reins tight in one hand while carrying my bow in the other. I'm not the scared little King's wife he knew back at Caerwent. Artagan nudges his stallion forward. Malcolm grimaces, recognizing the warhorse as formerly his brother's.

The Blacksword smirks, suddenly looking like the cocky hedge knight he was when he first crossed swords with Malcolm all those moons ago.

"You're a long way from your own borders, princeling," Artagan begins.

"I've urgent tidings, for the Lord of Aranrhod alone."

Malcom swallows as though tasting a bitter draught. Doubtlessly, referring to Artagan as anything other than a brigand leaves a sour taste on Malcolm's tongue. I narrow my gaze, closely watching Malcolm and his massive mace. Why the courtesy? Despite his royal blood, Malcolm has the breeding of a pig. He would sooner trade blows with the Blacksword than speak cordially to him. Artagan smiles back, enjoying the Prince's discomfort.

"The name's *King* Artagan now. I keep no secrets from my subjects. Speak freely."

Malcolm grips his horse's reins in a fist, speaking through clenched teeth.

"My brother, King Morgan, calls on you for aid. A Saxon army has crossed into the Welsh Lands. We need every man we can get."

Artagan and I exchange glances. Malcolm cannot be serious. Since when does the mighty Hammer King call on other kingdoms for aid? Something must be terribly amiss in South Wales for Morgan to send his own brother to beg troops from his former enemies. Artagan utters a quick laugh.

"Your brother calls on *me* for aid? Me. Doesn't he still have a price on my head?"

"Old squabbles must be put aside," Malcolm retorts. "Ten thousand Saxons attacked the Dean Fort yesterday. They slaughtered the garrison and razed it to the ground. They march on Caerwent as we speak."

My skin turns to ice. Artagan's knights murmur amongst themselves. Ten thousand Saxons? Malcolm must exaggerate. With a force that size they could conquer all of Wales before harvest time. I lean forward in the saddle, still unable to fathom Malcolm's tale.

"You're sure the Dean Fort has fallen? What of Lord Griffith?"

"Taken hostage by Chief Beowulf, last we heard."

I shut my eyes. Such a sorrowful fate for such a worthy man. Lord

Griffith was always kind to me. Artagan and I first danced hand in hand under his roof. Now the old nobleman is doubtlessly chained like a dog to the Wolf's war wagons. A plaything for the barbarians as they ravage the Welsh countryside. Artagan aims a hard finger at the Prince.

"Ten thousand? Impossible. The Saxons on our borders don't even have that many men."

"They do now. It's no longer just the West Saxons under the Wolf who come against us. He has allied with the Anglo-Saxon king, Penda, who marches with him. Never before have the bickering factions of the Saxon kingdoms united like this against us. Our scouts report axmen, spear-throwers, and armored infantry amongst their ranks. Not since the days of Arthur have the Saxons arrayed such a force against us."

"And I suppose your brother thinks himself the next Arthur?" Arta-gan retorts. "Just snap his fingers and we'll come running to help him. Do you think me a fool, princeling? I won't shed the blood of my warriors to protect the Hammer King's castle. He'd just as soon plant spies in my court to capture back my wife. I ought to send your head back in a basket."

Artagan draws his blade. Malcolm's men raise their spears in re-sponse. Enid, Emryus, and Keenan draw their bows in turn. I might roll my eyes if all our lives didn't depend on the next few moments. These noblemen are fighters, but they've none of the nuances required for nego-tiation or diplomacy.

Nudging my mare between both groups, I extend my hands toward either side. South Welsh spears aim at me from one end and Free Cantref arrowheads from the other. I raise my voice.

"Stop this madness! I've more reason for grievance against King Mor-gan than anyone, but we will not shed blood here. Not under a flag of truce, not while every Saxon in Britain storms over the border into Wales. You would only be doing the barbarians a favor by fighting each other now. We're going to need every Welsh warrior we can get."

Artagan lowers his blade with an incredulous look on his face.

"You don't actually believe this liar, do you?"

"If he meant to deceive us, Morgan would've sent a raven or a cleric or someone from Dyfed," I reply. "Instead he sent his only brother, knowing full well we might kill him or take him prisoner. It's an act of desperation, but it's also an honest act as well."

Malcolm trots forward, making his men lower their arms.

"We've sent word all across Wales to gather our forces," he adds. "Vortigen of Dyfed has pledged to come, and Bishop Gregory has gone to North Wales to plead our common cause."

"The North Welsh will not come." Artagan waves dismissively.

"If you joined us, they would," Malcolm replies. "If not, the Saxons will gobble up our kingdoms one by one. If we do not make a stand against them now, all is lost. They'll raise their banners over each of our castles by Christmastide."

"And who's to command this combined Welsh army?"

"All the Welsh kings jointly, together as equals."

"I'll believe it when I see it."

Artagan sheathes his blade and folds his arms. Malcolm throws up his hands in exasperation. Both men would gladly rather draw one another's blood than fight back to back against an enemy. But the Prince has a point. We cannot sit behind our walls and wait for another endless siege. The Saxons will wear us down until we've run out of warriors and bread.

Several arguments break out simultaneously amongst the South Welsh and the Free Cantref warriors, each remembering past grievances and wrongs done by the other. I hold up a single palm and wait until both sides run silent. Turning in the saddle, I face Malcolm with the sternest queenly countenance I can summon.

"Prince, tell your king he shall have our answer in several days' time, beneath the walls of Caerwent. Our army will come or I will come alone myself."

"Saxons!"

Enid's voice carries through the forest as she points toward the plains beyond. Artagan and I halt our mounts at the edge of the woods, squinting into the misty dawn along the riverfront. At first, nothing but thin fog banks dot the gray river that cuts through the lowlands. The drumbeat of calfskin and timber shields murmur through the morning vapors. Tall pikes pierce the mists, some bearing bloody, golden, and orange banners. The colors of the Saxon tribes. I swallow hard. The heavy tread of men in chain mail echoes across the wetlands.

In the distance, the slate silhouette of Caerwent overlooks the river. Its imposing towers and fortified bastions array themselves like rows of stone teeth. If the battle should go ill, does the citadel have enough room to house our troops? That would be a slow death, starved out and bombarded by sling stones. No, far better to fight in the open and risk it all in a single contest with our barbaric foes. Artagan touches my arm, his gaze soft as blue felt.

"Are you sure about this?" he asks.

I clench his hand. When was the last time I was certain about anything? We've come too far to turn back now. Maybe we never really had a choice to begin with. But what kind of mother am I? What kind of wife? Leaving my child behind in Rowena's care to join my husband on the battlefield. I fight today not only for my own life, but for the life of my son. My place is here in the borderlands, battling for his future. If we fail today, there won't even be a free Wales for him when he grows up.

So, am I sure we've made the right decision? I nod toward my husband.

"I'm sure. The rest lies in God's hands."

Artagan kisses my cheek. Turning back toward his men, he hardens his features. No longer my softhearted lover, he wears the face of a warrior now, of a king. Drawing his blade, he calls out to the long column of archers on foot. Tall bowmen clad in green, interspersed with a few spear-wives wielding birch bows like mine own. Artagan raises his voice.

"For Aranrhod, for the Free Cantrefs, for Wales! For Mab Ceridwen!"

"Mab Ceridwen!" the warriors reply in unison.

Goose bumps rise along my skin. Their pet name for me has become something more. A battle cry, a plea for freedom. Artagan puts his heels to his stallion's sides, charging into the open plain while his troops jog close behind. I ride beside the column to make sure no stragglers linger.

Everyone we can muster has come. Amidst the crowd, familiar faces glance my way before taking the field. Farmers, huntsmen, and smiths. Fathers, brothers, and sons of the womenfolk who've helped make

Aranrhod what it is. Now we defend the approaches to Caerwent, not because we care for King Morgan, but because we care for the fate of Wales. All Wales. Emryus, Keenan, and Enid nod my way as they pass with more companies of green-clad troops in tow. Last in line comes a lone soldier on foot, his spear and shield immaculate despite his long beard and wild hair. Ahern halts beside my horse, pausing to catch his breath.

"Dungeon air has not done much for my lungs. You afraid I might desert, my Queen?"

"It was King Artagan's decision to offer you your freedom if you joined us on the battlefront."

"I ask no freedom for myself. Merely to fight by your side once again. Can things ever go back to the way they once were, sister?"

Eyeing him a long while, I turn my mount.

"Keep pace beside me, guardsman. Someone has to keep an eye on you."

He smiles and nods before abruptly regaining his stoic composure. Happy as a pup to be at my side once more, he jogs beside my cantering mountain mare. How strangely the fates twist and entwine our lives together. We've the same father and different mothers, once close as kin, then enemies, and now allies once again. The seesaw of fortune continues its ceaseless tilt.

Down in the plain, King Morgan's troops stand in square checkerboard formations beneath their red dragon pennants. Thousands of men-at-arms, their glaives and helms polished for the day. Let's hope it's enough to turn the tide against the Saxon hordes. A long line of drab spearmen with cowhide shields array themselves on the flank. Hearty sons of Dyfed. My heart beats faster with the rhythm of my pony's clacking hooves. Though long at odds with my father, it still lightens my soul to fight beside the people of my birthplace.

King Morgan's bannermen meet in the center of the field. Both Father and my former husband will be there. I swallow hard, clutching my bow tight. I'd rather go up against a hundred Saxons than face Morgan or Father again. A chill runs up my back. By day's end, I may get my wish.

Galloping forward astride my Gwenhwyfar, I join Artagan and his retinue beneath their green dragon banners. Ahern, although on foot, runs until red in the face in his effort to keep up. Artagan orders his warriors to halt, wishing to proceed alone. I ride beside him anyway. Whatever we must face, we shall face it together. Nonetheless, my spine tingles thinking of the hundreds of bowstrings and thousands of spears that will soon clash on these fields.

Morgan must realize we've far more to gain as allies than as foes. If not, all is lost. The jangling rumble of the nearing Saxon army looms louder through the fog, but aside from a few flags, their forces remain hidden from view. Like a sea serpent lingering just beneath the surface.

Artagan and I halt our steeds a few paces from Morgan and his knights. All eyes turn on me. Malcolm, the Bishop, Father, and Morgan himself. The Hammer King's dark gaze narrows on me, much the way a wolf might look at a guarded sheepfold. Both wary and wanting all at the same time. My flesh grows cold with sweat. So he still desires me in his bed? Probably wishing to embrace me and wrap his fingers around my neck all at once. Such are the mixed passions of men. I straighten my spine and sit high in the saddle. Morgan won't see me flinch, not this day. His deep voice greets Artagan, but his eyes never stray from my face.

"Blacksword. It's been a long time."

"I'm not here for you, Hammer King. I expect something in return for my participation today."

"You want me to relinquish my claim on Branwen, is that it?"

Morgan keeps his gaze fixed on me, but Artagan sidles his mount between us.

"I've brought a thousand archers."

"Pah! Vortigen alone brought a thousand spearmen."

"With ten thousand arrowheads? One of my men is worth two of yours."

Morgan looks Artagan in the eye for the first time. The two monarchs stare one another down. Artagan's force may be small compared to the thousands Morgan has mustered, but our archers will slay at least twice their number in the coming fight. No small balance in our favor against the Saxons. Morgan gives me a sidelong glance. Which matters to him more? Me back in his bed or a thousand Free Cantref bowmen on his side? Such is the price of maintaining a kingdom. But I'd sooner slit my throat than go back to Morgan, and every man here knows it. The Hammer King reins his horse back, eyeing Artagan's mount.

"That's my old warhorse. You ride two mounts I used to, one a stallion, the other a broodmare. Do you possess anything I didn't once fondle?"

Malcolm and several other soldiers guffaw behind Morgan. My face blushes crimson. That son of a bitch-dog. I clutch my bow until my knuckles turn white. Steely as ever, Artagan leans his face close to Morgan's.

"Have I your word, that you'll never bother us again?"

Morgan clenches his jaw, his venomous gaze piercing right through me. Artagan flexes his fingertips along the handle of his longsword. God help us. We may come to blows with the rest of the Welsh army before the Saxons ever reach us. Morgan snorts through his nose like a bull.

"I swear it," he says. "Place your archers on the left flank. I'll send Vortigen's spearmen to support you."

Nudging my mare forward, I cannot keep silent. Morgan holds something back, I see it in the twitch of his eyes. Something doesn't smell right, and I'll have it out of him if it's the last thing I ever do.

"Why so few men?" I ask. "Where are the rest?"

Morgan's eyes harden like rocks in their sockets. He and Father exchange looks before the Hammer King edges closer.

"Have you not heard?" Morgan begins. "We lost a thousand men at the Dean Fort, and a plague hit Dyfed not two moons ago. Many perished, including your father's bride, Queen Gwendolyn."

"My stepmother?" I reply with an open mouth.

I never got along with the old woman of propriety, but that doesn't mean I wished her ill. The plague in Dyfed must have been dreadful indeed if it took down nobles and commoners alike. Such maladies can oft strike a kingdom without warning and disappear just as mysteriously. I take a deep breath. Time enough to deal with such losses later. Today, we've a war to fight.

Morgan motions over his shoulder toward my father's spearmen.

"Thanks to that damnable pestilence, less than half your father's army is fit for the field."

"Then how many warriors do we have?"

"Five thousand in my contingent, a thousand from you, and a thousand from Dyfed."

"And the Saxons have over ten thousand? We'll be overwhelmed!"

Bishop Gregory raises his palm over his miter.

"Not if Belin's North Welsh come. He's pledged three thousand horsemen to our aid."

Artagan scoffs, leering at Morgan.

"The Old Man will never come. He despises you almost as much as I do."

"We'll see," Morgan says knowingly. "Just hold the left flank, Blacksword, and I'll do the rest."

The gathering of kings disperses, each heading to their respective portions of the battle line. Artagan and I ride back among our green-clad bowmen, but even from a distance, Morgan, Malcolm, and Father's stares make the hairs rise along the nape of my neck.

Ahern may have been the one who betrayed me in days past, but one of those lords across the field was the mysterious puppet master, plotting against me from the shadows. But who? The Bishop is the key, but I can't exactly question him now with thousands of men arrayed for battle and my hidden enemy possibly within earshot. *Climb one mountain at a time*, Morgan once said. We'll have to work together in order to deal with the Saxons first, but with God as my witness, I *will* root out the man who has been seeking my downfall. Sooner or later, I will. I must.

Artagan draws his blade beside me, bringing my attention back to the task at hand.

"I'm not sure whether to fight the enemy in front or behind me," he grumbles.

"We have to trust them," I counter. "We've no choice. Those are Saxons out there, coming to loot and plunder our homes. Deal with the treachery of other Welsh kings another day. Right now, it's the barbarians from across the border that are our greatest threat. They'll show us no more mercy than they ever have. Think of your father. Think of my mother. Think of our son."

Artagan's eyes glaze over as he puts a palm on my shoulder.

"Speak to the men. You have such a way with words, Branwen. Better than I."

"Now? Before the battle?"

"Give them the will to win. Show them that Mab Ceridwen is with them."

Drawing a deep breath, I canter out in front of our warriors. Seven thousand Welsh against more than ten thousand Saxons? What can I say to encourage them? Few will live to see sunset this day. As my white mare trots the length of the long line of yew bows, every man and she-warrior in the ranks quiets down.

Father leads his thousand Dyfed spearmen into line, well within ear-shot of us. It feels like ages since we have been within a hundred leagues of one another, yet I cannot bear to glance his way. Nonetheless, whatever I say, it must mean something not just to Free Cantref folk or Dyfed men, but all Welsh everywhere. I close my eyes, clearing my throat. May the Virgin give me strength.

"Bowmen, spear-wives, spearmen, hear me! We did not come here today to fight for ourselves, but for those who can no longer fight. Who here has lost someone to the Saxon hordes? Someone dear to them. A mother, a brother, a sister, a child."

One by one, each and every member of both the Free Cantref and the Dyfed contingents raise their palms. Artagan raises his arm, along with Enid, Emryus, Keenan, and Ahern. Water wells behind my eyes, but I blink it back. Thinking of Mother, of Padraig, and many others, I too raise my hand with my longbow and arrows clutched tightly in my fist.

"Let these be your tears! Your arrows, your slings, and spears. Weep for your loved ones with the blood of their murderers upon your steel. Show all Wales and all Christendom that today was the day we wiped the Saxon scourge from the earth forever!"

The Free Cantref folk begin to chant, many of the Dyfed spearmen joining in with raised weapons high over their heads.

"Branwen! Branwen! Branwen!"

Artagan beams at me from across the throngs of troops. Even Father, farthest down the line atop his horse, nods my way. I dare to return his glance, trying to remember that after all he is still my own blood. Despite the distance between us, his strong gaze makes me feel tall in the saddle. Never, *never* has he looked at me that way. Not as an ugly daughter, but as he might have looked at Mother. Maybe even how he might look at a king.

I look away, unsure what to make of the bittersweet taste of remembered hate and love stirring in the back of my throat. Does Father know of his grandson yet? Would it change anything if he saw the innocence and beauty in little Gavin's eyes?

A deadly quiet fills the field as the cheers die down.

The fog along the riverfront begins to clear. Across the fords, the splashing of water and the whinny of horses fill the air. The Saxons have already crossed the river. We should have struck them first, but for this damned fog. Heaven help us now.

Row upon endless row of spearheads emerge from the mists. The thunder of their chain mail and the heavy tread of their boots scatter crows across the field, like the gathering of clouds before a storm. On and on they pour, clad in furs and dented helms. The stink of their unwashed army wafts across the grass. I wrinkle my nose at the stench of musk, sweat, and piss. Rams' horns echo down the battlefront as two lead riders come into view. The Wolf and King Penda.

Small as they look from this vantage, the Wolf's towering frame and King Penda's glistening gold crown make them seem like lords of the earth surrounded by their massive army. No longer a collection of individuals, their forces swarm about the greens like a gigantic, living creature. A monster with ax heads and spear-points instead of arms and legs. The Wolf will want vengeance against us after Artagan slew his brother last summer at Aranrhod. He will offer us no quarter for certain. I cross myself as Artagan orders our archers to ready their bows.

A clatter of new horse hooves sounds far to our left. My pulse quickens. More Saxons? Have the barbarians somehow forged a second army out of thin air? If so, the buzzards will pick our bones within the hour.

Instead, Belin the Old comes galloping out of the dust, followed by his sons and a large retinue of horsemen riding under the black banners of the North. Hurrahs rise all along our lines as Belin's men take up positions on our flank. Now we have evened the odds against the Saxon brutes! Artagan grabs me by the hand.

"We've a chance now! I'll lead some of our men in with Dyfed's spearmen, to give cover for the archers. You stay here and make sure our bowmen get off as many arrows as possible. Belin's men will ride in to finish the job."

"But I want to come with you!"

"No, I need someone I can trust back here. Keep an eye on Morgan's half of the field to the right. Just in case he plays us foul."

I reluctantly nod my head. Artagan marches forward with the best of our woodsmen and his knights. Father leads Dyfed's spearmen beside him just as Morgan's men-at-arms far to the right advance. Lockstep, the Welsh contingents move out into no-man's-land between the armies.

The Saxons howl like wild animals, closing the gap as the two armies near one another along the fords and plains beneath Caerwent. Ahern stands by my side, intent on guarding me to the last. I raise my voice so that all our warriors can hear me.

"Archers, loose!"

The hiss of a thousand longbows sounds through the field. The sky grows dark under the mass of arrowheads, temporarily blotting out the sunlight. Sweat drips down my brow. The sun itself seems to stall in the sky. Both armies charge headlong toward one another, men shouting and roaring until my ears hurt. Our arrows land in the rearward ranks of the advancing Saxon columns. Their cries pierce the air.

"Archers, again!" I shout. "Loose!"

We fire two more volleys into the barbarian crowd. Downstream, the river runs red. I order our bowmen to hold their bows in check as both sides tangle with one another. I've no desire to hit our own troops while trying to get at the Saxons. My eyes search the mass of shoving, warring, bleeding bodies, but I can no longer see Artagan or any of his men amidst the fray. God go with them. It looks like a scene from hell itself beside the crimson-stained fords.

Risking another volley, I order our archers to pick off the Saxon horsemen far to the rear. King Penda moves his riders far to the other end of the field, well out of range. Those barbarian riders are Morgan's problem now. Hopefully, he has enough men-at-arms to repel them.

The Wolf's bloody battle standard wavers near where our own lines and Dyfed's intersect. Despite the back and forth of intermingled armies, the Saxon troops begin to give ground. More and more of them retreat into the shallows of the river, fighting hand to hand with Welshmen clad in green and red. We're pushing them back!

I notch another arrow to my bow. The Saxons' lines start to buckle. Ahern tugs my tunic, drawing my attention toward our own lines.

"My lady, look!"

Belin sits astride his fat horse, he and his sons still as boulders in front of their arrayed horsemen. Other than a few swishing tails and bobbing snouts, not a single horse moves. I blink, doubting my own eyes. What on earth is Belin doing? Why do his men not charge in like they did at the siege of Aranrhod? They're just sitting there, as though waiting. I suck in a sharp breath.

"No . . . no."

The North Welshmen dip their sackcloth banners. Far in the rear of the Saxon host, King Penda's horsemen likewise dip their golden and bloody standards in return. White-bearded Belin faces me and my archers. The old king smirks before drawing in his horse and heading to the rear. Rhun and Iago trail their father off the battlefield.

The North Welshmen follow en masse, retreating back into the wood. I pull at my hair until the roots sting. Ahern looks up at me with furrowed brows.

"What is King Belin doing?"

"Betraying us. He dipped his banners toward Penda's Saxons. The two kings have an understanding."

"You mean he sided with our enemies?"

"Worse than that. He has sealed our doom."

18

Rain comes down in torrents. Thunderheads rumble across the evening sky, gray as headstones. Soaked locks dangle over my face, my head down as my mare stumbles along the muddy switchbacks in the woods. My very bones ache under the relentless downpour. I list in the saddle before Ahern steadies me with his arm.

I nod in thanks, too weary to speak. He blinks up at me with his one good eye, the other hidden beneath a bloody bandage made from the hem of my tunic. My kinsman will probably never see through that eyeball again. He got off lightly. Glancing over my shoulder, I see the remnants of our tattered army stagger along the slippery trail. Most limp or cradle a bloodied arm. Some will not survive the march. Crimson footprints mark our path.

My fingers smart from the cold rain and my coarse bowstring. How many arrows did I loosen toward our foes? More than I can count. It mattered not how many Saxons we felled with our deadly darts. More and more poured over us until they overwhelmed the line. Raindrops run down my cheeks like tears, but my eyes have run dry. As the woods darken in the fading blue light, I sink farther into myself. This is truly the End of Days.

Like a good soldier, Ahern feels the need to report. I barely listen, not wishing to burden my soul with further heartache. But it keeps up his spirit to serve as an efficient guardsman, so I let him mumble on.

"I've garnered the figures in my head as best I can, my lady. At least half our army lies dead, dying, or captured on the battlefield. My last head count found three hundred bowmen left in our ranks, many walking wounded amongst them. The South Welsh lost at least several thousand men, and the Dyfed contingent was completely wiped out."

Ahern lowers his head. Even his stoicism begins to crack at the mere mention of Dyfed. I shut my eyes. The wet road lies long before us, a dark endless retreat into the night. It would almost be a mercy if the Saxons cut us down now, but the storm will probably finish us off if the rough forest trails do not.

Dyfed, Dyfed, Dyfed. My homeland will have nothing but widows left. Amidst the fray, I saw Father fall, pierced by half a dozen Saxon spears. His head probably lies atop a pike now. He was a drunkard and a bully, but it matters not what he might have been in the past. He was still ruler of Dyfed, and my father. The only one I'll ever have. Struggling to raise my voice, I lean down close to Ahern's ear.

"Any word of Artagan?"

Ahern bites his lip.

"Nothing certain. Rumor has it he was wounded. Our scouts think Belin's horsemen took him prisoner."

I ball my fists, grinding my teeth. Belin the Old. Belin the Traitor! His men deserted the line and watched as the Saxons swarmed over us like locusts. Falling into his hands seems as bad as being captured by the Saxons. I aim my forefinger at Ahern.

"Bring these scouts to me. I must have word of my husband."

"The scouts are spread out in the rearguard, my lady. We may not see them again until well after nightfall or even dawn."

I blow air past my lips. I doubt the sun will ever rise again. Not out of this foggy night. But I cannot fault a single warrior in our ranks, for each fought with valor and skill. The Saxons simply proved too many. Barely speaking above a whisper, I tightly clutch Ahern's shoulder.

"What of our own people? Do we know anyone's fate for certain?"

"Sir Emryus and Keenan both lie wounded. Their horses carry them now, farther back in the column."

Ahern looks down a moment, struggling to regain his voice.

"But I saw Enid Spear-wife fall myself."

I put my face in my hands. Enid. When I close my eyes, I still see her the day I came to Cadwallon's Keep. Stern as ever, she showed her strength and willfulness amongst the other male warriors and gave me the fortitude to stand tall when fate thrust a warrior's bow into my own hands. I never gave her credit for inspiring me so. Now I shall never have the chance to tell her. First Father, now Enid, maybe even my beloved husband.

No. Artagan must still live. I refuse to accept otherwise. But we must push on. No more thoughts tonight. We must make our way back to Aranrhod, where the survivors can gather.

Even in the darkness, the carrion crows caw through the night. The ravens and buzzards feast on the battlefields far behind us, swarming for miles to harvest the corpses of our loved ones. Before the moon rises, bats and wolves will join the unholy banquet.

My eyelids begin to sag when a thicket of sedge shakes nearby. Ahern immediately orders several men to investigate, leading them through the shadows despite his one good eye. Instinctively grabbing my bow, I realize I have no arrows left. A gruff voice growls from the brush.

"Unhand me!"

Ahern returns, tugging a man by the elbow. The rain lets up to a slight drizzle, a pocket of moonlight peeking through the cloud cover. An old, balding man in black sackcloth struggles under Ahern's grip.

"What have you found, Ahern?"

"A spy perhaps, my lady."

The man tries to shove Ahern's firm hand off his arm.

"I'm a priest, you blockhead!" the man answers, before bowing toward me. "Father David, Your Grace."

"Why do you spy upon us from the bushes, Holy Father?" I ask.

"I was shivering with cold. I'm a wandering parson and gave aid to the wounded at the late battle before the Saxon curs drove me off."

Ahern raises a skeptical eyebrow, but I can think of no reason the priest ought to lie. Many a cleric gives succor and last rites to the dying on the battlefield. Nonetheless, I give the priest a stern look.

"Well, I cannot let you go, Father. Should someone capture you they might learn our whereabouts. I intend to get my people home as safely and secretly as possible."

"I would not talk, your ladyship."

"Unfortunately, their blades would hack away at you until you did. I'm sorry, Father David. But you'll have to be our guest for now."

"You heard Her Highness," Ahern says, pushing the parson along.

The priest protests a moment before surrendering to the march. Turning my pony around, I halt in front of the cleric. Perhaps he saw more of the battle's aftermath than my scouts did.

"You say you saw the field after the fight was over? Did you see a man named King Artagan?"

David stops, the rain glancing off his bald scalp. He nods solemnly, his voice very low.

"I've news of both Kings Morgan and Artagan. One is captured and the other dead."

I waver in the saddle, the black woods suddenly turning into complete darkness.

The fire burns low in the grate. Flames dance along the peat logs, crackling embers echoing across the dark, quiet bedchamber. Folding my arms, I stand and stare at the flickering blaze. The orange fireglow shrinks from the empty bed behind me. A knock comes at my bedchamber door.

Ahern sticks his head in when I do not answer, my eyes still entranced by the blaze in the hearth. We stand silent in my tower room, listening to the crickets chirping outside. Droplets rattle the roof tiles high overhead. My kinsman holds his spear and shield, an eye patch over his left socket.

"The rains started again," he murmurs.

When I fail to reply, he paces toward the windowsill. A few hearth fires dot the otherwise dark confines of the castle. The halls of Aranrhod once echoed with laughter and revelry even into the wee hours, but not tonight. My guardsman frowns.

"I've watchmen patrolling the walls. All quiet tonight. The harsh weather will slow the Saxons."

Ahern sighs with exasperation as I continue gazing wordlessly into the fire.

"My Queen, you are the ruler of Aranrhod now. I need you to give me orders. The people need you to lead us."

"Maybe I don't want to. Maybe my days of thinking for everyone else have ended."

"You don't eat, you barely speak. You've hardly glanced at your son since our return!"

"Rowena cares for him. I love him dearly, but his face reminds me of his father too much."

Hanging my head, I shut my eyes. The movement of armies, shifting alliances, courtly intrigues all seem like some pointless chess game now. What does any of it mean without Artagan by my side? With the Saxons running amuck in South Wales and along the eastern borders, Aranrhod will soon fall under siege to the barbarians once more. It is only a matter of time.

The Saxons have broken the back of all Welsh resistance now. Since our defeat near Caerwent, word has spread of the slaughter and betrayal. The peasantry call it the Battle of the Bloody Fords. I call it a massacre. Most Welsh forces have either surrendered, fled, or perished against the encroaching Saxon onslaught. And I haven't the faintest idea what to do. What can a lone woman do when all the world turns against her? I heave a heavy sigh.

"Bring me the priest, Ahern. I wish to talk with him alone."

Ahern nods and exits the chamber. My kinsman has proven faithful since his return to duty. As de facto seneschal of the castle, the few guards remaining in the garrison seem to follow Ahern's orders without issue. It seems a small comfort when my most loyal warrior is a man who once betrayed me. But a comfort it is. Nonetheless, Ahern is no strategist. I cannot debate ideas with him as I might a true advisor. He said it himself: he wants to take orders, not give them.

A few minutes pass before he returns with Father David in tow. Ahern shuts the door, leaving the cleric and myself alone in my dimly lit chamber. Heavy rain pelts the roof as the storm intensifies.

"Have you any word from the outside world, Father David?"

"I sent ravens as you asked, Your Grace, but birds travel slow in such weather."

"But you have learned something."

"Aye. I received one reply yesterday from a layman I trust in a western monastery."

"Well?"

The balding priest hesitates.

"It merely confirms what I first told you. King Morgan was slain at the Bloody Fords by King Penda and the Wolf. Your husband, the Black-sword, remains a prisoner of King Belin in North Wales. They've taken him to the fortress at Mount Snowden."

My heart convulses, wrenched sideways. Snowden. The frozen mountain fortress of the North. Few outside of Belin's realm have ever seen it, but its reputation reaches far. Once brought to Snowden, there is no coming back. The fortress has never been taken nor any of its prisoners ever escaped. Second only to Belin's palace on the isle of Mona, Snowden typically falls under the sway of the heir apparent. Prince Rhun and Lady Olwen must be the lords of Snowden now. Keeping my voice steady, I turn back to the fire so that the priest will not see the fear in my eyes.

"Why does Belin hold Artagan prisoner? What does he hope to gain?"

"I'm a simple parson, my lady, but I can guess. Belin is Penda's ally now, no?"

"The Saxon king and Belin clearly have an understanding. The Saxons will leave Belin's kingdom alone while the barbarians gobble up the other half of Wales. Little does the fool realize, the devils will break their word once they've subjugated the rest of the country."

"Perhaps, my Queen, but Belin is as clever as he is pitiless. He may hold Artagan hostage in order to gain your allegiance."

"My allegiance? He betrayed us at the Bloody Fords and took my husband prisoner! Why would I ever bend the knee to him?"

"To save Artagan's life. Think about it, Your Highness. In exchange for your husband, he'll demand Aranrhod ally itself to him. In doing so, he could control half of Wales without losing a single soldier."

Raising an eyebrow, I turn toward the priest and look him over. For a wandering holy man, the priest has an unusually keen perception of things. Perhaps fate alone did not put him in my path the night he came across our retreating army. Maybe someone placed him here to spy on me. I've seen enough traitors around me these past few years to smell them out on sight. I narrow my gaze.

"How does a country parson grow so wise in the ways of kingly politics?"

"That's simple, Your Grace. Because I was a king once."

I blink in disbelief.

"You jest, Father."

"Nay, your ladyship. I'm cousin to the dying King Urien of the northernmost Free Cantrefs in Powys."

"You're kin to Olwen's father?"

"Many years ago, we both had a claim to the throne, but I ruled only a few years before Urien ousted me in a coup. He gave me two choices, either die a king or take holy orders and renounce the throne."

"And you chose life."

"It changed my life. God guided me through countless trials in the wilderness since that day many years ago. My soul belongs to Christ, but my mind has not forgotten the lessons of a kingship."

I nod, impressed. His story seems too outrageous to believe, yet I sense that a liar would have concocted a much more believable falsehood if they wished to deceive me. Father David holds my gaze. His simple cloak and callous hands bespeak a man who has indeed lived a rough rural life, yet his eyes sparkle like a true believer. A baptizer in the wilderness. I forgot such pious men of God still existed.

"We've no ordained man of God to lead our parish here at Aranrhod. You interested?"

"Does that mean you'll let me go if I decide to leave?"

"If that is what you wish."

David flashes a half-smile.

"God has led me to you. Perhaps I should stay and see if your flock needs a shepherd."

I smile back, the first time I have done so in many weeks. He bows slightly before excusing himself from my chamber. Ahern stands guard outside my door. I ask him to send for Rowena and my child. He grins broadly before seeing to my request.

When Rowena returns with Gavin in her arms, my little boy slumbers against her chest. I reach out for him, daring to wake him even if only to hold my babe close to my heart. He stirs and whimpers a moment before snoozing against my breast.

Rowena sits by the fireside with me, stoking the flames with fresh kindling. I gently rock Gavin in my lap.

"How fares my son?" I inquire.

"He thrives, m'lady. I've enough milk for both he and my Mina."

A pang of guilt sweeps through me. Although she doesn't mean it, I feel it as a rebuke. Instead of continuing to nurse my own boy, I rode off to war with his father. Now I've nearly made him fatherless, and I a widow. Stroking his soft cinnamon hair, I speak quietly with Rowena.

"Any word of Una? Is she still missing?"

"She turned up, m'lady. Joined a cloister of nuns over in Dyfed, she has."

"A nunnery? Why?"

Rowena blushes, looking at her feet.

"We shared Keenan between us, but once I got with child Una started to change. She said it was a sin, and if she took the veil it would free Keenan to marry me and set things aright."

"I'm sorry, Rowena. You two were close as sisters."

I suddenly miss Una with a pang, realizing I may never see the poor girl ever again. What kind of friend was I to her? What kind of friend have I been to anyone? Rowena sniffles.

"Worst of it is, Keenan lies in the infirmary still. His wounds may still get the best of him."

"Don't say that. He may yet recover. I'll see to him myself. He's a brave knight and will make you a fine husband someday."

Her eyes water over as she looks up and takes my hand.

"M'lady, do we stand a chance now, any of us? People say it's the end of the world and that the Saxons will come here to wipe us out."

"I don't know, my dear. I, for one, will not submit. Not so long as

I have Aranrhod, and my son to fight for. I don't know how, but we will save our homeland somehow. We must."

"I hope you're right, Your Grace. I hope you find a way. I hope we all do."

She dries her cheeks and rises to go, offering to take Gavin back to the nursery. I shake my head, preferring to keep him in the cradle beside me tonight. He has grown big for a baby, and after a good evening feed from Rowena, he can sleep through the night without getting hungry enough to awaken. Nonetheless, Rowena offers to come in the night should I need her. I thank her as she shuts the door.

Cradling Gavin in my arms, I stay up watching the fireplace. Rainfall brushes against the shutters and the wind whistles through chinks in the walls, but the hearth keeps the stones of my bedchamber warm and snug. Somewhere out there, my Artagan shivers in a cell atop Mount Snowden. And Saxons ravage the land from one end to the other with no one to resist them. The two greatest foes of the Saxons, Morgan and Artagan, are both defeated, one dead and the other in chains. My first husband is a ghost and the other in bondage. Who remains to stand up to the barbarian hordes? Just me and a handful of archers in an ancient castle. I whisper softly as I kiss my boy atop his sleepy head.

"I'll get your father back, my son. Somehow, I will set all the wrongs to right."

Before the fire dies down in the grate, I nod off with Gavin in my arms. The sound of the rain penetrates my dreams, thundering in my ears like the roll of the surf.

Like the sound of the sea where I was born.

The roar of the tide wanes, and I see Mother again. She smiles at me through the vertical threads of the loom. My fat, barefoot toddler feet bump against the small stone counterweights that dangle beneath the massive timber loom set. Mother moves the shuttle with one hand, poking me with a fingertip between the forest of taut, half-woven threads. I cackle in a high babyish voice, my mother flashing a pearly grin every time I laugh. She hums a lullaby while she works.

Her song suddenly stops. A man's voice murmurs from the chamber threshold. I cannot see him over the loom, but I know by his voice that he is not my father. Mother puts a finger to her lips to quiet me, her eyes sad. Something is wrong. I freeze like a hare in its hole.

Mother and the man speak in low, heated tones. The rumble of the sea outside Dun Dyfed masks much of what they say, but I can still glean something from their muffled voices. His words sound warm and stern by turns, yet oddly almost pleading. Mother seems angry, yet her voice remains smooth and calm as ever. The man refuses to go. Still hidden behind the loom, I start to tremble.

She rises, her voice growing loud. Mother tells the man to leave. He gets quiet, his feet shuffling away as he says something in a growl under his breath. Once he departs, I rush into Mother's arms and put my head in her lap. Mother pats my back, resuming her song, only humming much fainter this time. The stranger's footfalls fade down the stairwell.

Blinking my eyes awake, I find myself once again inside my bedchamber at Aranrhod. Yet my dream was no dream. It must have been something long forgotten, fragments that only a young child's memory can carry.

I rarely recall Mother ever entertaining any men without Father present. Even as a child, I knew Father's temperament could easily turn to jealousy. Yet who was this strange man who seemed to be on familiar terms with Mother, and why did his presence distress her so? His shadowy, formless face looms like a dark vision in the echoes of my memory. With a shiver and a yawn, I try and push such thoughts far to the back of my mind. Time enough to ruminate on such odd musings later.

When I arise at dawn, the gentle thud of the ceaseless downpour reverberates across the castle. Gavin wriggles in my arms and begins to cry for breakfast. I turn my head, massaging a crick in my neck. Rowena pads barefoot into the room with Mina already at her breast. She pulls out another large nipple from within her shift and begins to suckle Gavin. Ahern blushes from the stairwell, looking away as though he has not noticed. I might almost smile, but a shadow appears on the stairs.

Annwyn strides noiselessly into my room. Her once dark-and-silver hair has gone completely gray since news of the capture of her son. She smiles down at her grandson in Rowena's arms, even as tears form behind her sad eyes. She too sees Artagan in the little boy's face. I ask Rowena and Ahern to give us a moment. Once alone, I sit Annwyn down and pour us both some spiced wine. She doesn't touch her cup, hunched over the empty hearth. I rekindle the fire. Her cold palms linger near the budding flames. She seems to have aged a hundred years.

"I'm dying, Branwen."

My brows narrow, but something in her steady gaze unnerves me. She takes my hand to her breast. I start to pull away, but she keeps my palm there. A large, unnatural lump protrudes from her bosom. I swallow hard. A few times I've seen the same symptom in elderly village women. It often precludes a lengthy demise. Her ailment is beyond my skill to heal, or anyone else's for that matter. I shake my head, but Annwyn touches my cheek with a smile.

"No words, sweet child. I will be with your mother soon, and have no more troubles of this earth. But we must talk of what remains undone."

"I will get Artagan back. You should enjoy your time with your grandson."

"You cannot give in to Belin or the Saxons. If you do, my grandson will have no kingdom to inherit nor a homeland to grow up in. You have a hard road ahead of you, Branwen, but I am here to help you."

I sigh at the unending rain. What can I and one old woman accomplish?

"Whatever we do, we must wait for these unseasonable rains to pass. It bogs down all travel."

"No," Annwyn says firmly. "Whatever you plan to do, it must be done now. While our enemies are idle and bogged down by Mother Nature. Fate has given us this opportunity, and we must use it wisely."

Never have I heard her talk with such forcefulness before. Not once does she mention peace or compromise, but instead stares stoically ahead like a spear-wife. She has grayed into a stony-faced crone since the capture of her son. Before I might have flinched from the sight of such a transformation, but having a child of my own now, I know all too well what lengths I would go to in order to protect my boy.

These ungodly rains present both a blessing and a curse. They've worn summer away with heavy showers, flooding rivers, and swelling every lake and stream. They have made much of Wales impassable for the Saxon armies, as though the land itself were fighting back to save us. But they will only stall the barbarians for a season or two at most. Unfortunately, these very same storms will dampen the crops this year, making for a meager harvest. Come winter we will have a twofold problem, both war and famine. Yet I only see troubles and no solution. I shake my head, laying my hands in Annwyn's lap.

"What can I do? I've no army, no treasure, and no way to stall the Saxons or save my husband. I'm not even a great warrior. What can I possibly do to save us?"

"You are a queen! And whatever has come before you in life has prepared you for this moment. I feel it as surely as I do the coming storm in my bones or the call of my own mortality in my breast. I am here to help you, young one, but it is *you* who was born to lead."

Despite our impending doom, despite our losses at the Bloody Fords, a glowing warmth stirs inside me. As though my entire life has suddenly made a complete circle. As though all the travails of my existence somehow culminate in the abyss in which I find myself. As though if I simply step back and look at the whole, the entire picture might suddenly fit into view. My eyes slowly widen.

The Saxons, the assassin, my kidnapping, the defeat at Bloody Fords, all weave together with a common thread. How could I have been so blind? Holding a hand to my head, the gears in my mind begin to spin. I've been playing chess with my life for so long that I've forgotten to ask myself the most elemental question about my shadowy opponent.

What do they hope to *gain* from my downfall?

Despite all my travails, they have a single aspect in common that I have overlooked. A very select few could possibly benefit from *all* these misfortunes that have nearly befallen me. Shutting my eyes, the hazy silhouette of my true enemy begins to take shape. They would have to be a ruler, a noble who stood to benefit directly by my death or kidnapping. That narrows the suspects down to a handful of monarchs and their heirs. Secondly, they must somehow be benefitting from the Saxon incursions as it weakens their rivals. So that rules out anyone from Aranrhod or Dyfed, as the armies from those two realms have either been decimated or destroyed at Bloody Fords. It would also require someone merciless enough to risk using assassins and Saxons for their own ends, yet someone who also prefers to fight indirectly behind a mask of secrecy rather than challenge me openly. My list of suspicious foes runs short now indeed.

I can see only but one conclusion, but I must know for certain. I turn to my guardsman.

"Ahern, fetch me the priest! Quickly!"

Annwyn raises an eyebrow, flashing a knowing smile, as though she senses the change in me. Whatever spirit guides me now, I have no time to question it. Ahern returns with Father David at his side, the holy man panting hard. I snap my fingers at the priest.

"Father, did you yourself see Morgan fall at the Bloody Fords?"

"Aye, the Wolf struck him down with his own hands."

"But Malcolm got away with Bishop Gregory close beside him. Neither Belin nor the Saxons pursuing them?"

"As a matter of fact, they did, come to think of it. I thought it odd at the time, but the battle was all chaos. How did you know about that?"

"I didn't."

A frown creases my cheeks. It is worse than I feared. All this time, my shadowy foe has employed several highly placed conspirators in every plot against me. There may be a single author who has attempted to pen my demise, but this implacable villain has also arranged a small cadre of allies to ensnare me and all those I hold dear.

Wise old Annwyn leans her hard-set face close to mine.

"You sense now who conspired against you, child, from the very beginning, don't you?"

"Not just one, but multiple conspirators. But yes, I think I know the root now. But I must test my intuition to make sure before we strike."

Ahern and the priest exchange looks. Each of them questions me as to who my mysterious enemy might be. Malcolm? The late Morgan? King Penda? I shake my head, refusing to answer anyone directly.

"Just give me time to think, no more questions now," I reply. "I shall have some important tasks for each of you soon. But I need time to sort it all out first. When I'm ready, I'll call on each of you. The fate of all Wales and our very lives may well depend upon what we do in the next few days."

I shall have to risk everything on one last gamble. The time for playing it safe has long since passed. But will my enemies see this coming?

I bite my lower lip, contemplating how to best use the chess pieces that remain in this game of life and death.

Despite my troubled face, Annwyn flashes a half-grin.

"So you know what to do then?"

"I have a plan. Not much, but a plan nonetheless."

We gather our mounts beneath a broad oak tree outside the castle gates. Drizzling mists obscure the mountains that surround Aranrhod and the vale, filling the air with a damp, cool piney scent. Ahern and Annwyn sidle up next to me atop their mounts. Rowena and the priest remain on foot. My pony Gwenhwyfar sidesteps beneath me as I gently shush her and smooth her dew-covered mane. We've a long journey ahead of us, girl. You'll need every ounce of strength before the week runs out. I sit tall in the saddle.

"Does everyone know what to do?"

They nod their heads. Good. Father David glosses over a crumpled parchment.

"Another raven has come from my friend in the western monastery. Word has it that King Urien has died of old age in the northern Free Cantrefs."

I sigh. How will Olwen take the news of her father's passing? There will be more bloodshed once Rhun's horsemen try to claim Urien's Motte from the Free Cantref bowmen there. As though Wales hasn't suffered enough. But there's nothing I can do about that now. Father David clears his throat, still reading.

"Another piece of news as well: a knight named Sir Owen has claimed the crown in Dyfed."

Ahern smacks his fist into his other palm.

"The upstart! The coward should've died at Bloody Fords with his kin, instead of playing sick. I'd like to give him a taste of my cold steel."

I grab my kinsman's mount by the bridle.

"You've your own task, brother. You ride for Caerleon and Annwyn will go to Dyfed."

"And you, my lady?"

"I ride for North Wales and Belin's court."

Thunder rumbles in the distance. Another storm moving in. We've little time. Annwyn, Ahern, and I each nod toward one another before parting our mountain ponies. Let our desperate gamble begin. Each of us trots off in different directions into the wet woods. Calling back over my shoulder, I wave toward Rowena and the cleric.

"Look after my son and Aranrhod until I return. Pray for us!"

The priest makes the sign of the cross while Rowena stifles her tears behind her hand. As I ride alone through the dripping woodlands, a flash of lightning splits an ancient oak tree nearby. Halting my whinnying mare, I see the silhouette of Aranrhod's towers looming in the distance. Perhaps the closest place I ever had to a true home, and perhaps the last time I shall ever look upon it. Lowering my gaze, I dig my heels into Gwenhwyfar's flanks as the rain renews its strength. Godspeed.

Before an hour runs out, my soaked locks plaster themselves against my face. Biting, cold winds chill me to the bone. I urge my mare northward through the wilds. Winding through brambles and thickets, we push on during a letup in the rain.

In spite of the harsh weather, my stout pony moves fast as a hawk across the damp landscape, splashing through mud and mires. Yet with every mile I come to dread reaching my destination more and more. Despite my well-laid plans, I know I have overlooked something. The plot against me may be about politics and kingships, but there's more to it than that. Something personal lurks in the malice of these deeds set against me, whether from an assassin's knife or a Saxon ax. A knot tightens in my stomach, but still I spur my mare on.

After dark, a milky moon rises over the clouds and lights my way along the trail. Nothing but the sound of wind, dripping leaves, and my pony's clacking hooves sound through the still night. Despite my mare's panting breath, I push her harder still. We've so little time. My thighs ache and my head feels heavy as lead.

As I bob in the saddle, Annwyn and Ahern continually come to mind even though they're many leagues away by now. Did I give them clear enough instructions? Perhaps I have forgotten something important. I may never see either of them again. Maybe I've even sent us all to our deaths. Shaking my head, I struggle to stay focused. Ride, just ride on.

The time for doubts has passed. I've staked everything on this. We must succeed. We must.

The salty breath of the sea washes over the near hills. The scent of the ocean. Good. The castles of Belin the Old cannot be far. I've probably already crossed into their dominions. Despite the many ridges and rivers that intersperse our country, Wales isn't a large realm as the crow flies, at least not compared to the sprawling Saxon domains far to the east. A single rider unburdened by armor can traverse much of it if they throw safety to the wind.

Galloping through a ravine, my pony suddenly lurches beneath me and cries out. Sending me vaulting from her back, I collapse in the mud. Gwenhwyfar stumbles on a limp leg, her hoof entangled in briar snares. Damnation! Now I'll never reach Belin's castle in time. Certainly not on horseback anyway. Poor creature. I try to shush her and pat her neck. She perks her ears, still favoring one foreleg.

My gaze narrows. Those snares don't belong to anything natural, merely rough ropes with thorns woven into them. My eyes suddenly widen. I've stumbled into a trap.

The rumble of horseshoes fills the shadowy dell. Dozens of horsemen encircle me. Their tall pikes seem to pierce the overcast sky. The lead rider halts before me, lowering his long spear near my jugular. He grins as a sliver of moonlight cuts across his dark beard. My throat runs dry when Rhun edges his spear-point closer.

"What have we here? A princess pretending to be a queen? My father will wish to see you."

He nods toward one of his cavalrymen, the man drawing a short blade. Before I can blink, he slashes at my pony's throat. The mare's red blood spills across her white flanks. My heart twists sideways.

"No!"

I reach out for my dying mare as hands ensnare me from behind.

19

Belin laughs.

"You must be the stupidest little girl ever born."

He paces the stony floors of the empty castle hall, fierce winds howling through cracks in the vaulted ceilings. A lone hearth fire flickers in the corner while Rhun waits in the doorway behind me. The bald, white-bearded king stops and smirks. My drenched, frayed garments hang limp from my shivering limbs, bespeckled with mud and mare's blood. Poor Gwenhwyfar. I ball my right fist, wishing I could knock the old man's jaw off. If only Rhun's men hadn't taken my bow. King Belin grins, amused at my consternation.

"You're a fool to come to Snowden alone. Did you think I'd simply hand your husband over to you?"

"I thought you'd have some honor left!" I reply, only half-telling the truth. "To make amends for what you did at Bloody Fords."

Belin shakes his head with a laugh, pacing the floors again.

"Queens. So arrogant. Just like your mother."

My eyebrows rise.

"What do you know of my mother, old man?"

Belin stops, clenching his jaw. A frosty blue coldness in his gaze reminds me of a serpent. All the jovialness fades from his face.

"You look just like her. She was a beauty in her youth. But willful, arrogant, unyielding."

"She was a kind woman, a healer, and a stewardess of her people."

"Bah! She betrayed her people. She had the same choice you have before you now."

"What choice? What are you talking about?"

"She could have united our people, all Wales against the Saxons. Instead she spurned me."

An icy, prickly sensation wends its way down my neck. Suddenly an image of my dream the other night comes unbidden to my mind, the memory of my mother at the loom and the strange man who scared her. Belin. Younger, his hair was darker then, but it was definitely him in that half-forgotten memory of early childhood. It's as though my mother were trying to speak to me from beyond the grave. My gaze narrows on the old king.

"You offered her your hand in marriage? To my mother?"

Belin knocks a dish from a nearby tabletop, the pewter plate rattling against the cobblestone floor. I back up against a wall. Despite the airiness of the empty mead hall, it feels like a prison cell all the same. Artagan must be held captive here somewhere. One problem at a time. I must focus on the task at hand. Belin turns his back to me. The old man's shoulders sag with regret.

"She went and married that dog, Vortigen of Dyfed, instead! She and I could have changed Wales forever. With her people in the South and mine in the North, we might have bound up all Wales into a single nation. Like I said, she betrayed her people."

The old man bares his soul to me, almost on a whim. But why? Belin the Old, Belin the Cunning, Belin the Traitor, these are his names. He is not a man known for initiating a heart-to-heart. Quietly spinning his plots from his kingdom in the North, he has sought to subjugate all Wales under his rule before his rivals realized what was happening. And all the while my very existence as a queen of the Old Tribes has been a constant thorn in his side. My marriages to rival Welsh kings in Caerwent and later Aranrhod have provided an unwitting counterweight to his plans.

Belin walks to an arrow slit, staring at the cold barren crags outside

Snowden castle. Leagues upon leagues of upland wastes. The worn, time-carven land reminds me of the lines on his ancient face.

Coldness creeps into my bones. Belin would only tell me these things for one reason. He never intends to let me go. And there is only one reason he would keep me prisoner now. My lips tremble as I strive to speak.

"My mother didn't betray her people. She betrayed you. Is that what this is all about?"

"What is any of this life about? Power? Love? Power lost and gained. Love gained and lost."

Glaring at his back, I struggle to keep my voice even.

"You're the one who has sought to destroy me. All along, it was you at the root of it."

"I wondered when we would come to that."

He turns his steely gaze upon me. The spider at the center of so many webs. Like a fool, I have strayed into his nest. The man who sought to destroy me from the outset now has me in his power.

Sweat beads along my brow. I came here for two reasons, to free my husband and to find out for sure who has been plotting my demise all these years. And now I know for certain, but little good it does me in trying to free Artagan.

But Belin does not fool me now. His unrequited love for my mother was merely the seed of his enmity toward me and my family. I see it clear as day on his face. He fed his vengeful heart ever afterward on his lust for power and his greed for more land. A true warmonger, he only finds pleasure and meaning in life through wealth and dominance, all the while hiding it behind the mask of a quiet old man. No matter how much of Wales he takes, it will never fill the emptiness inside him. It will never be enough.

I swallow hard, stalling for time. Trying to think.

"How did you manage it?" I begin. "Saxons? Assassins? A lot to send against one young girl."

He paces around the fire, eyeing me with the calculating patience of a hungry wolf.

"By now I suppose you know of your guardsman's messages to your father, sent via Bishop Gregory."

"You were the one intercepting and reading those letters."

"It goes much deeper than that, little girl. I had my spies in several courts, men who sought the power I've now given them."

My mind races, trying to keep up. The signs were in front of me all along, but I had neither the insight nor the will to see it. I've been looking at the kings in power when I should've been looking at their next of kin, the heirs who would inherit their thrones once men like King Morgan and my father were dead.

I begin to pace, so as to keep the distance between us.

"Owen and Malcolm," I deduce. "They betrayed their kings so that they might rule in their stead."

"Very good. And now they will swear allegiance to me, because I and I alone have a treaty with the Saxons and can restrain them. I also have the only sizable army left in all Wales. Our entire country will be united under one banner. Mine."

"Not so long as I live. My marriage to Morgan united half of Wales against you. Even when I ran off with Artagan, that still posed too strong a threat to your power."

He merely scoffs in reply, not even remotely intimidated by my continued defiance. But something in his words still does not add up. After all, it was his army that came to our aid when the Saxons first cornered us at Aranrhod.

"But you saved us during the siege of Aranrhod," I counter. "Why?"

"For the same reason I offer to save you now. The prospect of marriage. I sent my son to woo you, but you proved as evasive as your mother."

"Rhun is wed to Olwen, and I to Artagan. That's marriages aplenty."

"But not to me. With you as my queen, the rest of Wales will fall into line. It is the choice I offered your mother once, and the choice I offer you now."

My stomach turns over. Me marry him? He's mad. Not to mention I already have a husband, who I'm sure would suffer an *accident* as soon as Belin took me as his bride. The mere thought of anything evil befalling Artagan lances my heart. Backing up against the cold stone wall, I wish I could run. The man before me is no king, only a monster.

"You cannot be serious! I've been married twice. That's more than enough. You've tried to kill me, for God's sake! Sending Saxons and as-sassins after me. You say this is all about uniting Wales, about kingships and kingdoms, but we both know that's only half the story. You see my mother when you look at me. This is your chance to set right the sup-posed wrongs you've suffered."

Belin bangs his fist against a tabletop.

"I can never right the wrongs that have been done! If I cannot have her, I will have the kingdom our marriage should have brought under my rule. The entire Welsh nation."

I slowly shake my head.

"I was wrong. You cared nothing for my mother. You only wanted the lands that her hand in marriage would've brought you."

He shrugs, lost in his own recollections for a moment.

"It was I who gave the Saxons their boats when they raided Dyfed all those years ago. They were supposed to take her prisoner after you and Vortigen had been killed."

My eyes widen, my hand rushing to my throat. Mother dead because of him? Because of him! Before I can think, I have my hands around his collar. I can see only red, the sound of pumping blood rising in my ears. The old man tries to push me off, but my palms tighten around his fat throat. A rough hand grabs me about the middle, pulling me off as I kick and shout. Rhun restrains me with an iron grip, but I lash out for Belin all the same. Damn him! Damn them both. Belin rubs his sore neck.

"Put her in the dungeons! She will wed me one way or the other. If she comes willingly, I'll let her precious Artagan live. Maybe. Otherwise, I'll hang him tomorrow. Let her cool her heels and think on that."

More guards hold back my arms as Rhun takes me down into the frigid dungeons. Thrown in a cell, I lie sprawled on the floor, cradling my wrists. The cell door shuts with a squeak. Rhun gives me a last smirk before clos-ing the dungeon entranceway. All turns to impenetrable darkness.

I hug my knees close to my chest, shivering in the frozen blackness. It cannot end like this. Belin cannot win. He decided long ago that if he couldn't have my mother, no one could. And now he has laid the same ultimatum upon me, the daughter of the woman he once both loved and hated. Now that he has me at his mercy, he'd rather keep me as a caged pet, the final feather in his cap after a life spent plotting and scheming, first against my mother and then against me.

The wheels spin in my mind, recalling every step of Belin's endless plots. When the Saxons first attacked me on the King's Road before my betrothal, it must have been Belin who unleashed the Fox and the Wolf against me.

Owen was already a herald in Father's court, but I hardly knew him then and paid him no mind. He could have easily gotten word to Belin, who in turn would've lent the Saxons the same ships they used against my mother all those years ago.

I shut my eyes, shaking my head. The same man who made me motherless would have had me rent apart by the very same barbarians. God, is there no justice in the world anymore?

The Pictish assassin had to also be Belin's doing. His long-dead queen was a Pict, or so Morgan always said. All the while, Morgan suspected Artagan when in fact his own brother conspired with Belin against him. Malcolm must have coveted his brother's throne as much as Owen wanted my father's.

With Malcolm, the Bishop, and Belin intercepting Ahern's messages to my father, they would've easily known my whereabouts at all times. Hence the Saxons lying in wait when we reached the Dean Fort. That was almost two years ago, and if not for Artagan's fortuitous appearance, I might have suffered death, capture, or worse at the hands of the Fox and the Wolf.

But even when I reached the safety of the Free Cantrefs, I could not entirely escape beyond Belin's long reach. Blinded by Morgan and Father's persistent efforts to recapture me, I never gave a thought to the king in the North who secretly worked against me all the while. But all my enemies still remain each other's enemies too, and even Belin didn't want the Saxons conquering the Free Cantrefs. After all, Belin wants to rule all Wales himself, and he certainly doesn't plan to share it with the Saxons. Both the Welsh and Saxon warlords use each other. Are we any better than barbarians ourselves?

When Rhun's horsemen lifted the siege, Belin seized the opportunity to try and wed his eldest son to me, thus securing his plans for dominating all Wales. But I would only wed Artagan and none other. So Belin changed his mind, once again seeking to kill me and remove me as a threat. Now that he has me in a Snowden dungeon, he can afford to let me live again. So long as I become his meek slave-bride.

I spit on the floor, drubbing my fist uselessly against the brick walls. Since his betrayal of our armies at the Battle of the Bloody Fords, Belin has the only army and diplomatic alliances left to save Wales. Whether they love him or not, the people will flock to his banners, if only to save their children from slavery at the hands of the Saxons.

Maybe the old King is right. Perhaps I am a fool. A fool to have come here alone, a fool to hope against hope that one woman could make a difference against a world of men bent on destruction and mayhem. All my best-laid plans have landed me in a dank dungeon, alone in a prison fortress high in the frosty peaks of North Wales.

I begin to pray, so utterly alone as tears stream down my cheeks. Hear me, God. Help me, please.

The prison door opens a crack.

A shaft of bronze light penetrates my dark abode. Blinking back my tears, I squint into the bright torchlight as a lone figure descends the steps to my cell. A woman with a round, pregnant belly stops beside the lock, her violet eyes reflecting the ruby torchlight. I rise to my feet.

"Olwen? Did you receive my raven?"

"That was risky of you. Anyone might have intercepted your message. You're lucky I'm one of the few who can read at this court."

"I had to try. Will you help me?"

"No."

My heart sinks. Staggering back, I steady myself on the bulkhead. All is lost. I was truly a fool to apply to Olwen for help. Heavy with child, she carries the next heir to the northern throne. She has no reason under heaven to help me. Has she come to gloat then? I'm the one in a cell while she is the mighty Queen. I won't beg, if that's what she's come to see. For Artagan or my boy, I might, but for my own life, no. I won't give her the satisfaction. Olwen lowers her face close to the bars.

"I won't do it for you, but for Artagan's sake alone do I do this."

She pulls a key out from beneath her robes and opens the lock. My mouth hangs open, but I do not budge. Still in disbelief, I walk into the light. Purple bags hang under her eyes, her Venus-like face and figure marred by the weight of pregnancy. And something else, I sense. Perhaps life as a queen in frozen Snowden has not proven as pleasant as she might have hoped. Olwen tosses the keys at me, but I still don't understand.

"What are you doing?"

"The third key will open Artagan's cell. Come quick. I relieved the guard, but he will return."

"You free him," I reply. "I'm not leaving just yet. I have unfinished business with Belin."

"You truly are crazy."

Olwen arches an eyebrow, looking at me as though I sprouted a second head. She takes the keys back from me. I pull her close, our breath fogging the other's face. I still don't know whether to trust her or not, but I have no choice. She eyes me warily. I ask her the only question that matters.

"You love him still, don't you?"

Olwen pauses a moment before answering.

"And I always will. Now go. You'll find everything you need out in the passageway."

We part, possibly never to see one another again. But our shared love for the same man will always bind us together. Olwen rushes noiselessly down the next hallway while I turn toward a small alcove. All my possessions lie wrapped in a small calfskin bundle, including my bow and quiver. Good. Let's hope this works. Otherwise, I won't make it past the first guardhouse.

Scaling the steps back to the main hall, I hear Rhun and Belin speaking together in low tones. It's well after midnight on a foggy evening, and no other guards stand watch. Probably a few soldiers man the watchtowers outside, but none patrol the interior corridors. Why would they? Threats to a castle normally come from without, not within. And we are deep within northern territory.

Tiptoeing noiselessly to the doorway, I eavesdrop on them. Rhun pours wine into a pair of goblets.

"Something still gnaws at me," Belin says. "Why did she come all this way by herself?"

"You said it yourself," Rhun replies. "She's a woman, and a foolish one at that."

"Nay, that was just bluster. She's survived too long to have that much folly."

"Whatever she planned, it matters not now. She's our prisoner, and that's that."

Rhun takes a full draught of his cup, quickly refilling it with a fresh flagon. Belin taps his chalice, too deep in thought to take a sip. Rhun's goblet suddenly clatters to the floor, spilling wine across the flagstones. The Prince clutches his throat, his cheeks turning purple. Belin grabs him by the shoulder.

"Rhun? Rhun!"

I loosen the calfskin bundle and withdraw my bow. Notching an arrow to the string, I step into the hall, silent as a wraith. Time for kings and princes to learn that a queen can be just as ruthless as a man.

Belin looks up at me with wide eyes as I stalk into the chamber with my bow. The hearth flames rise and crackle behind him just as the heat rises in my blood. I take aim at his heart. Rhun chokes on the floor, writhing like a fish out of water. Belin growls, knocking over his undrunk cup.

"You've poisoned the wine! But you couldn't have escaped your prison cell, not so quickly."

"The wine is Lady Olwen's, as are the jailer's keys, but the bow is mine own."

Red in the face, Belin stalks toward me, only to check himself as I draw back my bowstring. He grimaces, stopped cold in his tracks. One shout to the guards will kill us both. Even if his men come running, I can lodge a dart in his throat before they take me down. With one flick of my fingertips, I can send him to the next world. Rhun gurgles on the floor, no longer struggling. King Belin clenches his teeth, his pale blue eyes full of smoldering fury.

"Why? How?"

"Sorry, old man. No sweet speeches from me. This one is for my husband."

I loose an arrow into his gut. He staggers back against a mead bench, black blood pooling about his feet. It will take some time for him to bleed to death. He cries out. His guards will have heard and arrive soon. I notch another arrow to my longbow.

"This one is for my mother."

My next arrow embeds itself in his groin. The old man howls like a banshee, his screams echoing off the rafters. The footfalls of boots murmur through the corridors behind me. I've only a matter of moments. I string one more arrow on my bow.

"And this one is for me."

The third shot goes through his throat. Red spittle foams over his mouth. The light fades from his icy blue eyes, his head slumping back against the tabletop. So much for the cunning king who would've had me dead or caged while he ruled all Wales. Dead as a dog, he lies pinned to his own mead bench by a woman. No more shall Belin's plots haunt my steps or the steps of my child. I turn around, not even drawing my bow as the clatter of foot soldiers comes my way. There will be too many, and I haven't a chance. My deed is done. I'm prepared to pay with my life.

Artagan bolts down the hall with his longsword in hand. My pulse quickens as I rise on my feet. He rushes into my arms, his stubble beard grown scraggly and his hair wild. Olwen must have given him his weapons back. Blood runs down his blade.

"Come, I can't hold them off forever!"

"I thought I was rescuing you."

"Let me return the favor."

He blinks at Belin and Rhun's lifeless bodies on the floor. His eyes dart from my bow to the arrows riddling the old King. Artagan's mouth hangs open, but we've no time for questions. His wife is a killer, guilty as charged. I've done it to save us all, and I'd do it again. I take his hand.

Artagan leads me down several winding passageways until I'm quite lost. Obviously, he has learned plenty about the layout of this prison fortress since his incarceration. The roar of foot soldiers echoes behind us, their footsteps getting closer. If Artagan hadn't bloodied several of them, I doubt the rest would be so timid in trailing us. The Blacksword still strikes fear into men, even when he has languished in a dungeon for a fortnight or two.

We duck out a doorway into a side yard where a tall black stallion waits. Merlin! Olwen holds the steed by the bit, steadying the warhorse while Artagan and I mount the black beast's broad back. Artagan leans down in the saddle toward Olwen.

"We cannot leave you here!"

"Go!" she replies. "I'll lead them another way. Promise me you'll look after him, Branwen."

Olwen reaches up and places her lips against Artagan's. My cheeks flush hot as I grit my teeth. Before either my husband or I can respond, Olwen disappears into the shadows. Heavy with another man's child, her love for Artagan still gives her strength. I know the feeling.

Grabbing Merlin's reins, I shout into his ear. Astride our mount, Artagan and I gallop out an open side gate, left ajar by Olwen. We ride hard into the night mists while the clatter of steel and voices from Snowden castle rage behind us, all in chaos.

Artagan speaks softly in my ear as we ride Merlin through the wet woods in daylight. We've ridden many leagues without pause, but he can no longer contain his curiosity.

"So Belin was behind the attempts on your life all along?"

"He was the root, but many enemies still remain. Our work is not yet finished."

My husband halts our horse on the forest road, looking at me with incredulous eyes.

"Your entire plan to free me from Mount Snowden hinged on Olwen betraying her husband and King Belin? You conspired with her based on a single note sent by a messenger raven. That's beyond risky, Branwen. That's reckless!"

"I was desperate to get you back. I had no choice but to be reckless."

"But how could you have known Olwen would help you? You two aren't exactly friends."

"No, we're not." I smile. "But, you see, she loves you. Almost as much as I do."

He gives me another sidelong glance, probably wondering if I'm serious or not, so I explain it to him.

"Your mother was right," I begin. "Love is the most powerful force in the world. Warmongers like Belin and Morgan see love as a weakness, something that has no place in this harsh world of barbarians and plotting warlords. But you see how it has actually proven to be stronger than all their swords and armies and conniving put together. I used love, Olwen's love for you specifically, and I wielded it like a lightning bolt."

Artagan blinks as though seeing me for the first time. He smiles before leaning over to give me a kiss on the cheek.

"Thank you, Branwen. For saving my life. For saving our life together."

"Don't thank me just yet," I reply with a smile as I start our horse forward again. "We've much work to do yet if we are to save our kingdom and our people too."

The fog banks part over the valley as Aranrhod comes into view. My heart skips a beat at the sight of home. My husband's arms wrap warmly around me. Suddenly weary, I realize that I have not slept in two days. I've ridden hard, as though hell itself followed in my wake. Artagan guides our stallion down the switchbacks into the green vale as a hunting horn sounds from the battlements.

My ears perk up. That can only be Ahern's horn. He has returned! Perhaps Annwyn has as well.

Hardly able to sit in the saddle, I collapse into Artagan's arms once we dismount in the castle courtyard. Rowena blanches at the sight of us, rushing forward with a bucket of water. The Blacksword and I must look like a pair of bloodied beggars. My eyelids hang heavy. I stagger toward my bedchamber, intent on reaching my cot before I pass out. Ahern bows to both myself and the King, begging to report. I breathe in deeply, making one last effort to focus my mind. My temples ache.

"Well, Ahern?"

"It's been arranged. King Malcolm will meet you at the rendezvous tomorrow at dawn."

Artagan steps between us.

"What in perdition is he talking about?"

Waving my husband away, I reach out for Ahern. I've no time to explain just yet.

"Any word from Annwyn?" I ask my brother.

"None, Your Grace. None at all."

He frowns. I nod absentmindedly, the walls starting to swim in my vision. Heaving myself onto my bed, I sink into the mattress in my grimy and dirty rags. No matter. The world descends into a deep, dreamless sleep.

I awake after dark to the sound of pouring water. Rowena stands behind a steaming vat, much as she did the first time we met at Caerleon. Blinking at the fire in the brazier, I wonder for a moment if the past few days have been a dream. Maybe the past few years as well. Am I any different from that sixteen-year-old girl who first rode to Morgan's wedding?

My son's cries echo from across the chamber. Rowena quits prepping the bath in order to see to the child, but I raise a hand to stop her. I am a mother now, not some scared child-bride after all. It is no dream. This is my castle and my life. This is where I belong.

Rubbing my eyes, I stagger toward the hot water before I pause over Gavin's cradle. He stops wailing, his azure eyes smiling up at me. I flash a grin and touch his tiny nose. Removing my ragged garments, I slip into the bath and brush myself clean before taking Gavin into the lukewarm waters with me. Together we sit a while in the warm vapors, just looking at one another. Rowena wraps him up afterward in a towel and prepares him for bed.

My stomach rumbles. Gnawing on a plate of food beside the firelight, I devour three apples down to their cores, a leg of mutton, and a bowl of porridge. Enough provender to choke a pig, but after my recent journeys I seem to have a bottomless stomach. I pause to kiss Gavin on the brow before Rowena takes him to his nursery.

Alone in my room, I take a moment to peruse my bookshelves. After all my perils and near scrapes with death in the last few days, the comfort of a book by the fireside seems like heaven itself. I thumb through one of Abbot Padraig's old tomes, thinking on the late monk with a smile.

A passage from the legends of my namesake, Branwen the Brave.

And though all had come to naught, the strong and beloved Queen Branwen gave her life to save her people. Just as Our Savior did so to save the world, so too did Branwen know that the greatest act of love is sacrifice. And though her life ended, her people endure to this day.

My fingertips tremble as I put down the book.

I often wondered why my mother named me after such a tragic figure from the folklore of the Old Tribes. It is as though both Padraig and Mother speak to me through these worn pages even now. Such is the magic of books. They allow the living to converse with those long gone, but not forgotten. I ruminate over the passage again, hearing those words first in the Abbot's voice and then my mother's. The greatest act of love is sacrifice, indeed.

Footsteps on the stairwell suddenly draw my attention. Father David enters the room with Artagan and Ahern close behind. They all look grim. My spine tenses. Barring the door behind them, the priest speaks first.

"My Queen, a raven arrived while you slept. More news from my monastic friends."

"And what have the monks written that gives you that long face?"

"I'm sorry to bear such ill tidings, my Queen. Lady Annwyn is dead."

My throat stops up. Unable to swallow, I look up at Artagan. He turns aside, his profile cast in shadows by the orange glow of the hearth. Although cleaned and dressed, he looks more dejected than I have ever seen him. A lone tear streams down his face, his eyes red. He has been weeping. Rising to my feet, I embrace him from behind, whispering in his ear.

"I'm sorry, my love. So sorry. She wanted to go. She knew she was dying."

Artagan nods, unable to speak. Perhaps he already knew of her condition as well, but it doesn't make this any easier to accept. I hold him close, feeling his heartbeat through his ribs. Father David clears his throat.

"There is more, my lady. She was killed in Dyfed, by King Owen's guardsmen."

Ahern grimaces.

"Owen's no proper king, the blackguard! Tell her the rest, Father."

"The guards killed her because . . . ," the priest trails off. "Because when she met with Owen as your envoy, she drew a knife and stabbed him to death. By the time the guards intervened, both Annwyn and Owen had perished."

Artagan and I exchange looks, but neither of us speaks. So his mother forwent her famed pacifism in order to save her family. To save her son's life, and mine, and that of our child. I shut my eyes. This was her last sacrifice. I knew in my heart that it would come to something like this, but I never dared admit it aloud to myself. Nonetheless, both Annwyn and I knew what she had to do. My heart weighs heavy in my chest as I hang my head. I will never see such a woman of the Old Tribes again, the woman who taught me to believe in myself and to be the queen I was born to be.

Ahern grimaces as he cracks his knuckles.

"And now all Dyfed is in tumult," he adds. "Every bastard-born king's son claims the throne and none of them with more than a dozen supporters. No one rules in Dyfed now. All is in great confusion there."

I fight back the tears in my eyes.

"Then all has gone according to plan."

All eyes in the room turn on me. I can't tell if they view me with awe or as the next Medusa. Annwyn certainly knew what she was doing. I told her to take care of Owen and she did. I envisioned poison or something more subtle, like the drinking chalice Olwen used against Rhun. But Annwyn made her choice. She did not want the long wasting death that lay before her, a terrible blight that the lump in her breast foreordained. Now she sleeps with the angels or whatever spirits the old pagans worshiped.

The men still stare at me as though I have suddenly grown ten hands taller. No longer just mistress of a castle, I have had to become a ruler. A queen as conniving and adept as any king. Men use their advantages in battle and I employ my tactics in my own way. I need not explain my actions to any of them any more than I already have, nor do I intend to. One by one, I have dealt blows to our enemies, without the benefit of an army or even a sword. By cutting off the head of each enemy kingdom, I have thrown them into chaos.

So far, I have eliminated half my enemies. Belin dead. Rhun dead. Owen dead. And before the week is through, not a soul in all Wales will doubt who was behind each execution. It is a chess game of life and death, and I intend to win.

Sitting down, I give my orders. If Artagan wants to contradict me, he can. Instead he stands silent with the rest, trusting me to lead them even though only I know the full details of my plan. I aim a finger at each of them.

"Ahern, ready every available warrior to depart before daybreak. Father David, continue sending ravens to every friend you have in every kingdom. The more we know before our enemies do, the better. Artagan, I need your strong arm. Are you ready to lead our warriors in battle?"

My husband smiles, a bit of his cocky hedge knight countenance returning to his face.

"Against the Saxons or anyone else, the Blacksword will lead his men into hell if Mab Ceridwen wishes it."

"My lady," Ahern interrupts. "We've maybe three hundred archers at best. Whether facing King Malcolm or the Saxons, we will doubtlessly be outnumbered."

"Let *me* worry about that, Ahern. Our enemies will walk into our trap, and no amount of numbers can save them."

"You sound quite certain, Your Grace," Father David says.

I crack a tiny, wicked smile.

"Trust me, Father. They'll fall into my trap for one simple reason. Because I will be the bait."

20

Father David makes the sign of the cross, absolving me after my confession. Kneeling in the castle chapel, I silently make my prayers of penance for the lives that I've taken and those I am about to take. A wooden roof now covers the ancient stone church, its timber rafters shaking with the thunder of another coming storm. The rains have drowned away summer just before harvesttime. Perhaps the archangel will reap the final harvest from Wales soon enough. That, or the Saxon crows. I rise from the pew, my limbs rested, steady, and prepared for the task at hand. Tomorrow marks All Hallows Eve, and my nineteenth name day.

I pace outside the chapel as the stars begin to fade overhead. I gird on my quiver of arrows and longbow. It will be dawn soon.

Artagan lies asleep in our bed with little Gavin snoozing beside him. They look like a pair of angels sprawled amongst the coverlets. I bend down and kiss my son atop his warm scalp. Before turning to go, I press my lips to each of Artagan's soft eyelids. Covering my mouth, I stifle a sigh. If ever I live to see another day, I pray only for the bliss of this bed and my two boys sleeping in it.

Without fanfare, I steal into the stables and saddle my husband's stallion, Merlin. I'll need the strongest horse in Christendom today. Alone,

I ride out the castle gates and into the dark hills as the first flicker of blue light glows in the east.

The wooded foothills steepen as Merlin climbs the southernmost ridges, heading toward the towering mountain gaps. The rush of fast water murmurs through the dells. Waterfalls and cataracts swell with rainwater, dumping their tears down the many ravines along this stretch of green peaks. Foaming brooks splash about my ankles as Merlin fords the last streambed before reaching the highland pass. The whicker of horses echoes from atop the heights. Someone already awaits me at the summit.

A large company of horsemen graze in a mountainside clearing. Steam rises from their steeds' nostrils in the dawning light. Crimson dragon banners of South Wales snap in the cold breeze. Malcolm's voice emanates from the brush.

"Did you come alone?"

I nod, halting my horse a stone's throw away. The new king of South Wales trots forward, a brazen crown atop his head. He smirks through his trim brown beard, his eyes provocatively running the length of my silhouette.

At least a hundred men-at-arms accompany him on horse and double that number on foot, maybe more farther down the pass. My heart sinks. Even if I turn back now, I doubt I could outride all of them. Malcolm has me well in his clutches and he knows it. He snaps his fingers and waves a soldier forward. The guardsman holds something under his cape, cradling it with both hands. Malcolm waves the man away after handing me the shroud.

"A wedding present. Consider it a token of my fidelity."

Fidelity? This farce makes my stomach turn over, but I keep a cordial smile on my lips. Beneath the folds of the cloak a bird squawks. My falcon! Placing the raptor's talons on my leather glove, I click my tongue and make soothing noises at my winged pet. Vivian. How long since I last went hawking with her! Not since I lived at Caerwent. Back when I still called myself King Morgan's wife. My half-smile fades as I remember again why I am really here.

"Thank you. I have missed hawking with my bird."

"You can do so every day if you like. I shan't have much need of you apart from our bed."

The next words turn to ashes in my mouth.

"I agreed to marry you given certain conditions. Have they been met?"

"Your guardsman, Ahern, was quite clear about the terms. In exchange for your hand in marriage, I am to provide three assurances. Two I've already done. As my Queen, you will retain Aranrhod as your personal castle. Secondly, any children you had by previous marriages shall be recognized as mine own."

Assurances? Pah! Does he think me fool enough to believe his word? With me at his side, Malcolm would have a claim not only on South Wales, but Dyfed and the Free Cantrefs as well. With half of Wales under his sway, I doubt he would honor any of the assurances he gives me now. But like all warlords, his greed blinds him. The chance of me coming willingly into wedlock with him provides too rare an opportunity to forgo. But he has neglected the most important item I had Ahern request of him. Pulling my lips tight, I must let him know I won't bargain my life away so easily.

"What about the last request? I want the Bishop of South Wales delivered into my power."

"That I cannot do. The Bishop is dead. Slain by Saxons during the siege of Caerwent."

"What?"

"We had too few troops and the citadel fell. The barbarians plundered it."

"But you escaped?"

"I rallied my men at Caerleon, my new capitol. The Saxons lost many troops taking Caerwent."

Looking away, I try to take in all these changes. Caerwent fallen? One of the most fortified castles in all Wales now lies in the hands of the barbarians. This could upset everything. With the Saxons based at Caerwent, it will be near impossible to dislodge them from the Welsh borderlands now. With a barbarian stronghold so deep in our territory, the Saxons could send raiding parties against half of Wales with less than a day's notice. Malcolm has proven so greedy to solidify control over his brother's former realm that he doesn't realize he will soon lose half of his kingdom to the Saxons come next summer. His gaze makes my skin crawl.

"From my brother to Artagan then back to me. You're quite the ewe among such rams."

"I'm a queen," I reply through clenched teeth. "I do what I must for my people."

"Belin will never let the Blacksword go, nor would I let him. I can't have you running off again."

Arching an eyebrow, I struggle to keep my features complacent. So he doesn't yet know. Just as I hoped! He thinks Belin still lives and word of my deed upon Mount Snowden has not yet reached the South. Any hour now, a raven might arrive, informing Malcolm that Belin and Rhun are dead, and the Blacksword set free. If Malcolm learns just how badly I'm double-dealing him, he would have my head right here and now. A droplet of sweat trickles down my brow. Malcolm rambles on, his horse pawing the dirt.

"Your son will come to live with us at Caerleon, as an assurance that you will remain loyal. My nephew, Arthwys, will be a stepbrother to him. That will ensure the peace between you and me."

I swallow a lump in my throat. A hard bargain, but I must make it seem that it pains me to agree with him. I'd never send my son within a hundred leagues of Malcolm's court, but he must believe I will, even if grudgingly. I solemnly nod my head, pretending I am too spent for words. King Malcolm grins, seeing me so cowed before him. He thinks he has won. But who am I to judge? If things should go awry today, he may prove himself right after all.

The sun rises over the mountaintops, playing hide-and-seek between gray thunderheads. Another storm is brewing. Just another half hour, at most. If I can simply stall Malcolm long enough, my own forces can lay our trap down in the ravines below. But we need more daylight. Those gullies will prove treacherous and steep. Even the best Free Cantref warriors will need some sunlight in order to navigate those crevices and set up an ambush. Time. I need to somehow buy us more time.

A ram's horn sounds from the mountain passes, echoing eerily off the cliff faces. My spine tightens. It cannot be my own men, it's too early. Malcolm exchanges looks with me, his eyes suddenly suspicious.

"What devilry is this?" he demands.

"I came alone. Do you have more men in the woods?"

More horns bellow through the forest, the clash of ringing steel reverberating farther up the mountainside. Fur-clad warriors with round shields and broad axes storm the heights, charging headlong into Malcolm's companies of men-at-arms. A surge of lightning runs through my veins.

Saxons!

A lead rider emerges from the woods, a massive brute with a double-headed ax swung high over his head. His yellow eyes lock on me and Malcolm. The Wolf! I freeze in the saddle, unable to move or think for an instant. The Saxons aren't supposed to be here. Of all possible outcomes, this will spell the doom of us all. So much for my best-laid plans. I sought to lay an ambuscade and find myself ambushed instead. Malcolm draws his long mace.

"Shite. Welshmen, rally to me!"

Malcolm and his foot soldiers form a wall of spears and shields, but their lines break apart almost immediately against the ferocity of the Saxon onslaught. With hundreds of warriors at his side, the Wolf has brought more than enough bloodthirsty brutes to finish us all off. Ax heads and knives whirl through the air, embedding themselves in the helms and faces of Malcolm's men. Streams of blood redden the muddy hillside.

Releasing my falcon, I set her free. If only I could fly too. Save yourself, Vivian. Only death lingers here now.

I draw my bow, knowing I might lodge an arrow in Malcolm's neck and put an end to him once and for all. But the Wolf charges into the melee, downing Welshmen two at a time with his broad ax. What is a queen to do? The enemy of mine enemy is only my friend so long as the battle lasts. In another moment, Malcolm could be my foe once more, but right now I need to save my scalp from these blood-drinking Saxons. I aim my arrow for the Wolf, but mingled amongst so many Welsh and Saxons, I cannot get a clear shot.

Malcolm swings his mace at Beowulf, narrowly missing him before splintering the war-chief's shield. The Wolf growls, tossing his shield aside as he raises his ax with two hands. Before I can blink, he brings it down atop Malcolm's crown, splitting him in twain from skull to collarbone.

The spittle turns bitter in the back of my throat.

Malcolm's body wriggles, headless atop his mount before slumping to the ground. Already broken, the South Welsh flee in all directions as the Saxons loot the dead. Beowulf turns his steed toward me, his saffron eyes flickering like flames. My throat runs dry as I dig my heels into my stallion's flanks. Run, Merlin! Run faster than you have ever run before.

Bolting downhill into the undergrowth atop my steed, I charge through the foliage, heedless of briars and dips in the land. One false move and my horse will break his leg, and I'll go tumbling into a ravine. The crash of tree limbs behind me grows louder as the Saxons on horseback gallop after me. Daring a glance over my shoulder, I draw back my bow and loose a shot. My arrow scratches the Wolf's cheek, drawing blood, but he only growls all the louder. The venom in his stare curdles my insides. He will skin me alive and have me raped by his men before granting me death. I bellow louder in Merlin's ear.

When I face forward, a branch snaps across my nose. Reeling in the saddle, stars sparkle in my vision. Gripping the reins, I hang on as my nose throbs. Hot, sticky blood runs down my chin, but I do not stop, urging Merlin to fly all the faster. Rivulets of perspiration run down my back. There is no world, no conscious thought, no plots or plans. Only life and death. I must ride, ride unto the ends of the earth before Beowulf guts me like a sow.

Hand axes and knife blades whir past my head, some embedding themselves in tree trunks. The Saxons roar as they close in on me from behind. Their spearheads nudge into the corners of my vision, their sour breath and sickly musk permeate the groves. Merlin rears up with a shrill cry.

I crash through the treetops, my feet no long gripping my steed. No saddle sits between my legs. Slamming into a thicket of brambles and sedge, my arm bends backward with a snap. It takes a moment to recognize the screaming voice as my own.

Shooting, fiery pain runs from my fingertips to my shoulder, my forearm cocked at an unnatural angle. Staggering to my knees, the thunder of horses surrounds me. Merlin whinnies in a cloud of dust, a Saxon spear dug into his hindquarters. Beowulf lunges from his steed like a bird of prey, the sharp edges of his double-headed ax spread before him like talons.

His agility in midair seems impossible, but in a flash he is upon me. Clutching my broken arm, I stare like a hare frozen in a hunter's trap. I shut my eyes. Dear God, let this end my surging pain. Let it be swift.

"Mab Ceridwen!"

A roar of voices booms from the woods. Opening my eyes, I see a sword parry the ax rushing toward my head.

Beowulf and Artagan snarl at one another, their weapons locked together over my head. I try to rise between them, but sway with dizziness. My legs seem unable to move as well. Am I crippled or already dead? Artagan pushes the Wolf away with his longsword, the two battling like giants over my crumpled frame.

Arrows hiss through the trees, felling Saxons from their horses as their cries fill the wold. More barbarians arrive on foot, but many lose their footing as Free Cantref archers send them toppling down into the narrow ravines. Bodies riddled with arrows litter every gully and dell. Pawing the earth for my bow, I find it broken in twain from my fall. Blast. I must rise to fight. I must.

More cries of "Mab Ceridwen!" rise above the din, but the Saxons are many, and for every one we down, two more arrive to take their place. It is the same story over and over again. The barbarians always have more men, always. Meanwhile, we dwindle down to our last reserves. The priests were right. This is the end of the world. God forgive me my sins, I did it all as a mother, as a wife protecting her loved ones. I did it all as a queen ought. I've few regrets.

Artagan staggers back, his arms and head flecked with flesh wounds. Beowulf circles him, equally rent and bruised. The two combatants eye one another like wary predators, each trying to sink their fangs into the other for the final kill.

My bow may have broken, but my arrows still work. Limping forward, I lunge for the Wolf with an arrowhead in hand. Diving forward with my good arm, I stab into the soft flesh of his foot.

Beowulf howls with pain, kicking me aside. Sprawled faceup in the ivy, I stare up at him in a daze. Fresh blood runs down my cheek. The Wolf raises his good foot over my skull, his eyes red with rage.

Suddenly his head drops into my lap, his tongue lollygagging on my chest. Shrinking from his skull, I roll his head aside as his decapitated body collapses to the ground. Artagan stands over me, panting hard as the Wolf's blood trickles down his blade. He kneels and takes me in his arms.

"Branwen! Branwen, can you hear me? We did it! The Saxons are breaking, they're falling back."

Victorious chants of "Mab Ceridwen" fill the woods. My eyelids feel heavy as I collapse in his embrace. His voice seems far away as he doubles in my vision. Artagan keeps calling my name, but my lips refuse to move. The breath goes out of me. All turns to darkness. So this is the last of earth.

A lullaby murmurs in my ears. Soft, hazy light clouds my eyes, the world an indistinguishable aura of shadow and glowing effervescence. A hand caresses my face, materializing out of the blur.

"Branwen. My sweet girl. How you've grown up."

Blinking, I still cannot move. A fair-skinned woman with long raven locks and emerald eyes smiles down at me. Her purple gown and lavender scent seem somehow familiar, but I cannot place her. My gaze suddenly widens, my palms trembling.

"Mother?"

"Yes, child. It is I."

"But how? Am I . . . ? What is . . . ?"

She shushes me with a gentle finger to my lips. My limbs relax, my head suddenly lighter than a feather. My voice sounds no stronger than a child's.

"Mother, you won't leave me now, will you?"

"I never left. I've watched you, shared your suffering and your joys. I'm very proud of you."

"Can I stay with you?"

"Soon enough. But you must rest. Know that I love you and will always be with you."

I sense that despite what she says, she will leave me, but I cannot seem to voice it. Warmth radiates from her touch. I nuzzle her cheek.

"I don't want to be alone."

"No one with love is ever alone. And you, Branwen, you have many who love you."

"Mother? Mother!"

Everything dims. Awash in an inky darkness, I hear muffled voices surrounding me. They sound close but indistinguishable, as though I listen through a clay jar. Golden shafts of light glow behind my eyelids.

"Shh. She's coming around."

Blinking back the sunlight from the window, I see Rowena leaning over me with a careworn face. Lying on my cot inside my bedchamber, I find that I can barely move my head. A soreness envelops me, making me groan. When I try to rise, Rowena presses her palms against my chest.

"Easy, m'lady. You've been out for three days. I thought more than once that you'd left us."

"Rowena? Are you really here?"

"Of course." She smiles. "We all are."

Gavin coos from Artagan's arms as he sits on the bed beside me. Artagan presses his lips to mine, our little boy murmuring between us. I smile at my husband and my son. My men. Breathing deeply, I try to flex my wrist. I wince as a sting runs up my elbow. My left arm lies in a sling and my skin aches from a dozen different wounds, but at least I can wriggle my toes and sit up in the covers.

Familiar faces smile from across the room, all gathered around my bedstead. Gray-bearded Emryus and bald Father David. Sir Keenan with his infant daughter Mina in his arms. Ahern sniffles, wiping the tears of joy from his beard. I almost chuckle until a woman in a dark habit nods from across the alcove.

"Una?"

She curtsies.

"I prayed when I heard what happened, and received permission from the cloister to come here as soon as I could."

Rowena smiles beside her, one arm wrapped around her friend, now a woman of God. Pressing my lips together, I feel the water welling up behind my eyes. Their love, like their warm smiles, is as tangible as the blankets on my bed. So many loved ones no longer number amongst us though. Enid, Padraig, Cadwallon, Annwyn, Father, Mother. But I sense their presence with us still, arm in arm with the living who make this castle home.

Turning to Artagan, I kiss him again. My love. I've so many questions, but I don't know where to begin.

"Tell me everything."

"I shall," he says with a wink. "But first, we've a feast to attend, and you're the matron of honor."

I narrow my eyes. A feast? The unseasonable rains have dampened the harvest. I don't see how we could have much left to eat at all. But I shan't argue. My stomach growls, and I still feel a touch lightheaded. Artagan guides me down to the courtyard and out the castle gates. Despite my unsteady steps, it feels like heaven to feel warm sunshine on my cheek. Everything seems out of season, first rain in summer and now warmth in the early days of autumn. I seem to have strayed out of time entirely.

Villagers gather along the lawns outside Aranrhod, bundling sheaves of ripened wheat and toting sacks of grain. Womenfolk reach out to touch the hem of my robes, familiar faces of mothers and daughters who stood with me during the siege last year and helped rebuild the castle afterward. Bowmen salute by raising their longbows overhead, defenders of the vale in war and huntsmen in times of peace. Children scurry playfully about the blankets laid out on the greens, their ever-present focus untroubled by worries about the future or memories of the past. Minstrels pipe dancing airs as the peasants form circles for jigs. The scent of roasting meat permeates the grounds as venison sizzles over hearths and spits. Stopping to clutch Artagan's hand, I whisper in his ear.

"How is all this possible? Plenty of food, meat, smiles on every cheek?"

"All in good time. First we eat."

Mead benches from the main hall cover the lawns, reminding me of market fairs we once had in Dyfed when I was a child. I've not seen such gatherings since peacetime. Barrel taps fill flagon after flagon with glistening cider and foaming ales. Artagan stands atop a table, raising his goblet high overhead.

"To Queen Branwen, who gave us victory when all the world had turned to defeat. To my wife, Mab Ceridwen!"

"Mab Ceridwen!" the crowds reply.

My household joins me around the table, bringing over fresh plates of mutton, deer, and beef. Steaming barley bowls and tall piles of oat cakes fill the platters before me. Even with one arm in a sling, I manage to empty several dishes in a matter of breaths. Downing a cup of cider, I finally sit back with a belch. My fingertips buzz with a hint of inebriation. I pat my sated stomach. I've earned this day and I intend to enjoy it. But it all still seems a dream. I half-expect my mother to come walking amongst the tables. How *is* this all possible?

Father David appears with a scroll under one arm and leans down beside Artagan's ear. The King nods, turning toward me with a steer's bone in hand. He smiles at me between bites.

"Let the Queen hear," Artagan says to Father David as the priest shows him the scroll in hand. "These tidings may help answer some of her questions."

"As you wish, my liege," the priest says with a bow. "I've word from Queen Olwen. She has wed Iago, the new king of North Wales. King Iago reports pleasure in his new kingship and offers peace between our kingdoms. He also sadly reports that his father and elder brother perished in a mysterious attack by wolves, but that the matter has been put to rest."

I exchange looks with Artagan. Wolves indeed. Young Iago seems thirsty enough for the throne, so much so that he didn't even blink at the assassination of his father and brother. In some royal families, no amount of blood relation can quell ambition. Olwen must have Iago wrapped around her finger as well as in her bed. And yet it was love that drove her to help Artagan escape, allowing me to try to save Wales. She loves my husband enough to betray the father of her child and marry his brother. But how can I fault her? Artagan's love could drive any woman to any lengths. I stare into my empty cup.

"We owe Queen Olwen a great debt," I admit.

"She has one request of us," the cleric adds. "But it is no small matter."

"Anything. We owe her as much."

"Very well then. She recently gave birth to a healthy baby boy, and has sent us her newborn son to be fostered here at Aranrhod. I believe she fears what her new husband may do to his brother's boy, since it will be a rival to any heirs he plans to have. Meanwhile, our fostering of the boy will ensure the peace between us and the North."

"Does the child have a name?" I inquire.

"Cadwallon."

Artagan raises an eyebrow.

"Like my father," the King remarks.

"When did you say this child would arrive?" I ask.

"The infant is already here," David says with a bow.

Rowena sits beside a cradle and a basket, one with Mina and the other with Gavin sleeping soundly. In her arms she holds another tiny, bald baby wrapped in a swaddling cloth of royal purple. I tiptoe quietly beside Rowena. My goodness, our household will be boisterous as a cattle pen with three young ones soon running around within the next year. Gavin, Mina, and young Cadwallon. Perhaps Olwen's son and mine will have a chance to grow up together, close as friends in a way that Olwen and I never could. Perhaps this is the best way to unite Wales in the years ahead. By forging strong ties of friendship and fosterage from birth instead of marriage beds and assassins in the night.

"Forgive me, my Queen," Father David quietly interrupts, drawing me aside. "There is more."

"More?"

"I've word from Gwent in South Wales, although only a few ravens have gotten through. It seems a certain falcon nesting in the tower eaves is scaring them off."

Glancing up at my tower within the fortress walls, I spy a falcon circling the ramparts. Its cry pierces the azure sky. I cannot help but grin. Vivian. She has chosen to nest beside my own tower windowsill. Good. I shall take her out to hunt all the field mice she can stomach. Father David warily eyes the soaring raptor, doubtlessly concerned about his beleaguered ravens.

"Who sent us a message from the South?" I ask. "King Malcolm is dead, no?"

"The new ruler of Caerleon, Your Grace. King Griffith."

"Lord Griffith, now a king? I thought him captured by the Saxons."

"Evidently, he escaped and rallied the survivors at Caerleon where they made him their sovereign. He has accepted the role of royal steward until the boy, Prince Arthwys, comes of age. King Griffith has offered terms of peace between our kingdom and his."

Holding my good hand to my head, I blink incredulously. Could fortune smile on us so? A favorable king rules Caerleon in the South, an allied queen controls the monarchy in the North, and both have made peace with us. If only we had word from Dyfed, but I fear they have been made impotent by their own civil strife. Plague and war have weakened them as well. At least they no longer pose a sizable threat, not so long as they bicker amongst themselves. Putting a palm on Father David's shoulder, I give the old priest a kiss on the cheek. He colors marvelously.

"I take it you accept King Griffith's offer of peace?" the priest asks.

"I do, but what of the Saxons? We've slain the Fox and the Wolf, yet their forces remain."

"You've not heard, my lady? Of course not. You've been convalescing. After the capture of Caerwent, the beleaguered Saxon armies fought amongst themselves over the spoils. King Penda's forces and the West Saxons have begun feuding along each other's borders."

"You mean the Saxons are actually fighting each other?"

"Better than that, my Queen. Despite their victories, their armies suffered substantial losses. While the West Saxons remain our foes, they are much diminished in strength. As for King Penda, he has honored the peace treaty made with North Wales and extends his pact of nonaggression with any who call King Iago and Queen Olwen friends."

"Alleluia."

Just think of it. Barbarians fighting barbarians. Peace or no, the Saxons will doubtlessly break their word sooner or later, but for now, at least we will have a respite from war.

That's all I ask, Lord.

Just time enough to heal our country's wounds, for the next generation to grow up, and our fields to fill with crops again instead of graves. The threat to Wales has not vanished, but it has been held at bay for at least another generation. I close my eyes, a leaden weight lifting from my chest. At least my son will inherit the same country my mother and father left me.

And all my enemies are dead. This will take more than a few days to properly sink in. The year 599 has brought us much pain, pleasure, and promise all at once. God gave me a son, but also took many loved ones from us in the defeat at Bloody Fords. Yet he ultimately delivered us from evil and has given us peace in our day. The Lord truly works in mysterious ways.

Across the castle stables, a boy gives a bucket of feed to Merlin, my stallion limping from the spear wound he received from the Saxons. The horse will recover, but will bear the scars of this war for the rest of his life. Perhaps all we can do is thank God for the life we have, and do our best to live well with the days we've been given.

After thanking the priest, I return to the festivities. By now, many of the villagers have joined dancing circles, sloshing drink and porridge along the grass. Mingled voices, laughter, and song fill the meadows beside the castle and the woods. Wrapping my good arm around Artagan's neck, I kiss his clean-shaven cheek while he pours himself another drink. He cackles with glee.

"Can you believe the wonders God has bestowed on us? A fortnight ago, all seemed lost. Look at us now! And we all have you to thank for it, Branwen. You truly are an amazing woman, you know that?"

"One thing still puzzles me. With such a meager harvest, how did you manage such a banquet?"

"Did Una not tell you? Her cloister shared their grain stores with us. In exchange, I've offered them protection and patronage."

"Una arranged that? That will prevent us from starving this winter. And I thought she'd forgotten about us."

"Who could ever forget you? Everyone loves you! And I most of all."

His lips travel down my throat. It takes me a moment to playfully push him away. Women and men alike throw us knowing looks, smiling at their King's friskiness with his wife. I plant a long kiss on Artagan's cheek, whispering a few vivid scenes from our bedchamber that ought to tide him over until nightfall. He beams at me with the eagerness of a young stag in season. I cannot help but grin back at him.

The joyfulness on everyone's faces reminds me much of our wedding night. Like that festival, many more children will doubtlessly be sired tonight. And why shouldn't it be so? We've had enough widows and orphans to last a lifetime. The hills and dales of Wales will fill with the laughter of children once more, and the steady heartbeats of men and women in love.

Looking out over the rolling downs and verdant woods beneath the mountains, the vale has never seemed brighter. Green dragon banners fly proudly over Aranrhod's towers. A good castle, my castle. How far I have traveled from that long-ago day when I was a scared girl living by the sea, betrothed to a man I had never seen. Now I have my true love by my side, my husband and my child. I have many guises, yet within me they all coalesce into one.

Wife, mother, lover, friend, and, of course, queen.

Acknowledgments

Thank you to my family and friends, whose support and love continue to inspire me. A special eternal thanks to my wife, my muse. I love you.

I have to thank my agent, Rena, for first seeing the potential in my book, and giving me the wings to give it flight. Thank you a hundred times over, Rena. I will always be indebted to you.

I'd also like to thank everyone at Thomas Dunne Books and St. Martin's Press, especially Pete, Emma, Annie, Elizabeth, and Elsie. Your hard work and dedication helped make this novel what it is today.

Thank you to my beta readers and fellow bloggers, too numerous to count, but all valuable friends who offered their precious time and advice out of the goodness of their own hearts. I am truly humbled by your generosity and kindness.

Finally, I'd like to thank God. You really do work miracles.

5/31/17 pgs 159/160 - stained
pgs 41-48 - warped along edge

WITHDRAWN